Island of
Desire

Also by Lorie O'Clare

PLEASURE ISLAND

SEDUCTION ISLAND

TEMPTATION ISLAND

UNDER THE COVERS
(with Crystal Jordan and P.J. Mellor)

FEEL THE HEAT
(with P.J. Mellor and Lydia Parks)

Published by Kensington Publishing Corp.

Island of Desire

Nancy —
Always live for
the romance —

LORIE O'CLARE

Lorie O'Clare

𝒜
APHRODISIA
KENSINGTON PUBLISHING CORP.
www.kensingtonbooks.com

APHRODISIA BOOKS are published by

Kensington Publishing Corp.
119 West 40th Street
New York, NY 10018

ISBN-13: 978-0-7582-6139-7
ISBN-10: 0-7582-6139-X

First Kensington Trade Paperback Printing: February 2012

10 9 8 7 6 5 4 3 2 1

1

"The Mr. Desire Pageant is the fastest growing in the history of pageants." Windsor Montgomery spoke as if he were solely responsible for its success.

Andrea Denton stared at her red closed-toe heels that matched her Betsey Johnson dress, a bright red thing that was off-the-shoulders sharp. She crossed her legs and pushed the cool material down an inch, almost to her knees. "I'm impressed," she offered, knowing Windy, as he liked to be called, was waiting for her praise.

"In its six years, it's grown in popularity so that today each of the fifty contestants is loaded with sponsors." Windy paused, looking at his file.

Andrea had already looked over the figures, or she wouldn't be here. She also wouldn't be here if it hadn't been for her success working with the Miss Florida Beauty Pageant for the past six years. She knew why Mr. Tripp Sr., who'd recently bought the pageant, wanted her here.

"Miss Denton knows the facts about the Mr. Desire Pageant." Julie Ward, Andrea's lawyer and the closest person

Andrea had to a friend, leaned forward in her high-backed chair and slid the contract across the oblong table.

Her target was Mark Tripp Jr., but Frank Benison, his lawyer, snatched the stapled papers with his thick hand. Windy's eyes followed the contract from one end of the smooth, highly glossed table to the other. He shifted in his seat, looking rather proud of himself, as if his speech had secured this contract. Andrea had worked with Windy before and absolutely loved him. Although straight, Windy presented himself to the world as if he were gay, then acted baffled when more men came on to him than women. He was one hell of a good PR man and Tripp had been smart to pull him on board. She wasn't sure yet how she would like working with Tripp, but Andrea already knew she would have no problem having Windy around.

Andrea caught herself before she started fidgeting and remained perfectly still. Body language could be so misleading. It was one of many lessons this line of work had taught her. If she shifted, it would look like she were fidgeting, which indicated impatience. That would inevitably lead to Tripp and his lawyer taking more time with the contract. She'd already approved the changes Julie had made and now simply waited for Tripp to sign it. Unfortunately, Mr. Tripp Sr. wasn't here. Mr. Tripp Jr. had better hold power of attorney. They wanted her. They knew, and Andrea knew, she was the only one who could get them out of the pending disaster the pageant was about to face.

"I believe we made it clear Miss Denton's salary was non-negotiable." Frank Benison spoke with what almost sounded like a fake British accent. His white starched, button-down collar was cutting into his neck, and his skin was too red.

Andrea imagined it was due to high blood pressure. Mr. Benison had no idea how many lawyers tried intimidating her on a daily basis. All part of the job. She ignored his pointed glare and instead focused on Mark Tripp. She'd learned about Junior only after arriving at this meeting at the Tripp Mansion.

In spite of her impeccable track record of always showing up for a meeting prepared and knowing what she would gain from her time, Andrea was surprised to meet Mark Tripp Jr., who looked somewhere around thirty.

Apparently, although Mark Tripp Sr. had recently purchased the Mr. Desire Pageant and changed the venue at the last minute, he didn't see it as necessary that he attend the meeting where he would hire his new pageant director. A pageant director who would save his ass, she might add. Not many in her line of work would enter into a contract to direct such a high-profile pageant when the previous director had just walked off the job after the new owner changed the location for the pageant. Andrea was up for the challenge.

"I believe Mr. Tripp is well aware that this pageant will be the largest public humiliation he's ever endured without Miss Denton on board. Feel free to contact your boss," Julie said, leaning back in her chair as she poised her pen on the notepad in front of her. "I'm sure he'll agree the numbers I adjusted are incredibly reasonable."

"Miss Denton isn't being asked to do anything that any pageant director wouldn't do. The salary offered is on the high end for her profession."

Julie laughed. "You're asking her to do a year's worth of work in a month. According to your reasoning, she should get twelve times the amount you're offering."

"Miss Denton will hardly be launching this pageant from scratch." Tripp's lawyer scoffed.

"Mr. Tripp bought this pageant, then immediately changed the location where it will be held. The new location"—Julie glanced at her notepad, which was blank shy of her doodling—"hasn't been prepared for the pageant. Normally during the last month before the night of the pageant, the contestants are rehearsing on the stage, doing final photo shoots."

Andrea managed not to slouch in the comfortable, high-backed chair. At the same time, she didn't want to look stiff as a board. And as Julie and Mr. Benison continued arguing her worth and value, Andrea wished she was anywhere but there. She felt like a slab of meat on a chopping board being fought over by the butcher and a customer. Each one had their own opinion of its worth.

Junior didn't appear to be any more impressed. He stared out the windows that lined the west wall and offered a view of well-manicured gardens. Andrea studied his profile. He was distractingly good-looking but seemed rather distanced from the meeting. Maybe it was his father's money and not his that bought the pageant. Tripp Jr. might not care about Mr. Desire, or that it would be held on his family's privately owned island off of Key West. He hadn't spoken a word since their meeting began.

Which made him a mystery. And a damn sexy one at that.

Julie and Mr. Benison continued haggling over the details of Andrea's contract. Andrea knew every word of the contract and knew Julie wouldn't budge during the negotiation, unless it was for more money.

Julie was right. They wouldn't find a better pageant director than Andrea to pick up the pieces of the pageant and make sure the event went off without a hitch. It wasn't conceit but hard work that had earned her reputation and success. Modesty was a rare and unappreciated trait in her line of work. Realtors might continually use the mantra *location, location, location.* But in Andrea's world it was *image, image, image.* She let Julie continue singing her praises and remained quiet. They would eventually quit haggling, Andrea would sign the contract, then life as she knew it would be over. The Mr. Desire Pageant would take over her world.

Andrea knew everything about Mr. Desire. Six years ago, the Mercury Energy Drink company took the most eligible bachelor contest, as often reported in magazines, a step further, encouraging cities to hold their own pageants. No longer was the most eligible bachelor strictly a movie star or a celebrity. Now the guy in the next cubicle, or who taught kids in school, or who possibly delivered mail, might be the most eligible bachelor. With enough propaganda and the proper promoting—Andrea remembered the commercials being top-of-the-line—the Most Eligible Bachelor Pageants sparked to life all over the country. Within the year, almost every state was holding the pageants with as much reverence as Miss America.

Mercury had one hell of a marketing team, although she wasn't sure sales spiked all that much for their energy drink. What did spike was the need to take these pageants to the final level. The Mr. Desire Pageant was created. Each state presented their Most Eligible Bachelor to compete in the nationwide Mr. Desire Pageant. It had passed up Miss America's television ratings two years running. Andrea had no problem joining the winning team, especially when they had sought her out.

And she'd also done her homework on the Tripp family, although her focus had been on Mark Tripp Sr. She was now kicking herself for not researching Junior, as well. As in, was he dating anyone right now? Was he the long-term kind of guy or more into one-night stands? There weren't any good pictures of any of the Tripp family online. They were definitely old pros at dodging the paparazzi. Had there been, Andrea would have searched hard and long to learn if he laid out in the nude, if he had any kinks, and what nightclubs he frequented. She would have gone to that nightclub, stumbled into him, and pushed hard to take him home that night. Then, during all of this negotiation, she would be entertained by the casual looks he would have sent her way. And she'd be contemplating when and where to do him next.

It sucked that none of that had happened.

"I'll sign the contract." Mark looked away from the windows, proving he'd been paying more attention to the meeting than Andrea had guessed. He looked directly at her, showing off green eyes brimming with power.

Andrea had done what she'd sworn she would never do, judge someone on their appearance. Granted, how a person dressed, what labels they leaned toward, spoke volumes in this business, but she had no proof Mark was in the pageant business. As far as she knew, he wasn't. His casual attire of jeans, a button-down shirt with no tie or jacket, and loafers with no socks, made him look anything but a businessman.

"Excellent," Windy breathed, clapping his hands together and grinning a toothy grin as he looked to her and nodded.

"Mark," his lawyer, Mr. Benison, said under his breath, barely moving his lips as he turned to his client. "I'm not through."

"I am. Miss Denton is the only person we're willing to consider to run this pageant. Her terms are fine." He didn't look away from Andrea when he pulled the contract out of Mr. Benison's hands, lifted a pen from the table, and poised it over the contract. "You'll agree to give notice to your current employer and work exclusively for us within two weeks."

He didn't make it a question. Andrea wasn't sure he knew she'd been studying him, but she made a show of taking him in now. Mark's soft brown hair was long enough to wave around his strong facial features. He was tan, and not from tanning booths. He looked like the kind of man who was outside a lot more than he was in an office, if he ever was in an office. In addition, the top button of his shirt was undone, revealing a glimpse of enticing chest hair.

"You'll spend all of your time on the island," Mark continued, his voice crisp with authority. In the blink of an eye, he'd taken over the meeting as if he ran the show on a daily basis. "Of course, you'll be provided with living quarters I think you'll find suitable." He finally looked away from her, focusing on the contract and pressing the pen to the paper. "Contact Mr. Benison to schedule a move-in date."

Mark signed the contract, and a strand of hair fell over his forehead. He had a long, narrow, straight nose and just a bit of shadow lining his strong jaw. When he pursed his lips, his expression grew more serious. She now saw indication of a man capable of running the family ventures the Tripps were known for. His lawyer huffed, puffed out his chest, and grew even redder as he watched Mark sign the contract. Mr. Benison didn't challenge Mark, which showed he knew Mark was a man who could not be pushed.

"Andrea," Julie whispered, leaning closer.

Andrea blinked and quit looking at Mark. Julie's natural, golden light brown hair, a color to die for, reflected the sunlight streaming in from the windows. She had pretty blue eyes but downplayed them with the brown eye shadow she always wore. Andrea ached to do Julie's makeup but didn't want to offend her by suggesting she could do Julie's face better.

"What do you think about living on the island?" she whispered. "There's nothing in the contract about living arrangements. You don't have to if you don't want to."

Andrea liked the loft she rented, which was only a few miles from her office. She knew she would be giving notice as director of Florida Pageants, Inc., where she'd worked since moving to Key West from Miami. She hadn't considered moving out of her home.

"Your job requirements will require you be on the island full-time," Mr. Benison interjected, watching her and Julie pointedly. "We'll type up an amendment if necessary."

Mark was watching her, his eyes not moving from hers. Not once did she catch him checking her out. He was all business, something Andrea knew how to be as well. She worked in an industry that focused on beauty and sex appeal, and that was filled with manipulation, deception, and greed. She could always spot a player, a two-faced bitch, and a bad deal. Andrea knew how to think on her feet and go with the flow when plans changed.

"That's fine," she decided and forced herself to relax. Mr. Benison was right. She would need to live and breathe this job in order to have everything ready with so little time left. "Everything should be in writing."

The moment Mark finished signing the contract that sealed Andrea's future, a fifty-something woman wearing a straight-cut, gray wool dress entered the conference room from one of the closed wooden doors behind Mark and Mr. Benison. The woman moved silently, pausing when Mark slid the contract across the table to Andrea.

"Would you like a tour of the island?" he asked when Andrea accepted the pen Julie offered her.

"That would be a good idea." She realized it was the first time the two of them had spoken to each other directly, and she found herself being pulled into those commanding eyes of his.

"We can head out now. Your pageant headquarters need to get used to functioning without you," he added. "Give copies to Ms. Ward and Mr. Benison," he instructed the woman standing next to him and pushed his chair back. "Shall we?"

Andrea glanced at Julie when she pushed her chair back, as well. "Thank you," she said quietly.

"Give me a call." Julie gave Mark an appraising once-over when he appeared behind Andrea. "We'll get together this evening so I can go over your letter of resignation. You need to get that turned in before the press gets wind of this meeting."

Julie was right. Timing was everything, even when it came to resigning from a position. She would also interrogate Andrea about her time with Mark Tripp. Julie worked at least as hard as Andrea did, often putting in twelve- to sixteen-hour days. Very few people had a clue as to how much work went into a pageant. Unlike Andrea, though, Julie maintained a healthy social life, always having dates and often boyfriends, who at times hung around for months on end. Andrea was good at her job, damn good. She started working often within minutes of getting out of bed, and finished shortly before putting her head on her pillow at night. There wasn't time for dating. She wasn't sure how Julie pulled it off.

Mark's loafers didn't make a sound as he walked ahead of her out of the conference room and through his family's mansion to the front door. When they'd arrived, she'd been taken by the beautiful rooms they'd passed through to get to their meeting. Now, Andrea stared at Mark's broad muscular shoulders, the way they tapered down to a trim waistline, and how his blue jeans hugged his hard-looking ass.

"In spite of the popular opinion that all beautiful men are gay, it isn't true."

"What?" She stopped as they reached the front door and stared at him.

Mark's expression was blank, his eyes pinning her gaze so she couldn't look away. He was definitely a man used to controlling his surroundings. She was forced to tilt her head back in order to maintain eye contact.

"What's that supposed to mean?" Andrea saw no reason to hide her confusion. His statement came out of nowhere and made no sense. If he was making a comment about Windy, he was being too forward.

Mark opened the front door, not explaining himself. The butler, who had been so attentive when she and Julie had arrived, was now nowhere in sight. She stepped out into the early spring sunshine, welcoming the warmth of the day. Mark moved ahead of her but faced her when the driver came around a sleek black limo and opened the back door for them. Was every servant in this household able to foretell their employer's actions?

"You're an incredibly beautiful woman," he said, lowering his voice although the driver was easily in earshot. "Your mother was Miss Florida and your sister was a runner-up. You won three pageants by the time you were twelve. I look forward to hearing why you're a director of pageants, yet chose not to continue being in them yourself."

Mark ignored the driver and gestured for her to enter the car. He'd just told her she was beautiful, yet Andrea didn't take it as flattery. Nonetheless, she shot him a curious glance. Mark looked away before she could catch his expression. He had done a fair amount of background research on her.

It crossed her mind to tell him she would follow, then grab Julie, who had driven the two of them out to the Tripp Mansion. But Julie was incredibly perceptive. Usually her uncanny ability to read people was useful. Not this time, though. Andrea didn't want to be drilled as to why she was suddenly unsure about being alone with a gorgeous man.

Andrea gave silent thanks that the only person who knew her dreadful secret was mortified by it, and equally as disgraced as she was. No amount of research would unbury the truth. Today there wasn't quite as much pain, at least not as much as usual. She worked too hard to dwell on her past. Someone as sexy as Mark, and accustomed to having people jump whenever he moved, might think he could trip her into spilling information that wasn't part of the public record, but he wouldn't.

She slid into the car, the smooth, cool leather stroking the underside of her legs as she adjusted her red dress. She took a moment to regain her composure while Mark took the seat facing her.

"I love what I do," she offered, keeping her voice soft as she crossed her legs and watched his gaze trail down her body. "But, Mr. Tripp, it's rather late for an interview, don't you think?"

Mark had a smile that almost made her melt inside. She

fought the urge to clench her legs together when his bedroom eyes rose to her face.

"This is your business, not mine, but I intend to learn everything about it before the contestants arrive on the island." There was a shift in his expression, that commanding, rather dominating glint returning. It made his green eyes appear to glow. "I hope you're a good teacher."

Mark's cell phone rang, which he'd been holding in his hand. "Excuse me," he muttered, then flipped it open and stared at the number on his screen. It was too hard to tell if he was angered by whoever called or upset because they'd been interrupted.

Andrea pulled out her phone, giving him as much privacy as possible in the confines of the back of a limo and checked her messages. Julie had already left her a voice mail. Andrea kept her phone on silent, deciding if she took all of her calls while Mark took his, they would never get through their tour of the island.

"I've attached a file on Mark Tripp Jr. Since we didn't know he'd be part of the contract negotiations, I guessed you hadn't researched him. Now that you have some tasty-looking eye candy to ogle over, I bet you're dying to know about the goods. Check out the articles when you get a chance. There is some interesting stuff on Mr. Stud Muffin."

Andrea fought a grin over Julie's nickname for Mark. She also wanted to know what Julie viewed as "interesting." It had to be trivial information or Julie would have told her in her voice-mail message. Nonetheless, Andrea was anxious to get to her laptop once she had a minute.

"We'll discuss that later, Dad," Mark said, his tone unbelievably soft-spoken and gentle. If he hadn't just called him "dad," she would have guessed he was speaking to a child. "Yes, we're heading to the island now. And don't do that. I'll meet with you later and fill you in. Yes, I promise. Good-bye."

Interesting. Mark Tripp Jr. wasn't purebred hard-ass. There was a nurturing side to him as well. Andrea stared out the window so she wouldn't drool, or worse yet, try to get in his pants. Although the latter sounded like a pretty good idea.

Andrea hadn't been on a ferry in years. She enjoyed watching the waves splash against the side of it and listening to Mark exchange idle chitchat with the old man who captained the boat. It wasn't long at all before Tripp Island was in view.

The island was as breathtakingly beautiful as Andrea had imagined. But she wasn't prepared for long walks in her heels, and she was about to tell Mark as much when they stood at the dock.

"This way," he told her, and left her side before she could say anything.

Andrea followed him to a new Excursion, and Mark pulled keys from his pocket and pushed the button on his key holder to unlock the doors.

"Tell me something," he began after opening her door for her, then coming around to the other side and sliding into the driver's seat. "The increase in income you requested in your contract won't make it worth your while if we choose not to renew it after this pageant is over. Are you tired of being surrounded by sexy ladies and so decided an island of sexy men might be more appealing? They say a man who enjoys a pedicure from time to time, dresses to the nines, and spends more than five minutes on his hair each morning must be gay. That description probably fits more than half the men in this pageant. That still leaves the other half for you to hit on, if that is your nature. So, did you settle for less money because you thought you could sleep with the contestants?"

Andrea looked at him. Mark started the SUV and put it into gear. He focused straight ahead, not glancing her way even as she continued staring at him.

Was he seriously that big of a jerk? And if so, why did her tummy twist and her pussy throb when he burrowed into her soul with those intense green eyes of his?

She took a deep breath. It just figured Mark would be more asshole than nurturing and kind. Mr. Perfect existed in fiction, maybe, but not in real life. They started down a straight, paved, one-lane road shrouded with tall palm trees on either side. In less than a minute it grew darker in the car as they drove into an undeveloped, tropical jungle–like setting.

"Did I offend you?" he asked when a moment of silence passed between them.

"Were you trying to offend me?"

"No," he said and glanced over at her, making eye contact for only a second before letting his attention stray down her body. Heat ignited under her flesh wherever he looked. "But I am trying to understand your motivation."

Andrea didn't get it. She was usually good at reading people. She saw hard-ass in him. Mark definitely had a dominating, aggressive nature. She'd witnessed him speak to his father with all the loving-kindness of a doting mother. But how had she missed the part of him that was a complete and total jerk?

"I took this position because it was a smart career move. I haven't met the contestants yet, so I can't comment on that, and I'm not worried about my financial situation." If he'd phrased his question differently, she might have told him she never had sex with anyone she was working with, no exceptions.

Mark nodded without saying anything else. She wouldn't have noticed the tug of a smile at his face if she hadn't already been looking at him. Son of a bitch! He was learning what kind of person she was based on her answer to a preposterous question. His straight jawline and nose, along with his high cheekbones and that hint of a shadow from not having shaven, created the perfect mixture to make him easily the sexiest man she'd ever laid eyes on. And regardless of his accusation, Andrea had directed pageants for men in the past. None of the contestants held a flame to this man sitting next to her. And she'd just seen yet another side to his personality. Mark had created a scenario with his question. Andrea's answer gave him insight into her personality. She wondered if he knew that his question told her a lot about him, too.

His personality was complex, possibly too complex. Once she had time to look over the file Julie had sent her, she might have a better clue into his nature.

"What's your role in this pageant?" she asked, deciding if she knew how closely involved they would be while on the island, she would then know how much time to dedicate to figuring him out.

"Role in this pageant?" He cocked an eyebrow and shot her a quick glance. "I guess you could call me the boss."

Andrea wondered at the sudden pang of disappointment that clutched her gut. His father was supposed to be her boss, not him. The Mr. Desire Pageant was on the brink of disaster and it was her job to turn it around, make sure the change in owners didn't affect the event, handle the change in venue over to the island, and do all of this without letting anyone see her sweat.

So much for trying to get into his pants. Andrea had always stuck by her few self-imposed rules. Sleeping with the boss was a definite no.

The road ended in a parking lot alongside a very large home, equally as magnificent as the Tripp Mansion in Key West where they'd had their meeting over her contract. The house had a burnt-orange Spanish-style roof with tall, narrow windows symmetrically spaced in the smooth adobe, pale-orange walls. Instead of facing the parking lot, the home faced the ocean. A rock garden stretched out past the terraces and brick driveway to the beach.

Mark took the brick drive, which circled the mansion. He

parked on the far side of the house in front of several carports, all of which were empty. The structure was even larger than she had first thought. Andrea climbed out on her side of the Excursion as Mark came around the front.

"This place is amazing." Andrea couldn't imagine living in a house this big, let alone owning two this size.

Mark tilted his head, looking at the home as if it were the first time he'd ever seen it and was trying to decide if he agreed. "Thank you," he murmured, sounding serious. Then he looked at her, and once again the predator was apparent as he took her hand and pulled her closer. "Let's show you your new home."

2

Back on the mainland, Mark pressed number one for speed dial to call his dad. He watched Andrea walk away from him to her car parked outside her office building. The bright red dress she wore clung to her incredible figure. It had been impossible to keep his hands off her while on the island. He had given her a tour so she would know the layout of the place. Andrea had told him what she would need to do to get the pageant regrouped on the island. Once again she'd impressed the hell out of him. She had her work cut out for her, but she had looked vibrant and full of enthusiasm as she shared the details involved in running an event of this magnitude. Without giving it thought, he'd found himself running his hand down her back, gripping her shoulder, or placing his hand just above her ass to guide her as he showed her around.

Andrea was hotter than any woman he'd ever met. There was something about her nature, too. So assertive, confident, and relaxed. At least that was how she presented herself. He had also noticed her high-dollar brand-name dress and expensive shoes. He knew next to nothing about the beauty pageant business, but Mark could take an educated guess and surmise that it was an industry filled with cutthroats, backstabbers, and jealous manipulators. It was also a world where show mattered more than tell. His father had taught him a long time ago that the best way to see a person's true character was by throwing them a curveball.

Mark watched Andrea's ass sway back and forth in her form-fitting red dress. It ended above the knees and she had beautiful, long legs. Her bright fuck-me red shoes clicked against the pavement as she reached her car parked across the street. She pointed her key chain at her silver Mustang and the taillights flashed. Andrea reached for the door handle then looked over her shoulder at him and waved. Several strands of light brown hair sashayed past her chin and brushed over her bare shoulders. God, she was hot! He was going to have to fuck her. There was no way he'd be able to keep an eye on the island and watch over everything otherwise.

An hour later Mark had showered and left the wing that had been his section of rooms growing up. Although he'd moved out of his father's house over ten years ago, his dad still kept Mark's rooms just as he'd left them.

Mark headed down the wide hallway with the oversized family portraits, each hand-painted, hanging on the walls. His ancestors watched him as he went down the stairs to his father's den.

"Come in." Mark Tripp Sr. spoke with a deep baritone.

Mark pushed open the heavy wooden door and glanced at Robert Tiel, his father's personal nurse. It had been hell convincing his dad to have a nurse be a constant companion. At first Mark had guessed his father would want a young, pretty nurse. But in the end, after going through a handful of nurses, Mark's dad decided on Robert. He stepped into his father's large office and crossed the thick, bourbon-colored carpet to the wet bar.

"You're late," his father said in greeting.

"I'm right on time." It was a private game he and his father played. Mark glanced at Robert when he rocked up on his heels. "How are you doing today?" he asked his father, and walked around the large mahogany desk where his father looked a lot smaller in his oversized office chair than he used to.

"I just got the signed contract." Mark Sr. tapped his arthritic finger at the stapled papers in front of him. They were the only papers on his desk. "Job well done, son."

"Why didn't you attend the meeting?" Mark leaned over and kissed his dad's forehead. He seemed a bit flushed to Mark, which possibly answered his question.

"Contract meetings are boring," he said crisply. "I knew the negotiations were in good hands with you and Benison there." When his father smiled, there was still a bit of the devil in him. "She signed for twenty K under what I thought she would."

"It's still more than she's making a year right now."

"So you gave her a tour of the island." In spite of being riddled with cancer, and the old bastard refusing chemotherapy, Mark Sr. still managed to remain informed. "What do you think of Miss Andrea Denton?"

His dad had blue eyes that were so pale they were almost clear. When he'd been younger, they were attractive against his brown hair but today, they almost matched his white hair. Mark had his father's straight nose. It was a Tripp trademark, having been passed down from father to son more generations back than Mark could count. The portraits in the upstairs hallway were proof of that. Mark wasn't sure how much time his father had left, and on days like today, when his eyes were so watery and the chair dwarfed him, he worried those days were numbered.

"She's impressive." Mark didn't elaborate, primarily because he wasn't sure his dad's heart could handle all the adjectives

Mark could think of to describe Andrea. Luscious lips, bed-room eyes, firm mouthwatering breasts, and a tight ass were just a few that came to mind. "Your team did a good job in finding her."

"I had a feeling," his father began, speaking slowly, "that you and she might work well together. I just wish I could be there to watch you learn the beauty pageant industry."

"You're enjoying this, aren't you, Dad?" Mark took one of the two chairs facing his father and made himself comfortable. Mark hadn't wanted to leave his architectural firm to spend a month with a pageant director just because his father had taken a vested interest in the success of Mr. Desire. "I'm not working this pageant thing. I know nothing about pageants, nor do I really want to learn. Besides, I would be in Andrea's way and she won't have time to explain everything she is doing."

"But you do care about Tripp Island." His father picked up the contract and flipped through the first couple of pages, appearing absorbed in reading it. "What do you think of Windsor Montgomery?" he asked without looking up.

"He goes by Windy." Mark grinned at the look his father gave him when he glanced over the papers in his hand. "And he also appears to be on top of his act. Before the meeting began he told me about three new sponsors he's brought on board. Coca-Cola and The Gap have both signed on to do special commercials during the pageant. He used a lot of industry jargon I didn't catch, but the gist of it is that you were right," Mark said, nodding to his father. "The Mr. Desire Pageant will be a gold mine."

"That's gold for you and your sister, son."

"You'll reap the profits, as well." Mark hated it when his dad made it sound as if he would be gone anytime soon. "I am curious about something, though. Why did you insist on moving the venue for the pageant?"

"You've always thought Tripp Island was beautiful," his father shot back, sounding offended.

"We all did," he responded quietly. Mark had only been there in the past few years when he designed, and helped build, the mansion currently on the island. Ever since his mother died when Mark was a teenager, the island had lost its appeal. It had been his mother's favorite place to go.

"I hear the home you built on the island is beautiful." Which confirmed what Mark had already suspected, that his father hadn't gone to Tripp Island since his wife died.

Although now it made sense why Mark Sr. had insisted the old house that had been there be razed and Mark's architect firm design and build the new home that was ten times the size of the old one. "How long have you had your eye on the Mr. Desire Pageant?" he asked.

Mark Sr. placed the contract on his desk in front of him and cleared his throat. Robert moved silently to the wet bar. The clinking of ice could be heard before he brought his employer a crystal glass filled to the rim with ice water. Robert looked at Mark, raising his eyebrows in question. Mark shook his head, declining the unspoken offer for a drink.

"As to your questions," his father began and sipped at his water. When he placed the glass down, Robert moved in again and picked up the glass and placed it on a coaster. Mark Sr. ignored his nurse and focused on his son. "I insisted on moving the pageant because I knew if I pushed the old director enough, she'd walk off the job."

"You did that on purpose?" Mark knew how often his dad had been a son of a bitch during business deals when Mark was younger. The deals were fewer and farther between these days, but although he should be impressed that his dad still had it in him, he immediately thought of Andrea and all the work she would have to do because the event had been moved at the last minute.

"Miss Denton is the best in the industry. I took my time finding that out," he told Mark, then pointed a finger at him. "That's good business, son. If I put my name on something, it will be the best there is across the board. That is how the Tripps work. You should know that by now."

Mark had heard variations of the same thing said all his life. "There were other locations than the island," he pointed out.

His father leaned back in his chair, suddenly looking exhausted. Robert must have sensed the same thing because he again stepped forward, lifting the glass of water and offering it to Mark Sr. The old man waved him away. "Which is why I need you to help oversee this pageant."

"You know I'm always here for you when you want me."

"Good. Then it's settled."

"But I can't completely abandon TAC for a month." Tripp Architect Company, TAC, had been open two years now and was Mark's baby. The company was doing well, taking on new clients on a regular basis, but it was still in the infant stages of business and Mark didn't want to jeopardize its growth in any way.

"You've got a good staff on board over there, very loyal from what I hear. And you aren't abandoning your baby," his father assured him. It was uncanny how Mark Sr. always seemed to know everything about Mark's affairs as well as his son's thoughts. "Son, I need you. Now you know I don't say that often. My damnable pride has gotten in my way more times than I care to remember."

It wasn't often his father got up from behind his desk while talking business. He had told Mark once that it was important to have a strategic vantage point when negotiating or cutting a deal. Mark Sr. had his office set up in a fashion so his office chair was a few inches higher off the ground than the two chairs facing his desk. The large mahogany desk was intimidating in itself, but it hid the small rise that his father's chair was on. As his father had told him more than once, it was his helm. His father was the ruler of his empire, and all those who approached him were beneath him and should be prepared to appeal to his good graces to get what they wanted.

Robert was at Mark Sr.'s side before he was out of his chair. Mark watched his dad lean heavily on Robert's arm as he came around the desk and faced his son. When his father placed his hand on the edge of his desk, Robert backed off.

"Dad," Mark complained, reaching for his father.

His dad slapped at Mark's gesture to assist. "That was your mother's island."

"I know that, Dad." Mark decided to stand also, hating how fragile his father looked and wishing he could see the giant tycoon that he'd looked up to and worshipped all his life. That man had been eaten alive by cancer, and what was left was a shell in comparison.

"Your mother always loved beauty pageants." His voice was immediately softer as he began reminiscing. "If she were alive she would be ecstatic to have Mr. Desire happening on Tripp Island. There are memories of her that are sacred on that island. I mean for them to stay that way."

"So let me get this right. You moved the event to Tripp Island because it would have made Mom happy. But at the same time, the island reminds you of Mom so you want to make sure all the people who will be descending on the island because of the event don't trash it out."

Mark Sr. turned slowly and looked at Robert. "Give us a minute," he said.

Robert nodded and slipped out of the room, closing the door silently behind him. Mark watched until the nurse was gone, then frowned at his father.

"That is the case, son."

When his father looked as if he might fall over, and reached for the closest chair facing his desk, Mark stepped in and helped his father sit. He then took the other chair, turning it to face his father's.

"There's something else," he prompted.

"I believe so." Mark Sr.'s cheeks were hollow and his lips almost nonexistent when he pressed them together. His watery eyes would appear glassy one moment and clear and attentive the next. "Your mother had a rough go of it before she died. She was paranoid and often not herself."

Mark couldn't remember the last time his father had spoken about his mother. He didn't interrupt and listened attentively, not having realized until this moment that it meant a lot to him to hear what his father had to say about Mom.

"After her accident . . ." he began, then looked down at his hands. He'd never appeared unsure or hesitant in the past so it wasn't completely clear that was how he looked now. But he did hesitate for a moment. "I had her personal things gone through and organized. Some of it was auctioned for charity, other items were stored away for you and your sister. At the time, your aunt questioned me about some things that weren't accounted for once we had all of your mother's items in storage."

"You've never mentioned this."

His dad shook his head, looking sad. "I buried myself in work after her death. It was my coping mechanism. As well, I didn't care if all of her personal items were accounted for or not. Margaret was gone, and I didn't want anything of her around me to cause the pain of losing her to last any longer than it already had."

Mark studied his father as he, too, flashed back to those terrible months following his mother's car accident. It was hard remembering he'd only been ten when his mom died. In his mind's eye, it seemed he'd been much older. A shroud of darkness had seemed to fall over their home after her funeral. Mark had turned to servants, the grounds crew, anyone who would take a moment to see that a young boy was suffering through pain he didn't know how to cope with. Mark's father wasn't in his memory of those dark days. It dawned on him now that it was because his father hadn't been home. The years following, Mark Tripp Sr. had made the family billions as he became the ruthless tycoon Mark knew him as when he entered adulthood. Funny how before this moment, Mark hadn't attributed all of his father's financial success to being a way of coping with losing the only woman he had ever loved.

"I remember racing across the beach on the island with Mom." Mark wasn't sure why he voiced the memory.

Mark Sr. looked up, nodding and patting his son's leg. "She was so full of energy before she got sick."

Sick meant before his mother became an alcoholic and grew increasingly more depressed. Mark wasn't a psychiatrist, nor could he rely on his childhood memories or know what took place behind closed doors, but he would swear his mother and father had a wonderful, loving, and happy marriage. He wasn't sure what made her drink herself blind, or start popping the pills that she'd called her "happy pills." Mark did know the alcohol and pills killed her. He remembered overhearing that his mother shouldn't have been allowed behind the wheel the night she drove her car over a cliff to her death.

"And she loved Tripp Island." His father's hand was clammy and bony as he gave Mark's leg a quick squeeze before clasping both hands in his lap and staring his son in the eye. "It was just this morning that I was reminded about the claim that not all of your mother's personal belongings were accounted for."

"Like what?" Mark asked.

"She had a jewelry box. It was an heirloom in itself. But the box was full of jewelry passed down from her mother and grandmother, as well as a few items your mother purchased."

"Valuable?"

"Very." His father pointed to his water. "Would you pass my water to me, son?"

Mark stood and reached for it. The moisture clinging to the thin crystal moistened his hand before he passed it to his father. Mark also grabbed the coaster and slid it to the edge of the desk close to his dad.

"So we have a missing fortune?" he asked, trying for humor.

His father made a snorting noise, something akin to laughter, and held the half-full glass of water up between them. "This piece was also part of your mother's collection. She loved beautiful, rare, and incredibly expensive items, no matter what they were or how practical they were. I remember one of those pieces of jewelry was a hideous copper and bronze necklace with matching earrings. I think your mother wore it once and got mad at me when I told her I liked how it looked better before it was polished." He shook his head, then returned the crystal to the coaster without assistance. "There is a point to dredging up all of these sad, old memories."

Mark had a feeling. "You want to begin a search to find them? Do you have an inventory anywhere of all the missing items?"

"Honestly, they can all remain buried with your mother," his dad said with scorn. "I can't think of one damn reason why I would want any of that jewelry. You children will never want for anything. And the jewelry won't bring my wife back to me. But that isn't the reason."

"What is the reason?"

"Since I was just reminded that all of Margaret's most cherished pieces of jewelry were never found, obviously someone else reminded that person that all of it is still missing." His father's eyes were clear and alert when he stared at Mark. "If someone is curious where that jewelry box might be, it's possible they think a small fortune is up for the finding. It didn't bother me that your mother's jewelry is lost, but it would bother me if someone else found all of it and tried selling the pieces."

"Shit." Mark leaned back in his chair and crossed his arms. "Do you think it's possible that Mom hid the jewelry? You know she wasn't always thinking clearly before she died."

Once, if Mark had said something like that to his father, he would have been yelled at, if not given a harsh swat on the rear end. His father had made peace with his mom's death, although Mark was pretty sure he saw the pain of having lost her still there in his dad's expression.

Mark Sr. scowled as he nodded. "It wasn't her fault," he said, immediately defending his dead wife. "I should have given her more attention and not cared so much about making so much goddamned money." His father never used profanity. He claimed it was a sign of weakness and that a good, strong man took the time to know how to express himself without being guttural. "None of it prevented my Margaret from being ripped out of my life." He sighed, a bitter scowl on his face. Then, in less than a minute, the bitterness vanished. He relaxed and looked at Mark. "I believe your mother might have buried her jewelry box somewhere on Tripp Island. She loved that island. Right before she died she was increasingly agitated and growing more and more paranoid. It makes sense that she might have hidden what she cherished so much."

"You think it's buried on the island? Why did we move Mr. Desire to the island then?" Mark wanted to know. "Send a crew out there with metal detectors, or whatever equipment necessary to find out if it's there."

The sadness had returned to his father's face. He shook his head slowly. "Up until this morning, that jewelry box was all but forgotten completely. I was just reminded about it this morning. Which is why this will be my last business venture. I don't have the brain for it anymore, son. And this is why I need you to be on the island through the duration of the pageant. If I change the location of the pageant again, it will most likely not be the performance the public has come to expect from this particular event. Mr. Desire has to take place on Tripp Island."

Mark watched his father glance around his office, as if suddenly confused about something. He'd managed to make it home almost every weekend to visit, but this was the first time in ages that he'd really sat down with his father and talked shop. Maybe his father wasn't capable of making decisions that involved something of this magnitude, like Mr. Desire. A tightening in his chest burned inside him, but he wouldn't let his dad see his sudden panic that his father was a lot worse off than he'd realized.

"I'll arrange to have a crew sent out to the island to look for Mom's jewelry box," he promised his dad. "Don't worry. I'll take care of it."

"I have all the confidence that you will," his dad said. "But sending a large crew out isn't a good idea. Miss Denton will be moving onto the island soon, and already I've increased the staff on the island to help prepare for everyone who will be arriving. The less people who know about this, the better. Or, I guarantee it, son, greed will take over and everyone will be looking for that jewelry box and destroying your mother's beautiful island."

"We can be discreet."

"Nor will metal detectors work. The jewelry box was made out of a thick-cut crystal that had some kind of alkaloid in it." His father tapped his water glass. "The crystal collection belonged to some princess and is centuries old. I don't remember what country, Ireland or Scotland, possibly. But I do remember that it's impossible to detect what is inside this particular jewelry box, which was why your mother loved it so much. She believed all of her treasures were safe inside that crystal box."

Mark listened, and understanding slowly twisted his gut into a painful knot. "Who reminded you of the jewelry box?"

"Bernard," his father said, referring to the family's butler, who had run the household and overseen the staff his father kept on in their home for as long as Mark could remember. "I confess, he had to refresh my memory about the jewelry box. He'd overheard one of the servants who had returned from the docks mention it. Apparently, Silver and Marcia were talking about it when she was at the docks after a large shipment was delivered of things needed for the many guests soon arriving out there."

Mark cursed under his breath, but kept his concerns to himself. Silver was part of their staff whose current job was to man the ferry that took them to and from Tripp Island. Mark hadn't realized that Marcia Ald, one of his favorite cooks growing up, was now out at Tripp Island. All three servants were very loyal to the family, and had been employed by the Tripps most of Mark's life. He would have to talk to all three of them, learn who else knew about the jewelry box, and hear all of them swear they wouldn't discuss this missing treasure with anyone else. The sooner he took care of this, the better. Otherwise, fortune seekers would tear the island up searching for buried treasure.

Mark sat and visited with Bernard, who had his own home behind the Tripp Mansion but on the grounds so he was able to relax in his own living room when not needed in the "big house," as he called it. Bernard was in his sixties, about ten years younger than Mark's father, but still appeared agile and alert. After hearing everything Bernard could tell him about his mother's jewelry box, including Bernard's speculation on who would know about the jewels, Mark made the old butler swear to him that he wouldn't discuss the matter with anyone else. Of his own doing, Bernard also assured Mark that if anyone brought up Mrs. Tripp's jewelry box, he would immediately tell Mark about it.

Mark headed upstairs and to the south wing, where his bedroom, his private den, and an entertainment room were located. He'd recently arranged to convert the two rooms on the wing that were once a playroom and a study into space more conducive to him as an adult. Although no longer home, Mark kicked off his shoes and changed into shorts once alone.

He'd thought, after meeting Andrea, that overseeing the pageant and keeping his father happy wouldn't be such a bad deal. TAC had only been open for two years, and he had a good staff on board. But Mark had enough business sense to know his company was still new and it was a competitive market out there. It was imperative that every design, every proposal presented, was perfect. TAC was too young, and so was he, for him not to be present when clients walked through his door. Or, at least present most of the time.

So he would be running his architecture firm and watching Andrea organize a men's beauty pageant. While doing both of those things, he would also be checking out the island very carefully for his mother's jewelry box, and making sure no one else would be doing the same.

Mark jogged down to the kitchen and noticed his father had a couple of new, young housekeepers on staff, who both offered him shy smiles that were loaded with invitation. He opened and closed two of the pantries, went for the cabinets, and got chastised by the head cook for not calling down to be served. Mark managed to throw together a ham and cheese sandwich, promised to push the button on the house phone that was installed in his wing the next time he wanted anything to eat, and jogged back up to his rooms. His father had his home set up like a damned hotel. Mark would need to call for room service if he wanted to be fed again. More than likely, one of those two young housekeepers would bring his food to him. Neither young lady was as hot as Andrea.

Mark settled in his den with his sandwich and booted up his laptop. It didn't take too many searches to learn more than he'd known about Mr. Desire before eating his sandwich. Every contestant in the Mr. Desire Pageant had won the title of Most Eligible Bachelor in his home state. That much Mark already knew. This was the pageant that drew the ladies to it in hordes. They all swooned over the fifty young men, who probably all thought their shit didn't stink.

He skimmed over a couple of articles with pictures that made it look like *Girls Gone Wild*. Women traveled from all over the country, willing to behave in ways they never would back home while enjoying the Mr. Desire Pageant. Mark stared at one of the pictures of several pretty young ladies with the caption underneath that said, *I desire Mr. Desire!*

This past year, police reports had been filed in eight different states involving the Most Eligible Bachelor Pageants. Death threats as well as sabotage to personal property were reported by several of the contestants. This sort of thing might be common during pageants. Mark didn't really know. The competition was steep and the stakes were high. According to a couple different websites, scandal surrounding the Mr. Desire Pageant was worse than it had been in previous years.

There could be no bad press surrounding this pageant. His father was big business and had successfully made the Tripp name a household word. Which meant, if something went wrong in his father's business, it could easily affect clients' decisions to go with TAC over another architectural firm in Miami. Mark's dad wasn't an architect and had never done business involving any architectural firm. It was the Tripp name. Everyone associated it with money and success. Mark pulled up the picture of the ladies holding up the sign about Mr. Desire. There would be so many horny women in town.

He closed out the picture, wadded up the napkin he'd brought up with his sandwich, and tossed it into his trash can.

"Two points," he murmured to himself. Would he have time to score with Andrea? "It sure as hell would make this next month a lot more enjoyable."

Mark conducted a few more searches, learning everything he could about the pageant and its contestants. There were plenty of newspaper articles nationwide about each state's winner of the Most Eligible Bachelor pageant. Mark was surprised to recognize a few names. One of his father's politician buddies had a nephew who'd won Most Eligible Bachelor out of New York. Another of his dad's old friends, a congressman, had a son in the pageant—Mr. Connecticut. The senator and the congressman would probably be inviting Mark's dad up for dinner, or a night out, to do some schmoozing. A statement to the press that Mark Tripp Sr. wasn't judging the pageant, and would have no association with the judges, would be necessary.

Mark had always preferred fresh air to air-conditioning, no matter how hot it was outside. Today was perfect, though. On an impulse, he grabbed the suitcases that held a few changes of clothing he'd brought down with him from Miami, and headed out.

"Mr. T," Mark said jovially to their chauffeur, who was polishing the limo, which didn't look as if it needed polishing at all.

Theodore had been with the family since Mark was a teenager. The day Mark had learned that his friends called him Mr. T, Mark had immediately followed suit. Mr. T wasn't quite six feet tall, was thin, and looked nothing like the real Mr. T.

"Is there somewhere I can take you, Master Tripp?"

"God! Call me Mark, please." Mark rolled his eyes and grinned. Mr. T hadn't been with the family when Mark's mother had died. Mark would like to find out if Mr. T knew about the jewelry box, but he didn't want to bring it up unnecessarily. He needed a good spy, and contact, within the large staff his father employed. "And yes, actually, there is."

It didn't take too long to reach the beach where the Tripp's private ferry was docked.

"Gorgeous day, don't you think, sir?" Silver—Mark had never known his last name—might look ridiculous in his formal captain's uniform, but he stood so seriously at the end of the dock when addressing Mark that his uniform looked fitting.

"Absolutely beautiful." Mark didn't know Silver really well, although he'd worked for the family for at least five years now. To the best of Mark's knowledge, all Silver did was captain the ferry to and from Tripp Island, as well as man the family's private yacht, which Mark hadn't been on in years.

Silver stepped forward when Mr. T lifted the two suitcases from the limo's trunk and took them from him. Taking one in each hand, Silver paused when he stood next to Mark. "Ready whenever you are, sir."

"I'm ready." Mark reached for his luggage. "I can help you with those."

Silver shook his head. "They aren't a problem. I'll get them secured in the back. Just make yourself comfortable, sir. It's a perfect day to be on the water, if I don't say so myself." Silver carried the two suitcases, which Mark knew were fairly heavy, across the wooden dock, then stepped onto the boat. "It's hardly long enough a trip to offer cocktails, but if the mood suits you, sir."

"I'm fine, Silver."

He just wanted to get to the island and unpack in his personal wing. Then he had some phone calls to make. One of them would be to Fran, his office manager at TAC. She would gripe and complain, accuse him of taking advantage of her, but then she'd line up security for the island faster than he ever could. Mark might also have her do a thorough check online for anything mentioned about his mom's jewelry box. If it was as valuable as his dad claimed, and she had obtained it after they married, there might be something about its history. Mark wanted to know everything there was to know about the box.

He would also have to touch base with the two architects he had on staff. It would be a first for both of them, handling clients without running their every move by him. Mark had confidence in them, though, or he wouldn't have hired them.

Rob Brown was his senior staff member, one hell of a good architect and with only a few quirks—the biggest one being he absolutely refused to answer to anything other than Rob. God help the poor soul who tried calling him Bobby.

Cleo Tigman was his newest employee, a recent graduate from the University of Florida. She showed promise and had a flare for the unique and nontraditional floor plan. Mark felt she brought fresh blood to his company, not to mention she was a riot. Cleo had quickly earned the nickname Tigger, partially from her last name, but more so because she was tall, thin, and walked and behaved just like Tigger from *Winnie the Pooh*. Cleo didn't have an ounce of physical beauty to her name, but she glowed from the inside. She was the biggest klutz Mark had ever met, but she wasn't shy. If anything, what the rest of the world viewed as downfalls, Cleo saw as simply part of her unique nature. The fact that she really liked herself made her even easier to get along with.

Rob and Cleo were going to get the opportunity to show off their talents. He would need to do some shuffling around in the schedule. He'd already given thought as to which clients he would assign to each of them.

"Penny for your thoughts." Silver turned in his captain's chair and smiled at Mark. When he did, his leathery, tan face creased into wrinkles that went from cheekbone to jaw. Not one white hair on his head budged against the breeze off the ocean.

Mark stood from his swivel chair along the side of the ferry and moved to the front, joining Silver. "I'll give them to you for free," he said. "I hear you mentioned Mom's jewelry box to Bernard, who in turn, of course, mentioned it to my father."

Silver's smile immediately disappeared. He was solemn when he nodded once before commenting. "Yes, I did," he said, straightening and smoothing his hands over the thick white captain's jacket. "I never had the privilege of knowing your mother, but I have heard she was a wonderful lady, and that she loved Tripp Island."

Silver gestured with a nod. Mark looked ahead of them where the island was already visible, its greens contrasting beautifully with the blue ocean.

"When my father had business trips, Mom would stay out here until he returned. She truly did love this island." Mark wasn't sure why he shared the memory that had just popped into his head. "Who mentioned the jewelry box to you?"

"Marcia, the cook." Silver again nodded toward the island, which was growing larger by the moment. "She knew your mama pretty well from the sound of it."

"Yes," Mark agreed, not elaborating. "Silver, I want you to stay quiet about this jewelry box. Do you understand?"

"Yes, sir."

"I mean it. This island will be flooded with way too many reporters and all the contestants. There isn't any proof, or even evidence, that the jewelry box is here on the island."

"You have my word, sir. But speak with Marcia if you want your proof."

Mark settled into a small wing toward the back of the house. No one questioned his arrival or made a fuss over him. There were very few people around. That would change way too soon. He opened his terrace doors and took in the incredible view of the ocean and wide stretch of beach before him. To say this was therapeutic was an understatement. Mark drew a deep breath of fresh air and pulled his phone out. He wasn't here for therapy.

"Fran," he said when his office manager at TAC answered the phone. "I've got news for you."

"As long as it's good news," she informed him, sounding as if she were typing at the speed of light as she spoke to him.

"Might be." For all he knew, all of them might jump for joy hearing he would be out of the office for a while. "I'm going to be in Key West longer than I expected. I'll be back up at the office later today, but then I'm returning down here."

"Is your dad okay?" she asked, sounding concerned but not missing a beat as she continued tapping her fingernails against her keyboard.

"Yes, he's fine." Mark was concerned about his father more than he ever had been in the past. He hadn't looked well and had appeared all too eager to turn the entire pageant over to him. "But he shared something with me, and I need you to do a few things for me."

"Something must be wrong with our connection," she continued, her intentional drawl proving she was going to bring up her age-old complaint. "Because I know you aren't asking me to do non-TAC-related work for you again."

Mark ignored her suggestion that he took advantage of her as an employee. "I need you to make some phone calls and find out who can offer the best security for Tripp Island."

"Your father doesn't have security guards on payroll?"

"Not to the magnitude we'll need. Make some phone calls. Report back to me with all agencies who would provide twenty-four/seven security. I want to know about every single person who steps foot on Tripp Island, and when they leave."

"Okay," Fran said slowly. She was no longer typing, which meant not only did he have her attention, her curiosity was also piqued.

"One more thing," he added, before Fran started bombarding him with questions. "There is this jewelry box."

3

Andrea stood quickly at the sound of the car pulling up behind her. She'd been on Tripp Island for only a couple of hours and already she'd fallen in love. Mark had given her a tour when he'd brought her out here after signing the contract, but Andrea had been so incredibly preoccupied with him so close to her the entire time, she'd barely noticed the island at all. But today, after dumping her luggage in the incredibly large bedroom that would be hers while here, she'd hurried back downstairs for her first meeting.

She was supposed to meet with Brandon Fisher, the man in charge of the land crew on the island. Andrea needed to know where, and how, to put up temporary lodging for the contestants once they arrived. The mansion was huge, and way too easy to get lost in with its many suites and staircases that led to different sections of the house. But there weren't enough bedrooms in any wing of the mansion where all contestants could be put together. Andrea didn't like pageants where all contestants weren't together at all times. It made it so much easier to call them forward for different events, before and during the pageant. As well, camaraderie grew stronger when all contestants worked together in all aspects. Therefore, one of her first requests had been to build temporary lodging for her men. The request had been approved within minutes.

Brandon Fisher was in charge of all landscaping and maintaining the island outside the mansion. He would advise her on the best location for temporary cottages, kits actually, that would be brought onto the island by ferry, and, according to their website, assembled in a day.

An SUV parked a few feet from her and she stared at the driver. The last person she expected to see looked back at her. Mark Tripp's gaze was intense, hungry. God! Did he look at all women that way? And if so, how many responded? A distracting, raw need formed deep in her womb. The flowers growing alongside the road that she'd been curious about a moment before no longer mattered. A new urgency blossomed and matured in seconds. The hell with him being her boss. Could she pull off some type of casual sexual relationship with Mark while on the island?

"I didn't expect to see you here." Mark approached her with a slow, almost lazy stroll that belied the tightly wound urgency emanating from his body.

Andrea almost gulped. She would hyperventilate any minute now. Watching him approach was doing something to her equilibrium. He radiated sexual energy. Her flesh tingled and made the almost invisible hairs on her arms stand on end.

"I do believe your contract says your employment doesn't begin for another two weeks," he added and stopped when he was within reach of her.

For a moment she swore he would touch her, but his hands remained at his sides. His eyes didn't wander. The dosage of sexual predator in this man had to be off the charts. At least he wasn't sleazy about it. His gaze remained on her face.

"Are you here to meet with Mr. Fisher?"

His dark eyebrows pulled together as he frowned down at her. "Brandon Fisher?"

"I thought you were him."

For some reason Mark found that amusing. The corner of his mouth twitched and his frown faded. His eyes grew brighter. They were an incredible shade of green.

"Are you going to talk to him about where to put the men when they get here?" he guessed, pulling his attention from her for the first time and looking around them.

There were three rather nice-looking, almost quaint cottages set not too far off the road alongside her. The cook, Marcia Ald, had informed her that each of the cottages had three bedrooms. Normally, there were only six servants who remained on the island. So there were two of them living in each cottage. Andrea thought her meeting with Mr. Fisher would be best started here.

"The contestants arrive in two weeks. Lodging needs to be prepared for them immediately." There was barely enough time to convert the mansion into the setting needed for the pageant. "Unless you've hired someone else to get the island ready, I don't have the liberty of waiting two weeks."

Mark studied her, tapping his finger against his lips. Andrea saw the facade drop. The sexual predator disappeared and he looked grave. Her heart flip-flopped, then began a rapid beating in her chest. The sexual energy dripping from him had been intentional. He was as intrigued by her as she was by him. Otherwise, enlightening him on how much work needed to be done immediately would have impressed him, but not changed his mood this drastically.

"The job is all yours," he said. "Why are you meeting Brandon back here?"

She forced her attention to their surroundings and explained, "Fifty men need housing. Each man will probably have an agent with him. Many will come with family. Ample guest housing will be needed, as well. I understand that there are quite a few bedrooms in the mansion, but I'm not sure we want family members, who often have free time on their hands and begin wandering, having free rein of that magnificent home." Andrea waved her hand in the direction of the mansion, which was barely visible through the trees. "I'll probably create a cutoff number and allow contestants to have two people on the island with them. Even at that conservative number, we'll need to accommodate one hundred more people." She began pacing along the edge of the road and gesturing at their tropical surroundings. "I don't know what you know about building cabins, but pulling all of this off in two weeks is asking a lot."

"Yes, it is," he said, almost under his breath.

She faced him. "The contestants' arrival dates cannot be adjusted. This is everything I plan on discussing with Mr. Fisher." There were still ten minutes left before he was supposed to show up. Based on their phone call earlier that day, he was coming in from the mainland. Andrea looked at her cell phone, checking the time. "There isn't time to build anything elaborate," she continued, and held up her hand, anticipating his interruption. "And I have no intention of doing any major construction on your island."

Andrea waved her hand at the land, already seeing square cottages with their fake siding, more like trailers than homes, lining the side of the road.

"I think this is a perfect location." She gave him a quick look. "Also, we'll need some type of ferry service, possibly running every half hour to start, but as we get closer to the date, it will probably need to run back and forth nonstop as needed."

"Oh." She snapped her finger and turned to face him, her mind rolling now as she went through her mental checklist of everything that needed to be taken care of over the next couple of weeks. "When I was talking to your cook, she was under the impression she would be feeding fifty people for a few weeks. That's not right. With family members, agents, photographers, the press, representatives from sponsors"—she took a breath and waved her hand in the air—"just to mention a portion of the list, there will be a lot more than fifty people here. When I told her to anticipate a couple hundred over the next couple of weeks, but on pageant night to at least double that number, she muttered something about having words for Mr. Tripp. I thought I'd give you a heads-up."

"Okay," Mark said slowly.

"You did tell me you were the boss, right? Do you not want me telling you all of this?"

"No. I need to know all of this. It's just that I have a feeling I should be taking notes." He looked amused.

Andrea took another breath. When it came to her job, she took matters very seriously. Mark Tripp might very well be the best-looking man she'd ever laid eyes on, and his sex appeal still had her tingling all over. But these weren't trivial items she was discussing with him.

"This is my job. It's what I do. I make sure the pageant goes off without a hitch. By doing so, I will make the Tripp name sound as enticing as the Mr. Desire Pageant." Andrea studied the pretty flowers lining the narrow road as she searched her brain, trying to give Mark all information she could on what had already been done so far, matters taken care of by the previous pageant director. "There are two commercials airing starting this week promoting the Mr. Desire Pageant. A website is up and running where anyone can cast their vote for who they want to win Mr. Desire. The pageant has its own Facebook page, which I do believe already has over ten thousand fans."

She'd walked across the road to the other side and stared at the undeveloped land, picturing all the cabins with her men rushing in and out of them, all hurrying for their next photo shoot or interview. Two weeks would fly by. In no time, moments like this, when she could stand facing nature in its most raw state, and its most beautiful, would no longer exist.

"I'm impressed."

Andrea hadn't heard him approach. But when he spoke, he was right behind her. Her heart began beating hard in her chest as heat rose between her legs and swelled inside her.

"Good." She breathed in the perfumed air from the spring bloomers. "And thank you," she added. Andrea wasn't conceited and didn't want him thinking she was. "I love what I do," she added, realizing she wanted him to see her as hard-working and not arrogant and pompous as so many in her line of work were. "Normally preparation for an event like this happens long before the pageant begins. I can do this, but it will mean a tight schedule, and a very full next couple of weeks. My employment with you needs to begin right now."

She dared glance over her shoulder when he didn't say anything. Mark wasn't looking at her but studying the area in front of them. "This isn't the right place for your temporary lodging."

"What?" She frowned, once again surveying the land she'd picked out. "Yes, it is. It's perfect. We'll have to do some clearing out, but not as much as you might think."

"What kind of lodging do you have in mind?"

"They are small cottages. I plan on putting five men in each. So we'll need ten for the contestants." She gestured over her shoulder. "I have a printout in my car."

Andrea started toward the car and Mark grabbed her arm. "You mean easily installed kits," he supplied for her, then, keeping his grip firm, he turned her around so she once again faced the natural wildlife growing on the side of the road. "In order to put enough of those in here, this land would have to be cleared."

"Not all—" she began.

"No. Not all," he agreed. "But in between these trees here."

He gestured with his free hand. "And here," he indicated, waving in the direction of a group of trees to their right. "All of the undergrowth would have to be cleared out. That requires a landscaping crew. Once cleared out, the land would need to be leveled. Even for temporary lodging, we would need to ensure the land was flat and able to support as many cabins as you have in mind." He stepped forward, bringing her with him, and pointed at the ground. "This ground isn't as soft as you think. I'm thinking one, maybe two, bulldozers, and a few other excavators would do the trick. But a different crew would have to be hired to do that work. Once the ground is smoothed, paths would have to be put in. We're liable for these men as long as they're on this island. Housing codes, building codes, and insurance requirements all have to be met. We can't have someone tripping over uneven ground and suing us. Once again, our landscaping crew would be put to work."

Andrea was impressed. Mark had struck her as the international playboy type. It appeared he knew a thing or two about business, or at least housing. Mark stopped talking and looked at her. She fought off the panic attack threatening to close in around her. Fifty contestants would be descending on this island, and there was no way she would be able to accomplish what she'd had in mind. She needed a Plan B, and fast. If Mark saw her waver, sensed her hesitation, he would worry she was incapable of this job. And she wasn't. Her job didn't usually require she play general contractor, builder, or know about which codes would affect this island. Normally, putting up so many contestants meant being on good terms with hotel event planners. She'd toured the mansion. The available bedrooms in the different wings would be reserved for her judges, VIPs, and the entertainment, who would perform during the pageant. But she could handle this. Andrea had mastered a lot over her years in this line of work, one being how to think on her feet and be ready for the unexpected.

If he would just stop rubbing his thumb back and forth along her arm, Andrea was sure she would think of something. A car approached and she yanked her arm free from his grasp. For a moment, they looked at each other, and something in his green eyes created goose bumps on her skin. He knew he affected her and had no intention of stopping. There was a promise in his eyes before he looked away and acknowledged whoever was approaching.

One of the young men who worked at the docks parked a work truck behind Mark's Excursion and turned to look at his passenger. An older man, slightly balding, and around thirty pounds overweight, if Andrea were going to guess, said something to the young driver, got out, then closed his passenger door. The kid turned the stereo up and began thumping his fingers on the steering wheel once left alone in the truck.

"Mark Tripp Junior," the man said in a deep, rolling voice as he strutted around the front of the truck with long, purposeful strides. "And Miss Denton?" He raised one eyebrow as he gave her an appraising look, dropping his large, watery blue eyes down her body before focusing on her face.

"It's always good to see you, Brandon," Mark said, stepping forward with his hand extended to shake the older man's hand. His voice dropped an octave as he assumed that masculine, business tone men used when speaking with each other.

"I didn't know you were on the island." Brandon didn't sound as upset as he did conversational.

Andrea couldn't guess how well these two knew each other, and although it didn't matter, she suddenly felt left out of her own meeting. Stepping in next to Mark, she took initiative the moment the two finished shaking hands.

"It's very nice to meet you, Mr. Fisher," she began. "We're on a rather tight schedule."

"Call me Brandon," the older man interrupted, his tone softening when he addressed her.

He might be one of those good ol' boys accustomed to taking his orders from another man. She'd worked with her fair share over the years and knew how to handle him.

"Brandon," Andrea acknowledged, and smiled easily.

"So what do we have here?" Brandon shifted his attention from her to Mark as if he hadn't yet determined whom he would be taking orders from.

Andrea wasn't sure why Mark remained at her side either, and was acutely aware every time his arm brushed against hers. She'd called for this meeting, though, and this was her show.

"We need to set up temporary lodging for roughly two hundred people. And I need everything ready for my contestants to move in two weeks from now."

Brandon whistled under his breath and rocked up on his heels as his expression grew serious. "Okay," he said slowly, then shoved his fists into his large trousers. "Do you have a layout in mind? If not, I have a guy who can work up a few options for you," he added quickly before his first question could be answered.

Mark cleared his throat, but Andrea knew how to handle pushy contractors. "That won't be necessary." She walked around Brandon, leaving both men on the side of the road as she headed to the Volkswagen she'd been given to drive around the island while here. "This is what we're going to do." Andrea returned with the information she'd printed off the computer about the kits that were easily assembled into small cabins.

"Andrea had a really good idea," Mark interjected when she paused after showing the description of the kits to Brandon. "She's been hustling, trying to find the perfect place for her contestants' temporary lodging. Right before you showed up she thought of the old parking lot behind the house."

"The old parking lot?" Brandon rubbed the back of his head, his expression serious as he gave Mark his attention. "I'm pretty sure your father plans on bulldozing that under."

Mark shook his head. "That won't happen until after the pageant. It's the perfect location. We won't have to prepare the land or deal with half the codes we'd have to worry about if we actually broke ground."

Andrea was confused. Mark had taken over, and she wasn't sure how to grab a hold of the reins again, or if she should.

"It's in dire need of repair, but for this," Mark said, and tapped his finger on the printout Andrea held in her hand, "it's perfect. I can give us all a ride back there."

Twenty minutes later, Brandon was shaking hands with her, then Mark, and agreeing to place a rush on the shipment of temporary cottages to the island. The lodging for the contestants would be assembled within a week, which would leave plenty of time to furnish them and make sure there were clean linens and all the other amenities needed in each cabin. The young man in the pickup truck had followed them around to the back side of the mansion where a very large, abandoned-looking parking lot was partially hidden by a grove of palm trees. It was a ready-made, cleared-out spot just large enough for all of the cabins. Andrea wished she would have known it was here prior to meeting with Brandon.

"I'll give you a ride back to your car," Mark offered once Brandon had left.

"Why did you do that?" she asked.

He held her car door for her, then closed her inside his Excursion, which oddly enough seemed the perfect masculine vehicle to match Mark's dominating nature. After sliding in next to her and shifting the SUV into gear, he headed around the house to where she'd parked the Volkswagen on the narrow road to the servants' cabins.

"Do what?" he asked.

"Tell Brandon that putting the cabins back here was my idea."

"Men like Brandon Fisher aren't used to taking orders from a lady. If he viewed you as incompetent . . ." Mark raised his hand, as if expecting her to complain, or resent his words, and shot her a sharp look before continuing. "Let's just say I've known Brandon most of my life. This way he will work with you without provocation."

She wanted to tell him she could take care of herself and that she'd dealt with men like Mr. Fisher as long as she'd been working. "Thank you," she said instead, having also experienced more than one man with a strong protective instinct about them. "And just so you know, although I've worked with beauty pageants for women, that doesn't mean I haven't worked alongside men before."

Mark laughed. It was an easy, relaxed sound, not forced or condescending. "You've probably never built a house before, but I bet you have some kind of idea how one is built."

Andrea didn't have a clue what he meant by that. They slowed and parked behind her Volkswagen, and Andrea slid out the passenger side before Mark could come around the front of the truck. An odd sensation tripped over her, one that pulled forth the realization that they were pretty much alone on an island, and damn near anything could happen and no one else might ever know.

She paused at the front of the SUV, facing Mark, and studying those bedroom eyes of his. Would they look like that after having hot sex with him?

Andrea blinked, lowered her gaze, and started around him. "Why did you come to the island today?" she asked.

Mark seemed a bit too aware of how he affected her. His hand wrapped around her arm, this time grabbing the opposite one from the one he'd grabbed earlier. There was something guarded in his expression. The way he stared at her a moment before speaking, and how once he spoke, that comfortable, relaxed look returned, had to be proof that he was fighting to remain composed around her.

"You and I are going to be working very closely together during this pageant." His voice had dropped to a whisper.

For some reason it struck her as dangerous-sounding, too loaded with unspoken innuendos that made her flesh prickle. She managed to swallow as a sheen of perspiration broke out over her skin.

"You told me. You're the boss. But I can manage—" she said, but he interrupted.

"I know you can. I'm doing this for my father."

Mark Tripp Sr. was a very powerful man. When he bought the Mr. Desire Pageant, Andrea had watched closely, as did everyone in the industry. It was the talk of the town. When the pageant director walked off the set, her only public statement being there were irreconcilable differences, Andrea paid even closer attention. The previous director had left at a crucial time, just over a month from the pageant date. When Andrea was approached to take the position, she jumped on the opportunity. In her eyes, that said a lot about her nature, how determined, aggressive, and fearless she was when it came to taking something on.

"So I go through you if I want something from your father?" Andrea couldn't imagine Mark being a whipping boy for his dad.

"Yes. Or if you want something from me."

She swallowed. Definitely not a whipping boy. Mark had just laid the invitation out on the table. It was right there for her to take. All she had to do was step forward, drown in those powerful, lust-ridden green eyes, and let him know exactly what she wanted.

Mark was dangerous. Her rational thoughts were buried in a fog thick with lust and raw, unleashed need. Most men didn't affect her this way. Sure, she would acknowledge scrumptious eye candy along with the next woman, but no man stole her ability to function.

"Good to know," she said, her voice clipped and at a higher pitch than normal. Even when she turned toward her car, Andrea wanted to turn back around and demand he kiss her. "I'd like to think my reputation speaks for itself," she added over her shoulder, then reached for her door handle. "Your pageant will go off without a hitch."

"In certain areas it does," he said, his soft, deep voice a breath away from her ear.

Andrea's cell phone was sitting on the dash in her car, and it lit up as she watched. "Damn it," she groaned, as she opened the car door and was immediately berated with the chirping sound of the phone. "I left my phone in the car," she announced, needing the diversion, and slid into the driver's seat, leaving one leg out and her other open-toed sandal touching the edge of the accelerator. "And I've missed a few calls."

She looked up at Mark, phone in hand, and caught him looking down, but not at her face. She glanced down and noticed her dress had ridden up her thighs, damn near to her crotch. She could either yank it down and emphasize the embarrassing moment, or get all the way in, or out of, the car. Ignoring the almost inaudible voice of reason in the back of her head, she got out of the car, phone in hand.

"I need to return some calls," she explained. All three missed calls were from Julie. Andrea had just signed a contract, and often, afterward, there were minor details to iron out. "Thank you for helping with the temporary lodging. I'll let you know if I need anything else." *Like your dick buried deep inside me.*

Andrea had to accept the fact that right now she wanted to fuck him more than she wanted to continue organizing the preliminary necessities for the pageant. What if she offered a proposal—of the sexual kind?

4

Mark entered through the side door that brought him in on the second floor. It was a discreet entrance, and one he'd decided was necessary when building the mansion. There might be a time when he would want to get into the place without anyone knowing. He'd built four such entrances to the mansion, all barely noticeable unless someone knew where to look. The mansion was designed to entertain. This door allowed privacy and discretion, and a means to get to the private wings upstairs without anyone knowing someone had entered the home.

Mark spotted a maid vacuuming at the other end of the long, wide hallway. He waited until she was looking his direction before approaching her.

"I didn't mean to startle you," he offered apologetically after the woman pressed her palm over her heart.

His roguish grin didn't impress her. The maid, whom he didn't know and hadn't seen before, wore the traditional black dress with white apron his father had always preferred all his house servants wear. Although possibly somewhere around his age, she gave him a scolding look and returned to her vacuum, turning it and ignoring him.

Which was fine with Mark. The maid probably didn't know who he was, and obviously she didn't care. She might not even speak English. It would be a good idea to round up the hired help and introduce himself. He'd hate to think Andrea might be working up here and the staff would be indifferent to anyone entering the house this way.

Mark had done some catching up with Marcia in the kitchen after leaving Andrea. She had been the cook at their home in the Keys and had practically helped raise Mark. Reminiscing helped clear his head from the unbearable urge to fuck Andrea. She was one hell of a distraction. He didn't argue something needed to be done about that. But his days were numbered in finding the jewelry box, if it was even on Tripp Island, before the masses descended upon the place.

Marcia hadn't given him any new information he didn't already have. She had brought up the jewelry box to Silver during a conversation they'd had about forgotten treasures on islands. Marcia had remembered Margaret saying on several different occasions that she would bury her beloved jewelry box before ever letting anyone else get their hands on it. Mark tucked this bit of knowledge away and spent the next hour visiting and listening to how much Marcia loved the new kitchen she had here on the island.

If his mother had buried the jewelry box anywhere near where the old mansion had stood before he'd built this one, Mark was positive it would have been discovered as they tore the place down. The old home had been disassembled piece by piece, all wood stacked, and the rest of it organized and hauled off to be used for Habitat for Humanity houses, a program Mark was heavily involved with. The jewelry box had to be somewhere else on the island.

That meant covering forty square miles of land, which was roughly ten miles long. Some places were wider than others. It was more rugged toward the middle of the island, with rocky hills that weren't quite mountains. There were steep inclines, a lot of cliffs, more than a few waterfalls, and thick foliage everywhere.

Margaret had loved exploring the island. She'd hiked all over the island with Mark and his sister, Morgan, when they were children. They had picnicked on cliffs, made sand castles on the beach, enjoyed showers in the waterfalls, all of which Margaret Tripp had claimed cleared the city out of their heads. And none of which helped Mark decide where to start looking for the jewelry box.

Once Marcia had changed the subject and begun asking questions about Andrea, Mark had known it was time to leave his favorite cook and get busy on other tasks. Marcia managed to ply him with several questions before he was able to leave. And he had learned Andrea had set up shop in the north wing, which overlooked the front of the house. She was using the empty bedroom next to her bedroom suite as her office. There was a staircase not far from that bedroom, which made it convenient for anyone arriving at the mansion to quickly ascend to Andrea's office. The north wing had never been a popular wing because of this seeming lack of privacy, yet it appeared to be the perfect setup for Andrea. According to Marcia, Andrea had asked for very little help in setting up her space. Mark left the kitchen with Marcia calling after him that the young pageant director was not only a dear, but quite pretty, and he'd do himself well to spend some time with her.

If Marcia only knew how much time Mark wanted to spend with their pretty pageant director. The old cook would have a coronary if she knew exactly what Mark planned on doing with Andrea once he did get that quality time.

Mark headed upstairs and paused in the hallway. He

watched through the open door to the smaller bedroom Andrea was converting over to her office. Her back was to him. In the couple of hours since he'd seen her, she'd showered and changed clothes. Her hair looked darker damp. She'd twisted it into a long bun pinned to the back of her head. Loose strands of hair fell around her long, nicely arched neck.

The spaghetti straps to her tank top draped over her slender, slightly tanned shoulders. Her shorts hugged her ass. It was the most casual attire he'd seen her in yet, and he'd bet her outfit still cost a pretty penny. Andrea wore expensive, designer clothing, which told him she liked quality and was willing to pay for it. He wondered what she'd be willing to do for really good sex. He'd seen the desire in her eyes earlier. She'd wanted him at least as badly as he wanted her.

It hadn't bothered him when she'd walked away after he'd told her to let him know if there was anything she wanted from him. It only upped the stakes. Andrea knew it, too. He had no idea if the calls she'd missed were important or not. But she hadn't yanked her dress back down when it had slid a bit too high up her thighs. Another inch and he would have had a full crotch view. The flash she had given him damn near got her an eyeful of his very hard cock. Andrea had pushed his restraint to the edge. He'd argued with himself for a few minutes after she'd left him over chasing her cute little ass down or focusing on the main reason he was on this island in the first place. In the end, his mother's jewelry box had won over what he was sure would be damn good sex. There would be time to enjoy Andrea. She wasn't going anywhere.

In her current position he could focus on her upper thighs and imagine how she looked undressed. It didn't look like she was wearing a bra and he looked forward to her turning around to confirm if he was right. Until she did, Mark took his time drooling over that perfectly shaped ass and allowed himself to imagine spreading her open, enjoying the view, then burying himself deep inside her tight, scalding heat. It was suddenly a hell of a lot warmer in the hallway.

Hell! He ran his hand through his hair, tilting his head and taking in the view a moment longer. There was nothing worse than turning into an unruly horn-dog. As his father would put it, show a little class to get a little class. Mark had never fully understood the expression. He didn't want *a little* of anything.

The maid in the hallway turned off the vacuum, and at the same time, Andrea began tugging on the large wooden desk pushed up against the far wall. The grunting sound she made under her breath as she grabbed the end with both hands and pulled sounded as hot as she looked.

"Like some help?" he asked after watching her pull it a foot or so across the thick, plush carpet.

"Oh crap!" Andrea jumped, let go of the desk, and spun around, grabbing her heart. Strands of hair fell free and draped her face. Her mouth formed a rather enticing small circle. And she wasn't wearing a bra. "Damn it, you startled me."

He thumbed over his shoulder. "It was kind of hard to make my presence known with the vacuum going."

Mark entered the room and grabbed the opposite side of the desk. He grinned at her flushed and somewhat wary expression as he leaned into the desk.

"Where to, ma'am?" he drawled.

Her features relaxed and she exhaled, gripping her end. "In the middle of the room, facing the door." Andrea lifted, releasing an unladylike grunt as the small muscles in her arms flexed and bulged.

Mark lifted his end, making sure he didn't move too quickly. "Why the middle of the room?" he asked, watching her breasts flex, as well, and create firm, mouthwatering cleavage.

"It makes me appear more approachable," she explained. Andrea glanced up at him then focused on their task as she stepped gingerly backward.

"Maybe we should switch places." Mark noticed her muscles twitch in her arms.

"I'm fine." But then she lowered her end and brought her hands to her face, her fingers still bent in position from carrying the desk. "I didn't realize it would be this heavy," she admitted, giving him a meek smile. "Your timing was perfect. I appreciate the help."

"No problem." Mark came around to her side and moved into her space, forcing her to step aside. Then lifting the desk from that end, he yanked it back, half-carrying, half-dragging, until it appeared to be in the middle of the room to him. "How's that?"

"Playing macho will get you a sore back," she teased.

"If that's an offer to rub it later, I accept." He noticed her eyes warm to the suggestion and held her gaze for a moment. The vacuum turned on again, in a far bedroom, which meant for the most part the two of them were alone in this wing. "What else do you need moved? Maybe I can pull a muscle and convince you to give me an all-over body massage."

He was teasing but noticed when her breath caught and she exhaled between her teeth. "It doesn't matter what I need," she muttered under her breath, then pushed the office chair behind the desk and leaned on it, staring out the door.

"I can be very reasonable." Mark glanced at her bare legs, betting they would be silky smooth to the touch. He couldn't wait to learn if she was smooth in other places, too.

Andrea draped a free strand of hair behind her ear and looked over her shoulder at him. "Didn't you suggest my reason for leaving women's pageants for men's pageants was so I could seduce all the contestants?" she demanded, her lashes lowering enough to hood her gaze as she challenged him.

Mark loved a good challenge. "Only because if I'm going to seduce a woman I want to make sure she isn't sleeping with everyone else when I do."

Color appeared in her cheeks but they didn't turn a blazing red. He'd enticed her but not embarrassed her. Nor did she look away. Andrea was considering his unspoken proposition. Not that he had a problem speaking his mind.

"I've never had sex with a contestant," she informed him, her voice a husky whisper. "I take my job very seriously."

"I believe you, and good." He moved closer, then lifted the hair she'd tucked behind her ear and stroked it between his fingers. His knuckles brushed against her cheekbone and she raised her gaze, staring into his eyes. "How seriously do you take your downtime?"

She arched one eyebrow, her expression a mixture of amusement and wariness. Mark had a feeling the relaxed part of her was more for show than the truth. Andrea's breathing had increased, and he swore he felt her heart pattering through the tiny vein at her temple.

"During a pageant there is no downtime," she whispered. "What exactly is it you're doing, Mark?"

He was fairly certain his actions were perfectly clear. Andrea wanted him to spell it out. Forcing his hand and making him present his proposition to her in the form of a question would give her the upper hand, allow her to lay down stipulations. Mark had no intention of following some scheduled guideline. And if given the choice, something told him Andrea would create a tight and precise schedule. He wanted her a bit more relaxed and spontaneous.

Instead of answering her, Mark gripped her chin, angling her head just as he wanted it, then pressed his lips to hers before she could protest. If she had planned to make him say what was on his mind, her words were transformed into a sultry moan when he kissed her.

He touched his tongue to her lips and she opened her mouth, a barely audible groan escaping as she tilted her head further, giving him way to deepen the kiss. Mark let go of her hair and wrapped his arms around her, pressing her body against his as he explored her mouth.

God, she tasted good. There was no awkwardness as was so common in that first kiss. Instead she molded into him, her hands moving up his arms, and her tongue came out to greet his. They began a dance of lovers, full of promise and expectation.

As much as he'd love to bend her over the desk, help her break in her new office properly, and fuck her senseless right then and there, that wasn't how it was going to be. Mark fought to keep his dick from getting hard as stone. All blood threatened to drain through his body and flood his cock. The pressure would be unbearable, and only through years of practice and knowledge of women was he able to prevent himself from moving past this first kiss.

Not that kissing Andrea wasn't one incredibly hot experience. Her lips were soft and her tongue explorative, yet just hesitant enough to draw out his dominating side. It had been a long time since a woman pulled this part of him to the surface. Mark felt his aggressive side grow with the urge to control Andrea's actions, to give her just enough and allow her sensuality to blossom.

She leaned against him, her fingers softly probing his biceps, then his shoulders. Her full submission was right there, so close to releasing. When she moaned again, Mark pressed one hand between her shoulder blades and dragged his fingers through her hair, forcing her head back further so he could dip deeper into her sweet mouth.

A moment after she fully relaxed against him, Andrea straightened and her hands dragged to his chest. Mark wouldn't force himself on her, although the last thing he wanted was to let her go. She'd been right there, relaxed and trusting, but had refused to let go.

"Mark." His name sounded too damn good on her lips.

Her voice was husky and laced with desire when she pressed against his chest and took a step backward. "Mark," she repeated, and licked her lips.

He was fascinated by her tongue. What he wouldn't do to see it lazily creating a wet trail around his cock. His dick jumped to attention at the thought, in spite of his strict orders to remain flaccid. He didn't want to startle her or make her leery that he wouldn't respect her wishes. Although he didn't see signs of her getting ready to slap him, or sending him away, she had ended the kiss.

"Okay," she said, tugging at her tank top. She created enough space between them for her to look at him without tilting her head back as far. "We got that out of the way," she added with a slight chuckle.

The sound amused him. It sounded nervous but incredibly sincere and meaningful.

"We're not finished."

"I agree." She held her hand up, her actions in conflict with her words. "I have a proposition."

"A proposition?" Mark studied her large brown eyes.

Andrea focused on him, not blinking or missing a beat when she pressed forward. "Yes. Obviously you were as aware of the sexual tension between us as I was." She licked her lips again. It was the only sign of nervousness she displayed. Her tone was calm and cool. Her hands relaxed on either side of her. "My job is very high profile and any type of relationship would drag that person into the public eye, which isn't as fun as it might sound. I would like to suggest an arrangement."

"An arrangement?"

"Yes." She nodded once, then tucked a loose strand of hair behind her ear. "A sexual arrangement."

"A sexual arrangement." He sounded like a parrot. But Andrea, the sensual creature who'd almost completely submitted to him in his arms, now stood before him speaking to him as if she were demanding an amendment to her contract.

"We set times and locations to meet to have sex. We'll need a code, or some type of signal. We'll need one way of contacting each other for a specific time and location. Since this is your island, and your house, I'll leave the details as to where in your capable hands." She looked meaningfully around her office. "Very soon this room will be high traffic. Definitely not a good place for a quickie." She shot him a look. "Or something more drawn out if time permits."

Did she blush, just a bit?

"So let me make sure I understand." He caught himself pacing to the far window, parting the floor-length curtains, and staring down at the drive in front of the house. "You're suggesting we enter into an arrangement, a sexual tryst, with set dates and times when we'll fuck each other's brains out then go back to our lives." He turned around and met her gaze when she snapped to attention, her brown eyes revealing nothing. "And I suppose we'll be keeping this arrangement of ours quiet."

"That would be best."

Andrea was offering any man's ultimate fantasy, a repeated sexual rendezvous with no strings attached. His protective side, the dominating nature in him that had yet to subside since their kiss, still simmered hot just under his skin. He felt the tension increasing inside himself. Mark blamed that part of him, which he usually kept buried enough that it seldom affected his interaction with women, for initially not liking her idea.

"You've got yourself a deal, darling," he heard himself say. His mouth was tight when he managed a small smile and finally got the blush he'd been anticipating from her since they started this conversation.

*　*　*

Mark walked out of the building where TAC was located a week later. He swore his dick had been at least semi-hard since he'd last seen Andrea. She'd insisted all of their "dates," as she wanted them called, be arranged through text messaging. The less personal conversation between them, the easier it would be to keep their emotions out of it. Again he reminded himself how perfect this arrangement was. The discomfort in his gut he'd experienced each time he dwelt on how this affair might play out bugged him, though.

Mark had good sense about him. He made good business decisions, thought things through, and never jumped into a situation without researching it thoroughly. He'd obviously thought this tryst with Andrea through with his dick. Although he honestly didn't see it going bad, the tension inside him grew with each day as he anticipated returning to the island. Once he and Andrea fucked, his head would clear. Mark lived his life in control of everything around him. It was his comfort zone, and being in charge came naturally to him. He was currently living with an unknown. Unknowns never set well with him.

There was a second unknown, as well—the jewelry box. Fran had done a lot of research for him. Mark's father had given his secretary full rein of all documents on file pertaining to possessions the family had purchased twenty to thirty years ago. Mark didn't want to know how much digging Fran had to do, or how long a list she had to sort through, and Fran didn't offer the information. She'd simply handed him a printout of the pieces of jewelry believed to be in the box at the time of his mother's death. He was going to owe her one hell of a Christmas bonus at the end of the year.

Fran had also arranged for some top-notch professionals to meet Mark on the island. This team specialized in finding things. Not people, but things. According to Fran they specialized in treasure hunting, but not for the glory. Apparently they had worked for the FBI and had other impressive credentials.

Mark was more than a bit curious to meet these people. Since their dock was private, when Mark parked the Lexus he'd driven into Key West from Miami after leaving his office, the three people who climbed out of his father's limousine had to be the team Fran had told him about.

"Mark Tripp?" A man possibly in his midforties approached Mark. He had short-cut hair with tinges of silver in it and wore khaki shorts and a green T-shirt. His nondescript features had *cop* written all over them.

"Yes." Mark glanced at the other two. The second man could have been described just as the first. He wondered if part of their job description entailed having features that would blend into any crowd.

"I'm Steve Wright." The man gestured to the other guy next to him. "This is Carl Torres and this is Eve Hampton." Steve gestured to the woman with them. Her hair was dark red and cut in a bob around her tan, oval-shaped face.

Mark accepted the card Steve offered him. It was off-white and glossy. Mark tilted it in his hand so the sun wouldn't glare off of it. It said simply, *Steve Wright, Alpha 21, Recovery.* There was no street address but the bottom line showed they were based out of Key West

"Alpha twenty-one?" Mark questioned. "I've never heard of you. How long have you been in Key West?"

"It's Alpha, two, one, not twenty-one," Steve explained.

Mark looked at the card again, nodded, then shifted his attention to Carl, and finally Eve. Both stared back at him, neither appearing pleased or displeased to be there. They were an odd group and almost too tightly wound to appear normal.

"I've spoken with your secretary, Fran, several times on the phone," Eve offered, speaking for the first time. She had large brown eyes and when she blinked, thick black lashes hooded her gaze. "She insisted on discretion."

"Yes." Mark nodded. "I don't want anyone knowing about

this. Do you have suitcases? Silver captains our ferry and will help load any luggage you have. Once you're settled in your rooms on the island, we'll talk more."

Silver watched attentively as Mark approached with his new guests. His curiosity antenna was raised full-mast, but the old sailor had enough training in working for the Tripps not to ask questions. After loading quite a bit of luggage, they left on the ferry without talking and barely said a word to each other once they arrived on the island. The Alpha 21 group left with one of the servants to their rooms. Mark remained in the large entryway when Andrea started down the stairs. She'd been on his mind way too much. That proposal of hers had damn near driven him mad. He'd wanted to fuck her before she'd suggested their arrangement. Once she'd made it clear they would have sex soon, and on a regular basis, he hadn't been able to think of anything else.

"Who were they?" Andrea asked and slowed on the stairs.

When she reached the bottom step, Andrea watched the three Alpha 21 guests follow the servant down the hall and disappear around the corner before turning to Mark with an inquisitive look.

"I didn't think anyone was arriving yet," she added.

Mark moved to the steps where she remained, possibly staying on the bottom step to have an inch or so in height on him.

"They're talent scouts," Mark told her, using the story they'd conjured up as Steve, Carl, and Eve's cover so they could move around the island without being questioned.

She frowned. Her hair was pulled back from her face and long curls draped her shoulders and disappeared down her back. She wore a fair bit of makeup, which made her eyes look larger. "Talent scouts? What agency? Did they say?" When she looked over her shoulder in the direction they'd disappeared, her thick, light brown hair tapered down her back almost to her waist.

"Agency 21."

"I've never heard of them." She shook her head, still frowning. Then shrugging, she turned to face him, her expression transforming. All concern was gone, and instead she searched his face as she licked her lips. "You haven't been on the island the last few days. I started thinking you were avoiding me."

"Hardly." He couldn't talk to her about his mother's jewelry box, which was going to take a fair bit of his time. She'd wanted to keep things casual, though, so there was no reason to fill her in on what he'd been doing at work and with his father. "If anything, I'm more than ready for our first meeting."

He loved the color that filled her cheeks. Andrea was a tender soul, full of passion and sexual desires he couldn't wait to explore. She covered up her uncertainty with a dominating nature. She wanted the world to see her as a strong woman. In her line of work, running the show, Mark doubted many questioned her orders.

"Does tomorrow night work for you?"

"It should."

"Good. I'll text you."

Andrea had to step around Mark on the stair to go past him. His father had told him about the increase in staff in the past few days since he'd been on the island. Mark didn't hear anyone around them, but hired help was notorious for being incredibly quiet. A housekeeper could sneak up on him before he knew it.

He decided to chance it. Mark slipped his hand around her waist before she could move. The green, loose-fitting, sleeveless blouse she wore showed off cleavage. It hung to her hips and felt like silk when he pressed his hand to her side. Her leggings ended just past her knees and showed off her thin legs. In her closed-toe heels, she was able to look down at him. Mark imagined lifting her off the step and letting her slide down his body until she was forced to stare up at his face with those large brown eyes.

"Your place or mine?" he asked quietly, only because he couldn't think of anything else to say, but he didn't want her walking away from him yet.

"I'll let you know." She smiled. Andrea liked being in control and letting him know they would fuck soon, but holding out on pertinent details gave her the upper hand.

Mark decided to try tilting the scale just a bit. Grabbing her waist with both hands, he lifted her off the stair. When she slid down his body and her heels clicked against the glossy wood floor, it was all he could do not to pick her up again, haul her up the stairs, and give her a taste of what to expect the next night.

"Mark," she gasped, digging her nails into his shoulders.

"Yes?" He let go of her waist and brushed his knuckles against the underside of her breasts, then over her nipples before cupping her face with his hands.

"This isn't being discreet," she complained with a husky whisper, although she didn't try backing away from him.

"I promise, there are no hidden cameras." He brushed his lips over hers, tempting himself to the point where he could barely see from the blood boiling through his body to his cock.

It was all he could do not to deepen the kiss. There wasn't a servant under Tripp employment who would say a word if he devoured her right there on the stairs. Mark respected her wishes, though, and kept the upper hand when he dropped his hands to his side, gave her his best roguish smile, then walked away from her. He swore he heard her curse under her breath. His movements were stiff. Hopefully she didn't notice. He was more than ready for tomorrow night, and if her hushed complaints and ragged sigh, which was the last he heard as he disappeared down the hallway, were any indication, his new lover would be all over him the moment they were alone together.

5

Andrea stood behind her desk, tucking the files she'd pulled from the filing cabinet into the box on her chair. She'd damn near packed up most of her office within the last hour. It was her last day on the job. Tomorrow she would be a full-time employee for Mr. Desire, Inc., although she'd been working two full-time jobs for the past two weeks. There were boxes stacked on the chairs facing her desk, her wall hangings, one box had her two plants, then the other box had all the items from her desk. She stared at the dustless spots on the desk where her photographs, desk lamp, pen holder, and a few other items had been for the past six years.

Her cell lit up then buzzed. She grabbed it, glancing at her open office door and knowing none of the staff out there would come in. They were all rather upset that she was leaving but had moved into the mind-set that Andrea believed she'd outgrown them. Everyone thought she was out of her head to leave the solid security her job offered to take on the latest rage that might, or might not, make it to the ten-year mark. Andrea knew it would make it because she would see to it that it did.

"Hello," she said after glancing at the phone to see who called.

"Are you on the island yet?" Julie asked.

"No. I'm still in my office."

"Oh. Are you packed up? Didn't you say you planned on being out on the island by noon?"

"I did, but it took longer to sort through everything here at the office than I thought. At least I don't have any appointments today." Andrea couldn't say why she was dragging her feet. Honestly, she wasn't. Since dawn this morning she'd been running at full force. Mark Tripp Sr. had insisted on a teleconference that morning, which had lasted well over an hour. No sooner had she ended that call when the executive committee decided to meet with her. The board intended to give her a dignified farewell, but the meeting had turned into a harsh set of questions and answers with most of them demanding to know her plans for the newest pageant on the block. Andrea had been exhausted before noon after being raked over the coals by current and future employers. "My office is in boxes," she offered, shifting her attention to the boxes scattered around the room.

"Fun," Julie said. "I'd come help you but I'm in between meetings right now. Drinks later?"

Andrea thought of her seven o'clock *date*. Their first meeting. Mark had returned her text message midmorning and confirmed the time worked for him.

"Honestly, I don't know how easy it will be for me to come and go from the island once I'm out there. I'll have to let you know," she said, not wanting to mention she had a previous engagement. Julie would want to know what the meeting was about. Although she was Andrea's lawyer, she was probably the closest thing to a best friend Andrea had ever had. "I'll give you a call once I'm more settled. I promise."

Julie laughed. "I'll talk to you in a few months," she teased.

"I'll call you sooner than that," Andrea insisted, laughing. "I just need to get everything out of this office so I can think straight."

Julie understood. "When do the men start showing up?"

"Monday." She had three days to settle in and prepare for her contestants to show up, frazzled and full of questions. Andrea almost looked forward to it. Bringing peace and order to chaos always invigorated her. By Monday morning her mental chaos would be over. Then she would set order to fifty men's worlds. It was something she'd done hundreds of times now. Except this time she'd be reassuring them the pageant was in order and guaranteed to be their best ever. She had the speech down. Already she'd consoled agents, managers, and most of the crew already hired to handle the pageant. Fortunately, a lot of them were people she'd worked with before.

"I'll have to find a reason to come out to the island next week." There was humor in Julie's voice. "I want to check out these fifty hunks."

"Let me know and I'll make sure you're given a pass to come aboard. There is incredibly strict security up and around Tripp Island. No one arrives, or leaves, without showing a pass to these security guards." Andrea thought Mark had gone a bit overboard with the level of security, but she admitted it did make walking around on the island feel a lot safer. "By the middle of next week I'm sure I'll have a much better idea of my schedule and my life will be in order again." Andrea wouldn't focus on the many men who were about to enter her life. It was enough wondering how her life would be in the very near future with one new man entering it.

"Okay, darling. Go put order to your world."

It took longer than Andrea thought getting everything organized. She needed to drop everything from her old office off at her apartment. While there, she would pack more personal items that she'd decided she would need before heading to the island. She would only be on Tripp Island for a month, but she wasn't sure how easy it would be to go back to her apartment for an item forgotten. Better to have too many of her personal items, than not enough.

It wasn't that far from her apartment in the Keys to the docks. Andrea was so exhausted after packing that she didn't mind waiting for the driver, who would pick her up and take her to the docks. With everything she planned on taking to the island stacked by her front door, Andrea sat on her comfortable futon in her cluttered living room and opened the file Julie had sent her on Mark Tripp Jr. Boxes from her office were stacked around her. All of which she would sort through and decide what to do with after the pageant was over.

There were several articles inside the file. Julie had sent a write-up done on Mark in last year's *Architect* magazine.

"He's an architect?" Andrea mused, leaning back and holding her iPad in one hand while scrolling through the article with her finger. "And good enough to win an award."

The article was about the fifty-seventh P&A awards, which apparently were prestigious awards given out yearly to the most innovative architects. Mark won his award for his design of an underwater town that would exist purely off solar and hydraulic power. There was a small blurb singing Mark's praises. Andrea shook her head after reading it.

"Not what I expected."

The next article went back a few years and was a small piece from the *Miami Herald* announcing the son of the Florida tycoon Mark Tripp had graduated from the University of Florida with an architectural degree. It stated no one in the family was available for comment, but the reporter speculated the son of the reclusive billionaire wouldn't follow in his father's footsteps and run the family business. There was a small picture included with the caption underneath stating Mark Tripp Jr. was spending the weekends of his summer helping Habitat for

Humanity with pro bono blueprints for several different floor plans of houses that would be built that summer.

Andrea tapped the picture to make it larger and stared at a younger version of the man she'd agreed to have a purely sexual relationship with over the next month. "You've always been a hunk, haven't you?" she whispered and stared at the shirtless Mark standing on a ladder and laughing with the man next to him.

She stared a minute longer, her insides throbbing as she imagined running her hands over all that bulging muscle. "Just a few more hours," she whispered, stroking the picture, which made it disappear and a new screen pop up asking what she wanted to title the picture and where she wished to save it.

On an impulse, Andrea tapped the keys on her iPad and typed *my personal hunk*. Julie had sent a short message and Andrea speculated as she read it.

He's got my vote for Mr. Desire. LOL. Talk about good looks, brains, and money. What more could a lady ask for? You have my permission to go after this one.

Their arrangement would make it so she could not *go after this one*. Men loved slutty women. But Andrea had been around long enough to know any decent man wouldn't choose a slut over virtuous and classy when it came to a long-term relationship. She'd requested this arrangement so she wouldn't risk entering into a relationship.

Suddenly irritated and anxious, Andrea jumped off of the futon and hurried to her large front living room window. She lived in a gated community but could see the entrance where anyone could be buzzed through into the private parking lot. Tall, forbidding-looking black rods topped with iron spikes made up the gate, their sharp pointed tips dangerous and very protective. As she stared, a long, sleek black limo pulled up to the gate and a driver got out to punch keys on the pad that would announce him. A second later the keypad by her front door buzzed, letting her know she had company.

Andrea watched the driver load everything she was taking into the limo's trunk. It was a huge trunk and still the boxes of pageant supplies she liked keeping on hand, office supplies that were hers and easier for her to bring instead of requesting the Tripps provide them, as well as more of her wardrobe, quickly filled the trunk. It would take most of the day organizing and preparing for everyone's arrival on Monday.

In spite of all the work ahead of her, Andrea couldn't keep her mind off Mark. There was plenty to think about other than the articles Julie had sent her. She would have been better off not reading them. This no-strings-attached arrangement was so they wouldn't get to know each other. Andrea had enough to keep her busy while on the island. There wasn't time to think about a relationship. But damn, Mark seemed much more appealing to her now after reading those articles.

Already she knew Mark would demand enough of her attention. He was on her mind too much now, and she hadn't fucked him yet. The proposition had been her idea. She'd instigated the turmoil that now plagued her mind. The sooner they had sex, the better. Then their *dates* would fall into routine along with the pageant. That was all the relationship she needed.

Andrea swore she was more tired than the two young men who carried her luggage upstairs to her assigned suite. They were apparently part of the grounds crew but would be assisting everyone descending on the island over the next few days with luggage and other whatnot. This would be her home away from home for the next month. She plopped down in her chair behind her desk and looked around. There would be time to unpack, organize, and prepare for the following Monday. Her gaze fell on a plain clock hanging in front of her on the wall. It was six o'clock.

"Damn," she groaned, and pushed herself out of the chair. She had an hour to get ready for Mark.

Andrea made time to take her clothes out of her hanging suitcases and put them in the closet in her new bedroom. Then, standing in the large, walk-in closet, she stared at her outfits, mulling over what to wear. She wanted to look good, sexy, but not too anxious. How many times had she listened to designers advise contestants on how to dress to set a certain mood? Warm colors . . . cool colors . . . bright colors . . . knee-length dresses . . . short skirts . . . each of them spoke of a certain mood.

"Lord," she groaned, and rubbed her temple. All the explanations and examples floated around in her brain but nothing clicked. Finally, grabbing a simple strapless dress she'd picked up at Macy's on a lunch-hour shopping spree the previous summer, she hurried to the shower.

The hot shower helped. What water pressure! Andrea moaned with sheer pleasure as the jets pounded her back. Pressing her hands flat against the shower wall, she let her head fall back and closed her eyes. In less than an hour she would be exploring Mark Tripp's gorgeous body. She knew he was muscular and thin. His green eyes bored into her mind, watching her as she continued surveying his body in her thoughts. She bet his brown, wavy hair would be silky. The tight, small curls of darker brown hair that she'd caught glimpses of would be sprayed across his chest and tickle her fingertips as she played with it.

By the time she'd managed to wash her hair and shave every inch of her body, she throbbed and pulsated with raw, uncontrollable need. It didn't diminish when she dried with the thick, pleasant-smelling towels already hanging in the bathroom. She struggled to zip the zipper to her dress up her spine. After taking time to carefully apply makeup, her hair was still damp. Andrea carefully appraised her work in the full-length mirror hanging on the back of the bathroom door. Damp hair or not, she decided she looked pretty good.

"I could put a few makeup artists to shame," she muttered under her breath, pleased with how she'd managed to make her eyes look large without making it appear she had too much eye shadow on.

There was a firm rap on the door in the living room that led to the hallway. Andrea jumped and her heart skipped a beat.

"Shit," she groaned and grabbed her cell phone from the bathroom counter. It was ten minutes before seven. He was early. Rushing out of the bathroom, there was a second knock on the door when she reached it.

Her apartment had a peephole, but the door to her suite here in the mansion didn't. She hesitated when only the dark wood door blocked her from whoever was on the other side. Andrea didn't doubt it was Mark, but butterflies fluttered in her gut as she reached for the doorknob. She wasn't used to answering the door without knowing who was there. Worse yet, there wasn't a chain on the door either. The mansion probably didn't require more protection, or security, than minimal locks. Andrea required more. Born and raised in Miami, she needed to know she was safe when she relaxed at the end of the day. Reminding herself there were only a handful of people on the island right now, and twice as many security guards already stationed around the island, she opened the door.

All thoughts of security disappeared out of her head when she stared at Mark. The first thing she noticed was how good he smelled. He wore a plain blue T-shirt and dark, comfortable-looking jeans. His brown hair waved around his face, and his green eyes were exceptionally bright, even in the dim hallway light.

"You look good," was all he said before walking into her suite and taking her in his arms. Then his mouth was on hers.

Andrea wasn't sure how she ended up backed against the

wall. Hard, well-defined muscles crushed against her. His body heat sent her inner temperature to a feverish state within moments. Talk about a greeting!

This worked. Yes, he was definitely holding up his end of the deal. There was no conversation. Not that anything needed to be said. He impaled her mouth as his hands began roaming over her body. They started a wicked dance with their tongues and his cock throbbed between them.

If she'd had any notions of what to expect when Mark first got there, none of them mattered now. She wouldn't have remembered any of them if she'd tried. He kissed her the way a lover who had been missing her would. Andrea returned the kiss with equal enthusiasm.

Her heart raced. Her mind whirled, and she couldn't focus on any one thought. Her body tingled. Her insides pulsated. Already her pussy was wet, swollen, and eager for his attention. When she was sure he would raise her dress and explore where she needed him most, he gripped her hips and backed away from the wall, bringing her with him.

"Your bed or mine?" he whispered against her lips, then intensified the kiss once again.

Andrea didn't try answering, not when his tongue swirled deep into her mouth. She arched into him and her breasts grew heavy. Her nipples were painfully hard. The strapless dress she'd chosen, although not a designer brand, had always made her feel incredibly sexy. She hadn't had time to put on stockings or heels, which would have finished off the ensemble nicely, but now she didn't care. She stretched against his body, gripping his hard shoulders, and went up on tiptoe.

Mark was showing consideration, though, another redeeming comment. She'd asked for discretion, had even emphasized the fact on the stairs the day before when she worried he might have kissed her. Hell, she wanted him to devour her just the way he was right now when he'd lifted her from the bottom stair. He'd respected her wishes, and was doing so now. Much more of this and she would be falling head over heels in like. As it was, she was definitely in lust.

"I think mine is closer," she whispered the moment she could speak. Then nipping his lower lip, she sucked it into her mouth and scraped her teeth over the moist flesh.

Mark growled into her mouth as he scooped her off the ground.

"Oh!" she said, surprised, and her dress twisted on her, exposing quite a bit of cleavage.

He wrapped one arm around her back and slid the other under her legs. Cradling her against his chest, he kicked the door closed with his foot and made his way across her living room toward the door leading into her bedroom. Andrea didn't bother asking how he knew exactly where to go. The answer was obvious. This was his mansion. He'd possibly been in all the suites and all the wings of the giant house over the years his family had owned the place. Or maybe all the suites had the same layout. Andrea didn't care enough to ask.

Mark didn't bother with her light. He slowed his pace in the bedroom, weaving around her suitcases full of clothes she'd have to deal with before Monday. He released her legs and lowered her feet to the floor when they stood at the edge of the large bed. The wooden four-poster frame was high enough off the floor Andrea almost hopped to climb onto the bed. Mark, on the other hand, simply sat on the edge of it then took her in his arms again. This time, instead of ravishing her as he had at the front door, he turned her around so her back was to him.

She opened her mouth to speak but licked her lips instead when her zipper slipped down her spine. His knuckles brushed against her skin as the dress grew incredibly loose on her. Andrea either needed to grab the outfit, or allow it to slide down her body. Their arrangement wasn't about being shy.

Nonetheless, her heart hammered in her throat when she

forced her hands to remain at her sides and let the material slip over her breasts and past her waist. It crumpled low on her hips.

"Turn around, sweetheart." Mark took her hair, gathered it in his hand in the middle of her back, and held on to it, using it as if he might steer her where he wanted her. He tugged slightly but was gentle when he scooped her back into his arms. "Stand and face me." His raspy whisper made his words seem more of a request than an order.

Andrea was suddenly light as a feather, feeling like she might float back onto the bed. She stepped out of the dress and moved until she stood between his legs. It was the most wicked sensation being this close to such a gorgeous stranger, his eyes heavy with lust, while he sat facing her, completely dressed and her naked.

She ran her hands over his shoulders, forcing herself not to be shy. Although what did it matter if she was? It wasn't as if she were trying to give him a certain impression of her personality. There would be no feelings mixed in with this relationship. That way neither of them would get hurt. It was the best type of relationship to have. Muscles twitched under his shirt, filling her with a sense of power and confidence to explore. So much for being shy.

"I want your clothes off," she said, her voice raspy.

He raised his gaze but his lashes hooded his eyes from hers. She wasn't sure if he focused on her breasts or higher. Her skin was hypersensitive. She felt as if he were looking at every inch of her body all at once.

"Are you in a hurry?" It was more of a challenge than a question. As he asked, Mark moved his hands up her waist, under her arms, until he cupped her breasts.

"I'm not in a hurry." She tried leaning forward, encouraging him to take her nipples into his mouth. They were so hard. Even as he held them, lifting her breasts slightly in his hands, she felt the weight of them increase. He could so easily alleviate the pressure, bring it down to a level she could handle.

"Good," he rasped. "Your body is absolutely perfect," he continued, apparently satisfied that he didn't need to undress at that exact moment, and pinched both her nipples at the same time.

Lights flashed in her brain and Andrea hissed out a breath. She grabbed his wrists. They were thick with strength and although she didn't try too hard, Andrea suspected she wouldn't be able to move his hands off her if he didn't want them moved. Electrical shocks tore through her body straight down her middle until her clit swelled and throbbed as if it were the part of her just tortured.

"I want to see your body," she pressed the moment she regained her ability to speak.

She was so wet she felt the moisture cling to her shaved skin. Mark was ignoring her as he continued fondling her breasts. When she'd had all she could take, Andrea moved her hands down his shirt, tugging it upward as she did. She felt his bare back, touched his warm, smooth flesh, as Mark tightened his grip on her. It was as if touching him sent him closer to the edge just as tormenting her breasts did to her. She wanted to know just how sensitive he was to her touch.

Mark didn't give her the chance. He moved too fast for her to anticipate his next move. In one, quick fluid movement, Mark lifted her, turned, and tossed her in the middle of the large bed. Just as attentively, he was over her, spreading her legs. He stretched her open, exposing the cream clinging to her smooth, shaved pussy. His eyes glowed and a look of hunger in them made her insides scorch with need.

Andrea anticipated his next move as he positioned himself between her open thighs. She reached for him, willing to encourage his movements and place his mouth on her throbbing clit. Mark situated himself and looked up at her, past her belly, which rose and fell at a rapid pace. Andrea stared down her body, in between her full, ripe breasts, and drowned in his dominating gaze. As she tried to press her hands down on his head, he once again moved too fast for her to register what he'd do next. Mark grabbed her wrists and pressed her hands into the bed on either side of her. At the same time, his mouth descended upon her pussy. Andrea bucked against his face, howling as he restrained her.

"Oh my God! Mark!" She managed at the last minute not to scream, in spite of the incredible sensations tripping over each other and rolling up her body as Mark displayed amazing talent at oral sex. Loud howls of pleasure were always dead giveaways as to what was happening behind closed doors.

"I love a shaved pussy." His chin had barely visible whiskers that scraped over the most sensitive part of her body as he spoke. "Relax, beautiful. Every inch of you is tense," he instructed and let go of her wrists to run his hands up her body, then along her inner thighs. "How often do you let go, beautiful?"

His words spun around in her head. As soon as he finished speaking, his tongue dipped inside her then traced a path to her clit. His chin continued to brush against her skin. And he wanted her to relax?

Mark was doing things to her she fantasized about all too often when she stole time to masturbate with her favorite vibrator. He pressed his hands to the backs of her thighs and lifted her ass off the bed, stretching her wide open as he spread her legs.

"Don't worry about me," she managed, barely able to speak as she clenched the bedspread on either side of her. "I'm doing just fine." She smiled to prove her point.

Mark looked up at her and through blurred vision Andrea stared into his intoxicating green eyes. He wanted to manipulate her actions the way other men did. She wasn't surprised, but she just had no intention to give him that control. Andrea didn't let go for any man. All she wanted was for Mark to give her sexual pleasure. She would control how much and how often. She continued grinning at him and moaned, letting him know without words that he was making her feel incredibly good.

Her vision blurred more when his tongue stroked an exceptionally sensitive part of her pussy. It seemed his features hardened but not with determination. Other men she'd been with before liked turning sex into a competition, who could get whom off first and the most. It wasn't a bad game, but Andrea preferred not turning sex into a game with only one winner.

His long fingers pressed into her inner thighs and he stretched her legs further apart. "Just fine is how you are when you're at work, not when you're on the verge of an orgasm," he informed her. "And unless you think of this as part of your job . . ." he trailed off.

Andrea moved her hands behind her head, tangling her fingers in her still slightly damp hair and lifted her head, ready to shoot him a look to kill. At that same moment, Mark quit talking and captured her clit between his lips. He applied the slightest amount of pressure, just enough to cause the tiny nerve endings under her flesh to explode in a frenzy.

"Damn it." She wanted to complain and inform Mark he was out of line, and very far off base with his suggestion. "Oh!" she moaned, her mouth forming a small circle and staying that way when bright lights exploded into an array of color behind her eyelids.

Her world teetered. Andrea completely forgot what it was she was about to chastise him for. She slapped her hands against the bed on either side of her and twisted the bedspread with her fists, desperately trying to hold on when she swore the bed tilted, along with her entire world. Mark had her legs pinned. The skills of his tongue and the warm heat from his mouth continued to torture her. Finally the heat erupted inside her.

She leapt off the bed, or tried to, as she fought one last time to control her orgasm. It wasn't possible. She came hard, soaking herself as wave after wave of indescribable pleasure damn near tore her apart.

"Are you still doing just fine?"

Mark's words sounded as if they came from far away, moving toward her through a long, narrow tunnel. If she answered him, Andrea didn't have a clue what she said. Her body jerked several times during the aftermath of her orgasm. When she finally went slack, she was vaguely aware of him releasing her legs, letting them fall limp to the bed.

He moved away from her, standing. It took a moment to get her brain to work and when she did it dawned on her she was missing the show she wanted to see. Opening her eyes proved somewhat of a task and when she did, focusing on him took even longer. By the time she was able to stare at his virile, naked body, he was sheathing his rock-hard cock in a condom.

Immediately, as if in response to him preparing himself for her, Andrea's body began tingling all over again. The pressure in her pussy grew. Swelling started deep in her womb and spread throughout her when he moved over her.

She felt his body heat, studied the rippling, hard-packed muscles on his chest, and welcomed him by stretching her legs, then pressing her thighs against his hips when he positioned himself over her.

"Open your eyes."

She thought they were open. Andrea complied, words no longer seeming important. She wanted to see him, feel him, watch his face when he sank deep inside her. Mark allowed her all of those things, and more.

He didn't kiss her as she thought he might when his dick pressed against her entrance. She wasn't sure why she wanted him to, but she forgot about his mouth the second his cock slid deep into her pussy. He entered her with one quick, fluid thrust.

"Andrea," he whispered.

She hadn't realized her eyes were closed again. Blinking a few times, she focused and stared up at him.

"You're beautiful," he told her.

"You're good." Andrea didn't make it a habit of singing any man's abilities. If she got them this far, their ego didn't need stroking.

Mark didn't blink an eye at the compliment, nor did he respond to it. His facial features hardened, and he set his jaw in a firm, determined line as he increased his pace and moved swiftly in and out of her, building pressure, creating a sweet friction she didn't want to ever end.

As he impaled her again and again, Andrea came just as hard as she had when he'd shown her how good he was with his mouth. His cock was equally as talented. She cried out, tossed her head from side to side, and grabbed his arms, his shoulders, and his chest.

When he finally brought them both to an explosive climax, Andrea couldn't say if they'd fucked for hours or only a few minutes. She knew only two things. One, that he'd given her some of the best orgasms she'd ever had in her life, and two, that she wanted him to do it again very soon.

6

Mark wasn't sure what he had expected to happen once the men started arriving on the island. What he did know was he'd never given a lot of thought to the magnitude of the event, the amount of work involved in putting the pageant together, and how impressive Andrea would be as she calmly controlled the entire process.

Over the next few days the cottages behind the mansion, which had been assembled and prepared for their guests, then individually inspected by Andrea, began filling up with way too many incredibly good-looking men. At least each of them thought themselves handsome. The testosterone level inside the mansion was thicker than a gym locker room and strong enough to make Mark sick. There were family members, reporters, agents, and too many other professionals in this industry he knew nothing about filling the island with their wound-up personalities and high sense of self-worth. None of them were as haughty and arrogant as the contestants, though. It was hard to believe anyone would naturally like these men, yet the amount of schmoozing and ass-kissing going on around the place was disgusting. He was going to have to have the island disinfected once all this was over.

Through all of it, Andrea was a calm beacon of strength. There were calamities of all kinds, mistakes with luggage, cabins that weren't sufficient, and that was just from the contestants. Camera crews came to her with problems. Wardrobe designers flooded her with complaints. Andrea never broke a sweat. Every time Mark saw her, and he found himself watching her with intent interest, her smile appeared sincere, her posture and movements relaxed, and her soft-spoken mannerism enough to calm the most irate of people on the island. The papers had predicted the Mr. Desire Pageant would have a tough time pulling through a change in venues and pageant directors right before the event was supposed to happen. In the first couple of days, Andrea proved them all wrong. Saying he was impressed was an understatement.

Even with security beefed up on the island, they would possibly need a curfew. Mark drove the narrow road after dark that night and slowed a few times as people walked alongside his SUV.

"We have more than a few curious onlookers," Steve Wright commented, looking up, then standing when Mark approached.

"I need you to make note if the same person, or people, appear to be watching what you're doing," Mark said. He'd parked just off the road at the first beach past the house and glanced around him now at the darkness surrounding them.

"Eve can't work by herself," Steve added.

"*Can't* isn't the right word." Eve remained squatted next to both men. She used something that looked like a calculator as she punched buttons and stared at the screen. "I'm perfectly capable of working by myself, or with others. But apparently your contestants feel a woman alone on this island must be in dire need of their attention."

"They aren't my contestants."

Eve had an unusually shaped face, and a slight hint of an accent that might have been Irish. Mark wasn't sure if he would consider her attractive or not. But he understood her plight, and it was more cause to enforce a curfew, if not rules about where contestants could go on the island, and when.

"If you're Mark Tripp, this is your pageant, darling," Eve informed him with a sultry whisper.

"It is my island." He wasn't going to argue with her. He wasn't claiming one of those pumped-up, dim-witted contestants, but he would claim responsibility for anyone on Tripp Island. "I'll see that a curfew is enforced for all pageant-related people. I'm also thinking it might be a good idea to lay down a few ground rules on where, and when, anyone can traipse around the island."

"Good idea," Steve agreed.

"So what do you have for me?"

Eve stood, holding the piece of equipment she held in her hand out for Steve to see the screen. The backlight on it glowed against their faces, drawing out shadows against their solemn expressions.

"I am ninety-nine percent sure that your mom's jewelry box is not in the mansion," Steve told him, looking at Mark. "Nor are any of the pieces of jewelry you described."

Mark liked the fact that they were looking not only for the jewelry box with all its contents, but also each piece of jewelry. "Why ninety-nine percent sure?"

"I never claim one hundred percent assuredness."

Mark nodded. "What are you doing now?" he asked, nodding at the piece of equipment in Eve's hand.

She looked at him as he did, then turned so she stood next to him and held the piece of equipment up for Mark to see. "It's a good thing we work on commission and not by the hour," she began, looking up at him and smiling.

"What Eve means is our work is time-consuming, but seldomly not productive."

Mark caught Steve giving Eve a warning look. When Mark looked at Eve's equipment in her hand, he caught her studying him.

"I don't care how much it costs."

"I love that quality in a man." Eve brushed against Mark's arm with hers as Steve's phone rang.

Mark's father had sealed his first million before Mark was born. He remembered his dad telling him that he knew Margaret was the woman for him because she wasn't sure about marrying a man with so much money. It had been a lesson Mark learned at an early age. Any woman who showed interest in his money was guaranteed to bring trouble, heartache, or both.

"Hello," Steve answered. "Yup."

Mark focused on Steve, watching his facial expression change. Eve said something to Mark, but he ignored her when Steve met his gaze.

"Carl found something," Steve said, hanging up and stuffing his phone in his shirt pocket. "Let's go."

Mark met the crew behind the old parking lot that had been transformed into a fortress of cabins for the contestants. After parking his SUV back in one of the carports alongside the house, Mark trekked around the cabins where a variety of music filled the air and men's cologne competed with the fragrance from blooming flowers.

"We're definitely picking up on something," Steve announced when Mark came around the thick foliage and found the three of them huddled together over more equipment.

Carl scanned the ground with what looked like a metal detector. He looked up when Steve spoke and smiled a toothy grin.

"Hi, boss!" His face was lit up as if he'd just discovered

gold, which in this case, they hadn't. "She's going off like a Morse code secret."

Mark grinned at the analogy but was skeptical. "I was under the impression a metal detector wouldn't work in finding the jewelry box."

Carl glanced at Steve. Mark frowned when they seemed hesitant in commenting.

"What?" he demanded.

"We don't want to rule out any possibilities," Steve told him.

Mark nodded but got a strange feeling there was something else they weren't telling him.

"Do we have permission to dig?" Carl asked, again shooting a side glance at Steve before turning his attention to Mark.

One good thing about owning an island, Mark knew every inch of the land and what was underneath it. "Permission granted." He nodded in the direction of the house when they all hesitated. "I built that house," he told them, indicating the mansion. "Every pipe, every wire underground, I arranged to have put there. You're in safe territory here, gentlemen, and lady," he said, nodding to Eve, who flashed him a flirty smile. "I'll make sure no one bothers you."

Mark put in a call to his chief of security, instructing that no one disturb his crew digging behind the contestants' cabins. While he had him on the phone, Mark decided no one could wander beyond the immediate grounds surrounding the mansion after eight in the evening, and not before six in the morning. Anyone who wished to leave the grounds between six a.m. and eight p.m. needed to inform his chief of security where they were going specifically and how long they would be at that location.

The new curfew made it sound as if Mark simply didn't want to be held accountable for anyone on his island after it was dark. It also gave his Alpha 21 crew freedom to search the island without worrying about anyone else bothering them. Mark informed his chief of security that the Alpha 21 crew was exempt from the curfew, but they still needed to check in as to their whereabouts on the island. Mark wanted to be on top of everyone's movements on Tripp Island.

He paced while he spoke on the phone, keeping his voice down, and more than once he got the uncanny sensation he was being watched. There were enough security guards on the island to send several to make sure his crew wasn't bothered during their dig. After hanging up, Mark glanced back at Steve, Carl, and Eve, who were huddled together on hands and knees, scraping dirt delicately with trowels. They'd set up a high-powered light on a tripod next to them. None of them were looking his way.

More than likely, pacing the length of a very tall, overgrown hedge had his guard up. "Too many scary movies as a kid," he mumbled, then shook his head and turned toward Steve, Carl, and Eve. "Keep me posted," he informed them, having decided he wouldn't huddle over them while they worked.

"Were there coins in the jewelry box?" Eve asked, standing then holding her hand out.

She held her hand, palm up, in front of the light for Mark to inspect the three oversized coins. Mark took them from her, realized they weren't any type of currency he'd ever seen before, and squatted in front of the light, then blew at the dirt covering them.

"Here." Eve pulled what looked like a shaving brush out of her pack pocket and began gingerly removing dirt from one of the coins. "Now look."

She swapped coins with him and let Mark examine what appeared to be a gold coin, although he had no idea how old, or from where.

"Dad didn't mention coins."

"Take them with you," Steve suggested. "You can describe

them to your father. We'll let you know if we find anything else."

"Was this what you were worried about?"

"What?" Steve frowned at Mark's question.

"That the possibility existed the contents of the jewelry box might have fallen out."

Steve looked at him as if the thought hadn't crossed his mind. "It's a possibility. The description your father provided of the box suggested it had secure hinges and clasps. But time can wear anything down. I'm not ruling out a thing at this point."

Two security guards appeared from the other end of the hedge and hesitated in the dark. One of them flipped on a flashlight, aiming it at the ground, when Mark approached. He left the crew to their digging and joined the guards.

"Keep an eye on them," Mark instructed, and gestured over his shoulder with his thumb. "Make sure no one bothers them."

"Will do," a stocky guard said, nodding. "There were a few people on the other side of the hedge that we sent back to their cabins. One of them seemed a bit put out, and she told us she was the pageant director."

"Pageant director?" Mark squinted at the dark hedge. "Where?"

Mark took off in the direction the guards indicated. Had Andrea been watching him while he'd been on the phone? He doubted she would have overheard his conversation, especially after working his way around the hedge and coming up on the back side of the cabins. It sounded like a party was going on, and there were dozens of men lingering outside different cabins, drinking and laughing. That and the music would have drowned out any sound coming from beyond the old parking lot. But when he spotted Andrea, laughing and drinking with a handful of men standing in a circle around her, Mark opted for the long way back to the house. This was her party, not his.

And, he reminded himself as he made it back to the carports and the back entrance, she wasn't his woman, either.

The contestants entered the mansion by the patio that went around the back side of the place. Mark leaned against the railing in the shadows, enjoying a drink and trying to soothe his nerves. Less than an hour after staring at the star-filled sky and listening to the waves on the beach, Andrea came up the stairs not far from him. Mark pushed away from the railing, leaving his glass on it.

"Oh," she said, spotting him and showing her surprise at seeing him.

"Have fun this evening?" he asked.

"Yeah, I did." Andrea's smile was sincere and relaxed. "I always try to spend at least one evening with the contestants before the pageant begins. It helps to get to know them and let them feel comfortable with me."

There was a hint of alcohol on her breath and Mark wondered how drunk she was. Although he'd spent half his time alone brooding over her drinking with other men after making arrangements to fuck him, he saw now Andrea was doing part of her job. She didn't show any signs of being caught doing something she shouldn't be doing. But then, why would she? It wasn't as if they were in any type of relationship, nor were they trying to enter into one.

"That's good thinking," he said, then took her hand and stepped backward into the shadows.

"What are you doing?" Andrea wasn't upset when he tugged her out of view of anyone coming or going from the house. She grinned and laughed.

"I've decided it's good for us to know each other better, too, before your pageant begins," he whispered as he pulled her into his arms.

"Not here, Mark," she complained, although she was still

smiling as she looked up at him and collapsed against him once he'd resumed his perch on the edge of the railing.

"Here is perfect," he grumbled, and tangled one hand into her hair as he pressed the other into the small of her back.

Andrea didn't fight him when he kissed her. She tasted of alcohol and smelled nice, with a flowery scent to her. He held back the urge to ravish her, sensing she might balk and worry further they'd be spotted. He'd sat there as a few contestants had come and gone from the house and not been spotted. All he wanted was a taste. The thought of more instantly preoccupied his thoughts, though, as he deepened the kiss and slowly began feasting.

Andrea had skills of her own. She began a slow, sultry dance with her tongue that fueled the fire already simmering inside him. When she relaxed against him, her legs between his, her nipples puckered and rubbed against his chest. She moaned softly, running her hands up his arms to his shoulders and around his neck.

The minidress she wore rode up her ass. Mark felt skin, caressed her smooth legs just below her ass. He felt the soft curve of her rear end and dared run his fingers between her legs. He was inches from caressing her pussy. A groan tore from him and Andrea responded, moaning as she continued kissing him.

His cock raged to life in his shorts and Andrea rubbed against it. He felt the smile play at her lips as she groaned in his mouth. Mark broke off the kiss, damn near gasping for air as he tried deciding if he should hike her dress up high enough to fuck her right there, or toss her over his shoulder and make a dash for his private wing.

"You're pushing your luck, lady," he whispered against her neck when she let her head fall back.

She chuckled and didn't try moving when he brought her closer so he could kiss the top of her breasts. Spaghetti straps slipped off her shoulders and down her arms. Mark adjusted the material of her dress and exposed her breasts. He was barely able to focus through the lust tearing at his system. Andrea had beautiful light brown, large nipples. They were perfectly shaped and mouthwateringly tempting. Too tempting. Mark lifted her in his arms and pounced on the closest one to his mouth.

"Oh God, yes!" Andrea tangled her fingers in his hair, massaging his scalp. She pressed his head into her breasts, murmuring words to encourage him.

When she raised her legs and wrapped them around him, Mark adjusted his grip on her. His fingers slid between the soft moist flesh between her legs.

"Crap," he hissed. "You're soaked."

"And you're surprised?" she asked, and pressed her mouth to his ear.

Chills rushed over his body when she tickled him with her tongue. Mark growled and thrust two fingers deep inside her. Smooth velvety skin enclosed around him, sucking him in further. Mark swore his eyes rolled back in his head with the effort to maintain control and bring her to the edge.

"We can't do this here," Andrea protested, but arched into his touch further.

Her breasts were full and ripe and a view to die for as they bounced slightly when he impaled her further. She might have been saying one thing, but her legs remained wrapped around him and she clung to his shoulders. Her breathing grew more raspy. She let her head fall back all the way as she rode his fingers.

"This isn't right," she added on a breath.

"Feels right to me." Mark managed to focus enough to see they were very alone on the terrace. If someone were to come to the house from the lodging for the contestants they wouldn't see the two of them. But with Andrea moaning and breathing heavily in his arms, they might suspect someone was hidden in the dark shadows. "I promise, if anyone comes near, I'll make sure you're properly covered."

"Uh-huh," she murmured and tried creating her own rhythm as he continued thrusting deep into her soaked pussy.

His entire hand was wet and his dick throbbed in his shorts, anxious to feel all that heat wrapped around it. When Andrea moved her hands down his arms, then between them and gripped his cock through his shorts, Mark hissed. His entire world went dark, and blood rushed through his veins. Every inch of him tensed and he stilled inside her.

Andrea quit trying to ride his hand and chuckled. She lifted her head and stared at him through glassy eyes. "Fuck me," she demanded.

Mark wondered how drunk she was. They didn't know each other that well yet. He knew she was a professional and appeared to be good at what she did. If she was sober, would she make the same demand?

He was sober, though. Granted, damn near every ounce of blood was in his cock and his brain was fogged over with lust. Mark stared into her pretty eyes, focused on her pouty, full lips, and glanced one last time at her perfectly shaped breasts.

"Soon," he told her, already hating his decision and vowing at the same time that it would be real damn soon.

His cock was still hard as a rock when he woke up the next morning. Fresh air would do him good. He gave himself a very harsh lecture, reminding him why he had made the choice not to fuck Andrea the night before. She'd been drunk and he'd done the right thing. Another part of him insisted he should have followed through. It wasn't his responsibility to think for her. They weren't in any type of relationship.

Mark had the advantage of knowing the mansion like the back of his hand. Heading downstairs, he passed a group of reporters, who fortunately were too busy messing with their equipment to notice him. They were there to grab a few interviews with contestants. No one had formally announced his presence on the island. Mark had worked hard to keep his picture out of the papers. His efforts paid off when he was able to walk past reporters without being attacked.

Nonetheless, Mark made quick work along the hallway that stretched past two more large halls until he was in the back half of the mansion. He could head to the kitchen and eat, as well as have access to easy seconds. Or he could go outside. On an impulse he walked through one of the libraries and out opened trellis doors to the large brick patio where they'd been last night.

It wasn't quite as cool as it had been in recent days, but the warmth of early summer wasn't quite yet there. A wet bar that hadn't been there the night before was set up at the end of the brick terrace, with tables on each side where large glass bowls chilling in ice were full of shrimp and fresh fruit. Mark popped a cold shrimp into his mouth.

"Something to drink?" The middle-aged servant behind the wet bar appeared vaguely familiar.

Mark started to tell her no. It was too early. He'd just woken up. But he'd slept in and it was almost noon.

"Coffee sounds good," he told her, then eyeballed a few coolers stuffed with longneck bottles of beer. She had beer on tap, too. A dry-erase board was set up behind her showing prices. Once he woke up, got some caffeine and food inside him, those cold beers would sound even better.

Two men came up to the bar as the servant handed Mark a cup of coffee. "Miguel is perfectly primed for the auditions." A young man wearing a cheap suit and sporting a ridiculous haircut turned his back to Mark and spoke to the other guy with him. "You won't find that in Stephen."

"Miguel is from the wrong state." The man spoke in a hushed tone, making it difficult to be positive if that was what he said. "Stephen can just as easily be primed."

"Wrong state?" The younger of the two men made a scoffing sound. "How long have you been in this business?"

"Since before your first wet dream," the older of the two snapped. His hair was in more of a traditional cut but dyed an odd shade of black that looked as if it had hints of purple in it.

The guy next to Mark in the cheap suit and bad haircut leaned an elbow on the bar and waved his finger at the woman tending bar. "Would you get my ignorant friend here a draw, please, darling?" He didn't wait for her to acknowledge him but turned to his friend. "You should know as well as anyone there is no such thing as a wrong state."

"Just the right state of mind," both men said at the same time. Glancing Mark's way, they continued their conversation in hushed whispers. They took their plastic cups and cheap beer, paid for them, then left without leaving a tip.

Mark pulled a twenty from his wallet and dropped it in her tip jar. He winked at her when she smiled graciously. There were quite a few people on the terrace, all engrossed in their own conversations, and all lowering their voices as Mark passed them, as if they had an inside scoop on the pageant that no one else could know. Their conversations didn't impress Mark in the least. If anyone on the island knew about his mother's jewelry box and was there to search for it, it would be damn hard singling them out. They were all cutthroats. Andrea was either one hell of a good actress to appear so relaxed and happy when her world was packed full of backstabbers and behind-the-curtain deals, or she was the most naïve woman he'd ever met.

Naïve women didn't purposely arrange to have casual sex dates with strangers.

"Excuse me, Mr. Tripp?"

Mark glanced up as a servant approached. He acknowledged the servant, and at the same time those around him shot their attention his way. He'd just been outed.

"Marcia sent me to find you, sir." The woman wore the same black dress with white apron all the servant women on his father's payroll wore. "She asked if you'd come to the kitchen when you had a minute."

"That's fine." He started toward the library door and the servant fell in stride alongside him. There wasn't any point remaining on the terrace unless he wanted those around him to start talking to him as if they were dear long-lost friends. "Is there a problem?"

"I couldn't say, sir."

The two men who had been at the bar followed him inside, but Mark escaped through the servants' door to the kitchen. As he pushed through the swinging doors, the sounds of pots and pans clattering reminded him of his childhood and the many times he would plop onto a stool in the kitchen at their house in the Keys, in hopes of licking a bowl or being made official food tester to make sure everything was just right.

There were six women working in the very large kitchen. Mark entered and the chatter died. Noise from pots and pans clanging and knives hitting chopping blocks diminished to almost complete silence. He felt as if he'd just entered a world where he was the foreigner and the natives weren't sure what to think of him. It no longer reminded him of his kitchen growing up.

Marcia, an overweight woman pushing sixty, glanced his way. She gave sharp orders to the women around her in a thick, husky voice. As a boy he'd never been sure which had come first, the kitchen or Marcia. He still wasn't sure today.

"We can talk in here," she instructed Mark, then gestured for him to follow her into her small office. Without asking,

Marcia poured two cups of coffee, then led the way through her kitchen to the closed door on the far end.

Mark reached around her to open the door for the older woman, who once had been as much a mother to him as his real mom had been. Marcia didn't bat an eye at her employer waiting on her. After his mother had died, Marcia raised Mark and his sister. She did a pretty good job, too, if he were given any say in the matter. Their nannies didn't do anything with Mark or his sister, Morgan, without first consulting with Marcia. She handed his coffee to him then entered ahead of him, flipping on the light to reveal a cluttered office with a metal desk and filing cabinets lining the far wall. Mark didn't have a clue what she might have filed away in those cabinets.

"I heard something this morning," she began after closing her door and facing him with her back to it. She wiped her large, bloated hands on her apron and looked worried. "I thought I should let you know."

"What's that?"

Marcia sipped her coffee and walked alongside her desk, tapping stacks of papers with her finger as she moved to the well-used chair behind it. "If I told you half the things I've seen or overheard in all the years I've been working here, you wouldn't believe me."

Mark watched her over the rim of his cup. "I probably would."

Marcia smiled, her brown eyes embedded in her heavyset face. "What I'm saying is, I wouldn't be telling you this if I didn't think it was important." Marcia pressed her lips together and stared at Mark a moment. She was a good woman, hardworking, and incredibly talented in the kitchen. More so, she had management skills that made her an invaluable employee. With sometimes little to no notice, Marcia could feed any number of people. She could manage an entire staff and keep the mansion in order. As well, she was a good friend, something Mark didn't have enough of.

"What did you hear, Marcia?" he pressed.

"Earlier today while I was in the hall preparing for the banquet," she began, suddenly looking nervous. "I have no idea who they were but I'd know them if I saw them again. Two young men were talking about one of the contestants. They called him Big D." Marcia started to take a sip of her coffee but then put the cup on her desk instead. "I don't make a habit of eavesdropping," she insisted.

"I know," he reassured her. "What did you hear?"

Marcia looked really worried. Her coffee almost spilled out of her cup when she started to put it on the edge of a stack of employee log-in sheets. She caught herself at the last minute and situated her cup so it didn't spill.

"This tall, thin man, who wasn't as muscular as the other, although I could tell they were both contestants, told his friend that Big D was playing dirty. He said the only way to stop him was to make sure he suffered dearly from some type of accident." Marcia began wringing her hands together and grabbed her apron, twisting it around her big fingers as she continued. There was a sheen of sweat on her forehead when she looked up at Mark with nervous, watery brown eyes. "The other man, the taller and more muscular of the two, had a slight accent, but it wasn't ethnic. He sounded more like one of those rich country-club boys."

For all purposes, Mark himself was a rich country-club boy. He didn't ask her to explain her analogy but let her get her story out. They could break down details later.

"He told the shorter guy that Big D couldn't have an accident. He said it would stir up too much controversy and fingers would be pointed. But the shorter guy insisted a fatal accident would put an end to the deception going on in the pageant once and for all."

* * *

Mark was up early Monday morning. He had stored away the information Marcia had given him, and he had reassured her that what she heard was probably very common with pageants as competitive as this one. He made her promise to tell him anything else she overheard and to keep her ears open. Mark didn't mention Alpha 21. He hated seeing her so upset over what she'd heard, and used that as his reason for not sharing about the search for the jewelry box. In truth, he wasn't comfortable discussing it with anyone yet.

There wasn't any point in sharing what she'd told him with his father, not yet. It would only upset his father, and as with Marcia, he didn't want either of them upset further.

It wasn't hard to learn which one was Big D. His name was Denny, Denton Forthright, from Dallas. Mark had no idea if he'd obtained his nickname from the city he was from, or from his name and size. Big D was a good-looking black man who stood at least six and a half feet tall. It was impossible not to notice him in a crowd. Mark also discovered Big D was loud, assertive, and opinionated. At least that was the impression Mark got watching him during a photo shoot outside the mansion that afternoon.

Watching all the ripped, young men bored Mark quickly. They were all between the ages of nineteen and twenty-two, were way too muscular, and most of them looked fake. They were too tall, too friendly, at least to the right people, then practically backstabbing cruel as soon as the spotlight was off of them. He found it a lot more entertaining to watch Andrea, who seemed to be everywhere he was. The woman was a workaholic. She carried a couple of cell phones at all times, had two assistants rushing around her no matter what she was doing, yet she never looked stressed or unprepared. Her calm, soft-spoken, sultry voice soothed any situation instantly.

Mark's phone vibrated and he pulled it from his back pocket. He opened the text message.

What are you doing?

Mark turned around. He'd just seen her across the pool, sitting next to two older women, who had appeared distraught over something. The string bikini she had on with a silk scarf tied around her hips wasn't making anyone else at the pool distraught. He'd grown used to every contestant falling all over themselves to get even a smile from her. He'd also noticed that although friendly, Andrea kept a professional distance from everyone. Mark searched the pool area. She'd disappeared on him.

Where are you? he texted, instead of answering her question. *I've got some free time in about thirty minutes.*

Obviously neither one of them were answering the other's questions. Mark no longer cared. He almost ran into an older couple, probably someone's parents, when he about-faced and headed inside.

Meet me in my suite. He tapped his screen to bring up the time. *I'll be there at five.* After tapping Send he added, *Don't change out of that bikini.*

Mark had a dinner date with his father at seven. He wasn't so sure the crowded mansion and hectic atmosphere would be good for his dad, so he had agreed to meet him at his father's country club. They had sent the coins Alpha 21 unburied to have them analyzed, and his dad had told him they'd determined their age and origin.

Trotting up the back stairs, he reached his private wing then headed straight to his bathroom. There was enough time for a shower and shave. Stripping as he crossed his suite, Mark walked barefoot across the cool marble floor in the bathroom to the shower and started the water. He stared at his reflection in the mirror and contemplated taking Andrea mainland to have dinner with him and his father. It wasn't as if he had to

worry about how to introduce her; she was their pageant director. But then he and his dad wouldn't be able to discuss the
coins, which his father had seemed rather excited about.

"The old man would be on to you in a second," Mark chastised his reflection. He then turned to his shower in disgust. On
to what? That he was fucking Andrea? Lord, he didn't do well
with this kind of free time on his hands. Already he was creating some kind of illusion in his head that he and Andrea had
something to hide. They'd had sex once. He was definitely
looking forward to round two, but that barely constituted the
title of fuck buddies, let alone anything else. He would enjoy
dinner with his father alone. Tomorrow he'd spend time online
and e-mail Rob and Tigger at the office and make sure they
were both doing okay.

His phone was still lit up when he walked out of his shower
ten minutes later with a towel wrapped around his waist. Grabbing it, he pulled up the text he'd just missed from Andrea and
checked the time; it was ten minutes until five.

I have to cancel. Sorry.

"Damn it," he growled, tossing his phone onto his bed.
Mark paced the length of his room, pausing at the closed glass
doors that led to his balcony, which overlooked a magnificent
view of the beach. At the moment, though, he didn't see it. He
scowled at the view, then exhaled. "Enough," he ordered himself. "Life is good. You're happy, successful, and two weeks ago
you didn't even know Andrea." He'd be damned if some
woman would affect his mood like this.

Stalking over to his bed, Mark snatched up his phone and
sent Andrea a text.

Don't worry, sweetheart. Let me know when you have time.

It was good seeing his father enjoy himself at dinner, acting
like his old self again. Mark Sr. wouldn't have let anyone at his
country club see him failing and weak.

Mark didn't feel he was failing, but damn he was beginning to worry he'd grown weak. Especially halfway through their meal when he felt his phone vibrate. His father would never have tolerated a cell phone being brought out during a meal. Mark had better manners, and restraint, than that. Or so he thought. He didn't make it through after-dinner drinks before excusing himself to the men's room and checking his messages.

Andrea had sent several texts while he was at dinner with his father.

Sorry about earlier. How about here in an hour or so?

Forty-five minutes later she'd sent another text. *I hope this doesn't jeopardize our arrangement but I can't make it . . . again.* It was just as well he'd missed those first two texts. He wasn't sure he would have been as forgiving a second time. It was the third text he stared at the longest.

I just heard you left the island. Where are you? Or is it not my place to ask?

Mark barely managed to focus on their conversation once he returned to his father's table. The coins were believed to be of Celtic origin and made out of bronze. Although they were each valued at several hundred dollars, apparently they weren't incredibly uncommon. The question was, what they were doing in the ground on the island? Mark had a hard time speculating on possible explanations and trying to figure out Andrea's last text message.

As he headed down to the main floor the next morning and entered the large foyer, Mark wondered what had possessed him to take these stairs and not a back route straight to the kitchen. It was damn near standing room only in the foyer. He'd thought of having breakfast in the kitchen, listening in on the hired help's gossip, then heading out to find the Alpha 21 crew. After learning what he could about his mom's jewelry box, he planned on checking in at work. Anything to keep his mind off Andrea.

Before reaching the bottom of the stairs, Mark caught sight of her standing close to the front doors. She was talking to a few suits and glanced past them to make eye contact with him. Mark never had answered her text message from the night before and swore he saw the question still in her eyes.

Her hair was pulled back on top of her head and fell in soft curls down her back. The ponytail was secured with a bright green scarf. It matched the figure-hugging dress she wore. Her dress was strapless and showed off how round and perfect her breasts were, as well as her narrow waist and slender hips. One of the suits shifted his weight and blocked Mark's view of Andrea. Instantly, he hated the man.

Mark turned at the bottom of the stairs, heading to the kitchen, but hesitated. The smell of fresh-brewed coffee lured him forward, yet he stood planted to the floor, his hand still on the smooth, round banister.

"Fuck it," he grumbled under his breath.

Mark turned around and started in the direction toward Andrea. At just over six feet tall he was considered a big man. But in this world with Neanderthals mingling with agents, lawyers, and the press, Mark could no longer see her, let alone walk across the foyer to get to her.

His nerves were wound tight. Coffee wouldn't help at this point. All he needed was Andrea's soft, warm body underneath him as he buried himself deep inside her. He excused himself and moved around a cluster of contestants surrounded by giggling women reporters. When he spotted Andrea, the possessive urges he'd managed to keep at bay since meeting her hit him with full force. He didn't care about civilities. He didn't give a thought as to how his actions would be taken by the crowd around him. All he focused on was grabbing Andrea and getting out of there.

Andrea shook hands with one of the suits, then offered her hand to the other suit and smiled. Mark had known Andrea just a couple of weeks yet he spotted the stress around her eyes. Her smile was tight and didn't meet her large brown eyes. They looked flat, possibly bored.

Mark was just behind the two men facing Andrea before she spotted him. Her expression changed from surprised to wary as he moved around the men who had been hogging her for too long.

"I've been looking everywhere for you," he said easily, although loud enough for the men with her to hear. "We're going to be late."

Mark wrapped his arm around her waist and escorted her out of the tight circle. He gave the two suits a gallant smile then left them standing where they were. Instead of trying to take her across the foyer, Mark opted for the front door. In the next minute he had her outside and was heading along the front of the mansion past a long line of limousines and lingering drivers who were either reading the paper or focusing on their cell phones. None of them gave either Mark or Andrea a second glance.

"What are you doing?" Andrea demanded, trying to dig her heels into the ground for the first time when they reached the corner of the house.

"Were you having fun?" he asked, keeping a firm grip on her as he glanced down at her spiked heels. It crossed his mind to scoop her into his arms but he didn't want to draw too much attention to them.

"Fun?" She made a decent effort to stop when they started across the grassy yard. "I was working, Mark. I think that much would be obvious."

"Very obvious." He nodded at her shoes. "You might want to slip out of those so you don't stain your heels."

"I need to go back inside."

"You'll be back inside having your ass kissed soon enough."

"Mark," she said, her tone exasperated. "The two men I was talking to are with the network airing the pageant. They weren't kissing my ass."

He almost said it sure as hell looked as if they were, but he managed to keep the words from tumbling out. That would have made him sound jealous and that was one emotion he was definitely not feeling at the moment. Mark was determined. He didn't care if she was talking to men from Timbuktu.

"Now you're talking to the owner of this island," he said instead. "I wasn't planning on kissing your ass, either." He looked down to catch her staring up at him with bright brown eyes. "Unless you want me to," he added, growling and enjoying the hell out of the flush that spread across her cheeks as she puckered her moist lips into an adorable pouting expression.

Andrea didn't take off her shoes. Mark led her across the yard and around a thick row of palm trees to a path that worked its way through the well-maintained gardens. She moved easily in her high heels, but he kept his arm wrapped around her waist to make sure she didn't trip.

The thick smell of saltwater and the soothing slap of waves against the beach didn't affect him as it usually did. Andrea's perfume was more of a distraction. She smelled fresh, her dress was silky, and her body was warm and compliant as he navigated them away from the house.

"I get it," she said, her voice breathy. "But I swear, work controls my life. And although, yes, I did cancel on you twice, you weren't even here last night. Where were you?"

Mark stopped and stared at a narrow wooden door almost hidden by the thick, tall hedge that ran that length of the property. "Son of a bitch," he breathed.

"What?" Andrea asked, winded.

"I'd completely forgotten."

"What? That you can't just haul people away from their work?"

"That this was here." Mark judged where they were right now in relation to where the coins had been dug up on the other side of the hedge.

"Okay. Right now. What is this all about?" She stepped away from him. "I need to be in the banquet hall during breakfast."

"How much time do we have?" He tested the door and with a bit of work it swung inward.

"Not enough. What is this place?" Andrea leaned forward to peer into the darkness beyond the doorway. "There are rooms in your bushes?"

"Not quite."

There wasn't anyone around them, but he glanced at the quiet, secluded part of the yard. Andrea followed his gaze, her expression crunching into a frown.

"Wait a minute." Andrea took a step backward.

"Where's your sense of adventure?"

"What is it?" Her curiosity was getting to her, but she still hesitated.

Mark turned, grabbed Andrea by the waist, ignored her cry of protest, and lifted her into his arms, then entered the small greenhouse he thought had been torn down a long time ago. His father had some explaining to do.

"It is a greenhouse," he explained. "The gardeners built the hedge wall my father wanted around the yard so that it grew up and enclosed the greenhouse." It wasn't quite a lie since he guessed that was what his father had done. And he hoped it covered his initial reaction to seeing the door in the hedge.

"You're taking me in here?" Andrea dug her fingernails into his shoulder and twisted in his arms. "Not in here. It's dirty and there are cobwebs. Mark!" she complained, twisting further in his grasp until he was holding her bare ass.

The thong she wore under her dress immediately had him hard as steel. Andrea stilled and quit scowling at the dirty, forgotten room. She stared at Mark, her face an inch from his as her expression sobered. He lowered his arm and let her legs straighten until she slid down his body, her eyes never looking away from his.

"I wanted you to know where it was," he managed, adding to his lie. "No one saw us enter from the trees in front of the hedge." He was drowning in her large brown eyes. It took him a moment to drop his arms once she was standing. For a moment, their surroundings were no longer there. It was just the two of them, two souls slowly blending together.

Mark blinked, and Andrea looked away. He knew instantly that her feelings were being drawn into this *no-strings-attached* arrangement they'd both agreed to. His insides tightened, and he fought the urge to pull her against him and ravish her. Instead he kept his hands at his side and stared at her long brown hair taper down her back as she turned to take in their surroundings.

She looked around, taking a moment to stare at the dirty glass windows. In spite of the hedge growing around them, enough sunlight filtered through the leaves to see around the room.

"We won't get you messed up," he promised.

"No," she said slowly. Her dress was still twisted and bunched up at her waist. She ran her hands down her body but made little effort to cover her exposed rear end as she continued looking around the forgotten greenhouse.

Mark reached for her, unable to keep his hands off her for another moment. He cupped her bare ass, then slid his finger underneath her thong.

"Mark, there isn't time," she protested, but sighed when he slid his finger over her ass then lower until he stroked her pussy.

He wasn't a bit surprised to find her soaked. "You're right." He nipped at her flesh next to her ear. "Like I said, I just wanted to show it to you. You have to get back." He moved to her ear, kissing her earlobe then torturing her ear with his tongue. At the same time, he dipped his finger into her hot, tight pussy. The words were right there to tell her that he had to see her, needed to touch her, was distraught with the urge to have her in his arms. Mark shoved the words out of the way. This wasn't about emotions. But damn, they were there, and they were strong. He almost shook from the intensity of them as he continued to stroke her, taste her, and breathe in her intoxicating scent.

Andrea moaned and dug her fingernails into his shoulders. Mark didn't feel any guilt over building her up like this. Her job was important, and he didn't want her to think he was discrediting it in any way.

"You'll have to forgive me," he whispered into her ear, then moved his free hand behind her head and grabbed her ponytail. He tugged and her head fell back, giving him free rein of her neck. When he pressed his mouth to her skin, her pulse beat strong against his lips. "This dress you're wearing did something to me the moment I saw it on you," he told her, which wasn't far from the truth. The moment their eyes had connected in the foyer, he had needed her more than his morning coffee.

He thrust a second finger inside her and her pussy clamped around him. She was so wet, her pussy walls hot and velvety as he glided his fingers in and out of her, feeling her constrict and relax around him.

"You're doing this on purpose," she moaned.

Andrea was a smart woman. "Well, I didn't accidentally slide my fingers inside you," he agreed.

She chuckled and tried raising her head. Mark tightened his

grip around her ponytail. The silk scarf wrapped around her hair tickled his arm, and her long curls tortured him further.

"Maybe you should stop," she whispered, although there was no conviction in her words.

Andrea continued clinging to him and made no effort to push him away. He pulled a bit harder on her ponytail and raised his head to enjoy the view she offered him. Her strapless dress lowered as he arched her body in his arms. Cleavage stretched above the neckline. Mark adjusted her in his arms then lowered his face to her breasts.

Andrea grabbed his head, messing up his hair. She kept him pressed against her breasts and moaned when he managed to free one nipple and suck it deep into his mouth. Then, driving a third finger into her pussy, he continued finger-fucking her as her breath came quicker. When he was sure he had her at the edge, he slowed his pace, raising his head and kissing her, his savage need for her releasing as he devoured her mouth.

Andrea didn't protest any further. She might not believe he understood the pressures of her job. She wouldn't be the first who thought he lived a life of leisure among the rich and famous. It didn't normally bother him when people drew the wrong conclusion about him and thought he had no clue what a full day's work was like. Now wasn't the time to explain to her how he knew what the stress of a high-profile job could be like. He wouldn't talk to her about anything but sex. In fact, the less talking they did, the better. It was the only way he could keep his possessive thoughts about her under control. Mark was cool with her thinking he couldn't wait to fuck her. That much was true.

He'd learned at an early age that knowledge was power. If someone else knew less about him than he did about them, it put the ball in his court. The same applied to women. Andrea might be exceptional in many ways compared to any other woman he'd spent time with, but she was the same when it came to mastering the upper hand. She wanted good sex on the side. At her work she ran the show, managed everyone, and called the shots. He'd already seen how good she was at it. But during sex, while in his arms, she would submit and turn herself completely over to him.

Andrea had tried remaining in control the first time they fucked. But he'd commanded her submission. On the balcony, she'd demanded he fuck her, and had pouted considerably when he'd decided they would wait. Although trying to take command, that night she'd allowed him to straighten her clothing and escort her to her room. Today, her submission came faster. Knowing what made her tick, where to touch her, and how to make her respond, gave him the power needed to turn her into his perfect lover.

"Mark! Damn it. Oh God!"

He held her, watching her face flush as her body quivered and her pussy constricted around his fingers. Andrea came, and watching her do so was a bit too satisfying. The pleasure that washed over her face that created a sheen of perspiration on her neck and her breasts made her glow. It filled him with an intense pleasure and satisfaction that didn't come from simply making a fuck buddy come.

"Turn around," he instructed and adjusted her before she could complain.

Then bending her over so that she didn't touch anything that might get her dirty, he focused on her soaked pussy for only a moment before releasing his cock and pulling a condom from his pocket. Mark sheathed his dick, barely able to function from the need to fuck her. He'd tortured both of them last time, but today, even if there wasn't time to enjoy long, gratifying lovemaking, both of them would leave satisfied.

When he slid inside her, Andrea reached for an old workbench and held on to the edge of it as she cried out. He filled her, feeling her stretch but then instantly constrict around him.

"I love how tight you are," he muttered, and grabbed her hips. Then watching himself glide in and out of her, he ached to feel her without the condom. He wanted flesh against flesh. But that would require a commitment and a relationship neither of them wanted.

"You're perfect," she gasped. "God, so fucking perfect."

He hated rushing, although after finger-fucking her the other night, he'd been on edge. As easily as he could have taken care of it in the shower, Mark knew it wouldn't be satisfaction like this. He'd waited and it would take nothing to come now.

Andrea's soft cries were music to his soul. She soothed his tattered soul. As he filled her with thrust after thrust, the burning need riding him the past few days hit a boiling point. Mark adjusted his grip on her, focusing on her soft round ass and how he disappeared into her smooth, perfectly shaped folds.

Small muscles inside her quivered around his cock. "Mark! Damn it, oh," she cried out, and shook her head back and forth as her body tensed. "It's good. Yes, so good."

Andrea was fighting for control again. Mark wondered how often she managed refraining from experiencing a real orgasm. She was cheating herself of real pleasure over an illusion that she would lose her ability to manage her life. Mark eased all the way inside her, slowing his pace just a bit and at the same time stretching her open further with his hands.

"Damn it," she hissed, and tried inching away from him without complaining further.

He held her where she was, and pulled out far enough so when he thrust deeply, he felt her world explode. Andrea's legs damn near gave out underneath her. He felt the shift of her weight and held her steady as he rode with her peak until he came, as well.

He wanted time to hold her. It would be perfect cradling her, protecting her from the dirt and cobwebs, and getting to know her better. Mark shoved the thoughts from his mind as he helped her stand, then straighten her outfit before putting himself back in order. They didn't say a word until she faced him.

"Okay, sweetheart. Let's get you back to work." Mark couldn't let her see his growing feelings for her.

Andrea smiled. "Do I look as if I've just been fucked senseless?"

"You look fine." If he elaborated she might guess his thoughts were leaning in a dangerous direction.

"Too bad," she muttered, and stepped gingerly around him to the door.

7

It was midafternoon, the sun was bright and hot, and Andrea had already changed clothes twice in order to maintain a cool, calm persona. Inside she was far from either. Not only was she so hyped up about the pageant, her insides were burning with desire. Mark had left her, after escorting her back inside the mansion, with barely a nod good-bye, as if he'd given her exactly what she'd wanted and was walking away satisfied.

She wanted more!

Even as she adjusted her ponytail and retied the scarf she had wrapped around her ponytail holder, she vowed never to wear her hair like this again. At least not when Mark was anywhere nearby. Her head tingled from the many times he'd tugged on it. And as she adjusted it into place, every time she pulled her hair doing so, every inch of her body reacted. Her pussy was so swollen and wet, she doubted even the worst of catastrophes would bring her down.

No man had ever made her come the way he did.

Mark had cheated. This wasn't part of their deal. There had been more than need in his eyes as he'd burned his gaze into hers. He'd released her desire from her the moment he'd touched her, but there was more. And he'd seen it. Andrea knew he had. They were connecting in a way that should terrify her. This wasn't part of their deal.

Andrea wasn't an idiot. She hurried down the stairs and outside, needing to catch up with the camera crew as they continued working on the photo shoots of the contestants. She'd been smart to change into tennis shoes and shorts. And the sleeveless blouse she chose was still cool from being in the air-conditioned closet. Nonetheless, as she trotted around the large hedge, recognizing it now for what it was, Andrea understood exactly what Mark had done.

He thought he was getting even with her for cancelling on him twice after texting and saying she wanted to meet him. Andrea wasn't sure if he'd left the island after she cancelled on him the second time, or earlier. One of the housekeepers had told her he'd left when Andrea had considered trying to find him to apologize. Andrea had wanted to hound the housekeeper with questions, demanding to know exactly where he'd gone and if he'd left to see someone else. More than likely she wouldn't have known. Fortunately, Andrea had refrained from asking anything at all.

Andrea didn't want him distracting her thoughts. All she wanted was good, raunchy sex. But damn it, even now she wanted to know where he was and what he was doing. No matter how hard she tried, she couldn't get him out of her head.

Mark was more than capable of providing incredibly awesome sex, and she didn't need anything else from him. As it was, being in his arms, surrendering until he brought her to the edge of an incredible orgasm, felt a little bit too good. When he'd pushed her over the edge, she'd barely been able to focus on him. But she'd seen the look of incredible satisfaction on his face.

No one controlled her body. Raunchy sex without any emotions. Sexual fulfillment, complete satisfaction with no strings or complications. *That* was what she wanted, what she needed. Nothing else.

Andrea reached the beach and broke into a run. She quickly took it down to a slow jog, her leg muscles reacting to the strenuous jaunt over the sand and around small rocks. At the end of the beach, a small creek crisscrossed into undeveloped land. The island was absolutely beautiful and the perfect setting for the pageant. She turned from the beach and trekked alongside the creek. The shade from the trees cooled her from the hot sun. But mugginess wrapped around her, and the bugs were suddenly everywhere. Paradise came with a price. Skin So Soft was a wonderful repellent and smelled a lot nicer than insect spray. Andrea could hear a waterfall ahead. Just as she reached it, the land transformed into a rocky paradise.

She wasn't exactly surrounded by mountains, but a good cameraman could make it look that way. Dave Small, who was a rather large man, was one of the best in the industry. She was thrilled to have him working the pageant and knew he would take these natural surroundings and turn them into breathtaking backdrops that could easily compete with the gorgeous young men he was photographing.

"Andrea!" Dave waved her over when he spotted her.

Nodding, she kept her eye on the small group and occasionally on the uneven ground and worked her way closer to the crew. "So this is paradise," she said in way of greeting and grinned the relaxed, professional grin she'd mastered as a teenager. Created for the judges, and practiced daily to get her through life, Andrea knew she could convince anyone that she didn't have a care in the world other than their personal situation.

"It makes for creative challenges, but the camera loves it." Dave walked over to her, crossing his arms and placing one hand on his cheek. "Tell me you brought more bug repellent."

Andrea held her grin and pulled a non-aerosol bottle from her purse. "You know I always think of you," she assured him, handing the bottle to her head cameraman.

"You're a gem." He made a gracious bow before amply applying the spray to his exposed body parts.

Andrea took the bottle and finished the job, spraying the back of his neck and arms. "There's a chance of storms early this evening."

"You hate me after all," Dave said, giving her an over-dramatic sigh.

She patted his sticky arm. "You know I love you." Then, shifting her attention to the shoot, she studied the young men and their agents. There was her Georgia contestant, Paul Sanders, and Roy Porter, from Connecticut, who stood alongside a larger waterfall. Water trickled over their bare chests and dampened their hair as they posed for the camera in swim trunks. Big D, Denny Forthright, Texas's contribution to the pageant, stood on the sidelines with a large white towel around his shoulders. His dark skin glistened in the sunlight that filtered through the trees.

These three men were probably the best candidates in the pageant. Dave saw that, too. He'd brought these three men to the ideal setting for a reason. These shots would bring out the best in the men and their surroundings.

Mark would be in so much trouble the next time she saw him. Her insides were already on edge with the urge to climax again, and he'd left her to spend a day with these young studs who would all fuck her with a moment's notice if she suggested it.

"Need me to spray you down?" Dave offered.

"I've already applied it pretty thick. I'm not sure they make a spray that is one hundred percent effective against this many bugs."

"Probably not," he agreed.

There were a handful of photographers, each shooting from a different angle. The men focused on them, each one squatting in front of the contestants, their cameras clicking and humming.

"Come sit over here in the shade," Dave gallantly offered and gestured to Andrea as he headed back in the direction he'd come. "Time to climb, men!" he shouted and pointed at the same time. His photographers quit shooting and all began adjusting their cameras.

"This is my shot," Big D announced, his deep baritone loud and demanding as he shoved the white towel off his incredibly muscular body.

A small, too thin woman jumped to catch the towel before it could fall to the ground. Andrea was here for moral support, something she did with all the off-scene shoots. Taking the folding chair underneath a very large white umbrella, Andrea watched as the three contestants began arguing, the agents at their sides jumping into the battle in support of their clients, determined to get their man up the rocks for the ideal shot. Big D was the only one willingly fighting his own battle as his agent stood back and watched.

If the same scene was used over and over again, it underplayed the shot. The men were fighting for the perfect backdrop. Andrea understood this. She'd learned years ago, however, to pick and choose her fights. It didn't matter to her who was shot at the base of the waterfall and who was shot on top. She relaxed in her chair, which was actually rather comfortable, and crossed one leg over the other. Her bare skin was shiny from the ample amount of Skin So Soft she'd applied before leaving the mansion.

"They are not climbing up those rocks," Dave announced, storming in among the agents and contestants and taking charge. "The rope pulley is ready to go. You will use it. Wrap these towels around you to avoid rope burns."

"Isn't this fun?" Windy was next to her, squatting and taking over one of her armrests. He shot her a quick grin before turning his attention to the men and women who were quickly getting wet from the waterfall. "I just love a good shoot, don't you?"

He had white stuff smeared over his nose and wore a straw hat that looked to be more for fashion than practicality. Its narrow rim didn't create enough shadow to cover his long, straight nose. Windy's bright red and orange shirt and equally bright trousers made him appear more the happy tourist than a liaison between the Mr. Desire Pageant and their sponsors. Which was so Windy. Always in the scene for appearance's sake, yet an encyclopedia of facts and knowledge when needed.

"The humidity will kill them if the rocks don't," she confided under her breath.

"You know it, sister." Windy nodded gravely. "Dave insisted I come," he enlightened her, rolling his eyes with his well-known air for dramatics. "If it weren't for my incredible skills at keeping peace in the family, so to speak, I'd be enjoying a piña colada by the pool right now."

"You suffer it well," she teased, grinning at him.

"A martyr, I know," Windy wailed, although he kept his voice quiet, making her an audience of one. He waved his hand in a limp effort to cross himself as he bowed his head. When his straw hat tipped forward, he grabbed it and looked at her with wicked hazel eyes. Amusement glowed in his gaze as he pursed his dry lips. "Do all these pageant men annoy the tar out of you as much as they do me?" he whispered. "At least with the Miss Florida Pageant the ladies pretended to like each other and only talked bad about each other behind their backs."

Andrea hid her grin and looked toward the shoot, deciding Windy's question had to be rhetorical. The two of them had hovered over cocktails after fifteen-hour days and dogged every contestant during pageants in the past. Windy already knew her answer.

Paul's agent was giving Dave a piece of her mind. Andrea couldn't hear the conversation over the rushing water from the waterfall but she read body language pretty well. She not only appeared willing to go to battle but to be enjoying herself as she gestured at the waterfall and her mouth moved, looking as if she were speaking very fast. Dave didn't look happy. When he turned from the woman and gestured to the other two contestants, she returned to her spot in the shade, looking satisfied.

Paul Sanders, the Georgia contestant, grabbed a rope Andrea hadn't noticed until that moment. It turned out to be part of the pulley Dave had mentioned, which in truth was a harness contraption that would lift the man to the top of the waterfall. The photography department was one of many underneath Andrea, and all of her employees had it drummed into their heads the first day on the job that all measures must be met to avoid any and all liabilities. Contestants couldn't get injured. Lawsuits weren't pretty. Beauty contests weren't about scabs and ugliness. They were about happy, perfect, gorgeous people.

She was impressed with Dave's intuitiveness in creating the contraption that lifted the men to the most scenic part of the waterfall. This wasn't a boot camp, and just because these men were ripped with muscles didn't mean anyone wanted to see them put their strength to the test, especially behind the scenes, when the slightest scratch on their perfect bodies would mean all kinds of headaches for her.

A couple of men helped secure the rope harness around Paul. Big D returned to where he'd been before and took his towel from his agent. She hurried to grab him water. He didn't look at her as he accepted it but watched Paul being secured, then slowly lifted in the air as he began ascending the twenty feet or so to the top of the waterfall.

Roy Porter slapped at a bug on his bare shoulder and walked away from the shoot, his back to the cameramen and Paul. He made his way toward two other men Andrea didn't recognize and pulled a shirt over his head. Andrea only watched him for a moment. It was her job to know something about all her contestants, at least enough to be able to make pleasant conversation and see to their needs while they all prepared for the show. Unlike a lot of them, Roy hadn't asked for any special needs when taking his room, and he didn't groan over the roommates he'd been assigned to bunk with on the island. That made him one of the good ones in Andrea's eyes.

Paul had requested his roommates not smoke. Smoking wasn't allowed anywhere on the island, other than at the docks. Paul was relatively new to the pageant scene or he would have known that no one smoked during pageants, at least not so that it could be seen or detected. She'd seen a few men disregarding the rule and smoking outside their cabins the other night when she'd spent time with them, drinking and getting to know them. Cigarettes made people look ugly.

Two men were pulling on the ropes as they hoisted Paul closer to the top of the waterfall. The island offered an incredible backdrop for many great shots, but this spot was definitely ideal for promotional photographs that the men could also use in their portfolios.

Paul reached toward the rocks, almost to the ground above them, when his body contorted. Andrea continued watching but it took a moment before she realized something was wrong. Suddenly Paul was waving his arms around him frantically. He swung away from the waterfall and the ropes seemed to cut into his chest.

Dave rushed to the two men hoisting Paul, working with them to steady the ropes. The ropes had somehow slipped on Paul's body and now were wrapped around his body and neck.

Andrea didn't remember standing, or covering her mouth with her hands. She couldn't even say if seconds passed, minutes, or even an hour. Paul's body continued to gyrate alongside the waterfall. More people hurried to help, desperately trying to get the rope to loosen, or release, so Paul could be lowered to the ground.

His torso went from a bronze color to streaked in red. Everyone was yelling, and it seemed the rushing of water grew louder until it was roaring in accompaniment to the nightmare playing out before her.

Andrea jumped to her senses and lunged forward at the same time. She didn't know how the pulley worked, but she knew what needed to be done now. Paul needed to be cut loose from those ropes. She ran to the men, determined to cut her contestant down. No one got hurt on her watch, unless it was their feelings.

"Someone get a knife, scissors, anything!" She screamed orders, struggling to get around the men who continued battling the ropes. "I need something to cut him free with," she yelled even louder.

Either no one had anything sharp that could be used, or they were ignoring her. Andrea tried getting underneath Paul but was shoved backward for her efforts. When she thought to climb up the slippery embankment alongside the waterfall, two men were already scurrying up it, looking like crabs climbing a wall, as they hurried to assist from the other end.

The waterfall was even louder this close to it. It drowned out everyone around her. The only thing that sounded louder than the rushing water was Paul screaming. When he quit it took another moment for Andrea to register. She'd been looking up the entire time, but her eyes hadn't been focusing on any one thing. Now, she stopped. Apparently she'd been darting in and around the men surrounding her. She stared at the buckle on Paul's belt and the dark leather laced through his jeans' belt loops. The shape of Georgia with the name of the state was printed in it. For some odd reason it hit her that Paul probably wouldn't normally wear a belt buckle with the name and shape of his state on it were it not for this competition. There was a slight gap between his jeans and his flat stomach, which was stretched taut as he hung upside down. His hands were reaching for her. His green eyes were open and staring just to the side of her. His red hair was tousled and hanging upside down along with the rest of him.

Andrea had the most uncanny urge to take a step to the side so she'd be in his line of vision. Maybe if she did she could get his attention so he'd keep fighting until they could get him down. Instead she remained frozen, her feet stuck to the ground where she stood. Paul had quit struggling and instead swung slightly from the right to the left a good four feet over her head.

As noisy as the waterfall had been throughout their struggle to free him, it faded into the background and everyone around her started yelling. A rush of urgency attacked her system and Andrea began hurrying, too. She raced back to the chair where she'd been sitting, watching a perfectly normal photo shoot just minutes ago. There was no going back in time. Instead she needed to think fast. Maybe he wasn't dead. Possibly he wasn't even that hurt. Andrea prayed for a signal as she yanked her cell phone out of her purse and dialed 911.

The rich and powerful always managed to have every modern luxury at their disposal when, and where, they wanted it. Later she would give thanks for that fact of life when her call went through and she explained to the dispatcher what had happened and where they were. GPS was a small godsend, as well. The dispatcher picked up on Andrea's signal as they spoke and verified coordinates. Other than Tripp Island, she didn't have a clue how to explain where they were.

"There will be someone at the docks ready to bring an emergency crew to the scene," Andrea offered, which the dispatcher accepted.

As she barked orders to everyone around her, she continued to divert her gaze from Paul's body, which still hung upside down.

"Someone get him down!" she screamed, stamping her foot.

He wasn't moving, was no longer struggling, and his color was turning a very scary shade. Andrea sent three errand boys, who she knew hadn't signed on for something like this, to the docks to wait for help to arrive. Up until now the boys had rushed to get coffee, or rap on doors of contestants who overslept, and had hauled equipment all over the island. All they were doing now was staring stupid-faced at the fiasco occurring around them. Andrea put them to work. It wouldn't take three of them to escort a team across the island to where they were, but just in case at least one of them wasn't thinking right at the moment, three was a good number.

Andrea stepped around Windy, who looked like he needed to sit down, and left him standing where he was. This was a nightmare, but it was her nightmare.

"Maybe he isn't dead." She continued repeating that to herself under her breath as she watched the men struggle to free Paul from the ropes.

Andrea felt as if she walked alongside her body when she left her office a few hours later. She needed her act together now. Andrea went down the stairs and headed to the kitchen. She needed strong coffee now. The press would be descending on her like the plague before she was ready. Andrea would never be ready for a press meeting like this. As she pushed open the door to the kitchen, she was greeted by what smelled like a fresh pot of coffee and an array of other aromas that any other time would probably make her stomach growl. Right now it simply twisted into more of a knot.

"I hope I'm not interrupting." Andrea was technically in charge of everyone on the island until the pageant was over. Nonetheless she hesitated when Mark and the head cook, Marcia, were hovering over steaming cups with their heads together as they spoke quietly across the well-scrubbed counter.

Both of them turned and looked at her, their eyes immediately filled with concern.

"Not at all." Mark jumped to his feet and was next to her before she was halfway across the kitchen. "Sit down before you fall down," he ordered.

When he put his arm around her it was all Andrea could do not to collapse against his powerful chest.

Mark planted her on his stool and Marcia pulled up another stool alongside it for him.

"How do you take your coffee, miss?" Marcia asked, already grabbing a cup from her cupboards.

"Black, please. And thank you," she said, adjusting herself on the stool. She was acutely aware of Mark taking the stool next to hers and his incredibly masculine body brushing against hers. She'd been surrounded by masculine bodies all day, but none of them did anything to her like Mark's did. Waves of charged energy seemed to rush at her as she tried getting comfortable next to him. "I should leave you two alone. I just wanted coffee."

"You could have called down for a pot." The cook wasn't scolding. Her expression was friendly as she slid the cup over the counter and in front of Andrea.

She tried for a congenial chuckle. "I thought of doing that." Taking the cup she greedily sipped at the hot brew, indifferent to the heat in her throat. "I think I needed to get out of my office, and I thought the kitchen might be a good place to escape for a few."

"It's definitely my best hiding place." Mark leaned against the counter, facing her, as he held his cup up in agreement then drank with her. "Fill me up again, my dear," he ordered, although his tone with the cook was one of someone speaking to a lifelong friend and not a servant.

"I'm cutting you off after one more cup." Marcia wagged her thick index finger at Mark but smiled as she brought the coffeepot with her to the counter in the middle of the kitchen. It was almost an island but Andrea decided it was more like a peninsula since it extended from the counter along the wall. Marcia took her stool on one side and faced Andrea and Mark, who sat on the other side. "It's late and you won't get an ounce of sleep at this rate. You know I don't have any slackers sleeping the day away on my shift," she continued to scold.

Andrea grinned with her mouth to her cup. The old woman spoke to Mark as a good friend and a bit motherly. Mark's eyes glowed as he focused on the old woman and extended his cup to be refilled.

"A slacker, huh."

"Don't try for sympathy from me, Mark Tripp Junior." There was the slightest of accents noticeable when she snapped at Mark. "Just because you . . ."

"Just because I'm filthy rich and can do whatever I wish all day long?" Mark interrupted.

Andrea met Marcia's gaze when she shifted it her direction. "I see how it is," she said softly, then clucked her tongue in her mouth. "Drink your coffee so I can clean up my kitchen. Some of us work for a living," she stressed, topping off Andrea's cup with a wink before scuttling across the room to return the pot to its warmer.

"I don't mind rinsing out my own cup." Andrea got the oddest sensation that Mark wanted her to think he didn't work that hard. If she hadn't read the two articles about him, she might have bought in to his playboy act. It made her curious why he would want her thinking that. Believing him carefree, with no schedule, or no concern other than how to spend his millions would definitely lower her opinion of him. Maybe Mark didn't want her to think highly of him. But why? Her brain was already too racked from enduring the worst day of her life to figure out his act.

There was a large, round clock hanging on the wall and she looked at it, not having realized until now how late it was. "I guess I wasn't paying attention to the time when I came down here," she said, needing light conversation so her brain wouldn't explode.

Mark held up his hand as if he guessed she might try getting up and leaving. "Don't let Marcia get to you," he advised, his look turning conspiratorial when he looked at Andrea. "Her kitchen is already completely spotless or we would have heard the heads roll before her staff went home for the night," he stated, narrowing his eyes on Marcia when he shifted his attention her way. "And two cups doesn't take more than a second to clean. Hell, maybe I might lift a finger and give menial labor a try."

"Oh for the Lord's sake in almighty Heaven," Marcia wailed, throwing her hands up in the air as she rolled her eyes to the ceiling. "There's no bologna on the menu for tomorrow, young man."

"Sit back down, Marcia," Mark said, pointing to her stool. "You can't leave me alone with this beautiful woman. You know what a scoundrel I am."

Heat rushed to Andrea's cheeks but she wasn't sure why. She managed not to choke on her coffee when Marcia sat and the two of them continued their friendly banter.

"Listen to us carry on." Marcia patted her forehead and pudgy neck with a napkin and grinned at Andrea. Her teeth were crooked and stained probably from years of coffee and maybe cigarettes. In spite of her hefty figure, ashen skin, and imperfect teeth, there was something very appealing about the old cook. "You came down here to get a piece of mind in order and we're not letting you do it."

Andrea guessed the qualities in Marcia were what had Mark spending his evening with her instead of out bar-hopping or hitting the city nightlife for a woman to spend his time with, of which he probably had several. Andrea was glad he hadn't, though.

"Actually, this is exactly what I needed." Andrea had managed to pour herself a second cup during Mark and Marcia's antics and sipped at the incredibly good brew as she smiled over the rim of the cup. "Listening to you two and drinking some of the best coffee I've had in years sure beats dealing with the press." She worried her words sounded callous and added quickly, "I do have matters under control, though. It was just time for a short break so I could keep thinking clearly." She wasn't sure at all whether she'd had a clear thought since Paul died hanging upside down just above her head.

"Well, let me say that although I obviously don't know a thing about beauty pageants," Marcia began and patted her wiry gray hair that stood on end around the small bun at the back of her head, "with all the people on the island right now everything is sailing along on smooth waters. You're an incredible organizer." She faltered for a moment. "Of course, not including today," she stammered and looked to Mark for help.

"No one could have known something so terrible like this could have happened," he jumped in quickly and reached across the counter to pat the old woman's large, round hand. "Even with the god-awful tragedy taking that contestant's life," Mark continued and stared at Andrea, "most people wouldn't have been able to function. But you had emergency crews in here in no time, guides helping them across the island, then even more men at the docks to prevent reporters from swarming the place." His hand covered Andrea's and his warm strength soaked through her skin and floated up her arm into the rest of her body. "You deserve a break, darling."

His eyes were a magnificent shade of green, and Andrea worried she was too vulnerable at the moment to stare into them for too long. Marcia might be an old woman but her senses were intact. Andrea had been acutely aware of her attentive brown eyes watch Mark's hand wrap around Andrea's. She didn't want the old woman conjuring up ideas about the two of them when there was nothing between them. Well, other than incredibly good sex.

"I do believe that is what I'm taking." She smiled at Mark as she pulled her hand free from his. Then for good measure, she patted the back of his before clutching her coffee cup with both hands. "It helps backing out of a situation for a bit in order to handle things better."

"What else do you have to take care of?" Mark asked.

She'd already taken care of speaking with Paul's family and signing way too much paperwork when Paul's body was shipped off the island. Her list of things to do before the matter was closed was far from complete, though. "I hate to sound callous," she began. "But I need to replace Paul. The bylaws of the Mr. Desire Pageant state if the winner of the Most Eligible Bachelor Pageant isn't able to participate in the Mr. Desire Pageant, his runner-up will stand in for him to represent their state. I'll probably wait until the morning, but then I'll have to contact him and invite him to participate."

"So, there is no investigation?"

"I don't see why there would be."

"So, it was an accident."

Andrea studied Mark's serious expression for a moment. "I watched him die," she whispered.

She prayed nothing in her expression instigated Mark's next move. But when he leaned forward, reaching for her, then pulling her into his arms in a tender embrace, Andrea couldn't swear that she hadn't met him halfway. She relaxed for a moment, her cheek pressed against his chest. Already she was familiar with his smell. Or at least her body was. In spite of how trying everything had been since the horrible accident, her insides quickened sharply when she breathed in Mark's familiar smell and felt his powerful, warm body envelop hers.

"I can't even imagine," he whispered into her hair.

Maybe Mark realized his actions were a bit too personal because he straightened, rubbed his finger across her cheek, and brushed a strand of hair behind her ear. Then, giving her a solid look, he patted her knee before retreating to his stool and relaxing against the counter.

"I'm sure if there had been something wrong with the contraption he was in when he died, you would have heard by now."

"There was obviously something very wrong with it," Andrea countered. "Or Paul would still be alive. I have no idea what, though. And if they even try pressing charges against Dave, my head cameraman, for what has happened, I'll throw a holy fit. I promise. I was there. Dave was so devastated he couldn't function. I kept his crew together, waiting to the side, after the medics showed up."

She stifled a yawn and was surprised to do so with all the caffeine pumping through her system. And although Andrea probably would have been wise to request herbal tea at this hour, all she'd wanted was the sanity the aromatic coffee had brought her.

"I'll walk you up to your suite," Mark offered, standing and taking her cup without asking, then carrying it, along with his, around the counter toward the large double set of kitchen sinks.

"Take her on up," Marcia instructed, relieving him of the two cups. "And keep me posted if they learn anything," she added, lowering her voice to a rough whisper.

"I will," Mark promised, then returned to Andrea. "You'll feel better in the morning."

She didn't want to think how she must look at the moment for him to say what he did. It dawned on her that she probably looked like crap, something she hadn't given thought to while they'd been sipping coffee together. Which was proof of how out of it she must actually be. Furthermore, she honestly didn't care what she looked like. That in itself was proof she should call it a day. She wasn't herself at the moment.

Andrea dwelt on thinking straight, and not on Mark's virile body, when he helped her off the stool. He held her close as he escorted her out of the kitchen and up a flight of back stairs that led to her rooms.

8

"Mark?" a woman asked when he answered the phone a few mornings later. "This is Sylvia Conkin, with KWPD. Remember me, darling?"

Mark stared at his ocean view as he leaned against the balcony ledge. "You're taking me back a few years," he said, trying to sound happy to hear from her, although he wasn't sure why. If she was pushing for another date, that would never happen.

A few years ago Mark had asked her out and they'd gone on two dates. On the second date she'd all but raped him. Mark had taken her home, had barely managed to keep his clothes on, and hadn't seen her since.

He'd known after the first date that Sylvia wasn't his type of woman. Her incredible body had distracted him into asking her out, but when she'd pushed for the second date, Mark knew she was too aggressive, too dominating, for their personalities to be compatible. Sylvia had all but ordered him to pick her up and take her to dinner on their second date, then had informed him what she planned on doing to him once they returned to his place afterward. When at first he'd laughed her off as they'd finished dessert, Sylvia had leaned forward, shown off some incredible cleavage, and had told him that if he didn't start behaving, she would handcuff him to her bed and spank his rear end until he begged to do everything to her she wanted done. Mark had ended the date at that moment, but still had to take her home. He wasn't the kind of guy to leave a woman stranded, no matter what type of kink she enjoyed.

"I've just been handed the Sanders case and figured I would call you as a courtesy."

"The Sanders case?"

"The young man who was killed on Tripp Island," Sylvia clarified. "I need to go out to the island today and interview everyone who witnessed his death."

"I thought it was ruled an accident."

"I'm not ruling it as anything yet." Sylvia was all business, her tone sharp and aggressive. She hadn't changed a bit. "Like I said, this is a courtesy call since this is your family's island. I'd like it if you were out there when I arrived."

He had half a mind to tell her that wouldn't be possible. Mark thought of Andrea and how fragile she'd seemed the night before after dealing with the poor kid's death all day. There was no way he would let Sylvia come barging out here and bulldoze into Andrea.

"I'm already here," he told Sylvia. "When will you be arriving? I'll clear you through the dock security."

"Perfect," she purred, the aggressive cop suddenly transforming into a sultry tigress. "I'm not sure why we faded apart," she added, her voice dropping to a husky whisper. "It will be great seeing you again, sweetheart. I should be there around noon."

After hanging up, Mark watched the waves rush over each other as they raced up the beach, then recede back into the blue abyss. He had over an hour before Sylvia would arrive on the island. Maybe he would seek Andrea out. Since Monday night, after glimpsing a side of Andrea he wondered if many ever saw, Mark hadn't seen much of her. He knew what she'd been doing, though. Everyone on the island did.

Andrea had called for a mandatory meeting of all pageant members the next morning and had given a moving speech, talking about Paul, explaining to everyone how he died, and as she'd said during her speech, alleviating the many rumors that were popping up all over the place. Andrea had done a good job of putting everyone's mind at ease and at the same time offering a moving eulogy for the death of a young man struck down before he'd truly had a chance to live.

At the same time, she'd successfully put enthusiasm back in everyone about being on Tripp Island for the Mr. Desire Pageant. Andrea had impressed upon everyone how Paul had been given an opportunity most men just dreamed of experiencing. He'd won Most Eligible Bachelor in his state. Since everyone else in the room had also won that title in their state everyone understood what she was saying. Within minutes of expressing how Paul was torn from life when he had everything in his hands, before the pageant had officially started, when all fifty men were equals and all there to achieve the same goal, the mood in the large meeting room had noticeably changed by the time she had finished speaking.

Mark had lingered in the hallway where he couldn't be seen and had listened to some of her speech. Her oratory skills were off the charts. Andrea had a gift for being able to speak to a large crowd as if she were speaking to each person in the room on a one-on-one basis. Since her speech, Mark guessed she'd focused on damage control, and trying to keep the momentum up among all contestants since "the show must go on."

Possibly Andrea would be ready to escape, even if just for an hour or so. It was day three of her damage control and assuring all contestants that as terrible of an accident as this was, in all the years of pageantry nothing like this had ever happened before and she promised them it wouldn't happen again. Andrea had no grounds to make such a promise, yet her assurance to all the contestants seemed to have done the job.

Although Mark had only gone downstairs briefly this morning, he immediately noticed the morose attitude had faded and once again all the young men who'd taken over his island were as cocky and arrogant as they'd been before Paul's death. His father had made a wise move in seeking Andrea out to manage the Mr. Desire Pageant.

Just as he was trying to decide if texting Andrea, or simply seeking her out and sweeping her away from whatever it was she might be doing, would be the better move, Mark's cell phone rang. It vibrated across the small, round glass table next to him as Mark reached for it and glanced at the screen.

"Hello," he said, calming himself so he could sound reassuring for his father.

"How is everything going out there? I'm still in shock over that poor boy's death."

"Paul Sanders's death was a terrible accident. I was just thinking about how well Andrea handled the matter and helped keep everyone out here calm and focused. You did a good job hiring her."

"I'm not in my deathbed yet," his father said, and laughed. It quickly turned into a raspy cough. "Key West's finest will have their detectives all over my island whether it was an accident or not." His father paused and took a breath. "Tell me what you do know," he instructed, lowering his voice. "Did you know this Paul Sanders at all?"

"I don't know any of the contestants." Mark stood and stretched. He glanced at the gardens below and took a moment to look at the small groups of people who were at different spots among the well-manicured landscape of exotic flowers and shrubbery. He couldn't identify any of them. "All I know about Sanders was that he was a kid. He was nineteen."

"Lord," his father groaned. "You've contacted the parents?"

"Andrea did," Mark said. "Immediately," he added, not wanting his father to worry, or think they weren't being compassionate over the situation.

"I got my hands on a police report." There was a shuffling of papers. "It describes some type of pulley thing that malfunctioned."

"I did see the pulley. I guess they use it all the time and have never had any type of accident prior to today." Mark wasn't surprised that his father was on top of things. He might be slowing down, but he had a staff who could pull off connections and get answers probably faster than the police could.

"You haven't heard anyone mention anything about suing us over this misfortune, have you?"

"No, Dad, of course not. I don't want you worrying about anything like that."

"I'm not dead yet, son," his father scolded. "You know I'm always on top of things."

"And will be until your last breath," Mark said, laughing.

"That's right," his father said with conviction. "Keep me apprised of things. How is your Alpha two, one team doing?"

"They haven't contacted me, but I know they're searching the island," Mark began, heading back into his bedroom and sitting on the edge of his unmade bed. "Dad, why didn't you tell me Mom's greenhouse had been buried in the hedge?"

"Buried in the hedge?" His father sounded confused.

"The hedge that runs the length of the back property line behind the house."

There was silence for a moment and Mark pressed the phone to his ear, listening and waiting as he stared at the floor and his bare feet. He wanted to prompt his father on but was seeing quickly that his dad wasn't remembering things that well, which bugged him. Mark Tripp Sr. was a rock, a financial tycoon who held the respect of men around the world. Mark didn't want that rock crumbling.

"I know the hedge runs along the back property line," his father said, sounding upset. "But your mother's greenhouse was torn down. I had that done years ago."

"No. It's not. I was in it last night."

"You're not making sense," his father snapped. "Brandon oversaw it being torn down years ago. I told him to tear it down."

"I see," Mark said slowly, wondering why their groundskeeper on the island didn't do as he'd been instructed.

"You sure it was her greenhouse?"

"I'm sure," Mark said. "I was at the edge of the yard last night and saw the door in the hedge. I went inside. I remember Mom's greenhouse. Furthermore, Dad, the coins that Alpha two, one found were directly on the opposite side of the hedge. I'd swear to it. I was going to investigate it further today."

"Interesting." His father sounded coherent now. "I'll call Brandon right now. He's been with us for years. What you're saying doesn't make sense. He wouldn't disobey my instructions."

Mark would have agreed. But if his father had ordered the demolition of the greenhouse, Mark was more curious as to why the order hadn't been carried out.

"Don't call him," Mark decided. "Let me look into this a bit further, first."

"Well, okay," his dad complied, although once again, he sounded confused.

Mark pinched the bridge of his nose, hating hearing his father not sounding on top of his act. If Brandon didn't tear down the greenhouse, and the coins were found just outside it on the other side, Mark wondered what else might be found in that greenhouse. His father should have pieced that together, too, yet didn't. Worse yet, his father broke into a wheezing fit that Mark waited out.

He was still breathing heavily when Mark added, "Get some rest, Dad. I'll call you back as soon as I figure this out."

"Don't patronize me."

It took Mark a second to realize his father was speaking to his nurse. His dad mumbled a few more complaints, then came back to the phone.

"Learn what you can and call me back. This man is going to lose his job if he keeps picking on me," he complained.

Mark laughed. His father had one of the best nurses in Florida at his personal beck and call. He wasn't going anywhere.

"Hang in there, Dad," he said, then added his good-byes and ended the call.

Mark was over in the wing where Andrea's suite was before he'd even realized that was where his feet took him. His father's phone call had him worried. Mark had a police investigation to keep focused on, and he needed time to learn why his mom's greenhouse had been buried inside a very thick and tall hedge that apparently Brandon had arranged to grow up around it. But why? He needed time to clear his head so he could sort all this out.

"What are you doing here?" Andrea sat behind her desk, the door to her office open. Her eyes widened when she spotted him in the doorway, and she pushed her chair back, stood, and touched her hair with her fingers as she gave him a small smile. In spite of her question sounding terse, she didn't look disappointed to see him.

"I wanted to check on you." Mark had an official reason for showing up unannounced. But he was telling her the truth in that he needed to see she was hanging in there. He would get to his other reason soon enough. For some reason it was important Andrea saw that his concern for her was legitimate.

Andrea continued brushing her fingers over her hair, making sure it was in place. Today she'd put her hair up in a tight bun at the back of her head. Long, neatly wrapped curls fell out of the bun and along her nape, giving her a very classy look.

The dark lavender high-neck, sleeveless dress she wore clung to her incredible figure. This outfit was out of character compared to her usual bright splashes of color. She'd probably gone for a more demure color to pay her respects to the recently deceased. She wasn't wearing black, but the soothing dark shade might still offer sympathy and made Andrea appear more serious and composed than anything else he'd seen her in since they'd first met almost a month ago.

"I'm fine." She moistened her lips as she tried to make her smile appear sincere.

Mark didn't miss the slight fog covering her large brown eyes. "Are you busy?" he asked.

She gave him a knowing look. "When am I not busy?" she countered, let out a soft laugh, and shook her head. "Needless to say, this week has been exceptionally trying, but I'm managing." Andrea sat against the front of her desk and crossed her arms over her chest. If her outfit wasn't so high-collared with a knitted choke fitting perfectly around her long slender neck, she would probably be offering him one hell of a view of her full, round breasts. "I might end up having to replace my head photographer."

"Really?" Mark moved to stand alongside her and rubbed a silk leaf on a fake plant Andrea had on the corner of her desk. He liked the settled look her office had even though she would only be here for the duration of the pageant. Although, already he would argue in favor of signing her on as the permanent pageant director for the Mr. Desire Pageant. "Is it for another reason?" Mark glanced over his shoulder at the door to the hallway although he knew they were alone. "Or was it his fault somehow that the boy died?"

Andrea focused on the hallway, which meant looking straight ahead instead of at him when he stood next to her. The pageant staff and all its employees might be Andrea's, but the house staff was his. Mark had found the young maid at the end of the hallway when he'd reached this suite. She'd been leaning against the upright vacuum and texting and damn near jumped out of her shoes when he had approached her from behind. He knew if his father had walked up on any of his hired help texting they would have been fired on the spot. The look on her face showed him she knew that, too. Mark had told her to turn on the vacuum if anyone entered this wing. Otherwise she was to leave it off and leave Andrea's rooms alone until he told her otherwise.

Andrea's tone was flat when she continued staring at the open door. "A Detective Conkin called me this morning and has opened up an investigation. They think there is some suspicion around his death. The detective told me she will be interrogating the head cameraman, which is Dave Small. I guess someone has to take the blame, and it was Dave's set. He's been photographing contestants, and models, longer than I've been in this business," she added, her voice filling with emotion when she looked at him. Her pretty brown eyes were moist. "Dave is beyond destroyed by all of this. I'm not sure he can do his job, and we're too close to the pageant beginning to give him time to get it together. Needless to say, nothing like this has ever happened to any of us before."

Mark knew what it was like to have to let go of an employee who had also become a friend. "You've got a way of talking to people. I see he was your friend but you'll find a way to let him go and still hold on to the relationship the two of you have," he consoled, stroking the side of her head as he spoke.

Andrea let out a dry laugh and shook her head slowly. "I don't know about friends. We never spent time together outside of work, although neither of us really had that much time outside of work." She stopped talking and stared Mark in the eye. She took a moment before she started speaking again, slowly. "I need a head photographer who can do the job. But if I let him go I'm worried it will imply his guilt."

"Does he have an explanation for what happened?" Mark asked, trying his hardest to sound neither threatening nor accusatory. Andrea obviously believed her photographer innocent of any foul play. Mark didn't have a clue who Dave was, but it didn't make sense someone who was so set in their career would sabotage it in such a public way. Either way, Andrea needed to bounce her thoughts off someone. He was glad to be there for her.

She shook her head and her eyes turned glassy. "The ropes had been pulled over the pulleys wrong. Whoever would have gotten on that contraption next would have died." Andrea sucked in a breath and straightened. "There was an argument before Paul was lifted to the top of the waterfall over who would ride to the top of it for the next round of shots."

"Who argued?" This wasn't information he had already heard.

"Dave, the photographer, of course, and he had two other cameramen working the shoot, too. There was Paul, Conroy Porter, who goes by Roy. He is out of Connecticut. And of course, Big D. He thought the shot from the top of the waterfall should be his and stepped forward to say as much." She frowned, lowered her gaze, and appeared to study his stomach. Her long twisted curls swept over her shoulders and hung forward, offering a natural shroud around her face. "His agent didn't do his arguing for him," she muttered under her breath.

"Whose agent?"

"Big D's," she said. "Which is odd, but I didn't think it through at the time."

"What seems odd?"

"The contestant's agents did their arguing for them. Which is how it usually is. But Big D's agent didn't come forward fighting for him to have that ideal shot at the top of the waterfall. And I know her. She's a pushy little—" She cut herself off and looked up at him.

"So you're saying if she'd fought for him, it would have been Big D in that pulley?"

"No. I'm not." Andrea walked around him to the wet bar alongside her large desk. Her hips swayed in an enticing invitation when she walked away from him. She bent over behind the bar and opened the small refrigerator he knew was there. When she straightened she held a chilled bottle of water. "Water?" she asked.

"If that is all you're offering."

"Oh. Well." Andrea looked at the clock hanging on the wall. "Maybe I . . ."

Mark moved in on her before she stammered herself into a fit. He came around the counter and took her wrist in his hand. Her pulse beat frantically against his fingers. "I meant if that was all you were offering to drink," he explained gently.

Andrea's mouth curved into a small circle when she looked up into his eyes. To her benefit she didn't blush. Her eyes were haunted, though. Death, intentional or accidental, wasn't something she dealt with on a daily basis. Very few people did.

He took the bottle of water out of her hand and placed it on the counter, then glanced into the small refrigerator hidden behind the bar. He helped himself to another water bottle, straightened, and blocked her path back around the bar.

"I noticed the mood among the contestants appeared more relaxed this morning." Mark opened her water and handed it to her.

"That's good to hear." When she smiled and offered a small laugh, both sounded forced. "The buck stops here, you know," she said. "It's my job to smooth out all wrinkles and make sure this pageant goes off without a hitch. Yet at the same time I keep seeing Paul hanging upside down, his hands reaching for the ground and his eyes open, but not seeing."

Mark knew, and had agreed, with the terms of their *dates*. The point of setting them up as they had was to prevent the possibility of anything other than physical connections existing between them. He didn't give a rat's ass about any of those terms at the moment.

Taking her opened water bottle from her hand, he put it on top of the bar then pulled Andrea into his arms. Not only did she not fight him, she collapsed against him. He wrapped his arms around her, pulling her in close, and rested his head on top of hers.

"Something terrible has happened," he whispered into her hair and breathed in the smell of lavender that seemed to match her dress and her mood. Sultry, distractingly beautiful, yet a bit of a mystery, and one Mark looked forward to unraveling until he understood every expression, every body movement, everything about her. "Andrea," he murmured, and as he spoke her name she relaxed against him. "Take care of the pageant. Paul's death is in the hands of the police. That was the other reason I came here to see you."

"I've already spoken with the chief of police on behalf of the Tripp family and the Mr. Desire Pageant," Andrea said, tilting her head back and searching his face as she spoke. "He's agreed to maintain a very low profile and do everything in his power to keep this out of the press, at least until the pageant is over. The Sanders family is grief-stricken, but they won't offer any trouble. I didn't sense anything other than grief when I met with them last night."

She'd been running all bases, fighting with everything she

had to keep the walls standing, not only for the pageant but for his family's good name, as well. Mark wanted to run his hand alongside her head, cup it in his palm, and promise her everything would be okay. Andrea was one hell of a strong woman. She'd witnessed the young man's death up close and personal, and she was the one standing here fighting to maintain her composure and show him everything was fine. If it weren't for how she'd just collapsed against him, Mark would have guessed her to be Superwoman. As it was, he'd bet she was barely holding on.

"Andrea, I promise you that your job is very safe."

Something shifted in her expression and she stepped backward, pushing away from him. "Are you saying I won't lose my job because I'm sleeping with the boss?"

He wouldn't say she sounded pissed, but the flat edge that sliced down the middle of her words was enough to show Mark he'd just said the absolutely wrong thing.

"That's not at all what I'm saying," he informed her.

Andrea pushed her way around him and stormed to her desk. Apparently she'd forgotten she'd put her hair up that morning because she blew out a loud sigh and dragged her fingers through her hair. Immediately her bun sagged behind her head and several long, tight curls twisted to the side.

"Crap," she hissed, turned on him again, and this time stormed into the bedroom half of her suite through the connecting side door of her office.

Mark was on her heels before she could slam the door in his face. He closed it behind them, realizing now he probably wouldn't hear the vacuum if it were started but not really caring anymore.

Andrea marched through her bedroom and into the large bathroom and stopped in front of the mirror. She jabbed at her hair, yanking out pins and allowing her long curls to tumble past her shoulders.

He leaned against the bathroom doorway, crossed his arms over his chest, and watched her. "You took what I said the wrong way."

"Did I?" She looked at him through the mirror. "Good thing."

"I told you how impressive you are. When you looked at me, worried, that is when I assured you that your job wasn't in danger, not because of anything other than the simple fact that you kick ass doing it. Regardless of what conclusions you've drawn about me, I know good business isn't managed by affairs of the heart. Paul's death wasn't your fault. Nor do I want you trying to handle the police and doing your job at the same time. I'll take care of the cops."

Andrea studied him through the mirror, glancing away to make sure she was putting her hair back together properly, then focusing on him again. "What makes you think I've drawn any conclusions about you at all?" she asked, appearing satisfied her hair was once again in place when she turned on him, defiance rimming in her eyes. Apparently when Andrea got mad, she didn't calm down quickly.

Mark was pretty sure he could soothe that temper of hers. But just in case she decided to take a swing or two, he made his move swiftly. He stepped into the bathroom, trapping Andrea. Her eyes widened but he doubted being trapped was the first thing that entered her mind. She licked her lips, stared up at him as her brown eyes grew wide and bright. He'd come to understand the flush in her cheeks when her mind filled with lustful thoughts. It would be one hell of a good day when she grew comfortable enough to share those thoughts with him.

He cupped her face in his hands, holding her in position with her head tilted back. Then taking care not to mess up her hair, in spite of the sudden urge that gripped him to tangle his fingers into it, Mark lowered his mouth to hers.

It had never occurred to him to keep track of all the women

he'd kissed in his life. There had been some women who really sucked at kissing and other women who had mind-blowing skills. At least he'd thought that until now. Andrea's lips parted the moment he touched them with his tongue. But when she opened to him, her body arching against his and her hands gliding up his arms to rest on his shoulders, it was all Mark could do not to tear her clothes from her body and take her right there, over the bathroom counter. She did something to him no woman had ever done before.

Saying Andrea had skills put her in the same category as every other woman, even if it did put her at the top of that list. Mark had never met anyone like Andrea. Her job was her life. There were many out there his age who had no life because of their careers. He was one of them. Yet Andrea embraced life and her work with class and grace unlike anyone he'd ever seen.

She embraced her sexual interests with the same elegance, the same fervor, although not with the same style. Andrea kissed him as if she needed to in order to survive. There was an energy sizzling over her flesh, a heat so feverish it singed his fingers when he touched her.

Andrea slid her tongue against his, encouraging a wicked, sultry dance full of desire and promises. Her kiss wasn't skilled through years of practice and mastering the art. She was good because she loved having sex. She loved sensuality. She craved it so much she went to the extreme of arranging taboo rendezvous with men she barely knew.

Mark was getting to know her, though. Andrea was getting to know him. She might not have a clear perception of who, or what type of person, he was. But the way she was kissing him right now wasn't close to how she'd kissed him the first time they'd had sex. There was passion in her lips. Her body moved against his with a very clear and precise invitation.

He wanted her. Damn it to hell, he wanted her so badly the need for her tightened every muscle in his body. Andrea must have noticed because she hummed with appreciation when her fingers brushed over the contour of his arms.

"I'm very good at what I do," she murmured and kissed him again.

Mark growled, willing to tell her she was far better than good, except he was too busy devouring her mouth. Her skin was soft and warm. When he moved his hands down her body, the cool silky material her dress was made out of was an enticing contrast.

Mark stretched his hands around her waist, gently constricting his fingers and feeling how thin she was. Not in an unhealthy way, though. He moved his hands to her hips, enjoying the curve of her figure, then reached behind her and cupped her ass.

"I imagine there isn't much you can't do," he told her, dragging his mouth from her lips to her neck.

"There's plenty I can't do." Andrea's laughter was soft, melodic, and free of the tension that had been threatening to fill her when she'd rushed into the bathroom.

"Maybe one is your inability to draw the right conclusion about some people."

"What wrong conclusions do you think I've drawn about you?" Andrea whispered, not bothering to raise her head.

Mark raised his head and stared down at her pretty face. Her eyes were still closed and her lips full, wet, and slightly parted. As he studied her, Andrea's lashes fluttered until she stared up at him through glazed eyes.

"What do you want me to know about you?" she asked, her hands still caressing the tops of his arms. "Or maybe I should ask, what image is it that you want me to believe?"

"Only the truth."

She lifted one eyebrow, arching it suggestively as she stared at him for a long moment. "I agree," she said slowly. "Honesty helps keep it simple."

"If we never had sex again, your position as director of the pageant wouldn't be threatened."

"Thank you."

Andrea ran her hands down her dress, smoothing it against her incredible figure. She walked away from him, moving in front of the mirror once again. They had other matters to discuss. But Mark made a mental note to learn what was on her mind later.

An unwavering flood of protective urges invaded his system. He took a step toward her, ready to yank her against him again. She wasn't angry any longer. Which meant she believed him.

"I own an architecture firm in Miami."

Andrea let her hands move slowly to her sides, staring at him through the mirror. Then slowly she turned around until she faced him. "Do you now?" she asked, her tone a bit too sweet.

"My father purchased the Mr. Desire Pageant and I agreed to be on the island during the duration of the pageant." Mark wanted her to know everything about him. He'd started and now wanted to tell her everything. Well, almost everything. Already the pressures of her job and the need to perform perfectly in front of everyone was taking its toll on her. There was no need to tell her about his mother's jewelry box. "My father's reputation precedes him, but he isn't as young and healthy as he once was."

There was no visible emotion on her face, but she didn't look away. Instead she looked as if she were willing him to continue. Hopefully her desire to know him better was as strong as his to know her.

"I have kept in touch with my firm and my two architects on staff since coming to the island. I really feel I should drive into Miami and check on things, but at the same time I need to be here."

Andrea cleared the space between them and cupped his face with her hand. "I'm sorry I suggested you would use sex against me."

"I would love to use my sex against you, and in you," he muttered, cupping her ass again and pressing her against him.

She opened her mouth but he pressed a finger against her lips. Mark didn't want to hear promises of sex later, not when it wasn't a promise Andrea could make.

"And I will, when we have time," he said before she could. "At noon I'm meeting one of the detectives and thought you might like to tag along, especially since you were there at the time. You can see what is going on, but after that I want you to let me handle the police."

"I have no problem delegating." She smiled and it lit up her eyes.

She walked alongside him back to her office and reached for her phone when it rang.

He waited as she sweetly answered questions for one of the contestants. "Do you think Paul Sanders's death was an accident?" Mark asked when she finally put her phone on the desk.

Andrea moved around the desk to the door leading to the hallway and closed it. She kept her hand on the doorknob when she looked at him.

"I don't have any solid ground to think anything," she began. "But nothing like this has ever happened before. The photographer on the shoot has been in this business longer than I have. I know him very well, professionally," she added, then sucked in a breath as she continued throwing out her theory. "Dave doesn't make mistakes. He's a perfectionist. He doesn't tolerate mistakes from anyone underneath him, either. The last thing he would overlook is the safety of a pulley used to lift contestants up a rock wall with a waterfall rushing down it. Not to mention, you didn't see him afterward. He was devastated. Dave is always collected, in control. The poor man could barely speak."

Which could be a symptom of guilt, Mark thought to himself, but didn't say anything. "Did everyone else act as you would expect after it happened?" Mark asked.

Andrea became contemplative, looking across her office with a faraway look in her eye.

"Honestly, I was so upset I wasn't paying attention to anyone else." She held her hand up when she shot him a look as if guessing what he would say. "The only reason I knew Dave's reaction was because he ran to me after . . ." She faltered. Then, clearing her throat, she held her head high and pressed forward. "When Paul quit moving I was directly underneath him, staring into his eyes. I now know that when someone dies their eyes really do dim," she added, her voice barely audible. "Dave rushed into me, damn near bulldozing me out from under Paul, and dragged me over to the chairs. We were both so upset."

Mark didn't remember walking across the room to her. He had her in his arms, kissing the top of her head when he held her close, and found himself wishing more than anything he could erase the horrific memory from her mind that would probably haunt her for years. Andrea was so damn strong, one hell of a businesswoman, yet with one sob she let down her wall of strength and let her vulnerability show. He wasn't sure how he knew, but he was certain she hadn't cried about any of this to anyone else. Something swelled inside him. It wasn't pride. He wasn't so pompous to take comfort in her pain.

They hadn't broken any rules—not yet. And they wouldn't. Mark assured himself, as he continued holding Andrea, that he could share parts of himself and be there for Andrea when she needed a strong shoulder, without risking taking anything to the next level. They were grown adults who had just evolved from fuck buddies into a friends-with-benefits relationship.

Right now they were indulging in the friendship part of that. Nothing else. Whatever it was swelling inside tightened in his chest. For a moment it was hard to breathe. He kissed her hair again, pulling her tighter into his arms. She wrapped her arms around his waist and sighed. The tightness in his chest erupted, and he recognized the overwhelming urge to protect her—from her own pain, from the misery she would have to endure if this got worse, from anything that might make her cry in the future. Again, he assured himself that was simply friendship.

"How do you think the pulley got sabotaged?"

Andrea looked up at him. "How do you know the pulley was sabotaged?"

9

Lieutenant Conkin was possibly a few years older than Andrea. She was pretty, in spite of the drab uniform she wore. The large black belt didn't help show off her figure, but Andrea knew the uniform was designed for practicality and not style.

"It's good to meet you." Conkin nodded her head briskly at Andrea, her tone all business. It softened considerably when she turned her attention on Mark. "You and I can walk to where this young man died. I need to rope off the crime scene."

"Crime scene? This was an accident," Andrea emphasized, and thought she saw something change in the officer's expression when she looked at Mark. Andrea shifted her attention to Mark in time to see him frown. "Did you know this was a crime scene?"

"No," he said adamantly. "And Andrea witnessed it." He stepped to the side, putting her in between him and the cop. Then, placing his hand on Andrea's lower back, he started them in the direction of the waterfall. "We both agree it's a good idea to go over everything with you again," he offered, glancing at the cop before looking down at Andrea. There was something odd in his expression.

"It's always a good idea to go over everything when it's still fresh in everyone's head." Conkin shifted when they turned toward the grove of trees and stepped in on the other side of Mark, making it harder for Andrea to see her when she spoke. "I understand you're the director of this pageant, Miss Denton," she said, her tone once again brisk with an almost harsh edge to it. "I imagine that keeps you incredibly busy. I can't imagine controlling so many men."

"I'm always busy."

"I'll vouch for that," Mark offered, his tone light.

The lieutenant almost cut him off with her next question. "Do you attend all the shootings?"

"Oh no, not at all. It would be impossible." Closing her eyes wouldn't block out the image of Paul hanging upside down. An unwelcome shudder rushed over her, and Mark rubbed her back, as if sensing she needed consoling. "Honestly, and I hate admitting this, but I wish I had been anywhere but where I was when Paul died."

"Where exactly were you?"

"Standing directly underneath him."

They reached the path that led them toward the waterfall. Already the sound of rushing water sounded louder than the different variety of birds chirping in the trees above and around them. It wasn't a wide enough path for the three of them to walk alongside each other. Andrea tried slowing her pace so she wouldn't be pushed off the path, but Mark simply slowed with her. The cop slowed as well, maintaining her position on the other side of Mark. Andrea was almost grateful when they got where they were going just so they could end the odd dance the three of them had seemed to be performing while walking alongside each other all the way there.

She stopped in her tracks when they entered the clearing.

The waterfall looked oddly beautiful. A picturesque scene lay out in front of them, grossly contradicting the ugliness that had occurred there just days before. She looked around and stared at the yellow police tape, which Lieutenant Conkin wrapped from tree to tree until she had the area marked off. She caught Lieutenant Conkin scowling as Mark lifted the tape and reached to help her into the blocked-off area.

There was white tape on the ground, roughly in the shape of a human body, but not as accurate as it was in TV shows. Andrea guessed there wasn't any way to tape off where Paul had actually died, since he had been in the air. When had the cops made this place, which once had looked like paradise, into a crime scene? The area taped off on the ground was probably where Paul had lain once he'd finally been cut loose from the ropes that killed him. She stared at the ground, then slowly raised her gaze until she was pretty sure she stared into the space where his body had been hanging.

"Are you okay?" Mark was hovering close, his arm now wrapped around her as he brushed her hair away from her face.

She realized quite a few strands were loose and wished she'd thought to take time to spray it in place before they'd come downstairs to meet the cop.

"Fine. I'm fine."

His concerned expression did something to her insides. A flutter started in her gut and swelled quickly, turning into raging need so strong she swore it had to be visible in her face.

Mark's small smile as he stared into her eyes confirmed her fears. He couldn't already read her that well, could he?

Looking past him, Conkin wasn't scowling anymore. She looked pissed.

"I'm sorry," Andrea offered, waving her hand in front of her face and moving around Mark. Granted, the close proximity was making it easier not to pay attention to where they were, but the lieutenant was obviously irritated and the last thing Andrea wanted was to appear uncooperative. This was bigger than her own feelings. An investigation was going on here, and it was part of Andrea's job to fully cooperate. "I'm not used to murder the way you probably are. But I'm fine. I can do this." She walked up to Conkin. "What exactly do we need to do?" she asked, and managed to laugh.

The lieutenant walked past Andrea and over to Mark. She stood next to him, facing him as she spoke, with her back to Andrea. "Since she is here with us, a reenactment would be helpful. We'll stand out of the way over here and let her show us exactly what happened."

Mark lowered his head and whispered something to the cop. In return, she giggled, sounding almost flirtatious. Andrea frowned, watching the exchange. It was almost as if they knew each other. Mark was beyond drop-dead gorgeous. The cop was quite pretty. Mark whispered something again, this time sounding more as if he hissed in anger. Again the cop laughed. When she slid her arm around Mark's and made an effort to move him to the side of the clearing, something nasty rose inside Andrea. She had a compulsive urge to leap forward and yank the cop away from him.

"Andrea, you don't have to do this." Mark finally looked at her and his impassive expression turned worried.

She managed to look up at both of them with a smile. "It's okay. I want to help."

"Good," the cop said, her voice sounding too sweet. Not to mention she was holding on to Mark's arm as if she were staking out her territory. "Walk us through exactly what happened."

"Okay." She looked around, getting her bearings. It shocked her how shaky her legs were when she started in the direction of where she and Windy had been sitting. "I was over here, sitting in a lawn chair in the shade," she began, reached the spot, then turned to face the waterfall.

Andrea saw the contestants, Paul, Roy, and Big D, along with Big D's agent and the photographers standing alongside the waterfall. The pulley was hanging amidst all of them. She sucked in a breath, blinked, and stared at the yellow police tape and the white outline on the ground.

"Everyone was over there. They were arguing."

"Good. Give us every detail. Don't forget a thing."

Andrea looked at the officer. Both her arms were wrapped possessively around Mark's. He seemed stiff, almost uncomfortable. Then it hit her. Like a heavy ball of lead swinging toward her and slamming her in the gut, the revelation came at her with cruel force. They were dating. That was why the cop was struggling to remain next to Mark as they walked along the path. It explained why they stood the way they did now. She was Mark's girlfriend and was letting Andrea know in no uncertain terms that he was her man and that Andrea would be wise to not forget that.

Anger seethed inside. Mark hadn't told her he was dating anyone. But then she hadn't asked before suggesting they fuck each other. Had he been weak and unable to refuse her all-too-convenient plan? After all, he would be on this island alone, without his girlfriend there to be suspicious. How would he know a crime would occur here and his girlfriend cop would show up? Or worse yet, did he stray often and his girlfriend knew it? Was she letting Andrea know without saying anything that she'd better stay away from Mark? Could she tell Andrea had fucked Mark?

Her voice cracked when she tried to speak again. Pulling her attention from the two of them, she focused on her surroundings, allowed the gory scene to replay itself in her head.

"Paul and two of the cameramen got the ropes around him," she managed, then walked on shaky legs toward the waterfall, pointing as she did. "Windy and I ran to the waterfall when Paul started struggling. Everyone did."

She stopped before she reached the waterfall. Cold drops of water splattered her bare skin. Did they hit her when Paul had been struggling for his life? She had been looking up, staring at him as he hung upside down. He had been reaching for the ground. Then his eyes, the eyes of a young man with his whole life ahead of him, had gone blank.

"He was tangled in the ropes." Andrea looked up and blinked a few times when more water sprayed over her face. It trickled down her cheeks. Or were those tears? "Paul was hanging right here, reaching for the ground when . . ." Her voice cracked and she let her words trail off.

"That's enough!" Mark had his arms around her.

Andrea shoved the horrific sight out of her head and started shaking. Strong, comforting arms pulled her against a warm, strong body. She blinked a few more times, took several deep breaths, and filled her lungs with Mark's familiar smell.

"She's rehashed this enough," Mark said sternly.

"It takes revisiting events over and over again sometimes to put the clues together," Lieutenant Conkin said cooly.

"I understand that. And Andrea just told you what she saw, which was awful." Mark was rubbing her back as he spoke.

Andrea blinked again and focused on the cop. She stood facing the two of them, her arms crossed and her expression fierce. That was when Andrea realized her cheek was against Mark's chest. His arms were around her and his hard body was pressing against her everywhere. She'd never felt better in her entire life. So much comfort. So much strength.

"What would you say the condition of the pulley contraption was?" Lieutenant Conkin asked, ignoring Mark's comment.

As good as it felt leaning against Mark, he wasn't her man. Nor would he ever be. He had some outstanding qualities and would be the perfect guy for someone. But there was something going on between him and the cop. That much was obvious. Andrea forced herself to back out of Mark's arms. A stiff chill wracked her body and she hugged herself, fighting to keep her cool. She needed to get away from the waterfall. And the sooner she put distance between her and Mark, the better.

"I honestly don't remember the condition of the pulley," she stammered. Then pulling her phone from her pocket, she fumbled with it for a moment, ignoring what Mark and the cop said to each other. "I've got to go," she announced.

"I'll walk you back."

"No," she said, and didn't care when she hurried away from both of them if her response was a bit harsh.

The next day, Andrea leaned against the door to her office after saying good-bye to her Idaho contestant and his agent and publicist. Each candidate's problems seemed to run together after a while. Either their living conditions on the island were unacceptable, they couldn't stand their roommate, scheduling conflicts existed, all of which she had handled so many times since arriving on the island she could mediate the worst of arguments in her sleep.

Sighing, she turned to her desk, slumped into her office chair, and picked up her smart phone. Andrea tapped the screen and the text messages she'd exchanged with Mark the day before appeared. She closed her eyes, but the damage was done. The text message burned into her brain. Opening her eyes, she forced herself to read the conversation. It was for the best, she told herself, as she scrolled up and down, reading the exchanged texts.

Why didn't you tell me you had a girlfriend? She had texted to Mark the previous afternoon after storming away from him and Lieutenant Conkin.

His response had been immediate. *Because I don't.*

Does your lady cop know this?

Six minutes had passed before he'd responded. Six excruciating minutes. Andrea stared at the time stamps between her question and his eventual response. Those six minutes had been telling.

It's one-sided, Dre.

Dre. No one called her Dre. And if anyone had, Andrea would have corrected them immediately. Yet for some idiotic reason, staring at the nickname he'd started using during their text messaging, a warm sensation formed in her gut.

One side is too much drama for me.

It was one thing about text messaging she hated. She had sent her response to his denial immediately, typing and sending without giving it thought. She'd condemned and turned him out. Worse yet, there was no text after that. Her final message sat there, hanging in text message air, ending their text session and their incredibly short relationship. Yet it was far from over.

Mark hadn't pushed the matter. He hadn't texted her since. Nor had she seen him. Granted, she'd been in her office since yesterday afternoon, although she wasn't hiding. The closer they got to the pageant, the more swamped she was. She was never alone for more than a few minutes before someone appeared in her doorway, asking to speak with her, and having a problem that needed to be solved immediately.

Andrea placed her phone on her desk and dragged her fingers through her hair. She'd worn it down today, primarily because she hadn't had the desire to do anything with it. It was also the weekend, although days of the week ran together sometimes. There was no clocking in at eight in the morning and out at six in the evening. Morning or night, weekday or weekend, her work continued. It was what she loved about this job. It wasn't a matter of getting her forty hours in but completing the project, which right now was the Mr. Desire Pageant, not Mark.

Since her hair was down, she'd accompanied the casual look with khaki slacks that ended above her ankles and a sleeveless cream-colored blouse. They were off brands, something she did when she couldn't concentrate on what label best suited her mood that day. Her wardrobe was her prize possession, and each piece of clothing had been hand-picked after excruciating time shopping to make sure she was always dressed for success. Today she might as well have been slumming it. It was sad to say no one who saw her would even notice, or care. Only a few of her select friends, Windy being one of them, would have taken one look at her and said, "Oh honey, we must sit and talk until you have it all off your shoulders."

She snorted. God, she lived in a world of snobs. But they were her snobs and they understood when her life wasn't co-operating with her.

Andrea looked sideways at her phone. "Nope, you aren't going to text him," she reminded herself under her breath.

"Miss Denton, do you have a minute?"

Andrea jumped and almost dropped her phone on the floor before managing to put it on her desk and look up at two excited, grinning faces.

"Always," she said cheerfully, although her face felt tight when she smiled at Barry Ortega, her Florida candidate, and Big D, her Texas candidate. "What can I do for the two of you?"

"I found this," Barry said.

"*We* found it," Big D corrected, crowding Barry when the two of them approached her desk.

"Found what?" Andrea didn't usually have candidates approach her grinning from ear to ear. She moved behind her desk and sat.

"This," Barry told her and reached for something in Big D's hand.

Big D yanked whatever it was out of Barry's reach, which wasn't hard to do since he stood over six feet tall and Barry was a good six inches shorter.

"I did find it," Barry said under his breath.

"I saw it before you picked it up but wasn't going to tackle you for a finder's fee," Big D pointed out, his smile intact although there was a slight warning tone in his voice.

"Damn good thing," Barry grumbled, his smile fading. "Give it to me. I want to show it to her."

Big D let out a very dramatic sigh and lowered his hand. Instead of handing whatever was in his hand over to Barry, though, he instead placed it in front of Andrea on her desk.

"Look!" he said, his voice full of excitement. "That's bronze and copper. I've taken a couple of archaeology classes," Big D informed her, his chest puffing out as he straightened.

Andrea only glanced at the big grin on Big D's face, and the rather put-out look on Barry's face that he didn't get to be the one to place it in front of her. She focused on the necklace they'd placed on her desk. Dirt fell onto her desk when she picked it up gingerly.

"It's an odd-looking necklace," she mused, brushing her thumb over what appeared to be thin leaves, every other one in bronze or copper. "Maybe it would look better cleaned up."

"I thought it should be brought straight to you," Barry informed her.

"Good afternoon, Miss Denton. Are we interrupting?" Lieutenant Conkin, who was with another officer, stood in her doorway and slowly entered, eyeing the two greased-up young men curiously.

Andrea picked up the dirty necklace and slid it into her bottom drawer, where there wasn't anything that would be ruined by a little dirt. Already Barry and Big D were backing away from her desk, both of their grins gone as they edged around the two police officers.

"Thank you for bringing it to me," she told both of them.

"If there's a finder's fee, remember who found it," Big D

said, his voice dropping a notch as he shifted his attention between her and the two cops.

"Which was me," Barry called out, although he was already in the hallway.

Andrea didn't acknowledge them, but studied Lieutenant Conkin and the tall, thick-chested cop who stood solemnly next to her. Lieutenant Conkin approached Andrea's desk, an angry scowl on her face. The woman didn't like Andrea, which was her own damn fault. Andrea hadn't done anything to her to deserve not being liked. It wasn't her fault if Lieutenant Conkin wanted Mark and he had given Andrea too much attention while they were at the waterfall. He'd never mentioned the cop to her before that day.

"You aren't interrupting." Andrea stood, tugged on her blouse, and came around her desk. "What can I do for you?" she asked, shifting her attention from Conkin to the other cop with her.

"We need to see Dave Small." Conkin stood tall and at attention, having a couple of inches on Andrea but not as tall as the cop who stood next to her.

Andrea nodded, shifting her attention to the man in uniform who looked a hell of a lot more dangerous than Conkin did with her hair pulled back in a short, blond ponytail that curled at the end just above her neck. The dark man in uniform next to her was her perfect contrast, Andrea mused when she turned to her desk and flipped her planner open. He was night to Conkin's day, dark to her blond, unreadable to her ice-queen demeanor.

"Today he would be over on the far beach," Andrea told them, after sliding her finger down her planner where she kept track of where everyone was and what they were doing at all hours of the day. "They're doing photo shoots over there. Why do you need to talk to him?"

"Our forensics team went over the crime scene yesterday afternoon and found fibers from the pulley ropes that show the ropes had been partially cut."

Andrea brought her hand to her mouth and was shaking her head as she spoke. "Someone sabotaged it?"

Lieutenant Conkin gave her a haughty look but didn't answer her question. "We need to speak with Dave Small," she said, her demeanor full of self-importance.

"Do you want me to call him for you?"

"No," the other cop answered, whose name plate on his uniform read Green. "We want you to take us to him." His harsh baritone, full of authority and commanding, brought Andrea pause.

She looked at the two cops slowly. "Do you need to see him immediately? He's in the middle of a photo shoot right now."

"We need to bring him in for questioning," Conkin told her.

"Questioning?"

"Yes, ma'am," Green informed her. "We would prefer you take us to him. We don't want him alerted we're coming."

Andrea almost started to tell them Dave wasn't like that. He wouldn't run from the cops if they were looking for him. Dave was a good man. He didn't have a criminal bone in his body and no reason to hide from them. Neither cop appeared interested in anything she might say. Both of them were tense, stiff, and looked ready to pounce. She returned her attention to her planner on her desk but no longer saw it. This couldn't be happening. Her brain had barely found the coping mechanisms to handle Paul's death, and now this?

No way would she fall apart with both of them watching her. Taking a silent, deep breath, she maintained her composure and didn't comment. Instead she grabbed her purse, then stuffed her phone in it. "We will need to drive over there," she said, impressed with how calm she sounded when she wanted to scream.

"We appreciate it." Conkin took a step back, then turned to the doorway as she spoke into a small walkie-talkie attached to her collar.

It was a silent drive to the other side of the island, which on the main road, the only paved road on the island, took almost a half hour. The island was ten miles in length but the narrow road twisted and turned, making it impossible to accelerate over twenty miles per hour. Her nerves were frazzled after the silent trip with the two cops. She pulled up to the edge of the beach, where the road ended, her emotions torn. She was anxious to end her drive with both of them but hated what would happen once they arrived at their destination. Her head cameraman, a man she'd known for years and respected very much, was about to be arrested, and she was taking the cops to him. It was wrong. They were arresting the wrong man. There wasn't a doubt in her mind.

"If you wouldn't mind waiting here," Lieutenant Conkin said after she'd climbed out of the backseat. Her blond hair was pulled back so tight into her curly ponytail it looked like it might hurt.

Andrea nodded, meeting the woman's all-business gaze only for a moment before looking at her partner, who stood with his back to the car and faced the men on the beach being photographed. After both cops started across the beach, Andrea left her car in PARK with the AC running and got out. She rested her arms on the top of the car watching the two cops struggle to walk on the sand.

Lieutenant Conkin was pretty, Andrea decided. She used tanning beds, it was obvious by the slightly weathered look on her face and the not quite natural glow of her bare arms. Her black belt did show off her slender figure and her slacks hugged her trim rear end. With her line of work she was probably in incredible shape. Andrea had spent her entire career judging women's bodies with each pageant she directed, yet for some reason she couldn't figure out what that woman had that Andrea didn't have.

"Obviously nothing," she muttered under her breath, since Mark had willingly agreed to the terms of their *dates*.

She needed to hate Mark. He was a scoundrel if he agreed to fuck her and had a girlfriend, who was a cop, in town. Andrea was good at spotting those who were taken. Or she always had been. There was something commonly characteristic about any man who was willing to cheat. Yet she hadn't noticed that in Mark. The night in the kitchen when he'd been so supportive. And in her office, then her bathroom when she'd tried keeping her hair in perfect shape while he'd seemed hell-bent on messing it up. Each time she hadn't once detected an ounce of distraction a man with another woman usually possessed.

He told you it was one-sided.

Dragging her hand through her hair, she combed it back, then held it in place with her fingers when the wind off the ocean picked up. Andrea walked around her car, letting out a jagged sigh, feeling the weight of remorse a bit too strongly.

What the hell was wrong with her?

First of all, she hadn't wanted a relationship with Mark. So it was a damn good thing that he did have another woman in his life because now that she thought about it, she was growing rather possessive.

Andrea stared at the photo shoot, which had now been interrupted. She was wearing sandals but didn't think about that when she started across the warm sand. The two policemen were turning a very astonished, and obviously shaken, Dave around and putting him in handcuffs.

"Crap," she hissed under her breath, picking up her pace. "What are you doing?" Damn it! She should have been paying closer attention. It hadn't crossed her mind that they would cuff Dave, and in front of the young men staring stupidly as the scene played out.

"Our job," Lieutenant Conkin informed her. "You'd be smart not to interfere."

"And I'm doing my job. You're upsetting these young men. Are handcuffs necessary to bring someone in for questioning?" she demanded, squinting against a glaring sun as her hair whipped around her in the heavy breeze.

"Stand back, Miss Denton." Lieutenant Green ignored her question about the cuffs.

Looking around at all the men, some holding volleyballs, others with straw hats on their heads, she ignored their props and saw only their panicked stares. The pageant was falling apart all around her, and it was her job to keep it from doing so. From somewhere deep inside her came a calm she would be eternally grateful for later. "Go with them, Dave," she said soothingly, as if he had a choice. "I'll have a lawyer meet you at the station." She stared at Lieutenant Green, who had his large hand on Dave's larger shoulder. "I assume you're taking him to the Key West police station?"

"Yes, ma'am."

She nodded once, then gripped her hair at her nape to keep it out of her face. "It's okay, Dave. I'll take care of this." She had no idea what she would do, other than contact the lawyers that were on retainer for the pageant. They weren't criminal lawyers, but they would know what to do. They had to know what to do.

Then it hit her she would have to drive them back to the dock. She stepped in front of Dave, preventing the officer from escorting him back to the Volkswagen, and put her hand on the shoulder where the cop's hand wasn't.

"Just stay calm. I know it looks bad right now. But we'll get this taken care of."

Dave's face was puffed, probably with anger, if not a fair bit of humiliation for being handcuffed in front of his team and the contestants. His body was tight, and she actually saw muscles bulging against his light-colored Polo shirt. All the years she'd worked with the man Andrea had always guessed him overweight. But now, standing so close to him and staring into his hard gray eyes, she saw he wasn't fat but thick and muscular. It was interesting all the years she'd worked with him and never had noticed before. And it was insane that she was having these thoughts right now.

Dave was pissed, and she didn't blame him. Andrea wasn't sure she'd ever stared someone guilty of a crime in the eye, but she couldn't believe Dave guilty of anything.

"Provano is my best photographer to put in charge." Dave didn't blink or even sound jittery. "He knows all the layouts and is up on our deadlines. But give Reece authority, as well. He's better with the boys. They need to keep working. There isn't time to waste with the amount of shoots we need done by the end of next week," he explained to her.

"Okay." She nodded, realizing this was information she needed to know and grateful for Dave thinking it through. They were taking him away, and she had delegated all matters pertaining to photography to him. Andrea could have found the information out, made it work, but it would have cut into her time to meet her other deadlines and Dave was right, there wasn't time to waste.

She glanced from Lieutenant Green to Lieutenant Conkin, who stood to the side. She had been on her radio again but looked at Andrea when their gazes met.

"I need a few minutes to talk to my contestants before we take him back," she explained.

"Take all the time you need. We have a ride coming."

As if on cue, the wind suddenly picked up, then turned almost violent. At the same time, a loud flapping sound, mixed with the rumble of an engine, grabbed Andrea's attention and she shaded her eyes, as did everyone else, and watched a police helicopter lower itself to the ground at the edge of the beach. It landed past where she parked, where the ground was flat and not sandy. That was when Andrea spotted him.

Mark leaned against the Excursion. He wore dark sunglasses, and his muscular arms were crossed against his chest. He was in jeans and a tank top that blew around his torso as the helicopter landed. Had he been out here watching the photo shoot, and if so, why? Or had he somehow learned the police were taking Dave and drove out here to watch it happen? Again, why would he do that?

Andrea caught herself staring and watched him turn his head in her direction when Lieutenant Conkin tapped her arm.

"I know this is out of place," the cop began, her light blue eyes searching Andrea's face.

Andrea stiffened, straightening to her full height, and tugged her sleeveless blouse as she waited for the woman to inform her to stay away from Mark.

"I just want to say you'd better take really good care of him. If you don't, there are other women who will snatch him up." The lieutenant turned and hurried to catch up with her partner and Dave as they headed to the helicopter.

Andrea stared after them, closing her mouth when she realized she'd been gawking. She shifted her attention to Mark and was positive he was still watching her. His attention wasn't on the three people now boarding the helicopter. She was also sure a moment ago that his mouth hadn't been in that thin, hard line it was in now. It was as if over the wind and the noise from the helicopter he'd heard what Lieutenant Conkin had just said to Andrea. Even with those black sunglasses Andrea was certain his look would say one thing.

You thought I was cheating. I'm a good man, the best there is, and you just blew it.

10

Mark stepped out of the shower, having been windblown and doused with sand after the helicopter had taken off from the island. He had called his lawyer and sent him over to KWPD to take care of the photographer, then he'd texted Andrea to let her know he'd done so. Now, drying off and wrapping the towel around his waist, he padded across the thick carpet, barefoot, and glanced at his phone where he'd left it on the edge of his bed. He'd received one text message and had missed one call while showering.

The call was from his father. The text was from Andrea.

I'm sorry.

Mark grinned. He wasn't sure he wanted to know what Sylvia had said to Andrea but something had told him, from the look on Andrea's face when Sylvia walked away, that it hadn't been work related. He tapped his screen and responded to her text.

Come to my room.

There was enough time between sending the text and her response for Mark to slip into a pair of boxers and shorts. More than likely Andrea was creating a list in her mind of the many reasons why she couldn't make time for him right now. She really did work as hard as he did. It was a Saturday and already he'd driven into Miami, spent an hour at the office just to make sure all was in order, and to take a look at the sketches Tigger and Rob had prepared to show clients on Monday. Rob had been in his office, catching up on work due the following week. The young man showed a lot of promise, and it was relaxing putting the pageant and Andrea out of his thoughts for a while and talking shop. Andrea didn't stay out of his thoughts for long.

Mark had made it back to the island in time to take the small ferry with Sylvia and her partner. He'd been pissed as hell when he'd learned they were taking Dave in over forensics findings that sounded sketchy at best. It had been pointless to argue. Ignoring the two of them had proven just as impossible to do. Sylvia had been shameless in her efforts to get Mark to notice her. His opinion of her nosedived when he told her, rather bluntly, he was interested in someone else and she still tried to get him to go out with her. Sylvia didn't care about him, his feelings, or anything else for that matter. Catching him was a game. Maybe if he had slept with her on their first date, she would have left him alone.

It wasn't until they were off the boat and Mark had taken off toward the mansion that Sylvia had jogged to catch up with him.

"Is Andrea Denton your girlfriend?" she'd demanded, her pretty blue eyes flashing with an air of competitiveness and insatiable hunger.

"Leave her alone," he'd warned Sylvia, then had marched into the house.

It hadn't surprised him when Sylvia hadn't listened.

Whatever she'd said to Andrea, it had obviously made it clear to her that he and Sylvia were very much not an item. And he should have been pissed that Andrea didn't believe him when he'd told her as much the other day. Mark saw the truth of it, though. Andrea had been jealous. And she'd been upset. They had an arrangement to meet and fuck while on the island, no strings, no stress of forming any type of relationship. At first it had been the perfect arrangement.

What he hadn't expected was how much he liked Andrea. More than liked. He had a damn good case of head-over-heels in lust with her. Obviously, it was a two-way street. If it weren't, Andrea wouldn't have cared how Sylvia had clung to him, and she wouldn't have sent him the accusing and cold text messages.

Andrea had ended their sex-only relationship. The deal was terminated. Now, with her apology, they would start over. This time he would offer an arrangement, but it wouldn't be sex only. Mark wanted all of her.

He walked over to the oval table in the corner of the living room. One of the servants had placed a silver platter with a carafe of hot coffee, Marcia's special brew, along with a platter of finger food. There was a hunger growing inside him that would take a long time to appease, but it wasn't for any of the small, triangular-shaped sandwiches. He poured himself a cup of coffee just as his phone chirped, indicating a text message.

Okay. Give me half an hour.

Twenty-five minutes later Andrea tapped on his door. He was struck dumb for just a moment at the sight of her. Her hair was down, recently brushed, but still held a slight windblown, tousled look to it. As always, her makeup was perfectly applied. She was dressed down today, but there were no clothes that could look bad on her incredibly sexy body.

Mark pulled the door open wider, allowing her to enter, and didn't say a word. When she'd taken a few steps into his suite, which varied only slightly from hers in that he had a parlor and a dining area off the large bedroom, where she simply had the oversized office, she paused and glanced around. She was fidgeting with her hair and shifted her weight but also said nothing. Andrea knew this time around would be different.

He closed the door quietly and came up behind her, stopping her when she would have turned to face him. Mark blocked her with his body then brought the silk scarf he'd prepared before she arrived over her eyes.

"What?" she gasped, her hands moving to pull on it.

Mark pushed her hands away and pulled the scarf tightly around her eyes, then tied it behind her head. "Today, sweetheart," he whispered into her ear, "we are going to have a lesson in trust."

"God. Mark." Andrea brought her fingers up to the blindfold, her fingertips brushing over it before he took her wrists.

"I won't ask what Sylvia said to you on the beach," he continued and found the button and small zipper for her blouse just below her nape and parted her hair to undo them. Then lifting her arms over her head, he pulled it off her. "Whatever it was apparently helped convince you there is nothing between her and me."

"Mark, I—"

"No." He took her by her arms and turned her around. "Don't speak." He didn't want to dwell on how she hadn't believed him. Her apology had been sincere and now she would learn to trust him in all matters.

Mark loved that she wasn't wearing a bra. He'd expected some lacy thing since her nipples had been harder than pebbles when she had stood in his doorway, but he loved that she was the type of woman willing to not wear one at all. Mark turned her around and cupped her soft flesh. He hissed in a tight breath, his cock already creating a tent in his drawstring shorts. Andrea's cheeks were flushed and her lips full and moist. As if she guessed he was looking at them, she ran her tongue over the top and bottom slowly, sensually, and he felt precum moisten the tip of his dick.

"She told me I better take really good care of you or some other woman would snatch you up," she whispered, her cheeks darkening further as she told him in spite of his instruction not to speak.

"Smartest thing I have ever heard that woman say," he growled. Already he knew Andrea would do and say whatever she wanted. She was willful to the core. No way would he break her nature. But with trust, Andrea would then be able to comply with his wishes.

Andrea grunted as her lips twisted into a smirk that was almost a smile. "I doubt I could have told you that if I weren't wearing this blindfold," she confessed, laughter in her voice. "At least I didn't tell her our mutual interest was over a sex-only relationship."

Mark wouldn't press why. There were too many easy excuses Andrea could have offered. She was being discreet. It was none of Sylvia's business. Any reason Andrea might offer would have been the truth. Just not all of it.

Already Mark sensed the feelings brewing inside him concerning Andrea were mutual. He was willing to explore slowly, patiently, and with well-guarded interest, as well as with a well-guarded heart.

"That might have been an interesting conversation," he drawled, then lowered his mouth to hers, kissing her as he fondled her breasts.

Mark tweaked her nipples with his finger and thumb. Andrea cried out into his mouth. She grabbed his arms, held on tightly, and arched her back. Blindfolded and surrendering already. Trust might be a lot closer than he imagined.

Her reaction fed his desire for her tenfold. Brain cells

erupted in his head from an internal heat burning him alive. He was sure of it. It lowered his line of thinking to an instinctive level, her body reactions spawning his actions. Letting go of her breasts, Mark grabbed her arms and lowered them, breaking off the kiss.

He missed seeing her eyes when he stared at her blindfold. But her full mouth, her lips still parted, were such a heavenly view he gave them all his attention. Andrea didn't know if he would kiss her again or not, and remained with her head tilted back, her mouth ready for him, and waited.

"What are you doing?" she demanded, her tone complaining when he had continued staring at her without moving or saying anything. She twisted her arms against his grip. "I'm not sure I like this."

Her breathing was coming hard, and her cheeks remained flushed. Mark doubted she was suffering. He let go of her arms.

"Stay there," he commanded and walked over to his dining room table where the other silk scarf lay. Then, returning to her, he moved behind her. "Give me your hands." He reached for them as he spoke.

"Oh Mark," she complained, this time her tone definite. "I don't think . . ."

"Shush," he insisted, taking her wrists and pressing them together just above her ass. Then, slipping the silk scarf around them, he wrapped it until her hands were bound and he was certain her circulation wouldn't be cut off. "Like I said, a lesson in trust."

"In trust, huh? Was there a point in time when you didn't trust me?"

"I want you to trust me." He moved his mouth against the side of her neck as he spoke and nipped the flesh under her ear.

Andrea jumped and almost started panting. "And you think restraining me will help me trust you? It seems to me you want to control me." There was a smile on her lips, a challenge in her tone. She didn't fight her hand restraints and continued standing there, not trying to move.

If she'd actually panicked or threw a fit not to play along, Mark wouldn't have forced her. Andrea was complaining only to try to maintain the upper hand. She wasn't nervous. Her hard breathing showed how turned on she was. Call it a lesson in surrender, as well. Mark decided not to tell her that, though. Labels might bother her, but her actions—and reactions—were what mattered.

Mark reached around her, sliding his arms through hers, and continued nibbling on her neck as he undid her shorts then eased them down her hips. He took her underwear with them and let them fall until they tumbled into a pile over her feet.

"Step out of them and slide out of your sandals," he instructed, then watched her footing and held on to her waist as she did so.

He then walked her forward, having her completely naked and bound. The view of her like this, completely at his mercy and trusting him more than she might realize, was beyond intoxicating. Mark turned her around then let go of her, stepping back and loosening his shorts. He slipped out of them and his boxers, his cock reaching for her, hard and swollen. As he faced her, both fully nude now, her full breasts, hard, puckered nipples, the soft curve of her hips, her smooth pussy, and slim, trim legs were a picture he would never tire of looking at.

"You are so beautiful," he whispered.

"You're just standing there staring at me." She walked forward, moving fast, and ran into him.

Mark laughed, especially when she felt how hard his cock was when she pressed against it after stumbling into him. "Guilty as charged," he admitted, then picked her up, tossing her over his shoulder before she could try wriggling her way out of it.

"Crap," she hissed, when the air left her lungs as her body hit hard against his shoulder. "I didn't know you were a Neanderthal!" she exclaimed.

"Every man has a bit of Neanderthal in him, my dear," he informed her.

Mark carried her into his bedroom, over to his bed, and flopped her off his shoulder. She fell backward and her legs went up in the air, then spread apart. He was certain he would never forget the view she offered him at that moment.

Lying on her hands made her have to work a bit harder to remain on her back and not roll to her side. Andrea pressed her feet flat against his bedspread and bent her knees, keeping her legs spread. He stared shamelessly at her perfectly shaved pussy, the slender folds of smooth skin curving enticingly and almost completely blocking his view of her hot, tight entrance. Mark didn't need to see to know she smoldered, on the verge of coming. He was damn near right there with her.

He might have grunted his approval if he hadn't thought Andrea might have flown off the bed, refusing to play with a brute. He did hum his approval and knew it sounded a lot like a growl.

Andrea's eyebrows moved under her blindfold. She was frowning. Her long hair splashed around her, falling over her face and fanning her shoulders. She spit and blew, trying to get it out of her face.

"Calm down, sweetheart," he whispered, soothing her before she grew too excited.

He was taking his time, and it was making her nuts. It was hard moving fast when standing before the most beautiful creature he'd ever seen in his life. Lust held a double-edged sword. As painful as it was to move physically, mentally he ached to rush just as he knew she wanted. But hurrying through these moments of staring at her incredibly beautiful, naked body, bound and waiting for him, would be a sin.

Mark came down over her slowly, being careful not to let their bodies touch. There was only so much torture he would be able to handle before he drove hard and deep inside her scorching heat. He picked up the strands of hair she unsuccessfully tried moving and brushed them away from her face.

"So you're going out of your way to prove why women have had to work their ass off to train a man just to make him suitable for a relationship?" she asked. "Many before me have concluded it isn't worth the effort," she added, maintaining a very solemn expression as she spoke.

"I'm worth your effort."

Andrea's mouth opened. Either her jaw dropped in disbelief that he might be suggesting her effort implied more than what they'd previously agreed upon, or she planned on saying something else and decided against it.

Instead of saying anything further, she stretched her legs and wrapped her thighs around his waist. She clung to him, laughing when he tried straightening. Andrea used all her strength to hold on.

Mark grabbed her legs. Andrea was in shape but he had the edge of sight, his hands, and the better position. He was naturally stronger but took his time, enjoying her struggle to win this small battle.

"And women wonder why we behave as brutes," he grumbled as he freed himself from her grasp. He stared at her moist pussy once he opened her up and held her legs spread-eagle. "Lord, Dre," he rasped, calling her by his pet name for her. He wasn't sure why he'd started calling her that, but he'd noticed every time he used the nickname it calmed her as music would a savage beast.

Andrea's smile faded but she didn't look upset. Instead she moistened her lips and sucked in a breath. "What?" she whispered.

She didn't question his nickname. It was on the tip of his

tongue to answer her truthfully, to tell her she took his breath away, that he'd never seen a woman who matched Andrea's beauty. Her body wasn't perfect. He'd seen longer legs on a woman. He'd been with women who had perfect tans. There were more than a few women he knew with much bigger boobs.

But Andrea, from head to toe, was a perfect package none of them could match. Their one or two attributes dimmed to Andrea's perfect ten. Her beauty glowed from the inside as well as out.

No, he wouldn't tell her any of that.

"You're making me very hungry," he mumbled, hoping the catch in his throat as he spoke would come off as desire and not longing for someone he feared he was already growing a bit too attached to.

She smiled quickly, but then fought to suppress it, forcing her mouth into a tightly closed circle as she continued pouting. Or at least she tried making it appear that way.

"I can't say the same since I can't see you."

Mark watched her forced poutiness continue as he moved so he was inches from her pussy, keeping a firm grip on her inner thighs in case she decided to clamp down around him again.

When his mouth was next to her smooth, moist skin, he breathed in her heady scent and immediately wanted to climb over her so he could plunge deep into her heat. His dick complained, throbbing and pulsing, but he ignored the desire, knowing the torture would be worth it, for both of them.

The sounds she made when he began feasting stoked his fire. His brain was electrified. Every inch of his body pulsed with need for Andrea. Before she'd arrived, he'd planned out exactly what he would say, how he would make it clear they were no longer just fuck buddies. He had made a very good argument for the two of them experimenting with what was growing between them.

But as he tasted her, drank her rich cream, and drowned in her sensuality, no words came to him. His brain was mush. Mark had never taken time to determine what qualities would make the perfect woman for him. For the most part, he didn't believe she existed. But Andrea was damn close.

The moment her legs clenched, Mark adjusted himself, knowing she'd knock him over if she managed to lock down on him.

"Relax, sweetheart," he said, caressing the soft part of her inner thighs.

Andrea rocked from side to side. "God, Mark!" she cried out. "Damn it, I can't move!"

She wasn't complaining. Her tone was more of a cry to resist. Which was something he wanted her to overcome. Andrea was always in control. She ran the show, literally. But with him, when they were alone, he wanted to see her enjoy the full extent of her orgasm, which meant letting go. He was convinced that she had seldom experienced the full pleasure she could enjoy if she'd completely relax and allow her body to take over in the throes of passion. Once she learned to trust him, she would then see how much more pleasure she would gain.

"Relax," he repeated, and pressed his hand against her abdomen. Then burying his face in her moist heat, he devoured her until he knew he'd brought her to the moment of pure, raw pleasure.

For a moment, Andrea didn't breathe. Her legs stilled and she quit rocking back and forth. There was a calm, almost serene expression on her face. Her lips parted and her frown disappeared. If he could see her eyes, they wouldn't be pinched shut any longer. He imagined them also relaxed with her lashes fluttering slightly over glazed, brown orbs.

He probed deep with his tongue and tasted a fresher, richer moistness. Then her muscles quivered around him. She exploded and cried out at the same time. If there was anyone else at this end of the house they would have known Andrea had just experienced one hell of a kick-ass orgasm.

"Oh my God!" she wailed, damn near coming to a sitting position.

Andrea came hard, flopping back down on the bed in the next instant. Her tousled hair was like raw silk sprawled around her and her cheeks were flushed crimson. The hard little pants she released tightened her belly and made her breasts jiggle.

Mark was sure he'd never seen a more beautiful sight. He rose over her, bringing his mouth to hers, and kissed her.

"I can taste me on you," Andrea whispered, and every inch of her relaxed underneath him as she opened for the kiss.

"Incredible, huh," he grunted, then impaled her mouth before she could comment.

Mark sat at his desk near the open glass doors to his balcony after Andrea left. He'd printed off reports from work and intended to go over them while he had some time. Instead, he found himself staring out the glass doors at his view of the ocean. He'd always been compelled to watch the foamy waves, the incredible stretch of sandy beaches, and the overwhelming blue calm that went on for so many hundreds of miles past what he could see. The ocean was beautiful and deadly. It all depended on how well the sailor knew how to handle her. Mark saw that a woman, and a relationship, were the same. Handle either wrong and they would eat you alive. But respect all of her power, admire her beauty and strength, and work with her instead of against her, and you had a partner for life.

For life? Was he seriously thinking about something long-term with Andrea?

His phone buzzed and pulled him out of his thoughts. Mark blinked and quit staring at the incredible view outside. Picking up his phone, he glanced at the caller before answering.

"Mark," his office manager, Fran, said crisply. "Sorry to interrupt."

He returned his attention to the vast blue ocean outside his open glass doors and smiled wryly. "It's okay." He didn't add that he had needed to be brought back down to earth. Anytime he started comparing any woman to the majestic ocean, someone needed to give him a hard slap. It might as well be Fran. She kept him on track most times anyway. "What's up?"

"You asked me to research your mother's jewelry box," she began.

Mark straightened and leaned on the desk, no longer caring about the ocean, at least not for now. "Yes. What did you find?"

"What didn't I find?" she retorted. "Your mother had a crystal jewelry box. It was about six inches deep, fifteen inches in length, and twelve in width. The crystal it was made of was very rare and believed to contain alkaloids that prevented most instruments from detecting what was beyond the crystal depths. In ancient times, it was believed if boxes were made of this crystal, anything could be put inside and protected from God and man." Fran paused, exhaled, then continued. It sounded as if she'd been reading. "Sound like your mother's box?"

"Sounds like what I've heard about it."

"You never saw it?"

"I think I might have, but I was very young. I'm not trusting my memory. That's why I want all you can find on it."

"I found all kinds of stuff, including a very old article." She hesitated for a moment. "It was published twenty years ago. So you would have been nine," she added, doing the math for him. "Margaret Tripp commented in this interview, and I quote, *'Jewels are pretentious. Too many women weigh themselves down with diamonds and rubies believing they are showing off their incredible wealth. I'm married to Mark Tripp. I can run around in cutoff shorts and a T-shirt and you would still know*

I'm incredibly rich, yet you wouldn't know me. The jewels I have mean nothing to me. It's the precious items I've collected that meant the world to women from our past, often given to them by kings or wealthy lovers, that I have kept safe over the centuries. My heart, and who I really am, are locked away in my jewelry box. All the diamonds, rubies, sapphires, or gold aren't worth protecting as much as my heart and soul.' " Again Fran quit talking. She muttered something, then grumbled. "It's the other line. Hold a moment."

Fran was the catch of a lifetime. She could run TAC without him, and had been proving as much since Mark had been on the island. The only problem was, she knew how good she was. And she was good. Ask her to do anything and she completed the task with 110 percent effort. That was the only reason Mark tolerated being put on hold without so much as asking if he minded.

"I'm back. Sorry. Got an office to run."

Mark shook his head, knowing if Fran had seen him do it, she would have carried on about how hard she worked. He knew all the work she did.

"And you can tell me what's going on at work in a minute," he said, feigning grumpiness. "Now go on about my mother's jewelry box."

"Yes, sir," she muttered, but there was no bite to her bark. It took a lot more than his pretending he didn't see all she did to get Fran bent out of shape. "The only other thing pertinent in that article is your mother's comment at the end of the interview, which is an interview of wealthy women in the Miami area, if you were interested."

He wasn't. He wouldn't go so far as to say he didn't care about all the money his family had. Mark knew his father had worked his fingers to the bone to build the Tripp fortune. He'd been smart and savvy. Mark respected and appreciated that. As his father had said, Mark and his sister were set for life, whether they worked a day in their life or not. His mother hadn't been quite so understanding. She had seen all that money as the reason her husband didn't fall asleep with her every night. Margaret Tripp had been a romantic, a dreamer, and she'd romanced and dreamed most of the days of her adult life alone until the tragic end. Mark hadn't seen that as a child, but now it was clear.

Fran took his silence as her answer. "At the end of the interview she says, '*All the pain and suffering so many women have endured can be locked away so no one can detect it. That is what I have done. Not just for me, but for every woman before me. There are no jewels or amount of wealth on this earth that need protecting as much as our souls. Without love and peace of mind, all the rest has no more value than a single penny.*' What the hell does that mean?"

Mark wasn't sure. "Maybe it means that material possessions didn't matter to my mom."

"Well, if they didn't there must have been another reason why she had one of the most valued collections of fine jewelry in the world." Fran hummed some unrecognizable tune for a second, and there was a loud crumpling of papers. "Here it is," she announced. "I'll fax this to you. Or I can scan it at my end to an Adobe file and e-mail it to you if you prefer."

"What is it?"

"A picture of all of her jewels and her jewelry box."

"Fax it over now," Mark instructed and stood to go over to his copying machine that also received faxes. "Hopefully you know the number."

"Yes, of course I do. I set all of that up for you out there on Tripp Island, remember?"

He'd forgotten at that moment but wouldn't let her know that. "And it was very much appreciated." He could have set up the computer himself, but not only did Fran run a show as well as Andrea, but if she wasn't needed at every moment, she would mope. Mark blamed it on a pretty woman who had raised four children alone and had never felt the unconditional love from a man she craved, or the security and self-worth that came from a solid, healthy relationship. "Send it over," he said, repeating his instruction. He stood over the fax machine expectantly.

"Okay, faxing now. I'm sending the itemization of everything that was in the jewelry box and its valued worth. That is, what it was worth almost twenty years ago, which was 10.8 million dollars. Can you imagine what it would be worth today?"

The fax beeped, then went through a series of sounds as it talked to his office's fax. A few minutes later, which seemed more like an hour later, it began printing. Apparently Fran had set it for high quality, which he would appreciate once he had the picture of his mother's jewelry, and the unique crystal jewelry box. But he tapped his fingers on top of the machine impatiently as it printed the picture and the following page that itemized the jewelry box contents and worth.

"You're worth even more than that to me, Fran. This was exactly what I needed. You're a sweetheart."

"I'll remind you of my value when it comes time for you to write out those Christmas bonus checks," Fran said dryly. "And you're very welcome. It was fun researching it. Now, let me know when you're ready for all of your phone messages."

Mark reluctantly set the faxed pages on top of the printer and returned to his desk. After jotting down his messages and numbers to call back, he listened as Fran gave him a rundown of all meetings and clients' statuses over the week. He would need to return some calls and spend time convincing a couple of prospective clients that their money would be best spent with TAC instead of another architecture firm. He would have to make those calls soon.

Mark stood, picked up the two faxed pages, and stared at the picture of all of the jewelry and the crystal box. He shifted his attention from the picture to the itemized sheet.

"You never tried living outside the money," he mused, seeing how his mother had spent without provocation. "You bought trinkets worth millions but hated how the world viewed you for having so much money. I wish I had been older. I wish I had been there for you, Mom."

11

"Max Azria would be so proud," Windy crooned, clucking his tongue as he moved around Andrea and admired her dress. "Darling, you are damn lucky this is a pageant of men. Otherwise the judges would want to crown you."

"Would you stop?" Andrea was grinning from ear to ear, though, as she stared at herself in the full-length mirror. She did look good. The BCBG dress fit her like a glove and was so damn comfortable she could cry. She wasn't sure Max would blink an eye at her, regardless of her wearing one of his designs. But she didn't care. She loved the dress.

"Eat it up, girlfriend," Windy said, laughing, then turned when Julie came out of the bathroom and spun in a circle to show off her dress for the night. "Well, color me lucky. There won't be a man in the house who isn't jealous of me tonight with you two beauties on my arm."

"You are so full of it." Julie wrinkled her nose but it was obvious she loved the praise. "I admit it's not that often I get to dress up like this, though. Do you know how much this thing cost, Andrea?" she demanded, her happy smile shifting into her all-business glare as she picked at the frilly material of her evening dress.

"A small fortune!" Andrea came up behind Julie and gave her a hug. "And you're worth every penny."

"I don't know which one of you is worse." Julie rolled her eyes but drank in the flattery.

Windy laughed and wrapped his arms around both women. "Andrea, definitely, darling," he said, grinning broadly.

"Am I interrupting?" Mark asked, standing in the doorway to her bedroom.

Andrea spun around and away from her friends, surprised and at the same time realizing that she'd forgotten to lock her office door. Mark gave Julie and Windy a quick glance but settled his attention on Andrea.

"Wow," he said under his breath, his eyes darkening as he moved in on her.

"I know, right?" Windy said, brushing imaginary lint from his shirt. "Just wait until you see me in my tux coat."

Andrea shot him a look of gratitude, thankful for his continual ability to ease sudden tension in a room with a light comment. Windy didn't notice her, though. As he moved away from Andrea and Julie and slid his tuxedo jacket from its hanger hooked over her bathroom door, his attention was on Mark. Andrea shifted her attention to Mark, as well.

"You clean up good," she said, grinning at him.

Mark's gaze sent scalding spears of desire shooting right through her. He took his time surveying her dress and for a moment she thought he might walk around her the way Windy had. She didn't realize she was holding her breath until his gaze locked on to hers.

"So do you," he growled. And there was no other way to describe it. His deep, baritone voice was a raw purr, like that of a mountain lion, or some other incredible creature whose strength was all that outdid their beauty.

"I thought you might like an escort."

The deadly, seductive whisper skated over her flesh, giving her a shiver, making her breasts swell with need and her nipples pucker painfully. Andrea moistened her lips and watched his attention move to her mouth. Even in the finely tailored suit that she bet was a William Fioravanti, there was that stubborn bad-boy look about him that turned her on beyond comprehension. Leave it to Mark to decide not to wear a tux to such an occasion, but instead put every man in the pageant to shame in his ten-thousand-dollar suit.

God, was she drooling?

Andrea cleared her throat, suddenly aware of Julie and Windy on either side of her. "You remember Julie Ward," she stammered, composed herself, and gestured to Windy. "And, of course, Windsor Montgomery."

"Yes," Mark said, barely giving either of them his attention.

"Do you want Mr. Tripp to escort you?" Windy's voice was deeper than Andrea had ever heard it before. He stepped forward, adjusting his suit jacket, which looked impeccable on him, and shifted his weight so he stood between her and Mark. "The press are in hordes down there," he said under his breath.

Since she'd authorized allowing them on the island, Andrea simply smiled at him, once again feeling in control of her senses. Mark had too much power over her, and not just her body. Andrea feared she'd just given that small bit of information away to her two friends. The concern on Windy's face was obvious.

"You look remarkable." Andrea adjusted Windy's collar and smiled at him. "One woman on your arm is enough, mister. I don't know if I can handle your ego any bigger than it is."

Windy's concern faded a bit, but he shot Mark a worried look. Andrea wanted to hug him for caring so much.

She released Windy and stepped around him. "We're going

to put those poor men to shame," she said, smiling at Julie, but then looking at Mark. "I'm ready."

Mark took her hand and wrapped it around his arm, then tucked her in close against his side as he escorted her out of her office to the hallway. The second they left her private rooms, the noise from downstairs increased greatly. The foyer would be packed. Everyone on the island had paid dearly to attend the Mr. Desire Pageant. The beachfront yards had been converted with lights and fiery torches surrounding the large stage, and hundreds of tables had been arranged for the multitude of guests now on the island. It had taken two days to prepare the outdoor event, and the star-filled sky, without a cloud in sight, would make for the perfect night. Andrea felt her first tingle of anticipation when Windy and Julie walked ahead of them and Mark waited as she locked her office door.

"We can go down the back way if you wish to avoid the mob." Mark spoke softly, and his attention was definitely not on her face when she turned to look at him. "Andrea, you are beautiful."

"Thank you." She warmed inside and knew her smile pleased him when his green eyes grew brighter as he stared at her. "I want to take that dress off of you later," he whispered and leaned forward to kiss her.

His lips were moist and so hot she almost teetered in her heels. It was all Andrea could do not to grab his suit jacket and hold on as she surrendered herself to him. Ever since he'd blindfolded and bound her hands, something seemed to have shifted between them. Or maybe it was her apology. Every time she tried figuring it out, her brain turned to mush and she ended up fantasizing about the many other ways they could enjoy sex. As much as her brain fought to keep her thoughts on the physical connection, her heart swelled just thinking about him.

This wasn't part of their deal, though. Andrea swore the

way his mouth moved over hers, then the way he ended their kiss, pulling back just a bit to stare into her eyes, created a lot more than just a physical longing between them.

"It's going to be a very long night," she heard herself say. Her voice was raspy, though.

"Yes, it is." He continued studying her and for a moment looked as if he might say more. Instead he straightened, took her arm, and wrapped it around his once again, taking the position of the perfect escort. "So, which is it? The flash of thousands of cameras or sneaking down a dark hallway?"

A hundred or so guests with VIP status had been invited into the mansion for cocktails and a chance to mingle with the contestants before the event began. Whether she liked it or not, she had to make an appearance and descend into the mob. Doing so with Mark on her arm would have the cameras flashing even harder. She bit her lip, took only a moment to ponder all possible consequences, and decided she could handle it. This was, after all, Tripp Island. Why not be escorted by the gorgeous Mark Tripp Jr.?

"The cameras," she said, and grinned at the skeptical look he flicked toward the stairs. "If you'd rather I walked down with Windy . . ." she began.

"No." Mark tightened his grip on her. "You're with me."

That swelling in her heart damn near cut off her ability to breathe. When Andrea turned toward the stairs with Mark, Windy and Julie were down the hall, watching the two of them. If she weren't so surprised by their expressions, she might have found it comical. To say they looked shocked was putting it mildly. Windy and Julie both gawked at Andrea and Mark, their mouths gaping with a mixture of stunned disbelief and bewilderment on their faces.

Andrea fell into stride alongside Mark, joining her friends. Let them be confused. Then she wouldn't be the only one.

"Best smiles, everyone," she said, using the coaching voice

the choreographers used while showing the contestants how to move around the stage. "It's showtime."

Mark kept a firm grip on her arm as they walked down the stairs. She swore the man had endured a few coaching lessons himself at some point in his life. He descended the wide staircase, remaining in the middle of the stairs, standing tall, and taking them a lot slower than Andrea knew he usually did. When they were still several steps from the floor of the foyer, Andrea noted it was indeed packed to the hilt with reporters and their cameramen from every local, regional, and national newspaper, as well as quite a few from magazines and major TV networks. This was the event of the season, and every known reporter as well as the not-so-known turned their eyes to Andrea and Mark.

One of *USA Today*'s top reporters slapped her cameraman, who immediately began snapping pictures of the couple. There was a small crew from *Us Weekly*, as well as *People*. As the cameras began flashing, industry professionals turned their attention to the stylish couple on the stairs.

Mark held her there for a moment longer, as if he already knew it was polite, and expected, to pose for a good picture before finishing their descent. The moment he moved her down the remaining stairs, his hand went to her back while his other kept her arm pinned to him. He didn't speak to her, spoke politely to the press who damn near stampeded them when they hit the floor, and kept Andrea moving, somehow managing to get the crowd to part for them as they headed to the large hall where drinks were being served and the contestants were mingling.

"You've done that before," she accused, when they paused inside the large room where even more industry people were smiling and laughing as they drank and called out their predictions of the pageant.

Mark looked down at her. "I promise I've never escorted my lady through a crowd of nosy reporters before."

Andrea stared at him. Mark didn't look away.

His lady?

That swelling in her heart was going to explode. "That's not what I meant," she choked out, her mouth suddenly dry.

"It's what I meant." Mark brushed his lips over hers, keeping his eyes open and watching her.

She couldn't help but respond. Mark was breaking every rule. They had an arrangement. He was breaking it. And . . . and damn it. She didn't care.

Andrea blinked several times, unable to focus on his face with it so close to hers. Moisture pooled between her legs. She was suddenly unsure of her balance. If Mark could read her mind, she was in serious trouble. He wrapped his arm around her waist, keeping her upright and against his body.

His lips met hers again, and her world exploded in an array of lights. It wasn't just from the cameras. She swore she teetered between her world and a place where it was just the two of them molded together, each supporting the other. Mark hadn't instigated a hungry, devouring kiss, either. His lips were pressed against hers, their mouths barely moved, then he straightened.

Andrea wasn't sure she'd ever be able to capture her breath. "That was dirty pool," she whispered.

Mark flashed her a smile she was certain the cameras would love. "It would only be dirty pool if I didn't mean it."

"You're breaking the rules." Now she was grinning, but not for the cameras. That swelling around her heart just burst with his declaration and the happiness inside had her giddy.

"I'm making new rules," he informed her.

"Mr. Tripp, Miss Denton," a daring cameraman said. "Please. A couple's shot for the cameras."

Mark didn't answer but instead turned her to face everyone and put his arm around her waist. Andrea was blinded by the explosion of flashes. She couldn't see a thing, and it didn't get much better when Mark announced that was enough.

"Miss Denton has a pageant to run," he announced.

He worked her through the crowd, keeping her close. Andrea squinted into the dim light, seeing the large room for the first time with its majestic glow from the incredible light system that had been wired in over the past few days. Getting her bearings, she spotted the opened double doors across the room and pointed toward them.

"We need to head outside." Already the intro music for the pageant had started.

"I can get us there." Mark swept Andrea through the room and outside, then around the many rows of tables already filling with people.

"Where to, my lady?"

She shot him a scathing look but couldn't help grinning when he smiled down at her. "I'm going to be needed backstage through most of the pageant. You'd probably enjoy yourself a lot more watching from one of the tables. I have several VIP tables reserved up front. Would you like the best seat in the house?"

"I'm flattered. But I think I'd prefer to stay with you. I'm sure the real action is backstage."

"Are you sure? Our emcee is quickly becoming the top ranking late night host. We're in for quite the treat. And there are several big stars performing in between the contestants' rounds."

"I'm sure. Shall we?" Mark draped her arm around his and started around the many tables. He had a skill when it came to moving through a crowd, not snubbing anyone, yet not talking to a soul and keeping them moving until they neared the large

draped curtain that blocked the audience's view of the backstage.

"It definitely helps having an escort who knows his way
around a crowd," she said when Mark guided them past the
mass of security guards, who seemed to acknowledge him over
her when letting them through to backstage.

Makeshift walls had been put up to prevent anyone from
seeing everyone backstage. As well, temporary rooms for
makeup, costume, storage, and tons of dressing rooms had been
assembled. There were people coming and going, some running, others almost looking lost. It was the night of the pageant.
A feverish adrenaline spiked the air. Andrea had always loved
this point in the event. Everything had come together, and it
was showtime.

"Impressive," Mark said, having stopped amidst the many
people rushing around him.

It felt too natural. Andrea was too relaxed next to him. His
arm brushed against the back of her shoulder before he
dropped it to her waist. It felt as if it belonged there. "What?"
she asked, glancing at him but then turning her attention to the
growing crowd who mingled near the entrance to backstage.

"I feel like I'm somewhere else."

She glanced around, realizing he possibly hadn't watched
the construction crew transform the large grassy area before
the beach into the mini-stadium with its elaborate stage and
light show.

"I'm surprised you didn't watch them build the stage. The
lighting crew did an equally amazing job. They followed my instructions to the T. There are sparkling lights all around the tables
and large torches that will keep the bugs away, and also make the
place feel more enclosed even though it's outside. It's really
hard to see past the torches burning at night."

"I stayed away." Now he smiled. "If I had come out here,

with all the hammering and noise going on, within minutes I would have taken over. This is your show, darling, not mine."

Andrea tried picturing him doing carpentry work, or setting up wiring, and found herself able to do it quite easily. In one month her image of the rich elitist she'd seen him as when first meeting him at his father's home had completely transformed. Mark had money and probably lots of it. But he worked for a living, and although they'd never discussed it, Andrea imagined he took to his job with a passion, very much like she did.

"Wait until you see the light show. I was really impressed when I was in here last night during rehearsal."

"With the lights?" Something darkened in his gaze. "Or with the men?"

Andrea made a face at him. "All that brawn walking across the stage is absolutely breathtaking. It was all I could do not to throw myself at each and every one of them."

She gave a huge, toothy grin at his brooding expression. Mark gripped her shoulder, pulling her toward him. The crowd filling the room faded away when their foreheads touched. Did he really have ideas about taking this casual relationship and turning it into something more serious? She was almost positive the charged energy in the air between them was built off more than lust. As she raised her lashes and stared into his eyes, she had her answer.

She'd felt her insides explode with happiness earlier when they'd still been inside. Now something headier filled every inch of her with an electrifying sensation. She sucked in a breath and Mark took that moment to tilt his head and nip at her lower lip. Instantly flames ignited under her skin. An ache between her legs turned into throbbing need so incredibly distracting she fought the urge to press her legs together and squirm until she found some relief.

"Quite a few of those men would seduce you in a second just to move their careers forward faster."

"That wouldn't ever happen. Not because of you," she explained simply, "but because I don't sleep with contestants." Then to lighten the mood between them, she added, "male or female."

One eyebrow shot up and she fought off a grin.

"How about because of me?"

"How about what?" There was no way she'd chance answering him without him spelling it out.

"Don't sleep with any other men because of me," he growled. It sounded more like a statement than a question.

"Girlfriend, did you see that crowd?" Windy sauntered up to them with his arm draped around Julie's shoulders. "Everyone who is anyone is out there. It took forever to work our way through it."

"You did it!" Julie grinned from ear to ear and grasped Andrea's arm.

If either of them had noticed the moment she and Mark were having before the two of them interrupted, neither of them showed any sign of it. They were both high off the crowd.

"You can write your own ticket now," Julie added. She sobered and looked at Mark. "You're going to have to give her the world to hold on to her now."

"I'll give her whatever she wants," Mark growled and tightened his grip around her waist just enough for Andrea to notice.

Mark's words bounced around in her head. He did want a relationship. He wanted something to build between them. She stared at Windy and Julie and was barely able to register on what Julie was saying.

"Why weren't you answering your phone?" Julie asked.

Andrea blinked, her words taking a moment to sink in with Mark's statement having pulled her so far out of her element. It took a second to come back.

"What?" she asked.

"We've called you several times," Windy added. "When we couldn't find you, we didn't know whether to continue milling throughout the crowd or head back here. There are some major players out there who want an interview. Now isn't the time to play around backstage when your career is ready to skyrocket into the six-figure bracket."

Windy studied Mark as he spoke, instead of looking at her. He was scowling, something Andrea seldom saw him do.

"I didn't get any calls," she said, and fought off the urge to defend Mark. Windy hadn't come out and accused him of keeping Andrea from the masses. "And you know my place is backstage. I'll do interviews once the pageant is over," she offered instead.

"Well, that's what I told them," Windy muttered. "Where is your phone?" he asked, this time not sounding quite as put out.

Andrea held up her empty hands. "Crap. I didn't bring my purse. My phone is in that small gold handbag I was going to wear. I left it in my office."

"I'll get it." Mark acted as if he might kiss her with Julie and Windy standing right next to them. Instead he tapped her nose with his finger. "Give me the key and I'll run and grab it. Where did you leave it?"

Mark's hand slipped off her and she stepped away from his virile body. "The key to my room is in that purse," she confessed. "But I'm positive I locked my suite. I bet you could still get in, though, right?"

Something shifted in his gaze. "I can let myself in if that's what you want."

He wasn't talking about a key, or was he? His eyes smoldered with raw, hard need. They looked just the way they had after he'd made her come harder than she ever had in her life. It was a possessive, carnal stare, and she was drowning in it.

"Yes," she said, although the one word came out on a raspy whisper. "I do."

The corner of his mouth barely moved when he gave her a small smile. But the triumph in his eyes was proof enough that this small exchange held a much larger meaning. For the first time in years, she'd just let a man into her life. Not as a sex buddy, but into her personal space, into her heart. Andrea almost teetered when he walked away.

"Well, that just made it obvious something is going on between you and Tripp, something more than sex," Windy said as soon as Mark was gone. He put his hand on Andrea's shoulder. "Unfortunately, most people aren't who they appear to be."

"Windy, everything is fine. I promise."

"You know I love you dearly, girlfriend, or I wouldn't worry about who you were with."

"And you don't have all the facts. Mark Tripp isn't on this island simply to be with you," Julie added. "And all that security isn't to protect your pageant."

"I'm sure it's to protect his island, too. That makes sense."

Julie moved closer, almost whispering except with all the activities going on around them she spoke more at a normal level just to be heard. "He brought in security so he would know who came and went, and to make sure no one left with anything that is his."

"Huh?" Andrea looked from Julie to Windy. He'd moved closer, as well, so that the three of them stood in a tight, little huddle. "Well, if he's worried about theft, that doesn't make him less of a person. You know, it's not as if he is idly playing his way through life. You sent me those articles, Julie. Mark works his ass off."

"This isn't about him working." Once again, Julie leaned in before speaking. "Apparently his mother went a bit crazy before she died. She had a crystal jewelry box, and it, along with the jewelry in it, are worth hundreds of thousands of dollars. He has a crew on the island searching for it."

"We spoke with the head security guy," Windy cut in. "This

isn't just idle gossip. His mother flipped out and buried all her jewelry here. Your Mr. Tripp Jr. is on the island trying to find the jewelry, and his security guards are nothing more than his henchmen making sure no one finds it before he does and tries to make off with it."

Andrea almost said something about the necklace Barry Ortega and Big D brought to her. It definitely appeared to be valuable. She would worry about it later. Right now she had a pageant to put on and no time to discuss buried jewelry.

"We'll talk about this later." Andrea patted both of them on the shoulder, then rushed past them to the curtain.

12

Mark reached the thick black curtain that blocked off the backstage just as Andrea pushed her way through them. She looked frazzled, pale, and distracted when she ran right into him.

Mark pulled her into his arms. "Is everything okay?"

"Yes, fine." Andrea kept moving, sliding against his body, then starting down the narrow walkway against the curtain to where a line of contestants, all in tuxedos, were standing and waiting their turn to be announced and parade across the stage.

"Here's your phone."

She looked at him, then the glittery gold bag. "Thanks."

Andrea took the small purse and draped the long, thin strap over her shoulder. The little bag that was barely big enough to hold her phone rested against her hip. If he didn't know her as well as he did, Mark would think she'd forgotten he went to get it for her.

"What happened while I was gone?" Mark wasn't sure now was the right time to tell her what had just happened. "Did it have anything to do with the sound?"

Andrea stopped walking as quickly as she'd taken off. At the same time, the hum of the crowd talking disappeared, which made the two of them seem very much alone. The lighting changed, draping them in darkness. Suddenly it was very quiet.

"The sound?" Andrea searched his face, her large brown eyes bright in the shadows surrounding them.

The black, skintight dress she wore had an oval neckline, but it didn't drop low enough to show any cleavage. Tonight she wore a bra with enough padding to not show a glimpse of hardening nipple. Her dress was short-sleeved with a straight cut to it that hugged her hips and ended above her knees. It was conservative, classy as hell, and looked as if it were designed just for her.

Mark didn't know a lot about labels, and never planned on learning. He was willing to bet the simple but incredibly elegant dress was probably one of the top-of-the-line designer's pieces. Somewhere, some incredibly important reporter would go on about how perfect she looked wearing it.

"Why would you ask about the sound?" The makeup she'd applied made her eyes bigger but didn't make her any prettier than she was without it.

"Do you know who is running sound?" As he asked, a crashing bass wailed and broke into a loud, thumping dance beat. He glanced past her at the line of men waiting to go onstage. "I can handle this if you're busy right now."

She glanced over her shoulder at the contestants. "I need to be over there making sure each of them is perfect before they go onstage. I have maybe two seconds. What are you talking about?"

"Did you hire the sound crew?"

Mark glanced up and down the dark hallway. Alicia Keys was singing along to a crisp, upbeat melody on the piano. It sounded like a fairly large band accompanied her. The pageant had begun. And by the sound of it, it had opened with an explosive act.

"Do you have a problem with the sound?" Andrea asked more out of confusion than anger. "Is something wrong with that?" She gestured at the curtain and toward the stage.

Alicia carried a high note, her voice blending in with the moody notes she played on the piano. When cymbals crashed, ending the note, the deep baritones of a bass and cello accompanied her as she hammered it out on the piano. Mark doubted anyone would question the superb quality of the sound system being used. It was most definitely top-notch. Which was probably exactly what someone would want the crowd to hear, and believe, so when it was altered later in the show, they would already believe in the incredible sound and assume the contestant lacked the ability to project onstage.

Andrea leaned in closer. "Why did you ask about the sound?"

Mark breathed in her perfume, a tangy, enticing scent he didn't recognize. Her hair teased the back of his hand when he placed it on her shoulder. She stimulated all his senses so easily. It was all he could do not to pull her closer.

He tilted his head, shifting so his mouth was close to her ear. "I heard that the sound guy was going to turn down the volume for some of the contestants during their performances so they wouldn't sound as good."

"What?" Andrea looked up at him, shocked. The look on her face was enough to show she didn't question what he said, but that she asked in disbelief.

Andrea's friends had appeared behind her. Mark glanced past Andrea and met Windy's scowling frown. Andrea's friends didn't approve of him. For whatever reasons, he hadn't passed muster.

Andrea studied him only a moment before a hard resolve made her dark eyes brighter. "Maybe you should stay here," she said, leaning in to him so he could hear her. Then before he could respond, she spun around and said something to Julie on the other side of her. She was scooting around her friends and past the contestants before Mark could follow.

He simply stared at her backside as her black dress glistened from the light show on the stage. It hugged her narrow waist and accentuated her round ass. The way it swayed before she got past Windy, then disappeared in the darkness, damn near made him hard. For a brief moment he contemplated letting Andrea take care of things. He'd brought a situation to her attention, and it was her job to fix it. She did her job well. Her credentials were incredibly impressive.

He didn't doubt for a moment more than a few candid shots of the two of them would appear in gossip magazines before the week was out, if not sooner. Mark had spent his entire life doing his best to remain under the radar and away from paparazzi who lived to distort and dissect his life so those who didn't have one could analyze and scrutinize his. Not only had he grown up hiding, he'd kept his father and sister out of the public eye, as well. The only way he'd managed his degree and landed his first job was to downplay who he was. Mark contemplated all of this for another moment before rushing past her friends and after Andrea. Let the cameras flash, although he hoped tonight he would be the least of the reporters' concern with the pageant in full force.

Mark wasn't able to get out of there as easily as Andrea did. Julie studied him as she took her time moving out of his way. She was a breathtaking beauty, but there was something calculating in her gaze that Andrea didn't have. It wouldn't surprise him if she were asked out on a very regular basis by guys of all kinds. She gave him a warning look that was clear. He'd better not hurt her client, who was obviously also her close friend. Julie had nothing to worry about. The last thing he would ever do was hurt Andrea—or let her fight this battle on her own.

Windy stepped in front of Mark. "Where are you going?" he demanded.

The song had reached its crescendo, but Mark was able to read Windy's lips. "With Andrea," he said, not bothering to raise his voice.

Apparently Windy read lips just as well. "Why?" he asked.

"Because I want to." Mark didn't elaborate but moved past the man and hurried to catch up with Andrea. His ears were ringing with monitors so close on the other side of the curtain.

If she were going to take care of the sound guy, the sound booth was behind the many tables on the other side of the stage. If she were going to find whoever might be in charge of the sound crew, it would be impossible to know which way she went.

Mark pondered which way to go for another moment, then headed to the left. It was a shorter route around the stage than to the sound booth.

The song had ended, and a local comedian who was gaining national attention, Willy Wright, was entertaining the audience with anecdotes as the stage was prepared for the next act. Mark spotted Andrea at the edge of the stage and back toward the makeshift wall talking to a woman. The lady was facing Andrea with her hands clasped behind her back and her expression blank. Andrea looked at Mark when he joined them.

"Cara Miles, this is Mark Tripp," Andrea explained, waving her hand gracefully between the two of them. "His family owns this island, and his architectural firm personally designed the mansion."

"Well done," Cara said, sounding sincere, and gave him a quick nod but didn't bring either hand forward to shake his. He didn't sign her paycheck, and therefore she would be polite and that was it. Cara turned her attention to Andrea. "I'll send one of my men around to the sound booth, but ma'am, I assure you, no one with Miles and Miles would do anything you just suggested. No one."

"I'm not accusing you of any allegations, nor do I plan on doing so." Andrea had assumed her calm, silky smooth tone. She was a perfect diplomat. "However, a conversation was overheard by one of my most reliable men. I'm sure you understand. If your most trusted employee expressed a concern, you would investigate, too. That's what I'm doing. And I think the best way to make sure this is a false allegation is to replace your sound guy in the booth with someone else."

"You can't fire us." In spite of the calm speech, Cara's hackles were up. The oversized vest she wore, with its patch that said Miles and Miles, hung slightly crooked over her bony shoulders. The woman was almost gaunt, with leathery brown skin gained only from years and years of living on the beach. She had a very toothy, brilliantly white smile, which she offered at the moment although her blue eyes were flat and her smile cold. "You and I both signed a contract."

Andrea held her hand up and Cara quit talking. She watched Andrea like a hawk. Mark surmised that Cara might be a tough business owner, but she wasn't going to do anything to upset Andrea, contract or not.

"Cara, replace your head sound guy in the sound booth or I'll take care of it myself."

Cara sighed, put her hands on her hips, and looked away at the steady activity around them. "Alright," she said finally. "It's an odd request and I don't like it. You're questioning our reputation."

"And what we overheard was just as odd." Andrea lowered her voice, stepping closer to Cara and added confidentially, "I'm the first one who would want to deny any scandal could take place on my watch. I've done this for years. But believe me, I would rather take precautions and never know if it might have happened, or not, than choose to disbelieve it and risk my reputation getting tarnished. Trust me, Cara, if I was questioning your reputation, you wouldn't be here."

Cara returned her attention to Andrea. "I understand." She stepped away from Andrea first. "I'll take care of it," she added and pulled a two-way from her hip and held it to her mouth as she hurried away from both of them.

"Think she'll take care of it?"

Andrea shot Mark a speculative look. "I have to make sure she does." It wasn't a complaint but simply a statement.

"Do you want me to go to the sound booth?" Mark slipped his arm around Andrea's shoulder and ignored the few people who took time to look at them curiously. He guided her toward the back of the wall behind the stage. He pulled Andrea deep into the shadows. "I'll take care of this one. There have got to be at least a handful of other catastrophes you need to handle right now."

"There better not be." She made a face but nodded. "Go ahead. I'll put my phone on vibrate so I'll know if you call me. Don't be obvious but watch and make sure someone replaces whoever is doing sound."

"Yes, boss." Then because he felt like it, Mark pulled Andrea into his arms and kissed her. Her dress was softer than silk and her hair just as smooth. She smelled incredible and felt even better. He'd be glad when this evening was over. Whatever it took, Mark was taking Andrea to bed with him tonight. It was all he could do not to run his thumb over the soft curve of her breast, or to pull her against him a bit tighter so he could feel every inch of her hot, sultry body against his.

Andrea instantly opened up to him and returned the kiss as her hands moved to his shoulders. She clasped her fingers behind his neck and began a slow, sultry dance with her tongue in his mouth. Mark ended the kiss reluctantly. Andrea stepped backward, touching her fingertips to her moist lips.

"Let me know when you've talked to the sound crew," she

said, then turned and hurried away from him before he could pull her back into his arms.

Mark stepped around the makeshift wall and wasn't the only man who watched her perfectly shaped ass sway back and forth as she moved through the crowded backstage area. He watched her until she finally disappeared from his view in the dark, long shadows against the curtain.

The contestants were parading across the stage when Mark moved past the hundreds of round tables enclosed by strings of white lights and tall torches with dancing flames emitting streams of smoke that headed up to the inky black, clear night sky. Everyone was applauding and cheers erupted when a favorite entered the main spotlight. The night was charged with excitement. Everyone was dressed to the nines. With a glance across the crowd, Mark could tell many people viewed this pageant as pure entertainment while others saw the political advantage of a particular contestant winning.

Moving past the tables, Mark received glances from a few but mostly was ignored by the guests who were focusing fully on the stage. He came to the boxed-in sound crew. Three crewmen stared at him.

The fourth one, sitting with her back to Mark, had both hands on the sound board. "No one is allowed in the sound box," she announced without looking at him.

"I'm Mark Tripp."

"You know Cara sent him," the man closest to Mark said to the woman's back.

"She was told to send him," the woman emphasized.

"Shit, Brittany, don't make a big deal out of it."

Brittany did look over her shoulder this time and glared at the man closest to Mark who'd just spoken. "It is a big deal," she whispered, which made her damn hard to hear. The thin walls built up around them served more as a fence to keep everyone out than to provide any type of soundproofing. "I'm not backing down." She finally gave Mark her attention. "Nice house. I'm sure you have a lot of clout with this pageant, but this is my job. I'm the best person to do it, and I'm not going to risk the pageant going off as anything other than perfect. I'm sure you understand."

When she smiled, as false as it was, Mark imagined she could be rather pretty if she wanted. Brittany struck him as the kind of woman who didn't do anything unless she wanted to. Like Cara, she was in slacks and not a dress. She also wore the same vest with patches sewn on it that said Miles and Miles. Her strawberry-blond hair was pulled up in a ponytail that fell to the back of her shoulders then twisted in a playful curl. With a slightly different expression on her face, Brittany might come across as a very sweet, almost bubbly young lady. Her eyes were large and bright blue, and her vest almost covered her large breasts.

There was a calculating defiance in those large blue eyes. With her looks, Brittany could probably present herself however she believed would gain her the most of what she wanted. At the moment, all she wanted was to remain doing sound. That much was very apparent. She pulled some weight in her company. Mark saw that in the way the three men behind her weren't going to challenge her. He guessed she cared about Miles and Miles, which meant if she had been bribed to lower the volume, the amount of money she'd been offered was large enough for her to not think about how her actions might affect their business.

"Whatever they offered you, I'll give you double not to do it," Mark said, deciding to go out on a limb. He ignored the puzzled looks on the men's faces, and stared at the curl at the end of Brittany's ponytail.

She looked over her shoulder as her fingers moved over the knobs, turning, adjusting. Mark knew little to nothing about a soundboard. He didn't focus on her hands, though, but on her face. The body language of a liar often revealed their tell. Brittany took her time lifting her attention to his face.

"I don't know what you're talking about," she said lazily.

She didn't ask him what he meant. Brittany didn't look confused or perplexed like the three men behind her did. All she did was deny knowing what he meant, and a bit too coolly for his taste. Mark was positive she was the one bribed to ruin some of the contestants' performances.

"Bret, escort Mr. Tripp back to Cara. The two of you can tell her that if she has a problem with how I'm doing my job she can come talk to me about it herself."

"You know she doesn't," Bret began but quit talking when Brittany gave him a scathing look. "Brittany," he pleaded. "Cara will be pissed."

That way-too-sweet smile appeared on her face. "Since when have you ever cared about your sister's feelings? I think I can take care of Cara. Now both of you, leave."

"No," Mark said. He didn't take orders from any of this crew. Brittany struck him as fairly intelligent. He had a feeling she wouldn't push him too far. "My offer is about to expire. And when it does, I'll fire you and have you escorted off my island."

Her scathing look turned outright venomous. "We have a contract," she spit out at him.

"Miles and Miles will continue to run sound. It is you who will be escorted off the island," he said flatly.

"You're going to have me physically hauled out of this sound booth by your security thugs, then off this island?" She grinned at him. "I can just guess the headlines on the tabloids now."

"You're going to prove to me I'm right, aren't you, Brittany?" He held her gaze. "How much are they paying you to destroy Miles and Miles? Because if you turn down that sound, it will be noticed. The Mr. Desire Pageant will publicly announce their lack of satisfaction in your company's work."

"What's he talking about, Brit?" one of the guys behind her asked.

"God, Brittany, just give up the board," Bret demanded.

Brittany finally stood, tugged on her large vest, and stared at him.

"Bret, man the board. I'll be right back." She shoved her way past Mark and left the sound booth.

Mark watched Bret take over the sound before leaving to follow Brittany. He didn't see her but moved around the outside of the lights and torches toward the stage. One look around at the entrance toward backstage told him she wasn't there waiting for him.

"Damn," he grunted, looking at the small clusters of people standing nearby. He didn't recognize any of them and the few casual glances sent his way were ones of indifference. No one recognized him. Which was good but the fact that Brittany had disappeared was bad. Mark pulled out his phone, knowing if she hadn't come this way, she'd gone toward the stage then had slipped backstage into the chaos there. More than likely to intentionally lose him and escape without being accused of a crime.

He'd been an idiot not to grab her and keep her with him. Mark pulled out his phone and glanced around checking for the most private area to call Andrea, without going too far from the stage. Brittany was probably pretty damn proud of herself right now. She might relax and make a stupid move, like call or go to whoever bribed her to see if she couldn't somehow still earn the money promised to her.

Mark watched one hell of an impressive light show as he pulled his phone out. He was beyond impressed with the stage, and the multiple lights attached to a metal frame over the stage flashed and strobed as the audience cheered. The contestants were flamboyant as they strutted across the stage to the explosive crowd. For a moment Mark stared, duly impressed. Then turning his back on the show, he placed the call to Andrea and struggled to hear over the heavy bass-driven music he could feel vibrating through him. After one ring it went to Andrea's voice mail.

"Shit," he grumbled under his breath and put his phone back on the clasp on his belt.

13

Andrea remained where she was, standing in the shadows. She wasn't hiding. This was her damn pageant. But she would stand there and let Big D and his agent finish their conversation without Andrea interrupting.

"So where did she put it?" Becky Sterling, Big D's agent, asked.

"The cops showed up," Big D said.

"You told me that. Think."

Becky Sterling had to crook her neck to look up at Big D. Nonetheless, she stared at him with shrewd, narrowed eyes. Becky had been in the business forever and had represented some winning contestants over the years. Andrea didn't understand why these two were having this conversation. They were obviously talking about the necklace Barry and Big D had brought to her, the necklace Andrea had shoved in her bottom drawer because it had been covered in dirt.

"I think she slipped it in her desk drawer," Big D said and rubbed his hand over his nearly bald head.

"Are you sure?" Becky demanded.

"Sure as I can be." Big D gave her a huge, toothy smile.

Becky patted him on the back. "Okay, get out there and shine. Remember, you're winning this pageant tonight."

"Yes, ma'am," Big D said and pretty much galloped away from her toward the entrance to the stage.

Andrea needed to head that direction, too. She wasn't sure what compelled her to remain where she was. But when Becky turned in Andrea's direction and pulled out her phone, Andrea stayed where she was and listened.

Becky faced the wall and cupped her hand up to the phone, trying to shield the noise from backstage so whoever was on the other end of the phone would hear her better.

"It's me," she said. "Do you still have the earrings?" Becky scowled at the ground and listened. "Good. There are still four more pieces. Find them. No, I know where the necklace is."

Becky said something else under her breath, then hung up. She didn't look around her but headed quickly in the opposite direction from where Andrea was standing. Andrea rushed out of her hiding spot, although she reminded herself she hadn't been hiding.

Becky's conversation with Big D, and with whomever she'd called, bugged Andrea. She took a few steps in the direction Becky had gone, wanting to confront her. In truth, though, Andrea had been eavesdropping. The conversation wasn't any of her business. Unless of course, the necklace they were talking about was in *her* desk.

Andrea turned toward the stage. As she headed over to the contestants hurrying on and off the stage, she pulled her phone out and placed a call, requesting security at her office door.

The contestants were performing a medley of pop hits. As ten of the contestants came off the stage and the next ten hurried on, the emcee began announcing each of their names over the thumping, toe-tapping beat. The men had rehearsed hard for this performance with a team of choreographers. Adrenaline and energy levels were high, and the air was charged as the men hurrying off stage began laughing and talking about their mistakes and triumphs.

The cameras weren't allowed backstage, but the many reporters who had been able to swing backstage passes now swarmed the men, blurting out their questions and sticking microphones in their faces. A few contestants stopped, anxious for all the attention they could get. Some of them used the pageant for exposure in a much bigger game plan. The reporters didn't bother Andrea. She was simply grateful that no microphones were being shoved in her face at the moment.

Andrea slapped backs and patted arms as she congratulated each contestant who came off the stage. Then, moving to the side, she did the same to the next group who were hurrying onto the stage.

As the group onstage began a well-choreographed dance routine, Andrea glanced down at her phone. There was a missed call from Mark and a text message from Julie. Julie and Windy had gone to the reserved table alongside the runway, the best seats in the house. The weird news about the jewelry wouldn't stop either of her friends from having fun tonight. Glancing around, she saw there wasn't anywhere to go to return Mark's call privately. She needed to head to the dressing rooms and make sure the next group of men were ready to go onstage when it was their turn. But why had Mark called? Was he not able to replace the person doing the sound?

Cara walked toward Andrea. "There you are," she said, pulling Andrea out of her train of thought. "Bret has replaced Brittany. Now I'm going to have to deal with her bruised ego." Cara looked disdainfully at Andrea as if this were somehow all her fault. "Apparently she took off," she added, shaking her head. "I don't think she's even in the building."

"She left?" That could imply guilt, but Andrea held her tongue. Obviously Cara wouldn't believe anyone on her team capable of such a thing. "Thank you for cooperating," she said, remaining serious and meeting Cara's hard stare.

Cara might not like replacing her sound person, but Andrea couldn't let anyone's personal feelings get in the way of the pageant's success.

"You're doing a great job." She decided to end the conversation and moved around Cara, patting her shoulder as she walked past her.

"Thank you," Cara mumbled and attempted a smile as she nodded, then retreated and hurried away from Andrea into the crowd.

Andrea caught a glimpse of the Texas contestant, Big D, on stage as she headed past the heavy curtain toward the temporary rooms lining the far wall backstage. He was an incredible dancer. She watched for only a second, then continued to the dressing rooms. He was definitely a crowd pleaser. Andrea usually experienced a wash of satisfaction at this point in the pageant. There would still be problems for her to solve, but at this point in the event they weren't usually major. She searched for that feeling and was proud of the success of her first Mr. Desire Pageant. But apprehension created a small knot in her gut that wasn't usually there so close to the end of an event.

As soon as she was along the far wall and heading to the group of rooms where her contestants changed costumes and where makeup and hair designers worked their magic, Andrea returned Mark's call. There was no answer. She listened to his brief voice-mail instructions, then said, "Tag, you're it," and hung up. Cara hadn't mentioned that Mark had removed the sound person who'd taken a bribe. If anything, she had made it sound no such person existed, but that she'd put someone else in charge of sound to make Andrea happy. Had Mark been at the sound box? If so, where the hell was he now?

As her heels clicked over the narrow hallway floor, she realized her Max Azria dress was worth every penny she paid for it. She felt like a million dollars. The dress was soft, moved perfectly along with her, and never felt too tight or restricting. As soon as she was through checking out the dressing rooms, she was going to find Mark. At that thought, her mood picked up instantly. Once this night was over, she would do some serious soul-searching and determine exactly what was going on between the two of them.

My girl.

Those two little words shouldn't make her heart erupt with fast-paced beats. They really shouldn't draw a small smile to her face. She didn't want a relationship. It would only end painfully. She didn't have time to seriously date anyone. She would have to completely revamp her schedule.

But this wasn't anyone. This was Mark. And already he'd played a nice little number on her, and he'd pulled it off well. Andrea liked being *his girl.* The thought of not spending time with him didn't sit well with her at all.

"Crap," she hissed under her breath and almost dragged her fingers through her perfectly done hair. As she reached the first dressing room door and opened it slowly, ready to announce herself so she wouldn't walk in on any naked men, she heard muffled voices speaking in concerned voices.

"Are you sure everything will go over smoothly?" Andrea heard a woman ask.

A familiar voice answered, "You worry too much. This isn't like planning some huge-scale event here."

Andrea wasn't sure what made her hold her breath, continue to grip the door handle, and not enter the room. She leaned against it, the door barely ajar, and listened.

"I know that," the first woman snapped. "But one fuckup and there go our careers."

"And how would anything go wrong? I'm the one who

took care of our only liability. Don't make me regret having you on board, too." Becky Sterling's voice had turned into a harsh whisper.

Andrea didn't think before pushing the door back open. She was ready to demand to know what they were talking about when her abrupt presence in the dressing room had both of them spinning around. As shock registered on a tall, big-boned redheaded woman's face, bone-chilling resolve appeared on Becky's.

"Talk to you later," the redhead said before rushing past Andrea.

"Wait," Andrea said but didn't raise her voice. She knew the woman heard her and chose not to pay attention.

Becky watched her companion disappear but simply crossed her arms over her chest and stared at Andrea. Although petite and somewhat mousy-looking, and with a wardrobe that did nothing to help out her delicate features, Becky Sterling managed to hold her ground in a world of high rollers and sharp dressers. Someone had told Andrea once to always watch out for the quiet ones. She stared into Becky's large, doe-like eyes and noticed for the first time how shrewd and cunning the woman appeared.

"Is something wrong?" Becky asked her.

"I'm not sure yet." Andrea wasn't going to let the agent off easily. Perhaps the woman intentionally dressed as if she were oblivious to fashion, and purposefully remained quiet while everyone else ranted. It definitely made people ignore her. Andrea wasn't ignoring her now. "I just overheard your conversation."

"Oh? What did you hear?"

The woman was playing Andrea, and it pissed her off. She kept her cool, just as Becky was doing, and smiled sweetly. "Quite a few things, actually, over the past thirty minutes."

"I haven't been in this dressing room for thirty minutes."

Instead of appearing flustered, or even embarrassed, Becky smiled. If anything, she looked even more relaxed.

"I know," Andrea said. "My questions begin with your conversation with Big D."

"Big D? Denny? My client?" Becky shook her head, looking confused. "What's your question?"

"Why were you asking him where I put the necklace he brought me?"

Becky didn't so much as blink an eye. "Because it's mine," she said coolly. "It's very valuable, and I wanted to make sure you didn't put it anywhere that might damage it."

"It's safe," Andrea said offhandedly, surprised by Becky's claim that the necklace was hers but unwilling to show it just yet.

"No offense. It will be safe once I have it back. I have time right now. Send someone up to your office to meet me," Becky said, her tone firm and pressing. "Where is it?"

"I'm not sending anyone anywhere." Andrea had a warped sense of satisfaction when Becky bristled for the first time. She pressed on with her questions before the woman could argue any more about being given the necklace this evening. "You asked someone on the phone if they still had the earrings, and told them to hurry and find four more pieces."

Becky's jaw dropped. "What were you doing? Eavesdropping?"

"You didn't bother checking to see who was around you when you made your call." Andrea shrugged. "Why were you demanding someone find the rest of the jewelry if all of this is yours?"

Becky laughed and shook her head. When she waved her hand in the air between them, Andrea got the impression this woman didn't laugh or show any emotion that often. Her actions were terse.

"That's what you get for eavesdropping," Becky accused,

wagging her finger at Andrea. "That conversation was completely unrelated."

Andrea wasn't convinced. "What was the 'liability' you just mentioned that you took care of? It must have been something pretty serious if your friend was worried both your careers would be destroyed if caught."

"You really should focus on pulling this pageant off and making sure all of your contestants are doing okay. That is your job, isn't it?" Becky sneered. She then walked toward Andrea and pushed her out of the way to reach the door. "My private affairs are none of your business."

Andrea didn't care too much for being pushed around. She grabbed Becky's skinny arm. "Watch yourself. I am the pageant director, and I don't care too much for rude behavior. Furthermore, if you are in any way trying to manipulate this pageant, or take anything off this island that doesn't belong to you, I will find out."

Becky glanced at Andrea's hand holding her arm. When she looked up, her expression had transformed. Once again she was the passive, mousy agent in drab clothing.

"You have nothing to worry about." When she shifted her weight, Andrea let go of her arm. Becky ran her hands down her brown suit jacket, which hung on her petite figure. "That is, unless you want to worry about what the tabloids might print about you and the young Mr. Tripp. I guess it won't affect your career since the Tripps bought the Mr. Desire Pageant. But I'm sure, if you are serious about Mark Tripp, you wouldn't want him having to decide between the success of his pageant and his woman, whose reputation was trashed beyond repair for having slept with him in the oddest of places while here on the island."

"I don't do threats," Andrea informed her and kept her temper in check. There wasn't a doubt in her mind that Becky was doing her best to change the subject—and piss Andrea off.

Becky shrugged. "I don't blame you. Have a good night."

Andrea was distracted when she went to the other dressing rooms. Knocking on each door was almost ridiculous since she couldn't hear anyone on the other side tell her to come in. So Andrea did as she always did, which was to open the door, announce herself, then start into the dressing room. This practice had never failed her then. And even after overhearing Becky's conversations, she wasn't sure it had failed her. Becky had been holding out on her, Andrea would stake her reputation on it.

"Did you see our routine?" Steve Oftenhaus, her West Virginia contestant, asked Andrea.

"How about my solo, Andrea?" Roy Porter asked. His father, a congressman from Connecticut, had stated more than once that he believed winning the pageant would build Roy's popularity as he started following in his father's footsteps. The sad part of it was that Roy stood a good chance of winning the Mr. Desire Pageant, or at least finishing in the final runners-up. Being a runner-up wouldn't satisfy his dad.

"Both of you were even better than you were at rehearsal." Andrea grinned at the two boys, who were both twenty, and didn't even look like full-grown men in her opinion. They were tall, lanky, and probably hadn't started shaving yet.

"You saw the routine?" Roy asked, looking at her seriously.

Steve also quit grinning and waited for her answer. Although she wasn't quite ten years older than both of them, this wasn't the first time during a pageant that contestants looked at her as a mother figure. She studied both of them and told them the truth.

"I saw the first minute, maybe less, when I was rushing from one side of the backstage to the other." She nodded to Roy. "Your solo had to knock the judges right out of their seats," she said truthfully, grinning. "And Steve, if you want a future in dancing, I'd say you're a shoo-in. Did you see all those cameras out there?"

"Yes, we saw them," Steve announced. "You didn't tell us all the major networks would be here tonight."

She didn't always know which networks or reporters would show up to snap shots or get footage of the pageant. "I know which network is airing the pageant. I don't have confirmation on any other networks yet."

"Well, I do," Steve announced, then put one arm around Andrea's shoulder and his other arm around Roy's. "They are *all* airing Mr. Desire," he shouted, then backed away from both of them as he smiled a toothy grin. "Every single person in the whole wide world is watching us tonight."

Both of them gave a loud hoot, which those around glanced over but didn't pay too much attention to. Hoots and hollers had been part of the evening since the pageant began, especially near the dressing rooms since contestants couldn't shout by the stage. Steve grabbed Andrea and lifted her into the air, spinning her around before putting her back on the ground in front of him.

"Someone will notice me. Many someones," he added, laughing. "Even if I don't win tonight, I bet I get signed."

"Steve, you stand as good a chance of winning as anyone," Andrea assured him.

"Sure would make my dad happy."

"As long as it makes you happy. That's what counts," she reminded him.

"What people keep telling me," he said, still grinning. "But my father says as long as he's footing the bill on my life I do what he says."

Andrea nodded. She'd met all kinds of parents in her years as pageant director, some incredibly controlling and others noticeably absent. Nothing surprised her anymore.

"Don't complain about the free ride," Roy told him and slipped his arm around Andrea. "Of course, some of us have that free ride for life. Care to join me on it, pretty lady?"

Andrea laughed, snuggled against Roy for a brief second, then eased herself away. "And give up all of this? Not in a million years," she said, laughing. "Now you two better hurry so you're ready for your next appearance. Suits and ties, my dears," she instructed, and turned both of them toward their dressing room.

"You'd never stand a chance with this gorgeous pageant director," Steve teased Roy, looking over Andrea's head as he did. "And I doubt your free ride compares at all to Mark Tripp's money."

"There are some people in life who don't care for a free ride. We find life a lot more enjoyable when we create our own ride," Roy responded.

"The true voice of the middle class," Steve said, lowering his voice as he spoke, then laughed. "As my father would say," he added, shooting Andrea a pensive look as if he didn't want to offend her.

"I'm sure being filthy rich is great," Andrea told both of them. "But don't ever lose focus on your goals and dreams. There is so much more to life than money. Don't ever forget that."

"I won't," Roy said, turning at the doorway and giving Andrea a hug.

"I wish you'd tell my father that," Steve said, then he also hugged her and gave her a kiss on the cheek.

"Get dressed, both of you." She made shooing gestures as she backed away from the door.

Andrea exhaled and patted her hair, praying it was still in place. There wasn't time to primp, though. One glance toward the entrance to the stage and she knew the first round of eliminations would begin in minutes.

Backstage was full of people. Even with their makeshift outdoor setup, the setting looked like so many other settings from her past. It was a good job, and one Andrea was blessed to have. There were times when she wished she could refuse all backstage passes and eliminate all the drama-seekers and gossip-catchers, who were in huddles behind the curtains. Each of them just waited for some small thing to happen so they could expound upon it and blow it all out of proportion.

As she looked through the many groups of people, she spotted Mark. He was watching her, his brooding expression immediately sending a wave of excitement rushing over her body. He didn't look happy, but it was dark and she very possibly was reading him wrong. Andrea started toward him, but an older lady stepped in her path, grabbing her arm.

"You're Andrea Denton," the older woman, who was doused with perfume, said and pulled Andrea into her small circle of friends. "Sweetheart, you've done such a marvelous job. We were all just talking about it."

"Indeed, we were," an older man agreed, his tone as stuffy as his appearance. "I'm Stephen Brigade. I'm sure you've heard of the Brigades," he said, giving her an appraising once-over with one brow cocked. "We're known for our substantial contributions to the arts. Damn shame Tripp bought this pageant, although I doubt you complain about the man who signs your paycheck."

Andrea despised people who tooted their own horn over large charitable contributions. Their money was always needed and therefore always accepted, but the self-importance those people displayed was beyond annoying. She managed a smile, shook the man's hand, and nodded to the others.

"Doesn't surprise me a bit that a murder occurs right here during the pageant with Tripp's name on the bill," the woman who still clutched Andrea's arm declared. "Have they pinned it to him yet, dear?"

Andrea wasn't sure which Tripp they were referring to, but then she decided it didn't matter. "Mr. Tripp had nothing to do with the terrible accident that happened on the island, and it wasn't a murder. If you'll excuse me."

Andrea shifted her weight in order to politely edge her way out of the circle of pompous jerks. She'd done her research. Julie had shown her the articles. There weren't any blemishes on the Tripp name that she'd noticed. She'd also spoken with Mark Tripp Sr. on the phone several times. He came across as a nice old gentleman. And Mark—she looked for him through the crowd. He wasn't standing where he had been.

A young man stepped in front of her. "Excuse me, Miss Denton?"

Andrea looked at the college-aged boy, who stared nervously back at her. "What can I do for you?" she asked, recognizing him from Dave Small's crew.

"I'm really sorry to bother you," the kid said, shifting his weight back and forth from one foot to the other and tugging on his tie as he looked nervously around them.

Andrea overheard the snobs behind her whisper a bit too loudly that this was Andrea's first year working under Mr. Tripp and she'd see soon enough. When an older man said something about her being too gullible to see the truth, Andrea almost spun around and demanded an explanation.

"I was asked to come find you," the kid said. "There's a situation at the other side of the stage."

Andrea glared at the snobs behind her and was glad when they all looked surprised, then she scooted off alongside the young man.

"What's the problem?" she asked.

"I have no idea. That's just what they told me to say to you."

14

Mark worked his way around props and groups of people in tight clusters, stepping over countless cords, many duct-taped to the floor or each other. Backstage was a huge cluster-fuck, and it seemed even more chaotic now than it had at the beginning of the show.

"Andrea!" he yelled, trying to catch up with her and the kid she'd started walking around the backstage area with.

She didn't respond, which wasn't surprising. The music on stage had to be louder than it was when the show started. His Alpha 21 crew had kept him held up longer than he'd planned. But their problem was serious. He'd instructed them to focus their attention around and in the hidden greenhouse once he'd learned it was there. If they didn't find anything there then they were to continue their methodical search of the island.

Mark wasn't able to hear his phone ring and so had instructed them to text with any updates during the show. Right after leaving the sound booth, his phone had started going off with one text after another from the crew.

We have a serious problem in the greenhouse.

SOS. Call 911. SERIOUS PROBLEM!
Come here as soon as you can!

Mark had sprinted around the mansion to the much quieter grounds on the other side of the house. There were a few people idly visiting with each other. Mark had slowed his pace, but he still hurried to his mother's greenhouse. As he arrived, two men he didn't recognize high-tailed out of the greenhouse, damn near knocking Mark on his ass.

According to his Alpha 21 crew the men had shown up and tried bullying his crew out of there. They'd had digging equipment and other paraphernalia and had told the crew that they had permission to search the old greenhouse for the jewelry box. His crew didn't know who they were, but the fact that they knew about his mother's jewelry bothered Mark. After making sure no one was hurt, Mark had pulled several security guards over to stand at the entrance to the greenhouse. He stationed two more men on the other side of the tall, thick hedge for good measure.

Mark had questioned the crew for several minutes, but the men hadn't said anything that would help learn who had sent them in search of the jewelry.

"They did say something about the pageant director," Eve had announced as Mark was leaving.

"Eve. It's not necessary," Steve snapped.

Mark had turned around in the doorway, dodging parts of the hedge hanging down over the entrance. "What did they say?" he demanded.

"They said Tripp would keep the pageant director distracted, or else," she told him, and smiled up at him. "Something going on between you and your director?"

Mark hadn't answered her or said anything else. He'd pushed past the security guards and run back around the mansion, this time avoiding the crowd by cutting through a side entrance. He raced through the house, ignoring several surprised servants. Coming out on the other side near the stage, he'd all but shoved his way backstage. The flood of relief when he'd spotted Andrea had quickly been replaced with a darker emotion he didn't want to readily acknowledge. Mark had watched the two young candidates pick Andrea up, spin her around, then kiss her on the cheek. They were kids—boys—he'd told himself.

When Andrea had left them and spotted him, her expression had transformed. Every inch of him had hardened. It had been damn hard to breathe, let alone move. She'd started toward him as if she hadn't seen the hundreds of people packed in backstage. Each time someone had temporarily blocked his view of her, Mark had wanted to roar, barge forward, and send the poor fool flying. He'd moved toward her before even realizing he was walking.

Then some old broad had taken Andrea's arm and lured her into their small circle of men and women. Whatever they'd said had upset her. It was uncanny how, across the dark backstage filled with way too many flamboyant jerks and assholes, Mark sensed her emotions. The protective urges inside him were off the charts. He'd pushed his way through the crowd, and almost gotten to her, when several hyped-up reporters had grabbed him, demanding an interview.

Mark wasn't in the same world Andrea was in. He didn't give a rat's ass if the reporters thought he was an asshole or not. In fact, the more unapproachable they viewed him, the sooner they would leave him alone. He'd brushed them off, telling them he had no time, and then he'd started toward Andrea again.

She wasn't anywhere to be seen.

"Where are you, sweetheart?" he whispered under his breath and was forced to stop when groups of contestants hurried to the stage.

Andrea's friends, Windy and Julie, were near the makeshift

wall at the back of the stage. It looked like they'd just entered through the door coming from backstage, and Julie held a pamphlet in her hand given to everyone as they'd been seated when the pageant began. If they'd been out in the audience, they probably wouldn't know where Andrea was, but Mark had lost her. He headed over to them, ignoring the cold look Windy gave him.

"Have you seen Andrea?" Mark asked.

"Lose her already?" Windy asked, and rose an eyebrow.

"I don't plan on losing her." Mark took advantage of Windy's double meaning to make that one point clear. "But there might be a situation." Now wasn't the time to express his fear over what his Alpha 21 crew had been told by the men who'd tried bullying them. "Help me find her."

Windy studied Mark only a moment, his hazel eyes enhanced with what appeared to be black eyeliner. Then, letting out an exaggerated sigh, he pulled out his phone and placed a call. "Straight to voice mail," he announced after listening for a moment. "Not that that should surprise any of us," he added with a dramatic flair.

"She probably can't hear it ring," Julie added.

"She came this way. I was following her and lost her in the crowd just five minutes ago at most."

"Maybe she doesn't want to see you," Windy countered.

Mark took a step toward Windy. The man backed up, a look of fear crossing his face as he grabbed Julie's arm and all but shoved her in front of him. Mark stopped himself, sighed, and ran his hand through his hair.

"This is a waste of time." Mark looked in the direction he'd guessed Andrea had headed with the kid. Mark, Julie, and Windy were at the end of backstage. There was a door in the wall and he knew stairs led to the side yard and beyond that to the beach. In other words, it led nowhere.

"We haven't seen her," Julie offered.

"Look," Mark said and pointed a finger at Windy, who was now next to Julie, although he still held her arm, "the sooner you accept that Andrea and I are together and that makes both of us happy, the better off everyone will be." He almost added, "Including Windy's well-being," but he let the threat go unsaid. Either it was clear in his eyes or his words had an impact. Windy straightened, his facial features relaxing, and he no longer looked as if he might scream at any moment.

"I don't have time to explain," Mark said, "but it is very important I find Andrea and make sure she is okay."

"There is a chance she might not be okay?" Julie asked.

Mark thought of the threats the men had given his Alpha 21 crew, then how they'd said that Mark would keep Andrea distracted. But Andrea and Mark weren't together. He wasn't distracting her from shit. Not that he had a clue what he was supposed to be distracting her from.

"I don't know," he said honestly.

There were fewer people standing between him and the far wall now. Andrea wasn't backstage. She hadn't gotten past Mark to return toward the stage area. He couldn't think of a reason why she'd leave. This was her night. She should be here in the middle of all the action, yet she wasn't.

He felt his phone vibrate and pulled it from his pocket. Steve Wright, with his Alpha 21 crew, was calling him. Mark's insides tightened. They were supposed to text, not call. He held a finger up to Julie and Windy, silently instructing them to wait, and rushed to the door leading outside. Mark leapt down the three stairs, slamming the door closed behind him, and answered his phone at the same time he landed on the ground.

"What?" he demanded, every inch of him prepared for more disturbing news.

"Mark, we have another situation," Steve began.

"What's wrong?"

"We found a choker necklace with sapphires all the way around it."

Mark hadn't taken a breath since landing on his feet outside the backstage door. He started toward a side door that led up a narrow flight of stairs to the east wing. It was one of his private entrances into the mansion, and right now he wasn't in the mood to see anyone, except Andrea.

"Why didn't you text me this information?" Mark growled and finally took that long overdue breath. This was good news. Possibly they would unbury the rest of his mother's jewelry now. "Where did you find it?" he asked before Steve could answer his first question.

"We found it just outside the door to the greenhouse inside the hedge. It wasn't more than a foot underground and we came across it during a sweep of the yard. Not ten minutes after finding it, we found what appeared to be a matching bracelet and a diamond that I estimate was a carat in size, on a silver chain."

"That's incredible!" Mark hoped he sounded enthusiastic. As important as it was to find his mother's jewelry box and all the jewelry, his excitement was hindered by not knowing where Andrea was. "What about the jewelry box?"

"Mark, we don't have the jewelry anymore."

"What?" he howled, and was grateful that he'd just slipped inside the side door to the mansion.

"We hadn't even cleaned each piece when two men in ski masks took them from us at gunpoint."

"Was anyone hurt?" Mark leaned against the wall, his head spinning. There was definitely someone on the island, if not several people, who were after his mother's jewelry. His father might not want the jewelry in other people's hands because of them making money off of Tripp property, but Mark took it a bit more personally—especially after hearing the article Fran had read to him over the phone. His mother had despised how money kept her husband away from her. Yet for whatever reasons, these incredibly valuable pieces of jewelry had meant something to her. Mark might not ever know what, but they were a piece of his mom that he wanted.

"No, but we're a bit shook up. We didn't sign on for this. I don't have to tell you that."

"Where were the security guards?" Mark asked. His brain started churning. "As long as none of you are hurt, I need a detailed description of everything taken."

"Of course," Steve said.

"Come up to the house. I'll arrange for one of the servants to meet you at the front door. She'll get the three of you whatever you need. I'll meet with you shortly."

"We need to pack up our equipment."

"You aren't quitting, are you?"

Steve made a sound that was a mixture of a grunt and a laugh. "Just for the night. Honestly, I've been through worse. Searching for rare valuables often results in competition."

That made sense, but Mark was relieved nonetheless. "I'm sorry you had to go through this. Head to the house and relax. Whether you want coffee, tea, or a strong drink, the servants will take care of you."

"Thanks," Steve said, then added, "Sorry, man."

"I'm just glad no one was hurt. I'll have my security come talk to you soon."

Mark hung up and put a call in to his head of security. As it rang, there was a crash of cymbals outside, then a drumline beat from the stage that made it impossible for Mark to tell if his head of security answered. Mark covered his free ear and raced up the stairs just as the emcee began speaking.

"Ladies and gentlemen, I have the judges' decision," the emcee announced, her voice crisp and easily heard even as

Mark reached the top of the stairs. "We have ten of the sexiest and brightest young men from across our incredible nation here on stage. One of them will be Mr. Desire 2012." The crowd began applauding, and she spoke louder when she continued, "Our fifth runner-up, and the winner of a ten-thousand-dollar scholarship is . . ."

Long narrow windows were open at the top of the stairs, and thin curtains fluttered from a breeze. They also made it impossible for Mark to hear when his head of security did answer. He hurried down the hall and further into the house, escaping the noise from outside. Speaking as he worked his way toward the north wing, Andrea's rooms, Mark barked out instructions.

"Search the entire island, every inch of the place, the mansion, every cottage, every fucking blade of glass." He barked orders as he stalked down the quiet hallway. "Lock down the island and find those bastards. The Alpha 21 crew will be up here at the house. Get a description of these two men, then find them. No one leaves for the mainland until that jewelry is found. Is that clear?"

Mark hung up his phone after being assured the jewelry would be found before the night was out. His heart constricted when he reached Andrea's wing and she wasn't there. Anger rose inside him so raw, so intense, he shook from it. He debated calling his security man back and telling him Andrea was missing, too. Retracing his steps, he ran this time, then cleared the flight of steps to the side entrance two at a time. He'd check backstage one more time and if Andrea wasn't there, he'd tear this island apart himself until he found her.

Andrea wasn't backstage. He spotted Windy and Julie and thought of filling them in as his panic grew that something had happened to Andrea. If someone took her, or hurt her in any way, because of that goddamned jewelry, he'd dismember the motherfucker himself. Turning away when Windy gave him a cold stare, Mark bounded out the backstage side door once again. He almost sent an anxious crowd of reporters flying as he hurried to the door to the mansion.

Mark's brain was on fire as he ran through the hallways once again, grateful for the fact that the mansion was practically empty as all servants and house guests were all outside at the pageant. Which, he pointed out to himself, would be an ideal time for someone to steal the jewelry, if they had discovered that it had been found. God, he should have seen this all through. It was clear to him now. There had been someone on the island wanting the jewelry box. They'd learned that Mark had a team searching for the items, too, and had simply sat back and watched until the jewelry was found, then they'd struck.

But why the hell was Andrea nowhere to be found? She should be at the pageant, backstage in the middle of everything. She wasn't, and the few stagehands he'd casually asked while back there hadn't seen her.

Mark headed to the kitchen, which was a whirlwind of activity. He'd never seen so many cooks or smelled so many different aromas before. Mark stepped to the side as two women wheeled carts filled with platters of food past him.

"Marcia," he called out, spotting her at the far end of the kitchen.

She glanced up, wiping her brow, and frowned at him. "What are you doing here? Where is your girl?"

Someday he might ask Marcia how she always managed to narrow in on the pertinent topic before it was brought up. "She's missing."

"What do you mean, missing?"

Mark pulled her by her pudgy arm out of the line of fire as more cooks placed finger foods on platters and sent them down an assembly line to rows of carts waiting to take them out to the guests. Marcia didn't fight him but freed herself and turned on him the moment they were away from the rest of the cooks.

"What's wrong with you, boy?" she demanded.

He gave her a summarized version of what was going on. "I need you to call through the house. I want to know if any of the staff has seen Andrea in the last thirty minutes."

Marcia walked over to the wall phone that was just above a small shelf built into the wall. A piece of paper was taped to the wall next to the phone. Marcia picked up the receiver as she ran her finger down the list. Then, punching numbers into her phone, she put the receiver to her ear and faced Mark. "If she has been anywhere in my house one of the housekeeping staff would have seen her. Jonathan Morrison hired so many extras. I swear, there is a girl to every four rooms in this place. They hardly have to work at all." She rolled her eyes but then cleared her throat and stared at the floor when someone answered on the other end of the line.

"Hi, dear, it's Marcia in the kitchen. Quick question," she began as casually as if she were asking if there was enough finger food for the crowd out in the yard. "Have you seen Miss Andrea Denton, the pageant director, in the past thirty minutes? No? Okay. No, everything is fine and thank you." Marcia hung up. Without looking at Mark, she pushed buttons on the phone, entering a new extension. "I've never seen you so worked up over a girl before," she mused, shooting Mark a side glance.

He was pacing, rubbing his jaw, and glaring at the ground. Mark credited himself for not growling at Marcia's observation. And to her credit, she didn't laugh or say anything else, but continued with the next call.

Marcia asked the same questions, going down the list and contacting each extension in the house. Mark didn't remember at the moment how many there were, but there were phones in each hallway in each wing so the staff could communicate with each other. He'd never used them but was damn glad they were there. She worked her way methodically through the house, announcing which wing, or floor, she was calling before she placed the call.

"Brenda," Marcia said, her finger on the piece of paper taped to the wall. "This is Marcia in the kitchen. No, dear, everything is fine. I have a quick question. Have you seen Miss Andrea Denton, the pageant director, in the past half hour?"

Marcia's eyes grew wide and she grinned, shifting her weight and waving to get his attention. She pointed at the receiver clutched to her ear. "You have? Very good. Where did you see her?"

Mark fought the urge not to yank the receiver from Marcia's hand. The old cook would probably box his ears if he tried. His heart beat hard in his chest and a nervous trepidation snaked around his spine.

"She was heading outside." Marcia searched Mark's face as she repeated what she was told. "Not alone? You didn't recognize the young man. Between twenty and twenty-five you'd say?" Marcia continued, then forced a laugh not many would recognize as Mark did. Marcia was now nervous, too. "I know. They are looking younger and younger each year. Thank you, hon. Get back to work; we just need to track her down. No, no, I'm sure she wasn't trying to sneak out on the job."

Mark did growl over the last insinuation and didn't care when Marcia scowled at him. She hung up the phone and crossed her arms, studying him a moment before explaining what she'd just found out.

"Brenda Atkins, one of the temp housekeepers, spotted Andrea and some young white boy leaving through the doors that head out to the carports."

"You're a gem," Mark said, grabbing Marcia and pulling her into a hug. He kissed her forehead before letting her go. "Thank you," he whispered.

Marcia grabbed him before he could escape. "What's going on, Mark?"

He shook his head, his nerves irritating him more and more as time continued to pass without knowing exactly where Andrea was or what she was doing. "I don't know. But I'll let you know as soon as I do."

"Something is wrong."

He didn't confirm or deny it. But he didn't have to. Marcia let him go and waved her hands at him. "Go find your woman. Make sure she's okay. I'll have hot tea waiting for the two of you after all the guests are gone."

Mark doubted he'd be able to swallow anything at the moment. Coffee and tea sounded repulsive. He raced through the house, all the way ordering himself to keep his head on straight. Mark was a businessman's son and an architect in his own right. He could do calculative thinking and determine the nature of the problem, who or what might have caused the problem, and what means or solutions would solve the problem. If he needed to play detective to find Andrea, he would damn well do it.

Whoever this white punk kid was, he'd be lucky to live through the night once Mark got his hands on him. Mark reached another flight of stairs and damn near slid down them to the door where Andrea and the kid had been spotted leaving. He entered into the carports, of which two stalls were used to store golf carts that were sometimes used to drive to different parts of the island. They had been used by his family in the past. For reasons he'd never bothered to learn, no one with the pageant used them but instead drove rental cars his father, or more likely his father's secretary, had arranged to have available during the pageant. Mark took a moment for his eyes to adjust, then stared at the parked golf carts.

"There are only two." He squinted into the yard and at the paved drive that went around the house to the parking lot. There should have been three. Mark couldn't think of why his father might have removed one of the carts. Maybe one of them was in for repair. Or Andrea was out here recently with someone else and they left on the third cart. "How do I know for sure?" he mumbled, keeping his voice low as he walked the length of the carport searching for any clue that might help him know what had happened when Andrea came out here.

There were no signs that were so often found in movies, tire tracks, something dropped by the missing person, bread crumbs left as a clue. Mark didn't find any indication that anyone had been here recently.

After walking along the driveway as it curved around into the crowd from the pageant, Mark decided Andrea and whoever she was with probably wouldn't have gone in that direction. A few reporters loitered behind the mansion, smoking cigarettes. They would have spotted Andrea and swarmed around her immediately. Mark remained in the shadows and managed to recede back toward the carport without being seen.

Mark squinted through the darkness in the direction where the cabins were. Beyond them the tall, thick hedge would have hindered anyone's ability to hurry past it. They would have to walk along the rows of cabins in either direction to get around it. He then glanced to his right toward the beach.

"Which way did you go, sweetheart?" he murmured.

He walked to the edge of the drive, then, squatting and studying the ground, he finally spotted narrow tire tracks.

"Yes!" he whispered under his breath, and hurried to the closest golf cart.

The golf cart didn't have a very good headlight on it. It wasn't designed to run around during the night searching for tire tracks. Mark hurried to the back of the carport where various household items were kept on shelves.

"This will have to do," he said after finding a flashlight and running its beam along the wall. It wasn't the brightest flashlight he'd ever used, but it seemed strong enough. Hopefully he wouldn't have to search so long that the batteries would die.

Mark took off on the cart, heading off the driveway and

bouncing through the yard as he trained the beam of the flashlight on the ground. Another cart had trampled through there recently. Thankfully the ground was soft from recent rain. The trail wasn't as hard to find as he thought it would be. He'd never considered being a detective, but figuring out which way Andrea had gone was easier than he'd imagined.

The tracks ended at the edge of the yard. Mark stared at the dark beach and the quiet, gentle waves rolling up and down the sand. Something tightened in his gut. He couldn't imagine why anyone would take Andrea from the house, especially against her will.

Mark kept the cart out of the sand and drove it along the edge of the beach over very uneven ground.

"Oh God," he whispered, when he pulled up alongside the missing golf cart—empty. "Andrea," he pleaded with the darkness. "Where are you?"

Climbing out of the cart, he left it parked next to the other one and started walking through the dark, the flashlight his only companion as his stomach twisted into uncomfortable knots. He was more pissed than afraid. There wasn't room inside him for fear. Andrea wouldn't leave the pageant and walk into the night with some punk kid. She wasn't out here on some tryst. Nor would she abandon the pageant in its final hour.

There was only one conclusion. Someone was messing with the pageant. He didn't know their motive yet, although he had a few suspicions, the main one being rigging the pageant so a certain contestant would win. But by fucking with the pageant, they were fucking with Andrea. And that meant they were fucking with him.

He didn't question the bond he'd formed with Andrea. The look on her face when he'd called her his girl let him know their feelings were mutual. Andrea's eyes had lit up at the term of endearment. A slight flush had spread across her cheeks. She hadn't said anything in response, but that didn't bother Mark. Their relationship was moving to the next level. Both of them needed time to adjust to where they were now.

"Andrea!" Mark yelled and sent the beam of the flashlight trailing across the beach and undeveloped land in front of him.

He listened, pausing as he did and letting the beam move across the beach and through the palm trees to his left. He was all alone. Looking behind him, the mansion glowed with light coming through its many windows.

"Andrea!" Mark yelled again as he continued walking across the level area before the land dropped down to the beach.

After walking around the curve of the beach and listening to the gentle slap of the waves against the sand, Mark wasn't sure he was going in the right direction. He kept sweeping the flashlight on the grass in front of him, but he didn't see any footprints. When he focused the beam on the ground behind him, he noticed he wasn't leaving footprints as he walked, either.

On a hunch, he trained the beam on the sand to his right. Maybe Andrea and whoever was with her walked in the sand. It seemed a stupid move since they would leave footprints in the sand, but they hadn't just disappeared after getting off the golf cart.

Mark retraced his steps, growing antsy and irritated. He built buildings. He wasn't a tracker. But he had to find Andrea. She was out here somewhere.

"Andrea!" he yelled with more force this time.

He was getting angry. It cleared his head, though, and he took his time checking out the ground in front of him as he re-traced his steps. This time he did see a footprint in the ground close to the beach. Mark stopped, squatted, and studied the prints he had just discovered.

"They're mine," he concluded, but he didn't get up right away.

If he'd left footprints, Andrea and the guy she was with would have left prints, too. Damn it! Mark almost broke into a run hurrying back to the golf cart. Once there, he began again, this time keeping the beam on the ground, moving slowly, and checking all directions until he found them.

"Bingo!" Mark said, some of his aggravation lifting when he spotted two sets of prints moving off to his right. "You did go down to the beach. Okay, motherfucker, be prepared to run, but you won't get far."

Mark was going to beat the crap out of whoever brought Andrea out here. He clenched his fists, aching for that first punch more than he'd ever ached for a fight in his life. Mark took a few more steps and stopped again.

He breathed in the night air. There was the smell of the ocean, the salt in the air, but there was something else. Mark inhaled again.

"Cigarettes," he hissed under his breath.

Mark stood where he was, trying to hold on to the smell of the cigarette smoke. As he squinted toward the ocean, he swore he saw two figures. It was dark and the beam of his flashlight didn't travel far. He could only start in that direction and pray he wasn't approaching guests who had escaped the pageant for a walk on the beach.

There were voices. The shadows he saw began taking shape. Mark could distinguish their clothes against the dark sky. He focused on the snug-fitting black dress hugging a perfect figure. Her hair was up but strands of it whipped around her face every time the wind off the ocean picked up. When he heard laughter, Mark stopped, something painfully tight wrapping around his heart.

"You're a stupid little creep!" Andrea was facing a young man and it appeared she was almost staggering, fighting to keep her balance, as she faced him and spoke a bit too loudly. "Do you think this will accomplish anything?" she continued, then the laughter began again.

It was the same laughter Mark had heard a moment before.

He'd thought he'd heard Andrea's sultry, happy laugh. But as he watched, Andrea was unsteady, continually stepping back and forth. Her high-heeled shoes were in one hand and she waved her free hand in the man's face as she yelled at him.

"When I organize a pageant, there are no mistakes. It will go on!" she announced, raising her voice and pointing to the sky when she finished speaking.

Something wasn't right. Mark began walking, heading toward both of them. "Andrea!" he yelled.

She spun around, then collapsed to the ground, laughing as she did. "I told you. Didn't I tell you?" She was either reaching for Mark, or waving at him. It wasn't clear. "My man is here to rescue me."

As odd as her behavior was, the young man, who had just taken a drag off his cigarette, behaved a bit more as Mark would have expected. He took one look at Mark, his jaw dropped, then he tossed the cigarette and took off running.

The kid was possibly ten years younger than Mark, but Mark wasn't that out of shape. He hauled ass after the kid, leaping through the air and tackling him. He needed that first punch too badly to let the little asshole get away.

"What the hell are you doing out here with her?" he demanded, grabbing the back of the kid's shirt and spinning him around to face Mark.

Mark didn't wait for an answer but hit the kid square in the jaw.

"My man loves me!" Andrea sounded like she was clapping. "He'll fight for me. You're in trouble now," she shouted in a singsong tone.

15

Andrea sat on the edge of her couch nursing her pounding head. No matter how many times Mark or Julie, or Windy, re-filled the cloth bag with fresh ice, her head continued to throb.

"Jay Forrester is singing like a bird, but he doesn't have a very long song." Sylvia, the cop, seemed to be speaking way too loud.

Andrea would have glared at her but lifting her head off her ice pack was too much work.

"What did he tell you?" Mark asked. He moved across the room and sat down next to Andrea, first rubbing her back, then placing his very warm hand on her knee. It remained there as he spoke to the lady cop. "I want him behind bars, Sylvia. You got that?"

"That's where he is," she assured him. "But I don't think he's our guy."

"He had Andrea out by the beach, drugged," Mark bel-lowed.

Andrea groaned, wishing she could bury her entire body in the ice pack. All of last night was a blur. She wasn't too clear on

how she got back to her room, or into a comfortable pair of
sweats. Her hair was still pinned up from the night before although thick strands fell around her face to her shoulders. She
was sure she looked a wreck and actually didn't care. All she
wanted was to fade into oblivion and wake up once the pounding ceased.

"I'm sorry, sweetheart." Mark's arm moved around her
shoulder. "Do you want to go lie down?"

More than anything she wanted just that. It felt good leaning
against Mark, though. She didn't remember much from the
night before, but she did remember Mark being there, holding
her, carrying her at times.

"No. I want to know what happened."

Mark leaned in to hear her, snuggling her even closer to his
hard, muscle-packed body. "Okay. Let me know when you
need fresh ice," he whispered.

Andrea would have nodded but just thinking about doing so
brought on more pain.

"She really should see a doctor," Sylvia said.

"My doctor is on his way out to see her." Mark continued
holding her.

Andrea was pretty sure Mark didn't take advantage of being
a Tripp too often. But to have a doctor who would make a
house call to an island this early in the morning was pretty impressive, and at the moment much appreciated. Andrea wasn't
sure she could go anywhere.

"Forrester told us he drugged her with La Rochas. It's also
called a roofie, or Rohypnol."

"How did he drug her?" Mark asked. "And why did he drug
her?" he demanded, raising his voice, but then immediately
turned to her. "I'm sorry, sweetheart. I didn't mean to yell."

"Most commonly it comes in a pill and is put in a drink. But
it changes the color of the drink. If she were drinking something with Coke, or another dark liquid, the pill would have

made the drink cloudy. If she were drinking something with fruit in it, the pill changes the color of the drink to bright blue. I've heard some cases where a girl accepts a froufrou drink and wasn't sure what color the drink is supposed to be." Sylvia kept explaining although her words seemed to fade in and out until it became too much work to listen.

When the doctor arrived, Windy and Julie, along with Sylvia, left Andrea's office. Mark continued holding her close as he helped her to her bedroom. She didn't realize he carried her until she was placed on her bed. Andrea immediately stretched, found her pillows, and held on to Mark's hand.

"Lie down with me," she tried to say, but her mouth was too dry.

Then she noticed the concerned look on the face of an older man standing next to Mark. He must be the doctor. She hated how her brain wasn't working. They had just announced his arrival and that was why Mark brought her to bed. It wasn't to make love to her.

The pounding in her head began again, and she couldn't hear what either man said. They didn't seem to mind her not answering but instead talked to each other. Finally, the doctor began his examination. When he was done, Andrea fell asleep.

There is a difference in the sound of a house when it's quiet from everyone sleeping, and when it's silent from emptiness. Keeping everyone on the island after the pageant was over would have proved more of a nightmare than it would have been worth. Hardly anyone tried to leave during the celebration that followed. Big D was the new Mr. Desire—how appropriate. The crowd had congregated around the tables in front of the stage, and Big D had graciously gone from table to table spending time with all the guests.

Steve, Carl, and Eve had given descriptions of the two men who had stolen the jewelry right after it had been found. Between the three of them, they had been able to give quite a few details. Mark's security team were looking for two Caucasian men who were both under six feet tall. They were thin, not muscular. Neither one of them had brown eyes. Carl had been pretty sure one of them had blue eyes. Steve had noticed one of them held his gun with his left hand. Eve had added that they appeared to be very young. In her words, they weren't "filled out" the way a man would be.

It would have been difficult for any of the contestants from the pageant to get away and steal the jewelry. Also, the description the Alpha 21 crew gave didn't match any of the contestants. All of them were tall and very muscular. So they were looking for two men on Tripp Island who weren't involved with the pageant. Mark had increased security at the docks and had allowed all guests to leave, but they were subject to searches at his security guards' discretion. They hadn't found the jewelry on anyone leaving the island.

After the guests left, Mark had the docks closed. No one else was leaving the island unless they knew how to swim really well.

His Alpha 21 crew didn't have their own wing. Mark had put them up in three bedrooms alongside each other on the ground floor at the back of the mansion. They'd been interrogated in the smaller library close to their rooms. He'd been informed they were still there.

Pushing the curtained glass doors open silently, Mark entered the library. The lights had been dimmed and dirty plates were stacked on a cart just inside the door. Mark let his eyes adjust, then focused on Eve, who was stretched out on one of the couches with her back turned to him. Carl sat on a lounge chair with his feet propped up on an ottoman. His arms were crossed over his chest, and he appeared to be sleeping, too, but he raised his head when Mark entered. Steve was sitting across the room from the other two in an upright chair staring out a window into the darkness. He looked exhausted when he glanced in Mark's direction.

"Any word?" Steve asked.

Mark shook his head and took the chair next to him. He'd been running on adrenaline all night and realized as he sat that if he remained there very long, he'd be out.

"I heard the pageant director was drugged."

"She's upstairs resting. She'll be fine," Mark told him without elaborating.

"Hell of a night."

Mark grunted and acknowledged Carl with a nod when he joined them and leaned against the wall by the window. "I had those necklaces in my hand," he said to no one in particular.

"I'm convinced they are still on the island." Mark tried sounding positive, but exhaustion was setting in quickly. "I've got over twenty men scouring every inch of the island. We'll find them."

Mark's phone rang, and it took him a moment to acknowledge the vibration against his hip. Even his movements seemed to be slowing down as he twisted and pulled the phone from his belt. But the moment he saw the caller on his screen, adrenaline kick-started him awake.

"What do you have for me?" he asked anxiously when he answered.

"We found them," his head of security announced.

16

"I feel like there are holes in my brain." Andrea attempted a smile as she and Mark entered the foyer downstairs.

Mark stroked her ponytail and instantly her body reacted, anticipating the pinch in her scalp when he pulled. Just the thought of it got her soaked. Her insides swelled with need, and for a moment she considered turning around and hurrying back up the stairs. She wanted to demand that he fuck her before she had to deal with the day.

Mark didn't tug her ponytail, but simply stroked it gently as he guided them across the foyer. "Did the doctor say if you'd eventually remember the details of last night?"

She shook her head, resigning herself to the fact that incredible sex would have to wait. "No. It's common for people who take this drug to never regain their memory." Other than a portion of the previous night, her memory was intact. Still, knowing a part of her life had been robbed from her tore her apart in a way she never would have guessed it would. Mark's body brushed against hers as they walked. Every time he touched her, heat rushed through her. It was going to be hell staying focused when all she wanted to do was rip his clothes off and force him down so she could ride his hard cock.

Mark pulled her against him and moved them together, as one, through the house. He didn't let her go when his phone buzzed but simply pulled it from his belt and glanced at it. "The police are making their arrests now."

"Okay. This won't take long. I need to do this, though. I wasn't there last night when Big D was crowned Mr. Desire, and I need to make up for that as soon as possible." It had been heaven waking up with Mark next to her. Even then she wanted to remain snuggled up next to him instead of rolling out of bed. It was barely eight o'clock, but her job as pageant director wasn't over. She needed to congratulate Mr. D and be there for him, especially now that he no longer had an agent standing by his side.

Mark led them through the open doors onto the terrace outside. The bright sun was blinding, and Andrea worried she would teeter. Mark seemed to know her body as well as she did. His hand dropped down and rested on the small of her back for only a moment before he took her hand and wrapped his long fingers around hers. She fed off his confident strength and put on her professional smile the moment they were noticed and recognized.

A fairly large group of photographers, reporters, costume designers, and publicists—every type of person in the industry imaginable—huddled around Big D. Mark kept a firm grip on her hand as they joined the relaxed chaos.

Big D leaned against the brick ledge surrounding the terrace. He wore muscle-hugging dark blue jeans and no shirt. Every inch of his exposed, dark-chocolate skin was covered with glistening oil. He was the perfect specimen of a man, the definition of sex appeal, the epitome of charm and youthful confidence.

Big D answered questions about his childhood, his education, his goals for the future, and the efforts it took him to win the pageant. She didn't see manipulation, satisfaction from victory, gloating, or anything conniving at all. The cockiness was gone. Big D stumbled over his answers and hesitated more than once. He was scared and nervous, and she understood why. She'd made the right decision in insisting they inform him before dealing with the police who had arrested Big D's agent and her two sons for stealing Mark's mother's jewelry.

Big D spotted her at the same time several reporters saw her.

"Miss Denton, Miss Denton," the reporters chimed.

She locked gazes with Big D and noticed his visible relief that she was there. Big D might be Mr. Desire and have the body and sex appeal of a man, but Andrea saw the boy who still existed inside. She found her own strength and let go of Mark's hand. For the next few minutes at least, she needed to be there for Big D. Walking through the reporters she joined the new Mr. Desire.

"Congratulations," she whispered, grinning up at him. "I'm so sorry I wasn't there for you last night."

"I've heard terrible rumors," he said, also whispering. "You're okay, right?"

Andrea gained inner strength and gently patted his arm as she continued smiling and forced herself to relax.

"It would take more than some young scumbag to take me down," she told him, and laughed softly.

Big D flashed a huge, toothy grin. "I'm glad you're okay." His expression sobered as he added, "I'm sorry."

"Oh my God, hon, you have nothing to apologize for."

"My agent had you drugged," he hissed under his breath and his expression transformed as fury etched itself in his face. Big D suddenly looked very dangerous and outraged.

Andrea saw the demons he'd been fighting alone since learning she'd been abducted. "Denny," she said softly and firmly, and turned her back on the crowd around them. It was something she would never let any of her candidates in a pageant ever do. But this moment was necessary. There were times in her line of work when a personal moment was necessary to keep her contestant focused. "No one has connected what Becky Sterling did to my being abducted. Something awful happened and it's over. Now we glow, rejoice in your victory, and put everything else behind us. Understand?"

Big D nodded and visibly relaxed. All his bulging muscle remained perfectly defined even after he exhaled and the anger disappeared on his face. His large brown eyes were suddenly glowing with happiness and a hint of mischief. Big D had worked hard for this title, and his training and professional nature glowed in his face as he finally pulled his attention from her and returned it to the reporters and other industry professionals around them.

Andrea managed to shift her weight and face the reporters again as if her back had never been to them. She wasn't ready for all of the attention to suddenly be on her, though.

"Miss Denton, Andrea, a few questions please."

"Miss Denton a quote for the *Miami Herald*, please," another reporter shouted.

"Miss Denton, would you say true love can be found during the Mr. Desire Pageant?" The reporter who asked went down on one knee in front of Andrea, and held an extended mike so that it was close to her face. A man next to him started snapping pictures, his bright flash blinding her.

The gaps in her memory seemed to expand with each flash. Other reporters joined in, closing in around her and Big D.

"The Mr. Desire Pageant isn't about finding true love," she responded, barely able to see the man who'd asked the question from all the flashes that now were attacking them from all sides. She placed a winning smile on her face and hoped her expression looked confident and happy. "Mr. Desire is the perfect man." She turned and held her hands out, presenting Big D to the reporters and hoping she shifted the reporters from her to him. "And you must all admit, isn't Mr. Desire absolutely perfect? He is sexy and has a winning personality."

"You'll never know what you'll find with the Mr. Desire Pageant," Mark said eloquently, somehow managing to work his way through the crowd until he stood next to Andrea. Then masterfully, he guided her away from the reporters.

"Mr. Tripp, did you and your coordinator find true love during the Mr. Desire Pageant, or were you a couple prior to the event?" someone called out. Other reporters shouted similar questions, a few of them uncouth.

Mark ignored them, didn't turn around, and purposefully headed into the mansion with his arm securely wrapped around her waist. Once inside the house, Mark locked the glass doors. Not once did he look at the flashing cameras or the reporters. His expression was nondescript and focused down as he flipped the lock then turned around and reached for her. Mark had experience with paparazzi. In his world, though, he didn't have to flash a smile and appear appreciative of the attention. Instead, he didn't allow them to snap a shot that revealed a reaction of any kind from him. The reporters wouldn't get a good picture of him that they could put in their newspapers.

Andrea was standing in the middle of the room as Mark locked the door. When he came to her, his brooding expression wasn't readable. He slipped his arm around her, tucked her in next to him, and led them through the mansion.

She noticed for the first time how incredibly large and quiet the beautiful home was as they walked in silence. Hallways went on forever, each time opening into a section of the house that had its own unique theme. Some of the rooms were dark with a gothic theme to them, others were filled with bright colors, flashy and pretentious. Another area of the house was full of pastels, soft mauve paint on the walls, and paintings hung that looked as if the artist had created them just to fit the mood of this part of the mansion.

They'd just entered this third part of Mark's home when he paused. The long hallway had opened into a room full of small oriental statues. They had the option of taking a hallway to the left or right. Mark did neither but stopped, faced her, then grasped her arms and sighed.

"There's something I need to tell you," he began, his hooded gaze impossible to see. "And I should have told you about this before. I don't know why I didn't." He sighed again and pressed his lips together as if trying to find words to continue.

"What are you talking about?" Her stomach immediately twisted into a knot as she feared the worst, although she wasn't sure what the worst might be.

Mark raised his focus to her eyes. Andrea suddenly saw how exhausted he looked. His face was lined with turmoil and aggravation. There were shadows under his eyes, which were cloudy and opaque. The beautiful green eyes that she could usually so easily drown in stared at her with no depth to them at all. He looked damn near ready to collapse.

She read him so easily. As he looked at her, Andrea wondered if he detected her confusion and sudden fear that whatever he had to say would hurt her. Where was her line of defense? The wall that had so successfully protected her feelings and her heart for years had disappeared. She stared at him, vulnerable and exposed. He had the power to make her happy and satisfied, or tear her in two and destroy her. Andrea trembled from the realization. If this was love, it was the most terrifying emotion she'd ever experienced in her life.

Mark dropped his arms and looked away from her. "Last night when I carried you upstairs to your rooms, something inside me ripped in two. It was bad enough searching for you. But anger and outrage that I'd left you alone long enough for this to happen to you kept me moving. When that little punk was facing you on the beach smoking that cigarette, I ached for him to try and run. He did. Chasing him down and punching his lights out . . ."

"You hit him?" she asked, interrupting him.

Mark turned on her, his exhausted look replaced with something dark and terrifying. "I wanted to kill him for what he did to you, Dre."

She reached for him, her heart painfully pattering against her chest in fear of what he had to say. Yet the need to console him, to make sure he knew how much it mattered to her that he not suffer superseded her own pain.

Mark grabbed her wrist with so much strength that for a moment she worried he'd cut off the circulation to her hand. "I can't begin to describe how worried I was. When I found you and you were so drugged you could barely walk, all that mattered, over everything else happening at the same time, was making sure you were okay," he told her, his voice gravelly with emotion.

Her eyes suddenly burned with tears. She swallowed a lump in her throat but couldn't find the strength needed to control her emotions. "I am okay," she whispered. It was the worst feeling in the world knowing she might never remember those moments when Mark took care of her. Running pageant after pageant for the past seven years, Andrea helped train so many young ladies, and now young men, to be the perfect illusion of what everyone dreamed they could be. It had allowed her to stand on the outside of all those hopes and dreams, instead of having them herself. Knowing she'd lived through that moment when the perfect man for her had endured so many raw emotions as he searched until he had found her, fought for her, then carried her to safety, and that she would never remember any of it, was the worst feeling in the world.

"Andrea, I think I'm in love with you."

"Oh God," she cried out, and couldn't stop a tear from escaping and soaking her cheek. She laughed and swatted at it. "Mark," she gasped.

His fingers were on top of hers, touching her damp cheek. "Which is why I need to tell you this," he added, his voice cracking.

She shook her head, still smiling and suddenly very giddy. If another man had admitted he loved her, he would expect her to voice the same emotion. But Mark, her man, brimmed over with so much confidence he was comfortable voicing the ultimate of all emotions without validation that it was mutual. He wasn't conceited. The notoriety around his name hadn't given him an attitude. If anything he was living proof that so much money made the world see one thing and not bother to learn the truth about the person behind the fortune.

"I know I'm in love with you, Mark Tripp," she said, and walked into him. When she pressed her body against his and went up on tiptoe, his arms wrapped around her.

She might have instigated the kiss but Mark devoured her mouth. Fire exploded between the two of them, creating a heat so intense it was hard to breathe. Andrea's breasts were too tender against his chest. Her nipples were painfully hard. The swelling inside her turned into a throbbing pressure that seized every inch of her body. When Mark ended the kiss and put her at arm's length, it was worse than not remembering part of her night. She needed him, with every inch of her body and with every breath she took.

"Mark," she complained.

His breath was ragged as he stared at her. The burning fire she felt inside glowed in his penetrating gaze. It stole her breath. She wasn't the only one exposed and vulnerable. Somehow knowing they were in this together created the strength she needed to face him and not demand he appease the searing need to consummate their newly declared love.

"I came to the island for another reason other than the Mr. Desire Pageant."

She straightened, suddenly focused. "To search for your mother's jewelry box?"

"How did you know?" He looked confused, but then the lines of worry faded, leaving only exhaustion. He looked as if he hadn't slept at all last night.

"Windy and Julie told me last night backstage. I had forgotten that they told me until just now when you said you were on the island for more reasons than the pageant."

"How did they know?" Mark asked, frowning.

Andrea searched her memory and more of the night prior to her abduction came back to her. "A security guard told them," she said. "Did you take care of whoever was going to mess with the sound? There weren't any problems after that kid came and got me, were there?"

Mark shook his head. "Why did you leave with him?"

His question wasn't condescending but he sounded truly curious to learn what she'd been through. Andrea dropped her gaze, squinting and searching her memory, trying to recall details. Every time she had since she'd woken, it had given her a piercing headache. The headache didn't come back this time.

"There was a problem," she began, but then shook her head. "I hate that I can't remember," she snapped, and stamped her foot on the ground.

"It's okay, sweetheart." Mark tried consoling her as he stroked her back.

Andrea realized he'd repeated those words and the enduring action many times since last night. Sighing, she looked up at him. Instantly her frustration was replaced with her need for him. The fiery craving from moments before was more subdued now. As soon as there was time, she wanted to make love to him for hours, until there wasn't an ounce of strength left in her. Maybe there was a side to love that wasn't so terrifying. The sensation washing over her now was more possessive, alluring. She wanted to claim every inch of him, make his body her own and put her mark on his heart so he would never want to leave her.

"When I couldn't find you last night, I realized how strong my feelings for you were," Mark told her. He then walked away from her, his movements lazy as he paused at one of the statues on display on an ornate stand. He picked it up and turned it around in his hand, studying it. "I was ten years old when my mother died in a car accident."

His words came out of nowhere. Andrea didn't know if she should go to him or remain standing where she was. Mark didn't speak as if the information hurt him. His words were more matter-of-fact. She stayed where she was, watching and waiting for him to continue.

"She drove her car off a cliff when she was coming home from a fund-raiser, or some kind of social event," he said offhandedly. Mark turned the statue again, studying it as if the painted ceramic figure of some mythical-looking creature really impressed him. "I remember all the speculation and gossip. The police said she'd been too drunk to drive and that there were enough sedatives in her system to have easily impaired her judgment. People whispered that she'd killed herself." He cleared his throat and added, "Committed suicide. My dad buried himself in his work after Mom died. It was business deal after business deal. I didn't focus on when he'd be home as much as I paid attention to what city he was in that week. It was just me and my sister, and she was only five at the time. Within a few years she barely remembered Mom."

Mark put the small statue back on its round pedestal. Then walking to the next one, instead of picking it up, he ran his finger along the smooth white face of an oriental woman, posed standing with her hands inside long sleeves that hung low against her floor-length plain dress. He studied that statue just as intently when he continued speaking.

"When Mom was alive, she brought us to Tripp Island whenever Dad left town on business. We would pretend we were explorers discovering new land as we walked through the forests and climbed the rocky hills. She would tell us the waterfalls flowed with magical water and if we soaked ourselves with it all our wishes would come true." His voice cracked and he made a fist. For a moment it looked as if he might hurl the small statue across the room. "There were picnics and parties and . . ." Again his voice cracked with emotion. "She seemed happy. I remember her so well. And yes, she drank all the time. I was too young to know. When she drank she was more fun. There were her happy pills. I remember that she was more creative with ideas of fun things for us to do together after she'd popped a few pills." He finally looked at her. There was pain and anger lining his face. "If I had just been a bit older . . . She despised all the money but didn't know how to get around it. I could have shown her."

Andrea took a step toward him but Mark stalked to the other end of the room toward the far hallway. "She had a jewelry box made out of a crystal that made it hard to detect what was inside it. When my father made his will some years back, his lawyers helped him itemize all the items in the different houses, the one in Miami, in the Keys, and here on Tripp Island. Everything was accounted for and willed to my sister and me after his death. We still don't know how, but someone remembered my mother's jewelry box, but apparently it isn't listed in my dad's will."

"I don't understand," Andrea said when he quit talking and simply stood there, staring at the ground and looking deflated. This time she did walk to him. "Somehow your mom's jewelry box was lost on this island?"

Mark shifted his attention to her. His eyes pierced her with aggression, the look of an outraged predator ready to roar his protest over a matter he then would set straight. Andrea wasn't sure she'd ever seen him look so dangerous. His hard features, the high cheekbones, his long straight nose, that stubborn jaw-line, and the tousled strands of his brown hair outlining his face made him look more like an untamed barbarian than the suave playboy image he'd tried selling her on when they first met.

"Before she died, Mom became more eccentric. Dad was gone more often. He didn't know how to handle her. As much as he loved her, my father wasn't good with strong, unpleasant emotions. He wanted everyone around him to be happy. When Mom wasn't happy, instead of consoling her, he thought if he made more money she would then be satisfied. They both loved each other so much, yet they tore each other apart with their inability to see what each of them needed. Mom wanted Dad to be with her. When he wasn't, and instead out closing another business deal, I think it got to where Mom started feeling jealous of the money, as if it were another woman."

"That is so sad," she murmured, then worried her comment upset Mark even more.

"It is," he said through tight lips. "She collected jewelry that once belonged to women who cherished the diamonds, rubies, gold, or whatever precious metal it might have been because their lover had given it to them. Those pieces of jewelry in my mom's jewelry box were gifts from men who were incapable of physical and emotional love, which was all each woman who originally owned the piece of jewelry truly wanted."

"Just like your mom," Andrea said. "How tragic."

"It really is. I didn't understand how incredible my mother's pain must have been until I was an adult. I think my dad saw the truth after she died. He's never quit loving her, and not once has he gone on a date, or looked at another woman, since her death. He has cancer, yet he refuses treatment. He does try to eat well and has incredibly qualified nurses and trained staff at his beck and call around the clock. But honestly, I think he can't wait for death because he believes he will be with his wife again. I hope he gets the chance to make amends."

"It sounds like he needs to forgive himself. Your mom might have been unhappy, but it was her choice to turn to alcohol and pills instead of telling your dad she wanted to spend more time with him."

Andrea braced herself against the cold stare Mark shot her way. "Your mom had choices, Mark," she said softly and remembered that day when she was seventeen as clearly as if it had just happened. "She chose to focus all of her attention on buying jewelry from brokenhearted women from the past. She chose to start drinking, probably to help numb her own broken heart, instead of trying to fix it. I am so incredibly sorry that you lost your mother when you were so young. And it sounds as if she left you with some wonderful memories of times with her that were fun and happy moments."

"If I'd been old enough to understand that her eyes didn't glow, but were glassy because she wasn't sober," he began. "Or if I had known and understood that her behavior was the result of missing Dad, I could have talked to him, shown him how much Mom needed him."

"Trust me, if you'd seen the truth of the matter and spoken to your father about it, quite possibly nothing would have changed. Sometimes people are only happy in the limelight. They aren't happy or willing to show love if that limelight goes away."

Mark's brow narrowed, and he studied her with a gaze that was possibly too perceptive. Andrea shoved her own tormented past back into its dark corner. "All I'm saying is possibly your dad craved those business deals. You said he was always happy but it might have been because the only time you saw him was right after he'd just made more money. If he had stayed home for a long period of time without closing those high-rolling deals, he might have been miserable."

Mark shook his head. "All of it is history now." He seemed calmer than he had a moment before when he cupped her cheeks and brought their faces close to each other. "History that won't repeat itself, I promise. I'm like my mother, millions of dollars don't matter to me. But unlike my mom, I learned how to exist outside the Tripp fortune."

17

Mark had never considered talking to anyone about his mother before, let alone a woman he was sleeping with. Andrea was so much more than a fantastic sexual partner, though. It hadn't seemed important in the past how much anyone knew about him as long as he understood how they worked. Mark wanted to know every detail about Andrea. And before they met with the police, his security team, and the Alpha 21 crew, Mark had wanted Andrea brought up to speed. It was interesting that he'd never considered leaving her in her suite and meeting with everyone on his own.

Andrea's reaction to the story about his mother and her jewelry box had been just as interesting and unexpected. Mark swore there was something behind her refusal to show compassion over his mother's tormented and sad life. It might take some time, but he planned on finding out what hidden scars were in Andrea's past.

Whatever they were, they were deeply buried at the moment. Andrea had asked for a moment to freshen up before meeting with everyone. She'd changed clothes, applied some perfume, and turned every head when they entered the library a short time later.

Sylvia and Eve were the only other women in the room, and it was fascinating how each woman looked when they noticed Andrea enter. Eve offered a small smile and her eyes lit up as if she understood and related to the power a beautiful woman could have on a room. Sylvia frowned, her focus traveling down and back up Andrea before she pursed her lips and looked away. She didn't give Mark a glance.

Maybe she was unimpressed with Andrea's bright yellow dress that was drawn tight at the waist with spandex-like material that stretched over her breasts. Andrea wore a brown belt and matching brown heels and handbag. Sylvia might be disgusted by Andrea's need to be a sharp dresser, but Mark saw how happy it made her to look nice. The way her face had lit up when Mark asked her who designed it had him thinking he might start taking a vested interest in the fashion world.

"We were about to leave," Sylvia said instead of greeting him. Her expression was tight and she was all business, which was fine. "Becky Sterling and her two sons have already been escorted to the docks."

"No helicopter this time?" Andrea interrupted and smiled sweetly.

"We have the jewelry that she is accused of stealing tagged as evidence. If you have documentation that it's yours . . ." Sylvia continued, and ignored Andrea's question.

"They were dug up here on the island, on private property." Mark wasn't sure if the faxed papers Fran had sent him would qualify as proof of ownership. Other than that, his mother's jewelry had never been documented, which had been the whole point of this search. "Isn't that enough to constitute ownership?"

"There isn't any proof what was dug up," Sylvia said flatly.

"I'll swear under oath that jewelry was dug out of the ground on this island," Carl stated, coming forward.

"And we have descriptions of some of the jewelry and the jewelry box from Mark that he gave us before any jewelry was found. Why are you trying to make this difficult?" Steve demanded, walking around Carl and facing Sylvia.

She held her ground well when they all faced her, but her voice didn't have the hard edge to it when she answered. "This is what a lawyer will tell a judge," she explained. "Mark, unless you have solid proof of ownership, this could go to court, depending on what type of lawyer Becky Sterling gets."

"What exactly is considered proof of ownership?" Mark asked.

"I'm not going to speculate on what the judge will accept. I just want you to be ready when you come in with your lawyer."

Mark shook his head, already disgusted. "Thanks," he told her.

Syliva nodded once, then started through the library doors. "Oh, I almost forgot to mention, we picked up Brittany Bender with Miles and Miles earlier this morning."

"What? Who?" Andrea asked, looking confused for a moment before she frowned. "She was the one on sound when you overheard they were going to lower the volume during some of the performances," she said, looking as if the memories were still floating in and out of her head. "Did she say who she had planned on turning the volume down on?" she asked Sylvia.

"Nope. She demanded a lawyer before we even had her in jail," Sylvia grunted. "She won't be telling us a thing."

"Thank you," Andrea said, and extended her hand.

Sylvia glanced at it for only a moment before accepting and giving her one firm shake. Andrea clasped her hands in front of her and stood with her back to Mark, looking as if she might actually play hostess and walk Sylvia to the front door. Mark stepped forward and wrapped his hand around Andrea's waist.

Sylvia watched Mark pull Andrea against him, then looked at him as if they were complete strangers. "I haven't heard that the kid who drugged you is telling us why yet. Some people just don't get how to make their lives easier." She shook her head and the small ponytail at the back of her head swung back and forth. "Speaking of which, why did you get rid of that cool old guy who ran your ferry?"

"I didn't get rid of anyone," Mark told her.

"The guy hauling us back and forth to the mainland won't talk and makes that short ride almost unbearable. I never thought I'd say this, but I miss your eccentric old sailor and the stories he always shared when we brought your private ferry to the island."

Mark shook his head. "Silver hasn't gone anywhere. And no one has told me that someone is working for him. I've had a crazy past twenty-four hours, though. If he needed time off, I can't imagine it being for long. I'm sure he'll be back in no time."

"Hopefully I won't be back on the island in no time." Sylvia sounded as if she meant it. She looked past Mark, nodding at the group of them. "I can let myself out," she added, then turned and disappeared down the hallway.

Once he no longer heard her footsteps, he turned to Steve and Carl. "Show me where you dug up that jewelry. I have a picture of all the jewelry my mom kept in her jewelry box, and a picture of the jewelry box. Maybe we can find the rest of her jewelry, and the box."

Mark appreciated working with a crew who didn't think him inept or believed him the kind of man who thought himself too good to get dirty. He was neither of those men. Steve, Carl, and Eve took him straight to the location where they'd found the jewelry the night before. Mark brought down the pictures Fran had faxed over and passed them around.

Andrea didn't have any interest in digging, not that Mark expected her to in her bright, pretty dress. She watched with half-interest for a few minutes then disappeared into the greenhouse where they had fucked after he'd discovered the old building was still there buried inside the hedge. Mark had still not learned who had decided to grow the huge hedge around the greenhouse instead of tearing the old structure down. It had crossed his mind more than once that perhaps his father simply couldn't tear it down, in spite of how dilapidated it was. But Mark Tripp Sr. hadn't been on Tripp Island more than a few times his entire life. Had he really known how much his wife had loved her greenhouse?

Mark glanced up when the metal detector Eve was using started going off. Its frantic-sounding beeps drew in everyone's attention, even the guards he'd instructed to keep post around them while they dug. Mark wasn't taking any chances.

"Give her room," Steve ordered, holding his arms out when everyone crowded around Eve, who was on her hands and knees going over the ground with a tool that didn't appear any more effective at digging than a fork. "Everyone back off. Carl, hold that light directly over her hand."

"Wait a minute. Hold on," Eve announced without looking up. "I've got something. Steve, it's tiny. It's a wire. No—wait."

Steve was on his hands and knees next to Eve. Mark went to his knees, as well. He watched anxiously as they meticulously removed dirt from something lodged in the ground. A few minutes later Eve held up a dangling earring.

"Does it match the one in the picture?"

The earring didn't look too impressive covered in dirt. More tools were brought out as Mark continually looked at the picture, then the earring. He watched in amazement as Steve and Carl patiently cleaned the delicate earring until it began to transform into one of the bronze and gold earrings in the photograph.

"I found the other one!" Eve was laughing with excitement as she brushed dirt out of the decent-sized hole they'd dug for the first earring.

Mark glanced around him and realized Andrea hadn't come out of the greenhouse during all of the excitement. He left the crew to free the second earring from the dirt and walked over to the open door of the greenhouse.

Andrea sat on a stool inside the greenhouse seeming indifferent to the dust and dirt gathering on her dress. "I was going to call for you," she began when he ducked under the hedge falling around the doorway.

"What?" he asked, then paused and stared at the opaque, crystal box resting on her lap.

Mark's lawyer, Paul Athey, was laid-back, easy to talk to, yet shrewd and quick to find ways to benefit Andrea, as well as Mark, and with the best interest of the Mr. Desire Pageant. Andrea decided within minutes of sitting in the conference room at Mark's office in Miami that she liked Paul. He didn't wear a tie. He laughed easily and had everyone on a first-name basis within moments. It seemed even Julie liked him. He wasn't in a hurry for Andrea to sign anything and took his time explaining every part of the contract she had questions about.

"This new contract supersedes everything on the old contract. Notice your six-figure annual salary." Julie flipped pages and pointed to the income amount in bold dark numbers. She tapped the page with her pen. "This is a good contract. Sign it quickly before Mark's lawyer tries talking some sense into him," she whispered and handed her pen to Andrea.

"If you'll fill out this form, we can do a monthly auto deposit into your bank account." Paul opened a folder in front of him and flipped through pages until he found what he was looking for. "Here we go. We just need your account information," he said and handed the form to Julie, who merely glanced at it then slid it in front of Andrea.

"Pretty standard," she muttered.

Andrea flipped through the pages in her copy of the contract. She read over it. Normally she and Julie would take any contract back to her office, then go over it together in detail before she signed it. But Julie had already slid the pen over to Andrea.

Andrea looked at Mark. He was watching her.

"Is there somewhere Julie and I can speak privately?" she asked.

Immediately both lawyers pushed their chairs back, except Julie nudged her as she did. Andrea looked at her and saw the question and confusion on her face. The contract was perfect, and Julie was ready for Andrea to make it binding.

"Of course," Mark said, standing then coming around the table. He stood in front of Andrea, ignoring Julie right next to her. "Is something wrong?" he asked softly.

"No, not at all," she assured him. "I just need a moment."

Mark escorted Andrea and Julie to a small conference room. He met her gaze as he leaned on the doorknob but said nothing when he closed the door. Andrea still saw his face in her mind as she stared at the closed door. She hated seeing his confused expression. But at the same time, she needed to sort through her own feelings.

"So is this relationship with Mark Tripp actually serious?" Julie asked the moment they were alone.

"I think so." Andrea moved slowly around the edge of the small table in the room, dragging her finger over its smooth surface. She didn't want to see Julie's expression right now. But at the same time, she needed to bounce her feelings off someone. This was all too new to her. "That contract doesn't give Mark an out."

"That contract will almost double your monthly income."

Andrea gave a dry laugh. "Sounds like the perfect deal, huh?"

Now Julie laughed, the sound relaxed and happy. "Damn, you're in deep. I've never seen you like this before. Impervious Andrea has been bitten by the love bug. Do I need to get out the Raid?"

"Might not hurt." Andrea straightened the contract on the round conference table and sat. "Honestly, Julie, he's made me feel like this since the first moment I saw him."

"That's lust, darling, not love. I'd agree with you one hundred percent on that one. Mark Tripp is sexy as hell."

Andrea rolled her eyes, then crossed her legs and fingered the edge of her skirt. "My mind is all messed up over him. But what I just said is the best answer I can give. From the moment I saw him, more than desire ran through me hot and heavy."

"So you two have had sex?"

This time Andrea let out a gut-clenching laugh. She leaned forward, afraid she wouldn't be able to stop. "We agreed all we would do was have sex."

"How did that go for you?" Julie asked, laughing along with Andrea.

"Oh, it went great. Fantastic. Best I've ever had."

"But . . ."

Andrea stopped laughing. There was a great big, giant *but* attached to her comment. She saw it now, plain as day. "But incredibly fantastic, wonderful sex wasn't enough. I'm pretty spoiled, huh?"

"I wouldn't say so. You're just not shallow."

Had she been shallow in the past? Andrea had set up sex-only relationships before. Her goal and motivation had always been the same. There wasn't time for a relationship. All she had wanted was sex. All of her efforts in the past had failed.

The first time she had met with a guy for sex, it always went fine, at least in the sense that they had sex. But Andrea had always been left feeling empty, craving more, and feeling too awkward to ever meet with him again for a repeat performance. God! She had been so blind, so idiotic, so stupid.

After sex with some guy she barely knew, she had been left feeling empty because what she'd just done hadn't been making love, it had been fucking. She craved more than just the physical interaction. Maybe at some point in her life, a very short-lived part of her life, Andrea had been content with just the physical aspects of sex. But that level of satisfaction didn't exist for her anymore. Her criteria, her needs, her cravings, were set at a much higher standard. Andrea never met any of those men a second time because they weren't who she wanted.

"I think I'm in love." Andrea couldn't take the words back once they were voiced.

Julie didn't say anything at first. Silence stretched between them. Andrea not only let Julie digest what she'd just said, but she also gave herself time to let it sink in. Their emotions had been off the chart when she and Mark had told each other they loved one another. But now, admitting it to another person made it seem even more real. Before Julie could say a word, lecture Andrea, offer advice, or simply drag the silence on as she tried to wrap her brain around it, Andrea pushed forward.

"Do you know what he said to me?" she asked.

"What?" Julie asked.

"He said I reminded him of his mother."

"Oh boy," Julie muttered and rolled her eyes.

"Earlier he'd gone into detail about her collecting all the jewelry. He also told me about her death. But I think what he meant was that his mother was married into all this money that she hated because it kept the man she loved away from her. So she tried separating herself from all the money by escaping to the island."

"I think I see what he means," Julie said, her expression serious. "You demand everything from every single contestant during each pageant you've directed as long as I've known you. But you're the pageant director. You have always stayed on the sidelines and have never made those same demands of yourself. In a sense, you are also hiding on your own island."

"So why would he offer me this contract with such an extravagant income and with no means of terminating it unless one of us dies?"

"'Til death do us part," Julie mumbled.

"Oh my God," Andrea gasped and her heart did a wicked dance in her chest.

Julie simply looked at her and shook her head. "You obviously don't care about how many people believe the Tripps are ruthless, hard-driving businessmen who will do whatever it takes to cut a deal."

"I think that was Mark's father when he was younger. After he lost his wife, he buried himself in his work. But he's an old man now and Mark isn't like that."

"Well then, sign the contract already and go live happily ever after."

Mark glanced at the stapled papers but returned his attention to her face. "Everything works for you?"

"'Til death do us part," she murmured, repeating Julie's double-edged words.

His eyes glowed. "Definitely," he said under his breath.

Andrea felt heat burn in her cheeks. Things had shifted between the two of them. They'd gone from fighting to keep things between them just sexual to something so much stronger. The sexual tension was too thick to cut with a knife. Her emotions were also spiraling out of control. Never before had she so desperately wanted to explore those feelings. Not only that, but she sincerely wanted to know what Mark was thinking.

She searched his eyes, wishing they could stop time long

enough for her to understand what he meant by what he just said. Did he want to be with her for the rest of his life?

The next morning Mark stood in the open doors to his balcony off his bedroom. A gentle rain splattered against green leaves and rocks lining the garden below. Spring was about to lose out to summer, and these morning rainstorms would end. He would enjoy them while he could.

He wasn't sure what woke him up but it was barely dawn. Andrea still had work to do with the pageant and had told him she would come to his suites once she was done. She'd never shown up. Mark planned on finding her in the very near future.

There was a tap on the door and Mark bounded across his suite, yanking the door open then hiding his disappointment when one of the house servants stood before him with a silver platter in her hand. She glanced at his bare chest and the drawstring sweatpants he had on.

Clearing her throat, she lifted the tray slightly. "One of the gardeners mentioned he saw you standing at your balcony. Miss Marcia said to bring you coffee."

Mark moved to let her enter and the servant hurried across the room and placed his coffee on the table. "Ring if there is anything else you need," she said and scurried out of his room, keeping her eyes diverted so as not to see his half-naked body.

"Send Marcia my love," he called after her, then helped himself to the sinfully perfect brew.

Returning to the opened doors, Mark sipped at the coffee and breathed in the smell of the rain. Something caught his eye and he stared down at the gardens just in time to see someone dart across the lawn and toward the house.

"Andrea?" Mark whispered, and watched as she ran barefoot into the house clutching something against her breast. "What the hell?"

Mark didn't give a damn if his attire made anyone nervous.

He marched out his door and down the hallway toward Andrea's wing.

He pounded on her door and she answered almost immediately. She was wearing a long, white cotton nightgown that was damp and clung to her body. It was transparent in places and he was instantly hard just looking at her. Her hair was also wet and tumbled down her back. She was barefoot and her face was flushed. But there wasn't a look of guilt or concern when she stepped to the side and let him in.

"Is that coffee?" she asked, her voice sexy with sleep.

Mark handed his cup to her and she drank greedily.

"I just saw you running through the rain."

She nodded and handed his cup back to him. "The rain woke me and I was scared it would get damaged if it got wet."

"What would get damaged?" He followed her through her office into her bedroom.

Andrea appeared indifferent to how wet she was from the rain. Mark damn near had a tent in his drawstring sweats watching her bare ass sway underneath her wet cotton nightgown. Her hair was tangled and free and fell to her waist in heavy strands. Even her bare feet, also wet and with a few small blades of grass stuck to them, were almost the sexiest thing he'd ever seen.

Andrea was beautiful from head to toe and by the time they were in her bedroom and she stood at the edge of her bed with her back to him, Mark didn't care what she was worried about. He came up behind her and wrapped his arms around her waist. Mark pressed his body against hers as he nibbled at her neck.

Andrea turned around and stretched against him. She kissed him with the savage need that he felt inside him. Everything exploded inside him. A pressure that had begun swelling in his groin made him dizzy from the extent that it filled him. His cock swelled and throbbed.

Mark walked forward with the limited ability he had to move. He shoved her backward onto the bed. At the same time he impaled her mouth. Andrea groaned, holding him tightly with her arms wrapped around his neck.

Her nightgown, clinging to her from the rain, was made of a thin cotton. It wasn't enough material to shield her full breasts as they pressed against his bare chest. Andrea's nipples were hard beacons brushing against his flesh. They tormented him into a needy frenzy he didn't want to try to control.

With a fierce growl Mark grabbed her nightgown on either side of her and started to tear it from her body as he pushed her onto the bed.

Andrea squealed, breaking off the kiss and gasping for air.

"No," she said on a heavy breath, twisting to the side of him. The fabric made a tearing sound as she let go of him and fisted her nightgown at her sides. "We can't. We might rip it."

Mark's head was clouded with lust. His dick stretched against his abdomen as she rolled her hips against him. With her hands moving to his chest, Andrea managed to hold his weight with her body and move them closer to the head of her bed.

"I ran outside and grabbed the book. It had been inside your mom's jewelry box," she began, speaking so fast as she maneuvered them away from the items resting on top of her crumpled bedspread at the foot of her bed.

"What? Huh?" He blinked a few times, still holding Andrea, but managed to turn his head and focus on what she was pointing at.

Mark managed to straighten. Most of the blood in his body was still drained to his cock. He teetered for a moment, digesting what she just said. At the same time he was still holding her and all too aware of the flimsy, wet fabric preventing him from having Andrea naked in his arms.

"Mark, let go of me," she whispered, and ran her fingers nimbly down his chest to his stomach. "Don't be mad," she added, her voice soft and sultry as she continued caressing his chest. "I pulled it out of her jewelry box when I was alone in the greenhouse and began reading it. It was so personal and full of raw, tormented emotions it almost made me cry. I didn't think you'd want all of your crew going through it, so I left it in the greenhouse when we brought out the jewelry box."

When Mark let go of Andrea and took a step toward the end of the bed, he was focusing on a leather-bound notebook, slightly warped with age. It was a thick notebook with pages appearing yellowed and weather-worn.

Andrea turned and bent over in front of him. He shifted his attention to her bare bottom, almost completely visible through her nightgown. Already his insides had shifted from a rush of boiling need to nervous anticipation and slight fear. When they began to shift back, his brain was mush for a moment. He turned, blinking, unable to handle the two extreme types of emotions warring inside him.

"Your mom had a journal at the bottom of her jewelry box." Andrea held the leather-bound book as she sat at the edge of her bed and looked up at him. "God, Mark. Don't be mad. I hid it in the greenhouse so no one but you could see it. I admit I glanced through it when I first found it. That's how I realized what it was." She held it up to him. "It's filled with all of her personal thoughts."

Mark stared at it, his brain working to comprehend what Andrea had just told him. He staggered away from her, all of it too much. He hadn't remembered placing his coffee on the top of her dresser. He grabbed it and gulped down the still hot, but incredibly rich blend. Closing his eyes for a moment, he allowed the caffeine to do its magic and clear his head. When he opened his eyes, Andrea still held the leather-bound notebook but looked incredibly worried as she watched him.

"Here," he said, saving some of the coffee for her.

"Thank you." Andrea set the notebook on the bed next to

her and did the same thing he had done, closed her eyes and drank.

There wasn't a more beautiful woman on the planet. Her hair wasn't brushed and looked tangled in places. When she downed the remaining coffee, she held the cup with both hands between her knees and stared at the floor, slightly hunched. Her nightgown was slowly drying and stuck to her body in places. It was crumpled from him grabbing it and she hadn't bothered to adjust it. Her legs were visible almost to her knees and her feet were still dirty from running barefoot through the gardens to the greenhouse and back.

Mark wished he could have watched her sprint through the rain. It dawned on him that she had discovered his mother's diary and had made a decision on his behalf on the spur of the moment. Andrea had protected him. It was hard telling what was in that diary, but if it had been documented, assigned a number the way all the jewelry had been, with official paperwork printed out declaring it the property of the Tripp family, Mark never would have known how many eyes might have perused through it.

His insides swelled once again. The raw, barely controllable desire to fuck her still burned in his groin. But a new sensation swept over him, powerful and overpowering anything else he felt. Goddamn, he loved her so much! The emotion taking over his senses was new, and the clarity of it no longer terrified him.

He embraced it.

Andrea raised her head. Thick light brown strands framed her face and fell in waves almost to her legs as she remained slumped over. She didn't straighten but stared at him with her sensual, large brown eyes. Mark saw her torment. He also saw how strong her love was for him. It had taken barely a month for him to realize he'd found his soul mate. Now, staring at her, his heart burned in his chest with a sweet pain he prayed he'd feel for the rest of his life.

"Thank you," he whispered.

"For what?" Her voice was as rough as his.

"For protecting my mother's privacy."

Her smile tore at his heart. Mark moved until he stood over her. His muscles ached. His dick was still semi-hard, and when she dropped her attention to it, it danced in his sweats eager for her to notice.

Andrea gulped in a raspy breath and raised her hand. For a moment Mark thought she would touch him and struggled for the strength not to explode on the spot if she did. When she put the coffee cup on the floor by her bed, then twisted and reached for something behind her, his cock stretched painfully. He didn't have the strength, or the desire, to force his need for her to recede.

"There's one more thing." She held something in her hand but didn't try showing it to him right away. Instead she stared at his cock through his drawstring sweats. She was at eye level with it and he was within hand's reach. "I feel terrible that all of this is what is left of your mother. She meant the world to you, and I know that, but hell, Mark, I want you so bad."

His entire body jerked from the rush of unleashed, carnal need that exploded inside him. Andrea had just surrendered to her needs. She raised her gaze slowly to his. Her face was flushed a beautiful shade of pink. Her lips were moist, parted, and full. Her eyes searched his, and their light chocolate shade allowed him to see deep into her soul. The love he saw for him there intensified his need for her, but in a way so strong it took over his ability to move.

Andrea raised her hand slowly, lifting something that draped over her fingers for him to see. "It didn't dawn on me until earlier. Two of the contestants brought this to me. There was so much going on, and it was dirty. I shoved it in my bottom drawer and forgot about it."

Mark gave himself a mental shake and drew in a breath. He

released it slowly. Andrea held up a necklace made of large, thin sheets of metal that looked like they were shaped like leaves. The metal was streaked with dirt and was dull, but he saw that a couple of the thin leaves were made out of copper.

"I think this is the necklace that goes with the earrings Eve found in the ground," she began, lifting it further for him to see.

Mark took it from her and used his thumb to brush dried dirt off the necklace. "You're right," he murmured. "This is the last piece of jewelry in the picture." He shifted his attention to her face. "That means we've found all of the jewelry. We have the jewelry box. Everything that was mom's is now safe."

Andrea nodded toward the journal that was resting on the edge of the bed next to her. "You might get to know your mom better now," she whispered, as if just saying the words was a sacred thing.

He looked at the book but didn't touch it. "I think Dad should read it first," he decided, and his heart picked up a beat.

Andrea nodded, accepting his decision. It wasn't her call. She would go with whatever he decided. Mark couldn't tell if his choice was one made out of cowardice or respect for his father. His heart began thumping against his chest the moment he uttered the words. Yet still, was he anxious to show his father and possibly bring peace to a man who'd mourned his dead wife for the past twenty years? Mark had mourned her, too, in a different way, but the journal might give him what he wasn't able to take after his mother died with him barely half grown.

Mark stepped forward, taking the leather journal. He walked across Andrea's bedroom and placed the necklace and journal on the small table next to her glass doors. Then, staring at the gray world outside, he unlocked her doors, pushed them open, and immediately filled his lungs with the damp, early morning breeze. His insides still burned with so many emotions. The morning rain, the salty humidity that wrapped around him, and the barely audible slapping sound from the foamy waves reminded him of the constant power and strength the vast ocean always gave him.

He loved Andrea. The pieces remaining of his mother were now united. The police were investigating all that happened on the island during the pageant, and thanks to his and Andrea's lawyer, there were legal documents verifying that the jewelry box and jewelry belonged to his family. All of it seemed overwhelming.

Mark turned around. Andrea had twisted her body on the bed to watch him.

"I had planned on showing the necklace and journal to you after we were more awake," she said, and her apologetic smile made her eyes glow with concern. "It's kind of early to have all of this thrown at you at once."

"I'm fine." He walked back to her side of the bed. "There isn't anything else on your bed that you don't want damaged, is there?"

The raw desire that had been on her face after they kissed returned. "No," she whispered.

"Damn good thing." Mark shoved his drawstring sweatpants down his hips until they fell to the floor.

Andrea's attention darted to his swollen cock. He stepped out of his sweatpants and came to her. She licked her lips at the same time the damp breeze swooshed around him and cooled his feverish flesh.

"You're so hard, so thick and long," she said on a raspy breath.

Andrea reached for him, took his cock in her hand, and wrapped her fingers around his shaft. When she began slowly stroking him, Mark's world centered until only the two of them were left. It was like tunnel vision, with the dark borders swollen as dark waves of powerful need for her tumbled around him.

"I hope you don't mind." Andrea's words were soft and sweet. Her meaning sunk in as she wrapped her lips around the swollen tip of his cock.

"God! Andrea!" Mark lowered his head to watch and grabbed her hair at the back of her head.

He wanted to fist thick strands around his fingers and hold her head in place while he plummeted deep into her drenched heat. Andrea hummed with delight, lapped at his shaft with her tongue, and gripped his hips, holding him where she wanted him.

Mark didn't dare move. He conceded to her controlling the moment. It took some effort to focus on her as her lips stretched around his dick. But he was rewarded with one hell of a view as she took over half of him into her mouth.

His world was about to explode. Andrea stroked him with her tongue as she sucked him in deep, then pulled back until she tortured the tip of his dick. It was the most beautiful sight he'd ever seen. This wasn't his first blow job, but women usually sucked, moaned a bit, then quit because it wasn't something they enjoyed. Andrea looked up at him and tried grinning with him in her mouth. His heart swelled with love so strong it consumed the lust burning inside him.

This was unlike anything he'd ever experienced. Andrea sucked his dick into her mouth again, then increased the momentum. She controlled how fast his dick fucked her mouth. More than once she gagged and her reflexes damn near made him come. He had to focus. The sensations tripping over each other were strong. Mark used all his strength to prevent coming and to enjoy her wonderful yet tormenting skills.

Andrea continued building the momentum. She sucked almost all of him into her mouth then pulled back. His soaked dick fell out of her mouth and she looked up at him and grinned.

"Come here." She wrapped her hand around his dick and tugged.

At the same time she crawled backward on her bed. Mark leaned over her and grabbed her long nightgown.

"I suggest taking this off before I rip it off of you."

"Oh yeah? You aren't going to tear my nightgown. I don't want you to." She grinned as she continued inching backward. Andrea thought she could control his actions. The delight in her eyes as she issued her challenge fueled the fire inside him.

"Then take it off," he grumbled, his voice harsh as he pinned her with a stare that showed her how far she could push him.

Mark understood that being in charge of her pageants, running the show, and always issuing orders that everyone around her followed without question, allowed Andrea to remain in a safe place where she never had to let go. He'd made her come hard several times now, and each time he did, he saw the surprise on her face over the intense pleasure it gave her. Andrea still feared letting go. The only way he could soothe those fears was to continually show her how surrendering wasn't unpleasant.

Mark didn't want to manipulate her. He wasn't the kind of guy who got off controlling his woman and making her do whatever he wanted. Their relationship would grow through mutual trust. Andrea was strong, hardworking, and intelligent, an equal match to him in every way. He didn't want to overpower her. Their love would grow if they remained alongside each other, both of them enjoying each other's strengths.

Mark began crawling over her. Andrea continued grinning. She lay down, and her fingers ran along the tip of his dick before letting go. As he moved, he bunched her nightgown up with one hand and pulled it up her body. It crumpled in a pile just above her breasts when she lay flat on her bed underneath him. Her expression was triumphant. The nightgown had become a game. Andrea believed she'd won because it was still on her.

Mark let go of the soft material, slid his arm underneath her back, and pressed between her shoulder blades.

"Oh!" she cried out when he jerked her into a sitting position.

He pulled on the gown until she was forced to raise her arms. Mark quit tugging when it was bundled around her face.

"I guess we could blindfold you with it," he mused softly. "There's enough material to bind your arms, too."

"Oh no, you don't," she cried out and finished pulling the nightgown off of her, then threw it across the room. "You had your fun once, mister," she informed him, her eyes flashing with defiance. "There is no way you're ever tying me up again."

"A challenge," he whispered, and forced her back down onto the bed as he kissed her.

Mark ravished her mouth. Andrea relaxed underneath him and pulled him closer. She wrapped her legs around his waist. Her hands clasped behind his neck. Their bodies pressed together, flesh against flesh, as they feasted and danced with their tongues.

The torture was sweet. The pleasure was off the charts. Their union was a powerful bonding. When his cock slowly sunk into her hot pussy, he knew that he never wanted to live without her. Andrea was his other half that he'd never known he was missing. With her by his side he was stronger, more confident, and more fulfilled than he'd ever been before.

They made love slowly. When the momentum built and the fire between them increased, Mark thought he would die from the heat searing the two of them together. Their lovemaking became frantic. He impaled her again and again. It was almost impossible to focus, but when he did, he stared at Andrea's beautiful flushed expression and his heart felt as if it exploded from the amount of love he felt for her.

He couldn't hold out any longer. "Andrea, I . . ." The words were lost as he started to come.

"I love you so much," she cried out and dragged her fingernails over his damp shoulders when she let go and exploded right along with him.

18

"Thank you," Andrea called after the three boys.

Mark stepped to the side just in time not to be bulldozed over by the three rambunctious children. They were Marcia's grandsons or grand-nephews. He couldn't remember which. One of the boys had a bill crunched in his hand. Andrea probably tipped them generously for hauling the boxes that held all of her things up from the docks.

He had been puzzled when Andrea returned from the docks earlier that morning and informed him the new man working had told her that Silver had been let go by Mark Tripp. He hadn't said if it was senior or junior, but that wasn't what mattered. Silver had disappeared and no one knew why.

"I think Marcia has some nieces who work cheap, as well," he teased.

Andrea held a Matisse in her hands. It was probably a high-quality copy, but with Andrea, it was hard telling. The painting was beautiful, and she grinned at him, laughing, before turning and stretching to hang the framed painting on the hallway wall outside of her office.

"I think a couple of them were up here earlier. I love how so much of her family comes out to the island to spend time with her."

Mark moved in behind her and pressed his body against hers, trapping her against the wall. He reached for the painting, covering her hands with his, and breathed in the lavender scent in her hair. "She's a good cook," he said, his voice rougher than it was a moment ago. "Besides, Marcia loves family. She's thrilled that you're moving your pageant office permanently to the island."

When she knew Mark had a hold of the painting, she lowered her hands and turned slightly, trapped between him and the painting on the wall. "Is she the only one?"

"Most definitely not the only one." Mark positioned the painting until he could tell it hung on the nail, then slowly let go of the frame. "I love the idea of my woman being on my island."

Andrea shot a quick look at the Matisse, probably to confirm he was no longer touching it, then play-punched him in the belly.

"Ouch," he wailed.

"The island is a piece of property. I am not," she seethed, although there was mischief glowing in her eyes.

Mark doubled over, taking a step or two backward. He was careful not to trip over the stacks of boxes that were everywhere in the wide hallway. Both of them had agreed it was best for her to take over this entire wing and turn it into the official office for the Mr. Desire Pageant.

"I didn't hit you that hard," Andrea complained when he remained bent over, clutching his knees with his hands.

The moment she was close enough, Mark sprang forward, grabbed her by the waist, and tossed her into the air.

"Damn it! Mark!" Andrea screeched, but she was also laughing.

He loved the sound. It had taken five weeks of not knowing, but earlier this week a jury convicted Becky Sterling for the murder of Paul Sanders. Apparently Paul had overheard their plans to find the jewelry and had threatened to tell Andrea or the Tripp family. Becky claimed Silver had been in on it, too. He helped bring over Becky's sons without anyone knowing. He'd also told Becky what he knew about where the jewelry might be located. Silver had already known about the greenhouse in the hedge and thought the jewelry box was hidden in there. Becky claimed under oath that Silver was the primary agent in their scheme to steal the jewelry. Silver had done one hell of a disappearing act.

Becky had offered Silver and Brittany Bender a sizeable amount of cash to do what they could to sabotage the pageant in order to steer the attention away from her and the theft of the jewelry. Brittany's court date was coming up, and she was locked up until then. Silver was the smart man. Mark wasn't sure if they would ever find the salty old sailor.

Dave Small had been released with no charges against him. Becky also admitted trying to frame Paul's murder on Dave. She had sung like a canary in order to reduce her charges. Florida was a death penalty state, and apparently Becky liked living.

"Put me down!" Andrea squealed in between giggles. She'd noticeably relaxed once they'd been able to put closure on the terrible things that had happened during the pageant.

Mark swung her over his shoulders, then gave her a slap on her rear. "How dare you suggest I'm some kind of Neanderthal," he exclaimed, then grunted for effect as he spun her around and contemplated which of the empty rooms they should christen first.

"Marcia! Do you believe this treatment I'm forced to endure?" Andrea cried out.

Mark spun around again, catching a glimpse of Andrea's long hair flowing toward the ground as he kept her firmly in place draped over his shoulder. He couldn't hide a smile at Marcia's disapproving glare and the way she fought not to break out laughing by puckering her lips.

"Mark Adelhide Tripp," Marcia called out, using a singsong voice. "Put that poor girl down right now. And to think you told my niece that you'd keep an eye on the children today. Should have known you couldn't pull off the task. They are probably all drowning in the ocean by now."

Mark grinned mischievously at her. He tightened his grip on Andrea when she squirmed over his shoulder. "I'd say it's probably more accurate that they're drowning in your home-made lemonade and oatmeal cookies."

Marcia successfully kept from smiling and rocked up on her toes. "And to think I thought you'd make a good family man." She made a tsking sound in her throat. "Obviously I was wrong there."

He beamed. Marcia had always been the only soul he had ever confided his dreams in, until Andrea. Lately, he was finding it harder and harder to keep anything personal from her. Just watching her unpack and slowly make this wing in the mansion he'd built her own had given him images of her giving their own home that personal touch. He'd thought of sharing blueprints with her of a house overlooking the ocean. He'd designed it as a home built for two—or maybe three.

"Neanderthals get really hungry and thirsty. Better save some of that lemonade and cookies for me."

"Mark, her face is turning red," Marcia complained.

Mark swung Andrea upright, capturing her in his arms and cradling her to his chest. Her hair swung in her face and he grinned down at her when she parted it and looked up at him, still laughing.

"You are so bad," she managed, her voice breathy.

"Just wait until I show you how bad." He wagged his eyebrows at her.

"She'll be waiting, too," Marcia exclaimed. "I have five children in my kitchen."

"Aha! So they aren't drowning."

Marcia turned toward the stairs. "Come on down, mister."

"I think you can keep them entertained for an hour," he prompted, and scraped his fingers over a puckered nipple through Andrea's shirt when Marcia had turned her back.

"Fifteen minutes!" Marcia yelled as she started down the stairs.

"Fifteen minutes?" he immediately protested. "No decent Neanderthal takes care of business in fifteen minutes."

Andrea snorted.

"Half an hour and not another minute," Marcia called from the bottom of the stairs.

Mark sighed. "You heard the woman." He decided on the far back bedroom, the one he was pretty sure Andrea hadn't decided what to do with yet, although it was hard to tell with boxes everywhere and her furniture having not yet arrived.

"Do you babysit often?" Andrea curled into him, crossing her bare legs and pressing one hand against his chest. Her cheeks were still flushed as she smiled up at him. "You know, I haven't even showered yet."

"Then it's decided," he said, entering the large master bedroom that was void of all furniture. "We'll start in the bathroom. And I babysit for Marcia's niece's kids every now and then. They're not so bad really."

She hummed and curled into him like a cat. "You said you were going into work this morning. But I see why you would rather be here. Those children were a lot of fun. They really got into helping bring the boxes up here."

"Most people see all those young children and run the opposite direction. Marcia says they have a hard time finding babysitters."

"They were a big help. I loved the youngest girl."

Andrea slid down his body after he'd carried her into the bathroom off the master bedroom. The bathroom was the size of some people's bedrooms. The marble countertop, with its double basin vanity, was lined with her toiletries. Two thick towels were folded on a console table next to the deep, sunken bathtub.

"Did the article run?" she whispered.

"There were actually three articles. The Tripps and the Mr. Desire Pageant are the topic of every breakfast table in Miami this morning." And more than likely most of Florida.

"Three articles?" She frowned and her hands ran up his chest to his shoulders. "I'm not too thrilled about first-degree murder being connected to the Mr. Desire Pageant. I will definitely have to focus on serious damage control. What is the third article?"

Mark stepped back, pulling the folded piece of newspaper from his back pocket. The ring bulged in his back pocket as he handed the clipping to her. "Maybe it's not so much an article as it is an interview," he confessed.

Andrea looked worried when she searched his face before unfolding the newspaper article he'd cut out for her. He watched her as she scanned the text. Mark had cut out the entire second page spread, his personal interview he'd given to hopefully downplay murder charges so the general public might not associate it with the pageant. He never would have thought he'd invite the press into his personal world. The public loved knowing how the "rich and eccentric" lived. And honestly, Mark didn't care if people he didn't know thought him a bit odd, or different from the average Joe. All that mattered was Andrea's happiness and the continued success of her pageant.

"This is good," she said, and began reading. *"This reporter was impressed with the thirty-year-old billionaire who calmly shared with me how he found his one true love—as Tripp said, his soul mate—in the most unlikely place, on an island full of men."* Andrea snickered and looked up at him. "When did you give this interview?"

Mark nodded at the paper in her hands. "Keep reading."

She narrowed her gaze on him suspiciously before returning her attention to the article. Mark took advantage of her focus on the paper and moved behind her, reaching around and freeing the button at the top of her shorts. She hummed in reaction but continued reading. He leaned into her, nestling his face between her shoulder and her neck. Her hair was tousled from hanging upside down. He loved how her hair always had that enticing lavender scent whether pinned up or draping her shoulders in a tangled mess as it was now.

She moved her finger to the top of the middle column in the article and he knew she was halfway through. "Oh Mark. This is hilarious." She began reading. *"Many would think when a person has so much money that no financial crisis anywhere in the world could affect them, that they would enjoy life traveling, throwing parties, or with days of leisure most of us only daydream about. Mark Tripp Jr. has always loved carpentry. He received his architectural degree from UF. Tripp told this reporter it took seven years for him to graduate. He proudly shared that he put himself through school, working full-time and balancing schoolwork. Tripp explained his father was his inspiration. 'My dad put himself through college, paid off student loans, and built his empire single-handedly. I haven't touched the trust fund although I am eternally grateful for how hard my dad worked to create a better world for me and my sister.' Tripp*

*is trying to follow in his father's footsteps and has already estab-
lished himself in the Miami community as a reputable architect.
Tripp Architect Company has been open for two years now. In
2010, Tripp won the prestigious P&A award for his model of an
underwater community that runs solely off solar and hydraulic
power. I was honestly surprised at his level of involvement with
Habitat for Humanity. Tripp admitted giving monetary assistance to the program but refused to disclose how much. His involvement with Habitat for Humanity dates back to his early
college years when he tore down the mansion on Tripp Island
and donated all salvageable parts to them for homes built in the
Miami area. He told me he plans to help build twenty homes in
the area, all of which will be from plans he's designed. With a
new love in his life—yes, ladies, the eccentric billionaire might
be the original Mr. Desire but he's no longer an available bachelor—Tripp told this reporter he hopes to have his girlfriend do-
nating sweat labor by his side."*

Mark closed his eyes and buried his face against her soft skin
as he listened to Andrea read. He placed moist kisses over her
shoulder blade, brushed her hair out of the way, and began
kissing the side of her neck. He hated that his personal life, or at
least parts of it, would now be scrutinized by so many people
who didn't have a clue as to what type of man he was.

Andrea kept reading, disclosing more information about his
personal life. Every inch of him was poised. He had sat for this
interview, he and the reporter in his office in Miami, and prayed
sharing information about him and Andrea wouldn't backfire
on him. Mark was covering Andrea's damage control, but he
prayed not at the price of losing her.

"What the . . ." Andrea hissed and her knuckles turned white
as she crinkled the edges of the newspaper page.

"Keep reading," Mark encouraged. He'd come this far and
needed to see it out. The ring in his back pocket started feeling

more like a rock stuck in his clothes that needed to be removed. He held his breath and waited.

"Mark Tripp and I visited in his Miami office for a couple of hours. We had quite a few similar viewpoints when it came to women. This reporter isn't sure he would propose to his woman the way Tripp has decided to propose to Miss Andrea Denton, the pageant director for the Mr. Desire Pageant. During our interview Mark Tripp told me he is going to propose marriage. Of course, I congratulated him. He asked if I would mention the proposal in this article. I assured him I would. Tripp then informed this reporter that when Miss Denton reads this newspaper article, just as the rest of Miami does, she will be learning about her marriage proposal for the first time. Tripp requested that I put in quotes in this article, 'Miss Andrea Denton, would you marry me?'"

Mark wasn't sure it would be that big of a news flash, but he had allowed the reporter his moment of glory. He prayed it wasn't likewise a moment of insanity on his part. Regardless of the next few seconds dragging out, and fear of rejection taking its toll on his brain, breathing in Andrea, feeling her soft body against his, had his dick hard as stone. Parts of his body already knew the two of them were united, and he couldn't wait to be deep inside her to prove his point.

Later, Mark would describe her reaction after reading as a soft squeal, but he couldn't swear it wasn't an erotic moan. A very enticing sound came out of her mouth as her body jerked.

Mark pulled his mother's engagement ring from his back pocket. He'd discussed it with his father, who had thought Mark's decision to propose to Andrea through the daily newspaper a bit bizarre. Still, he had agreed it would quite possibly be exactly what the pageant would need. The general public would focus on the proposal and associate that with Mr. Desire instead of the murder conviction.

The small band was slender, silver and not gold, and embedded with tiny sapphires. Andrea turned around, her mouth shaped in a small circle. Her gaze dropped immediately to the ring he held up on the tip of his index finger.

"Mark?" she whispered.

"Andrea."

Her gaze shot to his. Her large brown eyes were moist with tears.

Mark hadn't expected her to cry. He searched her face, hating the sensation that he was in uncharted water here. Maybe he should have done some research. It wasn't as if he knew many married women, or had friends who'd successfully proposed in the past. Something told him she wasn't supposed to cry, though.

He cleared his throat. "Andrea," he started again. "I want you to marry me."

It wasn't how he'd planned on proposing. For two days he'd paced, practiced, written down, and recited. Mark had come up with an eloquent, poetic proposal he'd been positive Andrea would love and remember forever. It hadn't been six plain, blunt little words.

But they were out. He stared at her. Andrea looked at him. She looked at the ring. More than likely a second or two passed, but it seemed like an eternity.

"Yes," she said, and a tear slid down her cheek.

"Oh God," he breathed, sounding anything but manly as he damn near gasped for air.

Andrea was laughing and crying at the same time when she jumped into his arms. Mark fumbled to not lose the ring.

"The ring!" she cried out, leaping backward and latching on to it with both hands. "I almost lost my ring."

Mark took her hand in his, stilling her. "I had this all planned out." He was back in control of his senses now. The fear of rejection had passed. Andrea had said yes. "I was going to give this perfect speech."

"Well, let's hear it." She eyed the ring greedily.

Mark began shaking his head. That speech hadn't been him. "When I was giving the interview, I told the reporter how my father proposed to my mother. He hired violinists and had a moonlit dinner for the two of them with at least a dozen servants zipping around them during the entire meal."

Her eyes were still watery when she spoke. "I think I like your proposal better."

Mark rubbed away the stain the tear had left on her cheek. "She had walked me through the yard so that we stood exactly where the table had been where they had dined. My mom told me he had strawberries and cream, champagne and oysters and fancy food that she never did learn the names of." He laughed but there wasn't any humor in it, any more than there was fondness in the memory. "I remember her telling me that my father didn't remember exactly where the table was where they had eaten that moonlit dinner. She told me with my father it was all in the planning. I didn't get it at the time, but she said when you spend all your time hunting and never stop to enjoy your catch, eventually it spoils."

"That's awful," Andrea gasped. Her eyes had dried out listening to his somber story.

"You're right. It is. And I knew it was awful for years after having heard it. What I didn't understand was why, until now. The real meaning behind what she was telling me hadn't sunk in."

"You didn't understand that she meant he went to all that work and then ignored her after they were married?" She was back to staring at the ring he still held. "Because believe me, I am not that easy to ignore." Andrea shot him a huge smile.

Mark tucked his finger into her shorts, touching her belly

button. Then dragging his finger up, under her blouse, he watched her brown eyes smolder, like hot, melting chocolate. "You will never be ignored. I promise. And she meant that my father worked so hard to have everything around him. But all his money became worthless when he wouldn't slow down long enough to enjoy what was his."

"I promise to take time to enjoy what is mine," she drawled in a slow, sultry whisper. Then dragging her finger down his chest and past his stomach until it hovered dangerously close to his dick, she added, "Are you ever going to put that ring on my finger?"

She was right. He wasn't his father, and Andrea was nothing like his mother. They needed to get this proposal part out of the way so he could make love to her. Marcia would hold true to their thirty-minute break. He needed several hours, at least, and knew already they would need to schedule the rest of their celebration for later that evening.

Taking her hand in his, he positioned the simple yet beautiful engagement ring at the tip of Andrea's ring finger. It slid onto her finger as if it had been made for her. Andrea gasped, pulling her hand free from his, and held it up, wiggling her finger as she admired the ring.

"It's the most beautiful ring I've ever seen in my life," she said, sounding in awe. "And I really mean that."

Grabbing her, Mark enjoyed the squeal that escaped her when he lifted and pulled her into his arms. Andrea wrapped her legs around his waist and finally quit looking at her ring as she kissed him. Mark held her close, enjoying how she tasted and how she smelled. Their thirty minutes might be about up. And he didn't doubt for a moment that Marcia would come marching up the stairs and inform him as much. Not that he cared. He and Andrea had the rest of their lives together. In spite of the trauma they'd recently endured, Mark knew there would be more. But there would be just as many good times. They were soul mates and as long as they walked together through life they would be fine. It was only when two souls meant to be together strayed apart that they would suffer. As long as he and Andrea were together, he was positive the two of them could endure anything.

Missed any of Lorie O'Clare's
other steamy island books?
Take a trip to an exotic location
for the ultimate beach read. . . .

Pleasure Island

*Travel to an island paradise where sensual delights
by day lead to hedonistic pleasures by night. . . .*

PERFECT VACATION

Paradise Island seems like the ideal getaway for Natalie Green. She can't wait to fulfill her secret sexual fantasies, and once she's read the contract, she's ready to sign on the dotted line for two weeks of pure carnal ecstasy. Now all she has to do is choose the . . .

PERFECT MEN

With their hard bodies and skilled fingers, Nicolas and Tomas take turns pleasuring Natalie in ways she's never felt before. And when the three of them embark on a wild ride of passion together, it's the most erotic experience she's ever felt. But that's when she discovers the . . .

PERFECT DECEPTION

Mind-blowing sex is incredible, yet Natalie senses something is not quite right with the men in her life. And when she explores the island, she discovers the truth—and the incredible secret about Paradise Island. . . .

Temptation Island

HAWAIIAN HEAT

Ric Karaka knows he can transform the rundown plantation house he's inherited into a profitable bed-and-breakfast, but he needs money to get things off the ground. Hopefully he can procure the financing from a wealthy old lady who's coming to Hawaii to meet him for the first time. . . .

TROPICAL TEMPTATION

So it's a shock when the woman who arrives is not only young but gorgeous and incredibly sexy. Ric figures he's got nothing to lose by inviting Jenny to come to the plantation and take a look around. . . .

SULTRY SURRENDER

Ric knows his future is at stake, but once they're alone he can't resist exploring every inch of Jenny's beautiful body. With each kiss and caress his lust is aroused and together they begin an erotic adventure they'll never forget. . . .

Seduction Island

Escape to a remote island destination where
one man is torn by the desire of two sultry women. . . .

A DARING TEMPTATION

Jordan Anton is the heir to a staggering fortune, but he wants nothing to do with the rich. When his grandfather insists on sending him to an island escape with the beautiful Sicilian princess Tory Alixandre to show him how stimulating money and culture can be, Jordan discovers his ideals—and desires— put to the ultimate test. . . .

A DAZZLING PROPOSITION

There's just one hitch when he meets event planner Amber Stone, whose curves tempt Jordan beyond reason. She can't reveal her true social status or the fact that she has no experience, but as she spends time with Jordan, she finds it more difficult to deceive him—and resist him—until she finally gives in to the lust consuming her. . . .

A DANGEROUS BETRAYAL

Yet Amber hasn't forgotten that there's another woman who's occupying Jordan's time. And when she discovers the real reason Jordan's grandfather wanted her on the island, Amber must risk losing the one man who's awakened a deep hunger within her. . . .

Turn the page for a taste of *Seduction Island.* . . .

1

Jordan Anton squatted on the edge of the volcanic rock and stared at the white foam as it raced up the sandy beach. It receded into crystal clear, bright blue water. Coral reefs added to the magnificence of the view. Too bad the small island was nothing more than a dried-up old volcano.

Jordan picked up a loose rock and hurled it at the ocean. Prisons came in many shapes and sizes. At least this one offered a view.

He jumped the three feet to the sandy ground and walked the length of the rocky wall. Beyond the thick grove of some erotic-looking flowering plant, a worn path led away from the beach. He started up the path, taking in the thick trunks of what might possibly be a hybrid of a palm tree. If he were in Montana he would know the names of the trees around him.

Jordan wondered how many Antons had been sent to this island when they didn't meet the approval of Pierre Anton, his grandfather. He would only be here a month, through all of January, and the terms weren't completely unbearable. But he was here against his will. He would be here in this warm tropical paradise, while everyone at the ranch endured the frigid winter.

He paused, tucking a thick black strand of hair that had come loose from the ponytail at the nape of his neck behind his ear. The long hair bothered his grandfather, but then, everything about Jordan bothered Grandfather Anton. Which, of course, was why Jordan was here.

"Why bother with a Harvard degree if you aren't going to use it, boy?" Grandfather had asked him more than once during their last visit.

Jordan wanted to ask exactly how he was *not* using his degree. There was knowledge in his head that hadn't been there before going to Harvard; life experience and memories that he wouldn't have had if he hadn't attended the Ivy League school. Jordan didn't have any regrets. He wasn't sure why it bothered Grandfather so much that he went to help Aunt Penelope with her ranch in Montana. His grandfather, of all people, should see and understand that Jordan was yet again learning and gaining life experience and memories by helping out on the ranch that his aunt would otherwise lose after divorcing her husband.

Of course, since she had divorced an Anton, more than likely Grandfather Anton didn't want her ranch to make it.

Jordan could spend weeks trying to understand the mind of someone like his grandfather. Or he could put those thoughts out of his head and figure out what the incredibly gorgeous woman standing no more than ten feet in front of him was doing on this island. His grandfather had spelled out the terms of their agreement very clearly before Jordan flew to the island. He would meet Tory, a Sicilian princess who possibly came from more money than the Antons. His grandfather wanted to merge the families, a business deal in his eyes, loosely called a marriage.

Jordan had no intention of marrying anyone but knew if he didn't agree to come here, spend a month with the princess on the pretense of possibly announcing an engagement, Grandfather would make it hell for Aunt Penelope and her ranch.

Princess Tory would arrive tomorrow, which meant the sexy little thing wandering from the castle was one of the hired help, probably taking advantage of her boss not being here and exploring. He hadn't been scheduled to arrive until tomorrow.

He finished tucking the strand behind his ear and watched her studying the bark of the tree she stood in front of. "What are you doing?"

She jumped, yanking her hand back from the tree she was about to touch as if it might bite her, and turned and stared at him, wide eyed. In the next moment she regained her composure, straightened, and narrowed her gaze at him.

"I'm not sure that's any of your business. Who are you?" she demanded, obviously clueless as to whom her employer would be while on this island.

There were advantages to people not knowing his identity. It gave him the opportunity to learn their true nature before revealing his name and watching the fake appreciation and respect gloss over their face like it did every time he mentioned his last name.

"I asked you first." He hid his smile when she appeared frustrated, obviously realizing she didn't have the upper hand with him.

Jordan moved closer, admiring her long brown hair that was pulled back in a ponytail. His guess was it fell close to her ass. And he'd bet she had a nice ass, too. The curves he saw from the front view were beyond mouth watering.

"I seriously doubt you have permission to be away from the castle. And I don't approve of breaking rules to gain information." She had an American accent, probably northeast—New York or one of the nearby states. The way her hackles rose, turning her dark blue eyes almost violet, proved she knew how to defend herself.

Definitely not old money. Not to mention, if she were from his class, or the class his family so proudly held on to, she wouldn't be out here without an escort. Jordan wouldn't put her much past twenty-five at the most. No rings on her finger, not even a school ring. Maybe he'd run into his social organizer, although Grandfather boasted that the reputable social organizer ran only in the best of circles. Jordan seriously doubted his grandfather would hire a social organizer who shopped at Wal-Mart and not Neiman Marcus.

"Sometimes there are advantages to breaking the rules." He decided not to ask further who she was, doubting she'd confirm anyway. The anonymity on both sides allowed him to see her in her natural form. It would go away soon enough and she'd start kissing his ass. At least for a little while he could enjoy the fiery temper he doubted she'd let him see otherwise.

"Not that I can see." She turned, walking away from him, along the path she'd probably taken from the castle. "And if you believe there are, I doubt you'll hold on to your job for long."

Jordan liked playing the rogue. In truth, he didn't feel he was playing too much. But his damn last name and supposed "position in society" got in the way too often to allow him to interact with another person like this. Especially a gorgeous woman. Hell, when was the last time a lady walked away from him?

"What's life, if you don't take risks?" He caught up with her easily enough. Although it didn't bother him a bit that the path wasn't really wide enough to walk alongside her. The view of her backside was as extraordinary as he'd imagined.

"A safe place," she said tightly, her ass swaying beautifully in her snug, new-looking blue jeans.

"You must know how to take risks if you're here," he pointed out.

"You'd be surprised what I know."

"We might surprise each other with our knowledge."

"Huh," she snorted, picking up her pace. "I know your type."

The path curved around thick foliage and sloped up and down as it brought them closer to the large castle, now visible ahead of them. It was an anomaly, the only structure on this small island, and probably built during a time long forgotten. Jordan wouldn't be surprised if it were the selling point when his grandfather decided to pick up this little rock surrounded by the Pacific, and not too far off the coast of New Zealand.

He remained a couple paces behind her. "Do you, now? And what is my type?"

"The type I'm not interested in," she said, her arms swaying on either side of her. He liked how her long thick ponytail flowed from side to side, matching the soft curves of her hip and ass as it moved to a tantalizing rhythm.

"You don't know anything about me. How do you know if you would like my type or not?" he asked.

She stopped, the edge of the path just ahead of her, where it broke off into the well-maintained gardens surrounding the castle. He had been amazed when, upon his arrival just a few hours ago, he'd learned that a skeleton crew maintained the land and castle. There were only a few household servants, and there had to be a gardener, with as magnificent of a view the yard around the old structure provided, although he hadn't spotted any outdoor staff yet.

Jordan snapped his attention from her ass to her face when she spun around and shoved her long ponytail over her shoulder. He decided he liked how the spaghetti strap to her halter top almost crept off her shoulder, aiding in showing off her small bone structure and slender shoulders.

She shoved a nicely manicured finger into his chest. "I know what I need to know about you," she hissed, stepping close enough that he could see cobalt flecks bordering her irises. They helped her blue eyes darken when her emotions were running strong, as they obviously were now. "You are the one who thinks acting like a badass will impress a girl, make her take a risk, invite an adventure. You think you can play me, take what you want, and then gallivant on to the next pretty girl who strikes your fancy."

"Ouch." Jordan noticed she said "girl" and not "lady." That would definitely make her not Harvard. Probably not Yale or Stanford either, although he wouldn't swear to the latter. He also concluded she wasn't from New Zealand, although her American accent had already given a hint to that. Kiwis were usually pretty friendly folk, and this woman came equipped with a double-edged dagger. He hated admitting his intrigue. What he did know was he couldn't let her see it, or she might very well hand him his head on a platter. "You've pegged me wrong, my lady," he drawled, using his best Montana accent. "And as well, you've offered me a challenge. One I'm up to, I might add. For now, though, I'll bid you good day." If only he wore a hat. Tipping it in parting would play the part out perfectly. Instead, Jordan stepped around her, forcing her to jump to the side to avoid brushing against him. "I'm sure we'll see each other again very soon." He picked up his pace, heading to the castle, and as an afterthought, opted to head to the back of the building instead of the front. Making it look like he would enter through the servant entrance, or possibly even head to the stables, would keep her guessing.

Soon enough she would know who he really was.

Amber Stone walked down the wide hallway, her tennis shoes making a dull thudding sound on the glossy stone floor.

Beautiful, ornate carpets, which were narrow and probably cost more than any paycheck she'd ever earned, silenced her footsteps when she walked over them. She paused and looked into a dimly lit library. Its tall bookcases filled with hardback books appeared ominous, as if all the secrets they held weren't for her. Amber never understood anyone who would willingly sit in a boring room all day reading a book, when everything anyone needed to learn came from experiences in living, not in fantasizing about someone else's life.

She hurried past the room, turning and hesitating at the glass doors, which closed off a room she wasn't sure what to call. Amber imagined royalty sitting in there, passing the time of day in accepted boredom while servants took care of their every need. It was a life she couldn't imagine, and honestly didn't want to try.

Walking quickly, she reached the far corner of the first floor of the castle and pushed open the thick wooden door, immediately inhaling something sweet mixed with the mouthwatering smell of coffee.

"Please tell me there is a fresh cup available," she said, smiling at the older woman who turned curiously and stared at her.

"Coffee, ma'am?" The woman's gray hair was thick and bundled up on her head. Her accent sounded Irish, making her the perfect cook for this kitchen, which stole Amber away to another time.

"Oh God, please. But I'm not a ma'am. Just call me Amber." She reached out and touched the woman's cool, soft arm when the cook hurried around the corner of the island counter, wiping her hands on her apron and then reaching for a cabinet. "I can get it. Just tell me where everything is."

"I don't think . . ."

"I insist. Whatever you're making smells so good I don't

want to interrupt you. And I don't need to be waited on," she added firmly. "I can get my own coffee."

The back door opened with a bang, causing Amber and the older woman to jump and turn to acknowledge a man, probably close to the cook's age, hurry in so quickly he slid to a stop. "You wouldn't believe . . ." he began.

"Jesse," the older woman scolded at the same time the man spotted Amber and clamped his mouth shut. "Mind your manners," she added, lowering her tone as if she didn't intend for Amber to hear her. "There is company in the kitchen."

"Lord, I'm not company." Amber opened two cabinets before finding enough coffee cups to serve an army. Grabbing one of them, she admired the white, eggshell porcelain as she walked over to the industrial size coffeepot and put the cup under the spout. "My name is Amber Stone. I take it you're Jesse," she said, glancing over her shoulder at the older man who stood planted where he'd stopped, staring at her with watery brown eyes. "And your name is?" she asked, nodding at the older woman.

"I'm Cook," the older woman informed her, returning to her task of kneading out dough.

"Cook, huh." Amber carried her cup around the island, set it down, then spotted a stool up against the far wall. She dragged it noisily to the island and propped herself on it. "You've got a name, don't you?" she pressed.

Cook folded the dough in half, pressed with the balls of her hands, then repeated the process.

Amber glanced at Jesse, but he still hadn't moved. Obviously these two didn't get a lot of visitors. Their social skills sucked. Amber sipped the coffee and hummed her approval.

"I don't want to call you Cook. What's your name?"

Cook straightened, her eyes as pale a brown as the man's behind her, although their accents were very different. "It's a name you want, is it?" she asked crossly. "Fine, then, you'll have my name. It is Anne Marie Francis Margaret McGillicutty."

"Wow, that is one hell of a name," Amber said, hoping she sounded sincere. She glanced at Jesse. "Do you have as long of a name?"

"Nope. Just Jesse," he said, still not moving.

"What do your friends call you, Anne Marie Francis Margaret McGillicutty?" Amber asked.

"Cook," she said, returning to her dough.

Amber stared at Cook's thick gray hair, which was loose around her temples in spite of many hairpins attempting to keep it in place. Then, laughing easily at the comical situation, and wondering for the one hundredth time what the hell she was doing here, she wiped her eyes, still laughing.

Cook looked up at her, stopped her kneading, stared for a moment, and then broke into laughter as well. As if that were his cue to relax, Jesse hurried around the island, grabbing a cup and helping himself to coffee as well.

"How long have you two been here?" Amber asked, feeling the tension in the large, spacious kitchen fade as she brought her cup to her lips.

"I've worked for Mr. Anton for many years," Cook informed her. "Arrived the same day you did, yesterday."

"You're kidding. This place is in immaculate condition, the gardens gorgeous. Who takes care of the place?"

"I'm sure he sent in a crew to make it look like this before Jordan arrived," Jesse told her, walking over to the stove, lifting the lid off a pot, and breathing in the steam from it.

"He?" Amber asked.

Cook and Jesse looked at her pointedly. "He," Cook stressed. "Mr. Pierre Anton, our boss. Your boss, too. He told us you would be arriving tomorrow, though—assuming you are the young master's social organizer, Miss Stone?"

Amber nodded. "He just hired me but I asked if I could

come out a day early to get settled in." She figured it might be worth trying to get any information out of these two concerning the mysterious Pierre Anton. She'd never been offered a job in quite the way he did, or with a job description like this one. And she'd been working since she was fourteen.

"You asked him?" Jesse asked, rubbing his gray hair as if trying to comprehend what she just said.

Cook's look was stern, as if Jesse's question was somehow rude. Her expression softened when she focused on Amber. "If you've come to discuss the menu, we can do that after dinner."

"The menu?" Amber frowned.

"The menu," Cook repeated. "You know, all the meals that will be served to you, the young master, and the princess."

"Oh, of course. Well, I'm sure whatever you decide will be fine. Whatever you're making now smells delicious."

"You are the social organizer, aren't you?" Cook looked at Amber like she'd grown a second nose. "Are you always so indifferent about the food served at your events?"

"Of course. Show it to me after supper. I'll approve it." Amber stared at her coffee cup, trying to think of something effective to say to cover her blunder. She'd been insane to think she could pull off being a social organizer. The servants in this castle knew more about her job description than she did. "I wanted to take time to get familiar with everything before our guests show up. But if you want me to go ahead and start my duties today, that's fine."

"That's what I came in here to tell you." Jesse suddenly sounded excited. "He's here already."

"Who is here?" Amber asked, more than willing to direct the conversation away from her.

"Jordan Anton, Pierre's grandson. I just saw him out in the stable with the horses."

"Oh really?" Amber jumped up, her stomach immediately twisting with nerves. The entire reason she'd been sent to this island was to provide the entertainment for Jordan Anton and his fiancée. Not that she had a clue how to do that, but she had successfully bluffed her way through the interview with Pierre Anton. And she would bluff her way through introducing herself to the millionaire's grandson. If she'd pulled the wool over the senior's eyes, junior wouldn't be much harder to convince. "So much for a day to prepare," she said, downing her coffee and walking her cup to the sink. "Where are the stables, Jesse?"

Amber ignored the comments from Cook about her attire not being appropriate. Jordan Anton would understand she didn't start working for him officially until tomorrow. She would keep the introductions simple, she decided, heading down the stone path Jesse had indicated led to the large, stone building behind the castle. It didn't look like any barn she'd ever seen before.

Amber didn't get why Cook thought she should put on a dress to enter this place. It had been all she could do to find nice summer clothes to buy during the dead of winter. She'd been excited to use her clothing allowance although every one looked at her like she was crazy when she wanted halter tops and shorts when it was snowing outside.

She pressed her hand on the large wooden door that was already open and breathed in the pungent smell of horses and manure. Everything smelled so different here than it did in Brooklyn, New York. But then, Amber wasn't sure she'd ever inhaled air that wasn't laced with factory smoke and carbon monoxide.

"Hello?" she called out, edging into the barn and looking warily into the nearest stall at the giant beast that glanced her way, looking bored. "Do you know where Jordan is?" she whispered to the horse.

Amber had never seen a horse in real life, and this creature was a lot bigger than she thought horses were supposed to be.

"Hello," a man said, walking around the horse, who continued staring at her with incredibly large brown eyes. "Beautiful creature, don't you think?"

Amber licked her lips, which were suddenly too dry as she took in the man she'd met while exploring the island. For a moment she wasn't sure of the meaning of his words. He stroked the side of the horse, his hands large, with long fingers and nails cut short. She imagined his touch would be rough, yet calming and confident. There was something about this guy, with his black hair pulled back in a ponytail and his relaxed, roguish stance, that screamed trouble in the worst of all possible ways. Yet he was compelling. Granted, annoying, too. But there was enough of a challenge in his eyes that she prayed he would spar a bit better this time without running away.

"I don't know a lot about horses," she admitted.

"I'm sure you know when something is beautiful." There was a drawl in his tone that was too soothing to be fake. Yet she couldn't grasp why someone who sounded like they were from the Wild Wild West would be across the world on this island.

"What one person might view as appealing another might find terrifying," she countered.

"True," he said, turning his attention to the horse. "Bess here isn't terrifying. She and I are becoming quick friends."

Amber almost asked why they were only now becoming friends, but decided she'd be smarter to focus on her job and not provoke a conversation with this man. He had trouble written all over him.

"Are you the only one out here?" she asked.

"Not anymore," he said, leaving the horse and approaching her.

Amber instinctively took a step backward. He took her arm, though, appearing indifferent to her balking, and guided her past the horse and deeper into the smelly barn.

"Now, tell me you don't find him gorgeous," he said, stopping in front of the last stall.

It was dark this far back in the barn, the only light streaming in through the two large doors opened at the other end. Amber jumped when the black creature in the stall lifted his head, meeting her gaze with a defiant look that gave her chills.

"Oh, my," she whispered, unable to stop herself as she stared at the large, sleek-looking, inky black horse.

"Put your hand here." The man reached over her shoulder, pressing his hand against the side of the horse. "Then calm, gentle strokes."

Amber was overly aware of the man touching her backside, his hard body like a steel wall pressing against her shoulder and her hip. She shifted her attention from the horse to his arm, noticing dark hairs on his forearm that she bet would tickle her flesh if he pulled her into his arms.

"Like this," he said, his soft baritone next to her ear when he took her hand in his and placed it on the horse. He kept his hand over hers, stroking the horse with her hand. "That's how you make friends."

She wondered if he meant with the horse or with her. "What's his name?" Her voice cracked and she cleared her throat, telling herself she should pull her hand from underneath his, but her body ignored the instructions. She wasn't about to show any interest by asking his name again.

"I don't know but can find out. Would you like to ride him?"

"I've never been on a horse," she admitted easily enough. She wasn't sure the thought appealed to her.

"We need to change that. It's obvious he likes you. I'll teach you to ride."

"I don't think—" she began, not seeing how riding a horse would help her to be a better social organizer.

"Don't run from something because you don't know about it," he told her, tightening his hand over hers when she tried pulling free. "Especially when your fascination is so apparent."

Amber yanked her hand from under his. The quick movement must have startled the horse, or possibly annoyed him. He raised his head, looking down at her with very large eyes. The whites of his eyes in contrast to his black coat made him look exceptionally pissed. She jumped back and the man wrapped his arms around her, stilling her.

God, the dark hairs on his forearms did tickle her, sending a rush of excitement over her body, while goose bumps traveled across her flesh just as quickly.

"Shh," he whispered in her ear. "What most people don't understand about horses is their intelligence level. Believe me, he reads you as well as I do. He just registered your fear when he moved, which confused him. And I'm sure he detects how aroused you are at the moment, too, which probably is annoying him because he's stuck back here without a female horse to enjoy."

"How dare you," she snapped, struggling to get out of his arms.

The horse moved in his stall, stepping back and forth while making a sound in his throat. Amber wasn't sure if the horse was agreeing with the dark stranger, who pressed against her backside, or announcing him an ass.

"Would you rather I lie to you?" he whispered in her ear, keeping one arm tightly around her waist while moving his other hand up her front. His fingers grazed over her breasts, causing them to swell, suddenly feeling heavy with need, while her nipples puckered painfully. "Would you not be interested in knowing how the first time I saw you I turned harder than stone? Before I said a word to you I ached to touch you, learn every inch of your body while exploring your mind at the same time."

There was something interesting about his vocal inflection. He held on to a drawl, reminding her of a ranch hand who possibly spent his entire life around horses. But there was a New England, almost aristocratic edge to his words, too, barely detectable but coming through more noticeably as he whispered in her ear, torturing her flesh. He cupped her chin, turning her head so she was able to see how deep his dark blue eyes were. She swore if she stared into them long enough, she'd understand the very depths of his soul. One thing she noticed, as she slipped deeper into his compelling gaze, was there was more to this man than just a hired hand who lived his life caring for animals and doing menial labor.

It crossed her mind that her month on this island, carrying out a job she knew damn good and well she wasn't qualified to do, might be more pleasant if she consented to a sordid affair with one of the servants. Especially one like this man with his powerful body and incredibly smooth way of speaking and manipulating her body so it was ready and eager to agree with his proposition before her mind could even wrap around it.

"No, I'm not interested in knowing that," she said, the words slipping out of her mouth from years of habit kicking in. It was second nature to turn down the advances of any man who came on to her strong and fast. Any man like that was a guaranteed heartache. She reminded herself firmly that she didn't have time for this, especially over the next month while she tried pulling off a job description that was more foreign to her than the damn horse who watched them with vague interest. Pulling off this job would give her enough money to put a down payment on a home, to finally own something. She ached to create roots, lay down a foundation, and quit throwing money away on rent.

Amber twisted in his arms, and was rewarded for her efforts when his cock stretched against her hip, hardening and throbbing while he continued staring down at her with his compelling blue eyes.

"I'll let you go," he informed her, although he continued holding her firmly against him, cupping her chin while his finger moved slowly along the length of her jawbone. "But first tell me why you're lying to me."

Amber smiled. Maybe being a social organizer, pretending to know what filthy rich people did for fun, was grossly out of her league. But handling this ranch hand, this rough and ready man, was definitely something she knew how to do. Just knowing he would willingly bend her over and fuck her right here and now should have her beating his chest, scratching and clawing until he let her go, and then running as far away from him as she could get. It was her pride, though, that had her relaxing in his arms, continuing to hold his gaze, and going as far as to lick her lips, although when he had her this close to panting, she couldn't moisten her dry lips.

"I'm not lying. Just because you've successfully discovered I'm a healthy young woman who is capable of sexual reaction doesn't mean I'm like that horse watching us. I wouldn't fuck someone simply because they're presented to me." She licked her lips again, liking how he watched her, searching her face and then settling his gaze on her mouth while she continued speaking. "I'm sure your horses are as intelligent as you profess, but what makes them different than most people—or at least, from me—is in order for me to fuck someone, the attraction must be mutual, not just physically, but also emotionally. Now, let me go, please."

He released her, although he didn't look appropriately chastised. Instead, when he lifted his focus from her mouth to her eyes, crossing his arms over his chest, the flicker she caught in his gaze created butterflies in her tummy. She held her breath, watching his lips part, and realized that, although free to walk away from him, she anxiously waited to hear what he would say next.

"Meet me here tonight at midnight and I'll prove to you I can stimulate your mind as well as your body." He walked away from her for the second time, while she memorized the view of his tall, muscular backside and focused on it even after he disappeared from her view.